Scribe:
the apprentice

ARGON PRESS

h.william ruback

Copyright

Published in the United States 2023
by

ARGON PRESS

www.ArgonPress.com

Scribe:
the apprentice

With the growing popularity of the fantasy/adventure genre, it's hard to find a book that's truly, 100% unique and authentic... "Scribe: the apprentice" by H.William Ruback is all that and more! The deeply flawed, complex, and intriguing character of Gareth, diverges so completely from the traditional and well known hero archetype, and enhances the intrigue and mystery woven into the creepily fantastic plot. Fantasy, adventure, and dark intrigue collide beautifully to create an immersive world for readers to get lost in. "Scribe's" evocative and rich text leaves readers waiting with baited breath... for this is just the beginning of what is sure to be an epic fantasy saga!

Dedication

for
Teresa

This book is as much yours, as it is mine.
You were more than the Alpha Reader, Editor... Muse.
You were the energy and soul that kept this tale moving onward.
I hope the rest of this epic is able to live up to the beginning that
you helped create.

and

Always for:
D.C.R. and B.A.R.
And Forever
E.A.R. and R.K.R.

And for my Little Darling

"Shied Mountains"
El' Athandria
Reekstown
L'uramentia
Mariv'
Sonesia
Predür
Delgar
"the Island of Souls"
Ba'sal
"Port of Crowns"
the LostRealms
the Push
"the throne of"
Alder
"the throne of"
Rhyce IV

Writing is like religion.
Every man who feels the call
must work out his own salvation.

George Horace Lorimer

Even in the darkness of the windowless room, it cast a shadow.

Its slow, undulating movement, could only be described as a seething pulse as it slowly crawled across the surface of the blackened, weathered, flesh.

Seeking out each character, it swirled and melded with the lampblack, slowly devouring each cursive form, as it left a part of itself to merge into the leathered surface.

When it had completed the task, it began to twist and pervert the text it had replaced.

Satisfied of its accomplishment, it slowly blended back.

Where it lay in wait.

1

It wasn't the first bump in the road, or even the second or third. His body knew the difference between every rut. It was that final, bone-jarring jolt that signified the transfer from the field path to the muddy main road that was used by merchants and customers alike.

Gareth opened his eyes to take in the sights around him, knowing full well that this may be his last time entering Reekstown's central market.

One would guess incorrectly at how the town had gotten its name. Gareth laughed silently to himself at the irony as he inhaled deeply. His senses immediately were overwhelmed with the sweetness of a hundred spices emanating from the various vendors who had set up shop on the outer edges of the market square.

Some of the smaller farms, that didn't have the rent to set up their wares in the central market, simply pulled their carts to the side of the road. It was here that Gareth knew you would find the sweetest basil, the perfect bite of ginger and the most aromatic myrrh. The smaller farms couldn't compete with quantity so they had to make sure theirs was of the best quality.

As they came closer to the gates of town, groups of younglings and would-be soldiers hounded the makeshift blacksmiths, interested only in the weapons of war. Several small groups began to practice as impromptu battles erupted across the fields.

Knowing what Gareth's thoughts would now be on, his father handed over the horses' reigns.

"You guide them in, my arm is getting tired."

Gareth reluctantly took control of the wagon. His momentary hesitation quickly dissipated with the image of his father's missing left hand. Although his sights were no longer on the activities of the wannabe warriors, his thoughts never strayed from his desire to be amongst them.

"I don't understand why I have to do this." Gareth protested.

"Yes you do. You understand this and many other things greater than I. That is why you must, do it."

"It's just not fair. I didn't even get a word in the decision. The choice was taken away from me."

"Do you think that you have choices when you are a soldier? War is the least fair pathway in life, a path which often leads quickly to death."

"Why can't you just tell me?"

"There is nothing more that needs to be said."

"But you know that I can do it. I've trained with some of the best swordsman. I've studied with the master tacticians. They all can give me a reason to become a soldier. You give me nothing but silence."

"You have a way with words." His father spoke the tired answer to the same drawn out questions that Gareth used every time he began the protest to his impending apprenticeship. And just like the answer, Gareth responded with the same old argument.

"I have a way with swords."

"A sword has never built anything, it only destroys what has been built by the bonding of words."

"You're telling me that you are a destroyer. That kings and queens once bowed at your feet because you destroyed the words of politicians?"

After a long painful pause, his father's head lowered and his response was an almost inaudible, "Yes."

Gareth pulled hard on the reigns. The horses struggled and almost bolted but the wagon came to an abrupt halt. His unsuspecting father was flung from the wagon landing as a crumpled heap in the muck and mud along the roadside.

Half out of worry and shame, half out of anger, Gareth bolted from the cart to his father who struggled to turn himself over in the mass of mud and horse droppings in which he landed.

"My father is not a Destroyer! He was the greatest warrior of all time and I am my father's son!" Gareth screamed at his battered and bloodied father as the man struggled to get out of the manure. His anger fueled his determination not to back down on this point, but his father's words thrust a chilling reality through his soul.

"Take a look around you. If I was such a great warrior, or builder of kingdoms and savior of souls, would all of those around us still be snickering with insult and staring in disgust, afraid to soil their hands to raise the greatest warrior of all time from a pile of pig shit?"

And even though he realized the truth. His anger would not let him focus on the sight of his father.

Then Gareth turned and walked away. Becoming just another of the uncaring crowd.

Several hours later, at least Gareth supposed that that much time had passed. He still wandered the town aimlessly. Pride had driven him away. Now embarrassment kept him from returning. His actions seemed to only reinforce his father's point. There was no honor in walking away from an injured ally. A true warrior would risk all to help a comrade. Wasn't that the action that had caused his father's disabling wounds in the first place?

Pity gave way to confusion, then back to anger.

As he continued to wander the back streets of town he picked up a large branch that at one time had been shaped as a canopy brace. He measured its length and balance in his hand. He couldn't believe that it hadn't been carved to be a practice sword. It felt perfect in his grasp. Slowly at first, then with the speed and grace of hours of practice, he twirled the makeshift weapon.

His body went through a succession of feints and parries, then a swift strike into the nearest object. A cloud of dust billowed from the stack of sack-clothe that had been the victim of his assault. Flecks of dirt and fiber, caught by the wind, momentarily blinded him. He reached up with his free hand, raking at his eyes. He shook his head and cursed as the burning caused his eyes to water.

He would not give in to the emotion. He tried to focus it, as his training had taught him, but it was to no avail. Instead his anger and frustration reached a fevered pitch. His practiced joust became a maddened succession of violent strikes onto whatever surface crossed his path.

Disused clay pots shattered.

All forms of vegetation splintered and were crushed by the onslaught.

His hands began to sting from the constant barrage and he felt the sudden pain as the newly formed blisters began to tear open.

In that brief moment of hesitation, Gareth heard a soft chorus of laughter. He turned his anger towards that sound and raised his wooden sword to strike at the mocking figure.

"Such a warrior, vanquishing trees and bushes and, now it would seem, portly misguided travelers."

Gareth was frozen in shock at the newcomer's statement. The rotund little man's eyebrows rose to an alarmingly funny angle and Gareth dropped to his knees with a laugh.

"You need not fear me, fellow traveler." Gareth choked out with a fresh bout of laughter.

"Indeed. I'm afraid to say that I don't think your weapon is up to the task anyway." The older man said nodding towards Gareth's sword.

Momentarily confused, Gareth looked down to see the shattered remnants of wood that barely extended from his fist. They both broke out into another chorus of laughter.

The man reached out his hand, which Gareth took, using it for support to rise from the dirt. He noticed a series of symbols and script, tattooed up the man's arm, which disappeared under the multiple layers of the man's shirts and jacket. Several gold and silver charms jangled as they clattered together hanging from his neck. The color of every piece of clothing and jewelry clashed with the one next to it. And yet, the overall effect seemed to draw his eyes away from the man, to dismiss him as if he wasn't even there.

The man's voice startled Gareth out of this momentary trance.

"Tell me, my young warrior friend, what ill did this alleyway cause you, to incur such wrath?" The soft tone of his voice seemed to rise in pitch at the end of every question.

Shame won out again.

"It showed me my true self." Gareth turned, bowing his head.

"It is truly rare to find a warrior who can learn such a lesson from a battle such as this." The portly traveler stated as he followed Gareth.

"I am no warrior." Gareth spun towards the older man, checking his anger once again.

"But I clearly see the training of the likes of Kanther or maybe Darius Thorn…"

Gareth interjected. "I once trained with Kanther." He spoke softly as he picked flecks of straw and debris from his tunic. "Then when I was home, my father implored me to continue with my training…"

"Quite right." The stranger whispered as his head bobbed up and down.

"Only then." Gareth continued, "He would watch and quickly berate my efforts. 'Why in the name of the Forgotten Realms would you commit to that move, unless you are begging to have your head separated from your shoulders'?"

Again the response from the stranger was, "Quite right, he would know."

Gareth paused momentarily, taking in a different view of this odd traveler.

"But I wouldn't listen. And that, amongst other reasons…" Gareth's voice broke into a strained whisper, "Is why I am definitely not a good son."

"You would be surprised to what length a father's forgiveness goes…to a beloved son."

"What if the son doesn't deserve that forgiveness?" He asked, his eyes pleading for a favorable answer.

The squat little man just chuckled as he began to walk past Gareth heading towards the market square.

"Even the most callous action deserves forgiveness, if one is truly sorry for the harm it has caused." He spoke, never turning around.

Gareth closed his eyes wishing that that were true. When he again opened them, the funny little man was gone.

Every step Gareth took brought him closer to the consequences he knew that he must face. It wasn't shame over the public apology he owed his father. He couldn't care less what the gathering public thought of him. Thoughts of glory faded as quickly as the comprehension of how he had disgraced his father came. Although he was intent on making amends for his actions, his body protested by dragging on towards its destination.

He was somewhat startled by the realization that his father was no longer where he had left him.

Why should he be, someone would have helped him back to the wagon, surely.

Though he doubted that kindness would include setting up for the day's bazaar. A new wave of guilt hit, realizing that he might have cost his entire family a day's worth of badly needed wages.

Surprise seemed to be the theme of the day. Before he had even turned the corner to the prime space his father always insisted on renting, he could hear the theatrical boasting his father used in a fevered sales pitch.

Indeed, when Gareth reached the stall, the crowd was four deep trying to reach for "The sharpest blade, the finest folded steel, hand tooled leather scabbards, et al." It was business beyond expectation, but sadly it meant no chance to beg for absolution.

As he approached, pushing through the crowd, Gareth overheard the exchange between his father and a distinguished looking customer.

"You must truly be proud of your ability to create such a fine blade Timeon; your craftsmanship exceeds all others." The nobleman said.

Gareth was not at all surprised by his father's response.

"I can't afford to spend time on pride for the things already made. I must find pride in turning away to begin creating the next one." And at that moment his father caught sight of him, a broad smile filled his face. "But truth be told, I do take immense pride in something I did have a hand at creating, may I introduce my son Gareth, my lord." And with that he reached out his arm to embrace his son.

Gareth never could understand his father's capacity to overlook and forgive the misdeeds of others. Which made his embrace, sting that much more.

The sun had sunk behind the lowest building, submerging the entire marketplace into shadow. A few vendors had lit torches for the extra light trying to preserve as much of the day as possible, to get that one last sale. For Gareth and his father, though, it was the signal to begin the process of packing up their wares.

Every task today seemed to spark a new wave of sadness as Gareth realized that this would probably be the last time he would ever be with his father in this capacity.

Then his shame would return at having not yet apologized for his earlier actions.

He was in the process of retrieving the last sword to be placed onto the wagon when he hesitated, feeling the perfect balance in his hand, knowing that this too was not to be.

Shaking off his desires, he knew now was the time and he turned to approach and apologize to his father. It was then that a now familiar voice called out from the darkness, startling Gareth and causing him to drop the sword.

"Now I would wager, that that blade might do a wayward traveler a bit of damage."

The charms and medallions clanked together as the strangely dressed little man stooped to pick up the dropped sword.

"You startled me." Gareth breathed out.

"Evidently. I wouldn't imagine a warrior such as yourself, dropping your weapon for any other reason."

"I told you before, I am not a warrior." Gareth nearly shouted, then regaining his composure, "But yes, there are several reasons for a warrior to drop his weapon."

"Do tell," came the polite, almost pleading response.

Gareth was momentarily taken aback by the request of the little man. He took a moment to gather his thoughts, which became more and more difficult. For every moment of silence that passed between them, the stranger's eyebrows rose and dropped in a comical symphony.

Finally Gareth looked beyond the little man and focused on the darkness ahead.

"A warrior may drop his weapon when coming to the aid of a fellow soldier at arms or a civilian in distress. He may drop his arms as a gesture of peace to a fellow soldier or dignitary. Or…" he began, with a wave of anguish. "He may be forced to drop his weapon as a gesture of surrender to save the greater good in a lost cause."

The final statement brought such distaste to his mouth as he spoke it, but it was that statement that brightened the alighted stare and comment from the little man.

"If only all warriors had your insight, intelligence and compassion."

Gareth quickly looked towards the wagon so his anger would not be so apparent. "I told you I am not a warrior!"

When his outburst didn't seem to get a response, he quickly turned. But the little man with the jangling charms was nowhere to be seen.

The call from his father broke his trance and he began to walk towards the front of the wagon.

2

It was another hour or so into the city, before they reached the guild house of the Scribes. Gareth was always amazed at the stark contrast between Reekstown and the heart of El'Athandria, the capital city of L'uramentia.

Dirt roads gave way to stone laid pavement, farms and fields to brick houses with plush green courtyards, trees to iron fences and statuaries. Every corner was lit by ornate oil lanterns, numerous times larger than any Gareth had ever seen in anyone's homes before.

The closer to the heart of the city they traveled the more elaborate the buildings became. Although grander in style, Gareth knew it was a product of their age rather than the financial wealth of their occupants. El'Athandria was the second oldest city in the Crescent Lands. Kings and Lords from all six of the kingdoms once held residence here. Those estates now having been taken over by the various guilds, retained all of the elegance they once had had.

Gareth wished that they had arrived at this part of the city earlier so he might see the Governor's palace while still bathed in sunlight. He always marveled at how the copper clad roofs of the six spires glowed in the setting sun. Their massive expanse and height allowed them to cast an amber glow across the heart of the city. Every building for several blocks seemed for a time, to be part of the palace itself.

Gareth's thoughts were interrupted by the wagon's abrupt stop. His heart sank as he realized that they had reached their destination. He knew that this may be his only chance to ever speak a lifetime of thoughts and regrets, but each time he began his voice caught in his throat and barely a sound was released.

His father clasped Gareth's thigh eliciting a brief jump and laugh.

Then a calming pat.

"I know," was all that was needed saying.

Gareth jumped down from the wagon and grabbed his sack as he circled the back end. He slowly headed for the large iron gate that surrounded the meticulously kept landscape. He stared in awe at the size of the guild house. It's scale easily equaling that of the Governor's Palace. The entire facing of the grand structure was bathed in iridescent light. Long silken banners hung the entire length from each of the turrets. Their golden symbols leapt from each field of bright colors.

Gareth stumbled as he pushed against the gate to gain entrance into the grounds. His thoughts were so drawn to the fact that he could not see what device was being used to illuminate the building; he almost forgot to give a final acknowledgement to his father.

Again, the words froze and his father broke the silence.

"I have, and shall always be proudest of you, my son." And without waiting for a response, he whipped the reigns and set the horses off at a trot.

Gareth continued to watch the wagon fade in the distance and even when only the slightest echo of hoof-beats remained, his gaze did not waver.

The creaking sound of the immense oaken door stirred Gareth from his thoughts. He saw no soul as he slowly entered into the vast gathering hall.

He felt a gentle push and turned to see a young boy, having nudged him through the entryway, begin to push the door closed.

Gareth was about to say hello when the young lad walked away heading across the hall. A small wave was Gareth's only indication that he was supposed to follow.

As he quickly caught up to and fell in line, he began to look around. Every surface of the entire chamber, save the polished marble floor, was hand tooled from the finest lumbers. Each wall was covered in slotted bevels that held scroll after scroll. No windows were present. The room received its lighting from the same unseen source as the buildings facing.

Gareth's gaze was drawn to the series of balconies that rose four stories above to a grand vaulted ceiling. The same banners, though on a smaller scale, hung from the edges of the surrounding railings, though now he noticed subtle differences. The thousand-year-old crest of the Order of Scribes was emblazoned on each. Every banner's field, though vastly the same, held a different band or shade of color. And the positioning and style of each symbol was altered. Some with the addition of a sacred animal or tree.

Gareth realized that these were the flags of the neighboring kingdoms. It was a way of establishing the home territory of each of the resident scribes.

They exited the gathering hall through a modest door tucked in the rear corner of the room. The dimly lit hallway they entered led to a spiraling staircase. Gareth quickly became annoyed at the droning echo of their footsteps as they ascended the stone stairs. His legs felt as if they would fail him by the time they reached what Gareth had guessed, was the sixth floor.

Silently the little child moved forward through narrow corridors. Occasionally, a nook appeared and Gareth briefly slowed to marvel at the number of scrolls that were stacked and gathering dust. In some cases the shear weight of the pile was causing the older, brittle scrolls to crumble and their brisk movement through the hallways stirred small clouds of parchment to swirl as they passed.

Suddenly the small boy stopped at yet another nook. This one was slightly larger, save for the bed and small desk that filled the majority of it. He reached out and took Gareth's sack, gently hanging it on a hook that overhung the foot of the bed. He reached over the bed to open the small window and as he turned down the blanket, spoke softly.

"Even at this time of the season, the upper floors retain the daylights heat." He nodded and disappeared quickly around another corner in the hallway.

Gareth sat on the edge of the bed, his mind full of questions, doubts and regrets. His body cared not of these things and before he knew it, exhaustion consumed him.

A minimal amount of sunlight and the cool morning breeze stirred Gareth from his fitful slumber. He screamed in pain as a sudden cramp tightened his calf. He tried to reach out to grab hold of his toes to flex the muscle but his recent growth brought his outstretched fingers short of their target. After a moment the pain began to subside and Gareth realized another sense was being assaulted. The overpowering scent of pepper made him want to sneeze as he turned his head to see a large plate filled with steaming food sitting on the desk beside him.

He stood and looked down the corridor in both directions expecting to see the back end of the deliverer, but only the occasional ray of dust filled sunlight was apparent in either.

Gareth greedily ate the meal, not caring that it was over spiced. He readily drank the fresh juice until it was gone.

As he finished his meal, he noticed the pile of fresh clothes on the foot of the bed. Though not a type of clothing he was accustomed to, he gladly discarded his soiled work clothes in favor of the softer, thinner fabrics. The ensemble was finished off by a finely combed leather vest with the crest of the Scribe Guild hand sewn onto the breast pocket.

Beginning to wonder what would be expected of him, Gareth set off in the direction in which he had arrived the night before. Though more was viewable in the morning light, no greater detail was visible.

He soon lost interest in the recurring scene and quickly descended the stairs. He momentarily stopped at each landing to peer down a hallway in hopes of finding a single person who would be able to tell him where he should be going.

As he reached the third floor landing he heard the sound of a chair scrapping the wooden floor. He walked in the direction of the sound only to have been tricked by the echo. Embarrassed he turned around and headed the other way finally coming upon an open doorway.

The brilliance of the morning sun blazed through the windows that filled the outside wall. His eyes watered as they tried to adjust to the glare as every surface seemed to reflect the amber glow. In the center of the room was an elongated table. Large enough to seat at least a dozen grown men, yet only a single chair stood at the head of it. Its surface held row after row of hollowed tubes, the majority of which were filled with brand new scrolls.

As Gareth turned to look at the opposite wall, he was startled by the silent appearance of an elderly man. Razor thin, he easily was the tallest man that Gareth had ever encountered. His brownish gray robes barely moved as he unclasped his hands and broke from his rigid stance. His body did not waver as he approached and it seemed to Gareth that the man might actually be floating on air.

"You are versed in the arts?" the raspy voice questioned.

"I can both read and write, if that's what you mean." Gareth snapped back. Not caring for the older mans tone.

"Which school?" No sense of offense shown.

"I'm not sure what you me..."

"Standard! Kurvish! Which do you know?"

"I know of each. My father felt it was important to..."

"We use Ornamental here. It is a combination of both Kurvish and the standard text. You need not know of it. It will come to you in time, if you will avail yourself~to~it."

Gareth's anger elevated with each stressed syllable.

The slender man did not seemed phased by Gareth's discomfort as he walked to the far wall.

"You will take an ancient text from here." He spoke as he slowly slid a worn scroll from one of a thousand notches imbedded into the wall. " And copy it anew." he indicated the new Scrolls sitting in the center of the table.

"You will start here," he said pointing at the first scroll.

"And end only when you reach...here."

Gareth strained to see into the shadows that the man had disappeared into, at the far corner of the room.

Again his anger flared at the realization that there must be hundreds of scrolls lining the wall.

"But there must be..." Gareth began to protest.

"You need not use your mouth. Only your hand. Begin!"

Gareth was so shocked he hadn't even realized the tall scribe had walked passed him and left the room.

Gareth unrolled the first scroll and at was immediately dismayed. The text was indecipherable. At first he couldn't read a single line, but as he calmed himself he found the commonalities he was familiar with.

It was mostly written in standard block letters, their tails ending in a more elaborate flair. Only the first word of any entry contained Kurvish. The loops and dots were overly exaggerated, doubled up passes and in some cases given shadows to emphasize their meaning.

He quickly caught on and was proud of himself at how easily he was able to mimic the grand sweeps at the beginning of each new passage.

It wasn't until his hand started cramping, that he perceived the passage of time. The shadows had shifted across the room signifying late afternoon. With this realization came the new sensation in his stomach. He was starving.

As he stood to stretch his legs, he noticed a tray sitting on the far end of the table. A plate, covered with fruits, cheeses and various meats, sat next to a bowl of broth. At first taste Gareth noticed how cold it was. He had to wonder how long it had been sitting there without his notice. Next to the tray, a pitcher of water stood next to a tall glass. Having only ever seen and used a ceramic mug, Gareth marveled at the clear smooth surface. He held it up to see the way it reflected the surfaces of the room.

Shacking his head in wonder, he slowly made his way back to the far end of the table to begin again.

Gareth quickly settled into this new routine. Every morning he awoke to a hot meal and fresh clothes. He then traversed the halls to the same room were he copied scroll after scroll. He learned to anticipate when his meals would arrive so he would not have to have cold broth everyday. Yet, he was unable to ever catch who it was that brought them.

He rarely had contact with anyone, let alone the other scribes. In passing he had seen about five different members of the guild. Once, when he felt adventurous, he went down to walk the second floor balcony of the great hall. There seemed to be some proceeding with a group of local dignitaries and though much was being talked about and argued. The acoustics made it impossible for him to hear what was said.

A sudden glare in his direction from the elder scribe sent him scurrying back to his tasks.

Again he resumed his writing. Eventually, he would lower his head in exhaustion and each morning he would wonder how he found himself back in his bed.

Weeks passed, and the solitude and monotony of his daily task began to wear on Gareth. He ate his meals much slower, delayed his return to work after each visit to relieve himself. The number of scrolls he copied each day decreased. He didn't care if the scribes noticed or not. They gave him no indication that he even existed except for an occasional stare in passing.

On this particular morning, he had had enough. He was going to finish this last scroll, find the first scribe he could and loudly proclaim his intention on leaving.

It was at this moment, for the very first time, he actually read what it was that he was copying. A single name, in ornamental, jumped out at him and caught him off guard:

Timeon's sword had vanquished yet another wretched legion of the pitch. Its gaping maul hidden within the confines of its glistening, ebon skin, released a scream, which quickly dwindled and the other members of its tribe and their loathsome human allies picked up the blood-curdling screech.

Several members of the Captain's ranks had been separated from the command, and upon recognizing this, Timeon raced to aid his men. He thrust himself between the injured souls that lay upon the ground and five of the brutish mercenaries employed by the evil ranks.

With speed that I have never witnessed on any battlefield, he dispatched three, forthwith. The other two gave up their attempts on the injured soldiers and charged the captain with a mighty flourish.

The action was hard to follow as earth and sweat and blood arced through the air with each new assault. Whose blood and whose sweat was not apparent until one of the hoardsmen slumped to his knees, falling face first into the chewed up ground.

The battle too long and the foe too numerous must have taken its toll on the Captain. With each parry, Timeon began to falter. A feint too slow and the crossing blade raked his cheek. Backing away from a blow, his unsteady legs slid in the trampled earth and, off balance, he was not able to defend the coming blow.

He barely managed to raise his arm in defense, but with no shield, flesh could not withstand metal. His left arm was cleaved from the mid-point between elbow and hand. It fell lifeless to the blood stained ground. The course of the blade continued until it bit into his hip. Ripping out a chunk of flesh.

Although a cause for a stagger, Timeon never lost his stance. Using that one brief moment that his attacker took to admire its deed, he spun on his assailant. Timeon thrust the tip of his broadsword through the oncoming man's throat.

It now seems that he is staggering in shock and I wonder how long it will be before the blood-loss takes him.

It becomes apparent though, that he has a definite destination in mind. He has staggered to the edge of one of the burning shacks, set ablaze at the beginning of this conflict. Without hesitation he thrusts his severed arm into the flames. I hear the flesh sizzle and the bone begin to pop from the heat as he silently withdraws the blackened stump. I witness a nod of satisfaction in recognition that the flesh has been sealed. He then calmly reached down and picking up the edge of a metal door hinge, he holds the glowing hot surface to his hip.

Again, no scream escapes his throat but I notice the tear this time as the pain overtakes him and he falls desperately close to the flames.

I cannot let such a hero, after all that he has been subjected to, to now be taken by the flames that spark from this horrific scene.

I break my oath, setting down both quill and scroll, to drag him several feet away to safety.

I no sooner pick up my tools, than an onrush of Timeon's soldiers and medicians descend upon him. Either they hadn't noticed my blatant disregard of protocol, or have chosen to ignore it. It is never mentioned.

And even as they attend to their captain, he is already regaining consciousness.

As Gareth read the final lines his eyes blurred from the flow of tears. He raked at them with the backs of his hands only to release another torrent.

It was some time before he was able to collect himself and he read the entire passage again. When he finished, he rose and shook himself. Trying to regain his focus. He grabbed the brightest scroll from the center of the table and began to copy the passage again.

The passage had to be perfect. He was determined to show respect to his father in this small way. When the pen slipped. Or his tear smudged the ink. He quickly tossed the scroll into the small fireplace and grabbed another.

From this point on, the words would not lose their meaning. Their history would not be forgotten. It was his personal vow to give a voice to all that had come before. In hope that he may one day deserve the pride that was placed in him and honor the ones he loved most.

A month had passed. Each day Gareth bolted to the study to delve further into his calling. He began by thoroughly reading each new scroll. He would not begin to copy any scroll until he completely understood the meaning and context of each passage.

Sometimes it meant going back to re-read and re-copy previous scrolls. He would not proceed unless he could clearly convey what was being said.

With this new attention to every detail, Gareth began to see how the history of the Crescent Realms had taken shape. He began to recognize how each word, whether spoken or written could affect change. How a government could topple because of a simple misspoken phrase, if the intent was not properly interpreted on the page.

He now understood why the Guild of Scribes was so revered. How their presence in all conflicts and acts of policy was crucial to shaping the future. He understood why some had chosen to change their policies and intents in the time it took for a delegated scribe to arrive to chronicle those proceedings. The worry of how the scribe, and history, would see the true nature of their deeds could often be enough to quiet any unrest or attempted acts of indiscretion.

Each day was an opportunity to learn something new.

To grow a little more.

To gain some new insight, or wisdom.

He began to believe that there would never be a situation that could ever make him doubt, the absolute truths written in the scrolls.

Then one morning he was summoned to the great hall.

3

Gareth arose to the sound of rattling dishes and he thought as he opened his eyes, that he finally caught the one who delivered his morning meal. But as he spun his legs around to sit up on the bed he noticed that the plain looking young lady was actually preparing to take the tray.

"Hey! I haven't eaten yet." Gareth protested.

"You have been summoned to the Great Hall by Lord Hadrion and the others. There will be no meal this morning for anyone." She flatly spoke, dipped at the knees and quickly headed off in the opposite direction.

Gareth sat bewildered.

The Great Hall.

He grabbed his new set of clothes and began dressing as he hurried down the hallway.

Gareth was tempted to stop at the second floor balcony to scout out the situation but he could clearly hear the disgruntled bellow of an unknown man.

"I am not accustomed to being told to wait. No King, is ill-mannered or bold enough to suggest it. So why I should allow the demand to come from a simple wordsmith is beyond..."

At that moment Gareth bolted through the door into the massive hall, narrowly crashing into a row of robed figures. They paid him no heed, but an unseen arm gently coaxed him toward the center of the gathering.

All eyes turned to him as he sheepishly looked around. There were no fewer than twenty scribes lining both sides of the hall. And in the center standing rakish and tall, was Lord Hadrion, Chancellor of the Scribe Guild.

Directly facing him, a single man, dark-skinned and massively built, equaled Hadrion inch for inch. His bulk was covered in gold-laced silk. And Gareth wondered how any man could stand up straight with the amount of adornments that hung around his neck.

Behind him stood two cowering aids. Their discomfort grew more apparent with each word spoken by their lord.

Two Columns of honor guards filled the rest of the hall, and on inspection Gareth recognized the crest of the Throne of Rhyce the IV.

Before the man could utter another sound, Lord Hadrion spoke. His voice matched the larger man's in intensity

"Lord Rhyce, in this hall, no man, has any more worth than the other. This simple and humble wordsmith commands as much respect as the most powerful of war lords." Hadrion spoke with a venom, that brought a sense of pride and respect from Gareth.

"If I am not mistaken, you are here to beg favor of this simple guild. That you, will be making a generous donation to this guild, in return of that favor. Am I mistaken in any of these thoughts?" Hadrion raised his full height in direct confrontation to Rhyce.

Rhyce slowly looked around, his gaze stopping at the figure of a scribe chronicling the events, and Gareth saw the realization overcome the large man. He had read about it, learned to anticipate it, but was amazed to see it actual happen to such a towering figure.

A slightly less bold response emerged.

"I, Rhyce the fourth, holder of the throne of all forefathers, do make a solemn plea to the Sacred Guild, in hopes that they may dispatch a member of the guild to help record for all time, the sacred deeds of man. I do so willingly with all of the noble grace afforded the Kingdom of Rhyce. I vow a pledge of finance in return of the granting of such favor."

Gareth had to reign in his laughter at the sight of the large man dropping to one knee. His aids rushed to steady the King and they in turn struggled to raise him.

Not losing any decorum. Hadrion again addressed the man.

"Lord Rhyce the fourth, it gives the Guild great pleasure to assist you in the action of preserving history. We command to your favor, our most gifted apprentice and most recently anointed scribe, in hopes that he will perform the duties prescribed to him as a full member of this guild."

Gareth found the pageantry of this exchange to be overdrawn until he realized that it was him, that Hadrion was speaking about. He was about to step forward and protest when the firm hand of one the scribes clamped down on his shoulder and long fingers bit into his collarbone. Gareth suppressed a scream as his eyes met the others. He quickly understood the unspoken meaning and dutifully turned to face the proceedings again.

Only they were done.

The air of formal grace quickly withdrew, as did Rhyce the IV and all else in attendance. Suddenly Gareth was alone in the great hall with only Lord Hadrion and a single guard.

"Wha… Who… I'm not a…" Gareth's mind and body went through every stage of confusion and disbelief trying to process what had just happened. His anger began to grow as he struggled to comprehend the implications.

"Wait!" He screamed as even Hadrion and the guard also turned to leave.

Gareth quickly reigned in his emotions in response to Lord Hadrion's ominous glare.

"I am not a Scribe. I'm not even an apprentice. All I do… all I have ever done, is copy text from some old dusty scroll and rewrite it on to another slightly newer scroll."

His frustration began to grow anew at the lack of any reaction from the Master Scribe. His attempt to out stare, out silence Hadrion failed, as his rigid stance gave way to the slumped shoulders of the defeated.

"Just tell me why." He pleaded.

"You say that all you have done since arriving nine months ago is to copy the ancient text, anew." His voice was soft and melodic.

"Have you bothered to stop and read, what you have written?

Gareth again was filled with shock and confusion.

"Granted, prior to that day, I had my doubts as to why you were here. But all things change. Even you, and ever since that day, your moment of clarity…" And he paused waiting for Gareth's understanding.

Immediately Gareth flashed back to the moment of reading the account of his father's final battle.

"All I tried to do was…"

"All you did was became a Scribe. You infused each word with the emotions that had accompanied the action. You gave life to the faceless souls. Heart. Honor. You made sure that history would not forget why the people lived and why they died. That there is reason behind every action… and reaction. You captured a moment in time and preserved it for all eternity, exactly how it was meant to be. Honestly, so that no man could dispute the account."

Gareth would have been moved to tears by Hadrion's speech if it had been meant for another. Instead he was locked in a battle of pride and embarrassment. By the time he had sorted it out and was ready to ask another question… Hadrion was gone.

"Shall we leave, Master Scribe? I fear that Rhyce will not wait very long before he departs."

Gareth refocused his attention to the one lone guard who stood before him. For the first time noticing the shield of the Scribe Guild emblazoned across his chest.

Still, he barely managed a gentle nod of assent.

4

Gareth was not unaccustomed to riding on horseback. He had trained on them, worked his family's fields on them and even traveled, what he thought, were long distances on them. Yet, he was ill-prepared for what the requirements were for a journey of this nature.

Even though winter was reluctant to give way to spring, Gareth felt overdressed. They had piled on layer upon layer of tunic and vest, jacket and fur. He was surrounded by packs of all shapes and sizes, containing foods, medicines and the tools of his new vocation. What he did not have… was the comfort of his sword or dagger. Instead, in their place hung the accoutrements of the Scribe Guild. He found it increasingly difficult to perform the simple task of hoisting the reins with each item that had been fitted around him.

Gareth stared down at the bulk of his shadow and compared it to that of his chain-mail encased companion. He began to wonder whose outfit would provide the greatest amount of protection.

Companion? Not in any sense that Gareth recognized.

Throughout the rush to be outfitted and the sprint to catch up to King Rhyce's party, the only piece of information Gareth obtained about his traveling companion was his name. Larec.

Another hour had passed and as the party had come to the edge of the city. The column of horses came to an abrupt halt.

Even with the height of the massive steed that Gareth sat upon, he could not see as far as the front of the procession to locate the cause of their delay. Although battle trained, both Larec's and his horse began to become unsettled standing exposed in a section of the boulevard that transitioned the paved road of the city to the chewed up earth, which coursed its way through Reekstown.

Larec silently dismounted and headed off to the front of the King's procession. Instantly his horse became rigid. Staring intently after his master, muscles tensing in preparation to aid him in a moments notice.

Gareth reached down to pat the massive neck of his mount, trying to steady the beast.

He spun around in the saddle focusing all of his training into scouting their situation. Perceiving every movement as a threat or distraction.

Every shadow as a potential adversary…

And then he nearly wet himself when he stared down into the smiling face of the mysterious portly traveler.

"What in the name of the Lost Realms are you doing? Sneaking up on me like that. I could have cut your head off." Gareth stammered as he dismounted on to unsteady footing.

"Then it's lucky for me that you have traded in your blade for that of quill and ink." The man stated as he nodded to the crest of the Scribe Guild emblazoned on the chamfrain draped across the chest of the horse.

"Still…" Gareth started as he tried to regain his composure. "You never can tell how someone will react to being set upon like that."

The chubby little fellow continued, ignoring Gareth's last statement.

"I do say that this suits you better. A mind such as yours was not destined to follow the dreams of avarice, or the paths of idiots. I took you to be far too intelligent to march blindly into someone else's battle. Though I do have to question as to why you sit at the ass end of a jackass' procession." And he silently chuckled at his own little pun, shaking from internal laughter. Triggering a cascading chorus from all of his various chains and medallions.

Gareth had to suppress his own laughter at his sudden realization as to the similarities between the traveler and the object of his jests, Rhyce the IV.

And as before, in every encounter, when Gareth turned back to speak to the squat chubby man…

He was gone.

Gareth had grown accustomed to the swaying of the saddle now that they had been moving at a consistent pace for some time. He tried to rest his eyes and allow his steed to steer its own course, but as his mind wandered, his anger increased at the lack of any explanations for their delay.

"Is there some hidden rule that says a Scribe should be kept ignorant of all events save, what he is traveling to document?"

Gareth's anger spewed forth into the question catching Larec off guard.

"And furthermore! Is there some reason the Guild is being so disrespected by shoving us at the ass end of this cordon?'

"I… I'm sorry sir. There was not, disrespect intended. I thought you might not care to hear about the King's tryst with a woman of questionable intentions."

"We had to wait so he could get his…"

Larec quickly interrupted.

"And seeing how I am tasked with your safety on this journey…" Larec gazed around to make sure no one would overhear. "I am not fully sold on the virtues of the King's intentions… so I chose the best defensive position one could have in a procession such as this. I am positive that there will come a time, when you are demanded to the front of this line. I only hope it will be for pageantry rather than the alternate."

Gareth was embarrassed at his own actions and was about to apologize, but just like his father, Larec quickly waved it off.

Another hour or so of sightless riding passed. Although, on horseback instead of a wagon. Gareth thought that he could judge the contours of the land.

Suddenly he bolted upright in the saddle and stared off to his right.

Faint wisps of smoke curled into the billowing skies. Today the fires of his father's forge, burned hot. Gareth felt the flush of heat. Not of the fires, but again, from that nagging feeling of guilt. He wished that he had the courage to race to that shack, and beg his father's forgiveness. The flush of shame then came… knowing that he did not.

"You must be from around here." Larec stated.

"How can you tell?" Gareth venomously asked never turning his head from the distant view of his home.

"Every campaign I have ever been on…every journey as scout or guide… there is always someone who gets that look in their eyes."

"What look is that?" Gareth turned, his anger mounting yet again.

"When their eyes glass over and every muscle in their body goes slack. A sense of loss or regret cascades over them. Then either the pall of remembrance of something dear, now lost. Or the fire of anger, at the ambush of their embarrassment for some ill-deed or wrong that they cannot right."

He stared intently into Gareth's eyes. Challenging the anger he found there. Then subtly he softened them with acknowledgement and understanding.

"I think most, who would call themselves a ranger or even a rogue. If they peered intently inside… would find the same thing."

He let that statement float on the cool breeze as he turned forward and coaxed his steed into a brisk gallop. Leaving Gareth behind to sort out his own thoughts.

Larec had set their camp on the outskirts of the rearguard of the procession. Gareth again was angered, but not at his companion, more so at the questionable situation in which he found himself. He hated the uncertainty of each passing moment. He found himself longing for the comfort of his nook, and the over-spiced plate that would awaken him every morn.

He had to suppress a small chuckle. Larec peered over towards him with a look of concern, which made Gareth smile even more.

Sometime later, after a rough but filling meal of dried fish and quick bread, Larec and Gareth laid back and toasted the completion of their first, uneventful day of travel.

"Why have we set such a path?" Gareth asked as he traced their journey on a pallet of stars, with his finger. "Wouldn't it have been quicker and less dangerous if we had made for the crossroads through Predür?"

Larec sat up and cautiously gazed around.

"It is well known that Rhyce the fourth, does not always choose the most diplomatic of approaches when dealing with those he perceives to be of a lesser stature. Which is most everyone he encounters. He has on more than one occasion crossed words with the High Chancellor of Predür. And…" he paused to finish his mead. "The border to the throne of Alder is not the friendliest of neighbors either." He let out a small laugh.

"I recon, we will partner more with the pitch than we will the lovely ladies of Alder." And this last statement brought a loud and exhausting round of laughter from them both.

The early morning of the seventh day found Gareth too restless to sleep. The sun had barely broken the horizon and the field grass was damp with a fresh layer of dew. The horizon, all around them was distorted with a remnant of the night's fog that had cloaked the camp. Only a few distant, faint sounds indicated that any one else was even awake and Gareth gazed through the veil of mist to see the king's servants begin their morning rituals.

As he quietly stretched, he took notice of Larec's long sword. The brocaded hilt was woven in a pattern that matched the crest of the Scribe Guild. The leather must have been treated with a substance that Gareth was not familiar with, because as he moved, the colors seemed to change. Giving it an illusion that it almost wasn't there.

Curiosity and a longing for his own blade got the better of him. He gently slid the sword from its scabbard and walked a few hundred passes from the edge of camp.

He began with a few twirls and flips back and forth from one hand to the other to judge the full weight and balance. He was surprised that his wrist could still handle the weight of a long blade, being that the only point he had held lately was on the end of a quill.

As soon as he felt comfortable with the sword, he began a succession of footwork exercises, varying the height and angle of the blade on each crossover. At that point, training and years of practice took over. His body, arms and blade moved freely of their own accord and he lost himself in a future that would never be.

Unlike the alley, this battle was choreographed perfection, never deviating from form or intent. Emotion held no place and would not dictate a failed outcome.

But the charge of a screaming Larec, just might.

"What in the name of the Lost Realms do you think you're doing?"

Gareth was taken aback by the venom in Larec's attack. He was momentarily dazed as Larec threw a shoulder into his chest and swiftly stripped the sword from his grasp.

Larec slammed the sword back into his already belted sheath, pausing only momentarily to give Gareth one last glare before stomping off.

Gareth raced after him, his own anger mounting.

"What the Rhüle was that about? I understand some swordsmen are protective of their own blades… but all you had to do was ask me to stop." Gareth screamed after Larec.

"Don't ever reference that vile place when talking to me." Larec spat as he raised his fist in Gareth's face. Then he spun again and began hastily packing up their camp.

"What? What did I do tha…"

"You truly don't have a clue. Do you?" Larec's voice maintained his fever pitch. "Didn't you learn anything at all in any of your teachings. Anything? A Scribe never takes up arms or a weapon of any kind. He never shows signs of malice in any situation. How do you think a scribe survives in the heart of a battle to record the history of it? No aggression from. No aggression towards! It has been the sacred law since history has first been recorded. Never. Just never…"

Larec's frustration prevented him from continuing, but that only fueled Gareth's confusion and anger.

"There were no teachings and there were no lessons. Just like I told Hadrion, I'll tell you, all I was, was a copy. I copied one scroll to another. I am not a scribe. I never have been, and one man saying I am doesn't make it so.

I am a soldier like my father. I bested every teacher I ever had. And if you ever… come at me like that again. I'll best you." The look Gareth burned into Larec as he pushed past him, left no doubt of the meaning of his words.

The day's ride was filled with a seething tension between the two companions. The passing hours of endless hoof-fall echoed into every thought Gareth held.

No aggression! What do you call that thrashing? Gareth thought of the hostility Larec had shown. *No aggression? How does any creature suppress a natural instinct to protect itself when there is nothing but danger all around.*

He shook his head in confusion as Larec let out a stifled laugh. Gareth abruptly turned, but quickly noticed that Larec, himself was lost in his own thoughts.

"It's a little ironic that the warrior finds humor in the situation and the supposed scholar only finds aggression." Gareth quietly stated.

"I wanted to be a musician." Larec started. "I found a poetry in every noise I heard. Laying, in the fields with my eyes closed, I could sort the sounds of nature into a glorious tune. The singing of the birds. The wind shifting the branches. The scurrying of every little creature. Even each crack of thunder played their individual notes in the symphony.

Then I turned twelve. And my father…" he turned towards Gareth. "Who was also a soldier. Demanded that I pick up a sword. I had no interest to hack upon another with a piece of steel. So I stood there. Motionless. With that blade extended in front of me.

He pulled his blade and slammed the metal out of my hand. Then screamed at me until I picked it up again. And he did the same thing. Over, and over.

I thought that I could outlast him. That my stubbornness, would peak his anger into frustration, and he would finally give up.

Well into the night it continued. The only pause was when he beat down my mother for trying to intervene.

It was at that moment I felt that I could hack at another. And I did.

Of course, I couldn't come close to matching a master at arms. But it didn't stop me.

I tried every day for three years to strike him down. I listened to his teachings. I struggled through his drills.

Then one day, I knocked the sword out of his hands. Swept the legs out from under him and slammed him to the dirt. My blade, a whisker from piercing his throat.

And he laughed.

He felt that he had won. That he turned me into a warrior. That I was ready to go on to learn from other Masters.

And I did.

But it was then that I realized that I wanted to, not to follow blindly into some fools campaign for wealth… but to protect those who could not pick up that sword for themselves.

So, what I guess I am saying is, that maybe we don't always get to choose our own paths…

…But, the right path, chooses us."

Gareth was moved beyond words. He wanted to acknowledge his understanding, but again the "Wordsmith" had none of his own. He was determined to struggle through an apology but as soon as his first words escaped his mouth their attention was suddenly drawn to a massive disturbance at the front of the line.

5

Gareth and Larec spurred their horses into a canter and headed toward a growing scene of confusion and disarray. The droning of men's yells and horses whinnying grew in intensity as the two companions reached the summit of the hill.

Gareth's horse almost bolted, as a panicked steed raced over the ridge, screeching in fright, and being chased by a cursing cavalryman. Pulling hard on the reins, Gareth quickly settled his horse to a halt, just as Larec brought his battle savvy mount to his side.

They both stood a moment to take in the sweeping scene before them.

The procession of King Rhyce the IV had reached the farthest point they would travel in L'uramentia. And in doing so, the whole company crested the hill into the vast ruins of one of the ancient towers of the Märkén Thraüm.

The breadth of what remained of the tower's base was larger than any coliseum Gareth had ever seen. The furthest of the horses and men, scattered about, looked like tiny dots. Even the oversized war wagons, that in this case housed the King himself, were dwarfed by the enormous stone blocks that remained.

Gareth had trouble trying to comprehend how massive the intact tower would have been. The largest building he had ever seen was the Governor's Palace. And that paled in comparison.

The moment their horses stepped over the ridge a brisk wind bit into them. It carried with it a sickening sweetness, like meat on the verge of rot. Gareth looked beyond the ruins to the borders edge, to the blackened point at which the last great battle against the darkness had ended.

The entire hillside seemed to emanate a broken energy.

Pockets of hope.

Gaps of despair.

A mixture of the last vestiges of magic…

And the rank air of pure evil.

A presence of thought, intent on repelling the dispossessed…

Which twisted back upon itself to be overpowered by a blood anguish consumed by hatred.

Both horses gave a slight tug of protest on the reins but dutifully proceeded forward.

Gareth continued to marvel at the stark contrast between the two Realms.

Light and Life.

Darkness and apparent Death.

The assault on his senses was overpowering. He felt a pull towards the darkness, then a warmth in his soul from the light. Everything else seemed to fade. He was lost in an echo of events that played out thousands of years before his birth. Time was irrelevant.

Larec's booming voice and a sudden tug on his horses reins, pulled Gareth back to the here and now.

He was startled to see that he was on the very edge of the border of the Lost Realms. A breath away from entering where none had ever returned. And yet, he was unable to look away. It was like staring into the heart of the night itself, even as the late afternoon sun began to burn his shoulders.

He sensed movement in the darkness and a sharp pain spiked in his temples.

Larec had seen enough. He grabbed the reins from Gareth's hands and using his own horse's girth, spun Gareth's beast around, tugging both rider and horse back towards the perimeter of the tower.

Still in a daze, Gareth sat, leaning against the inner portion of one of the tower's foundation stones. He felt a sudden warmth as Larec molded his hands around a steaming mug.

"Drink this." Larec stated as he helped guide the mug to Gareth's lips.

A few sips and a brief choking fit later, and Gareth snapped.

"What the Rhüle is that!"

Larec chose to overlook the poor choice in curses.

"It is a poultice of burroot, pepperspice and orange lilly."

"Aren't poultices supposed to be rubbed onto the skin… not ingested?" Gareth bitterly spat.

"Maybe so. But it certainly seems to have done the trick." Larec's face lit with a wry smile as he turned and walked away.

The following morning Larec was so intent on packing up camp quickly that at first he didn't notice that Gareth had wandered off again. He knew though, where he would find him.

He slowly came to a halt behind Gareth's sitting form.

"At first I thought the blackness was just scorched earth from the fires of battle." Gareth started. "And then things moved. The grass... and the branches of the trees. They glistened with the morning dew, but it was more like the sheen of black oil upon water. And I saw... something, in the distance... a form, a man, but it wasn't a man... couldn't be a man."

"The pitch" Larec softly interjected.

"It had no skin. I thought that it had been killed and strung up, skin peeled back in some macabre ritual. But then it moved. Its head bobbed slightly on the immense thickness you would call a neck. So, I stared into the darkness, searching for a face... Can anything stripped bare be considered a face?" He shook his head trying to clear the image.

"There had to be something..." Gareth continued. "Some indication that it was more than just a mass of living evil. So I looked into the ebony that was its eyes, searching... Then I felt as if I was being pulled in. I felt I had to outstare it... But how do you outstare eyes that have no lids, eyes that do not blink. I felt as if it was challenging me to do just that and its gaping maw clicked open and shut repeatedly to issue that challenge. Again it wasn't the mouth of any animal I knew, but a crude device that crushed and ground anything unlucky enough to get caught in its vice.

"It moved again. This time though it wrapped its long arms around its body then it swung them in a grand gesture as it spun around and slowly walked away. I was amazed that its viscera hadn't spilled from below its ribs. But they seemed to have been held in by some unseeable force. And just like everything else, it glistened blacker than black. As if the darkness was just an extension of the creature itself. That as it moved, it left a part of itself, coating and choking all it touched."

They both shivered.

Larec helped Gareth to his feet and the two travelers retreated to the tower and quickly mounted their horses, eager to depart.

Both riders had to wonder at the sanity of Rhyce's choice to skirt the edge of the Lost Realms for most of their journey. A slight discussion occurred pitting the argument of how much Rhyce had truly pissed off the royal houses of Predür to risk an encounter with the pitch. Or if his ego was such, that he needed to prove his courage by challenging such a conflict.

Either way, Larec was weary of the affect the realm had on Gareth. He made sure that whenever possible he and his mount were placed between Gareth and the Darkness.

But for the brief distraction of the long dormant volcano the company passed upon entering Predür, there was not much to divert any traveler's attention from the numbing effects of the endless shadow.

Larec continuously tried to focus the topic of conversation towards the familiar. Tried to keep Gareth's mind on thoughts of home and family. But every discussion had a tendency to weave its way back into an exchange about the towers, or the battle, or the Darkness. He finally decided to try to get Gareth to focus on all that he had learned at the guild house, to convey his own thoughts as they pertained to this moment in time.

"What would it say?"

"What would what say?" Gareth countered.

"What would that first scroll say? What new insight would it possess? What would I, even walking beside you, learn and discover about this very stretch of land on which we travail?"

"You're that concerned with my present state of mind, that you would intentionally invite me to narrate your every step?"

"Not that! I would like to assume that a member of the venerable Scribe Guild would be able to make a keen observation, one that all others would have missed."

"You mean…" Gareth spoke as he nodded off to the distant ridgeline. "That we have been under constant scrutiny by no less than six separate companies of Predür's Elite since the moment we crossed the border."

Larec abruptly spun in the saddle, straining to find any indication that Gareth might be right.

"What do you mean? I see no signs. How…"

Gareth chuckled. He broke ranks of the procession and urged his steed into a gallop towards the hilltop. Larec, taken by surprise, hesitated. His horse responded first and turned, quickly bolting after their charge.

Gareth shouted over his shoulder at the oncoming Larec. "How often do you see a Burroot tree with more than one trunk?"

And as Larec finally understood what Gareth was talking about…

A whole column of Imperial Elite soldiers emerged from the cover of the hill's crest. Try as he might, he could not coax his horse to overtake Gareth before he reached the line.

Gareth had already made first contact by the time Larec settled in next to him, hand on hilt.

"What say you? I shall speak with the Master Sergeant." Gareth demanded.

They were quickly dismounted and led, surrounded by eight guards, to a small canopy that had been set up some several hundred paces behind the ridgeline. The resplendent banners of the Kingdom of Predür waved furiously within the same sickening breeze that had been their constant companion since their arrival at the border of the Lost Realms. A lone soldier sat behind a makeshift desk staring in earnest at several maps. He paused briefly as the two travelers were brought forward. Slowly, he made a grand spectacle of his rising, deliberately looking in any direction but theirs until he was directly in front of them.

"When my men tell me that there are illegals on my land and that they demand to speak with me, I generally just tell them to dispatch with the interlopers and cast their bodies to the pitch. But then I am also told that these illegals ride under the colors of the Scribe Guild... And I must stifle a most hardy laugh."

All those around Gareth and Larec began to laugh in concert with their leader.

This time it was Larec's anger that began to mount and he was on the verge of protest, when he was waved down by the Master Sergeant.

The man, clearly several years Gareth's senior, stood uncomfortably close. Staring down his slender nose at Gareth, he paused, letting the tension mount.

Larec was almost at a boiling point, but Gareth didn't waver.

"So, Gareth! Son of Timeon. Self-proclaimed, soon to be the Cresent Lands' future, greatest, warrior. And yet, I see you ride under the colors of the quill-pushers."

All those around laughed.

He then circled Gareth in a grand gesture, searching for weapons.

"And I see you seem to have lost your sword. But wait! It is your companion that wears the crested colors upon his chest. Surely that does not mean that you are the said, quill-pusher?"

Larec had had enough. He was just about to set upon the Master Sergeant when both the man and Gareth broke out into an ear shattering laughter and grabbed each other in a bone-crushing hug.

"You did it! You actually let that old smithy sign you away."

Gareth broke the embrace and turned and swept his arm towards Larec.

"May I introduce the man who is tasked to be both my guide and protector, Larec."

The Master Sergeant nodded at the dumbfounded Larec.

"Not an easy task, is it?" he said with a smile.

"And Larec…" Gareth continued. "May I introduce to you Predür's Master of Sergeants, Voyga D'ianto."

Voyga reached out to take Larec's arm, clasping a massive hand around the base of his elbow. A definite sign of kinsmanship.

So taken aback by the turn of events, Larec hadn't even realized that all of the guards had departed. He walked slowly behind Gareth and Voyga under the canopy. The desk was now gone, replaced by a low-set table, full of drinks, and surrounded by three chairs.

"What say you?" Voyga prompted Gareth.

"A wise man I recently met, showed me that sometimes, the path chooses the man."

"Good, good, good! A wise man indeed." Voyga bellowed.

Larec glanced over to Gareth who was in turn nodding his head in acknowledgement.

"You were always too sharp for us. Would have never followed our lead. Right or wrong that doesn't work when at arms. You will make a far greater scholar and I must say, we will all, be the better for it."

Gareth was actually starting to feel better about fate's chosen course.

"What say you Larec of U'Glendon?"

"How did you know..." Larec's voice trailed off, again taken aback by Voyga's ability to quickly turn a moment to his advantage.

"This master would not be doing his Lords any favors if in turn he did not know all of those adept with a sword, who might one day, be counted as friend... or assessed as foe." He plainly stated, then continued.

"Lord Hadrion must value your abilities to charge you with such a task as this." Voyga mocked as he nearly slapped the cup from Gareth's hand.

"Hey now!" Gareth protested.

"I mean no disrespect to the fledgling scribe. My qualms are with that ill-tempered sloth with whom you ride. You're wise indeed, Master Larec to take the positions you do. Not one among us believes that any movement he makes is pure. Something dirty is always lying underneath. Will you be keeping charge of my impetuous friend?" He spoke the final question directly at Larec coupled with an intense stare.

"I am unable to answer that question to your satisfaction. Lord Hadrion and the Guild have directed me only to place my Master within the palace walls in the Kingdom of Rhyce the forth. I am then to return to El'Athandria." As he answered the question his own apprehensions grew.

"This is no longer a game played in the haystacks, my friend." Voyga sternly stated to Gareth as he clasped onto his shoulders. "Please tell me you understand this and that you will take the utmost care."

Gareth was moved by the sense of true concern his friend showed for him.

"I will do my best in all things that I can control." Gareth pledged.

"Those are not the things that frighten me."

Having said his good-byes, Gareth mounted his horse, eager to catch up to Rhyce's procession. He expected to hear Larec's heavy sigh, a sign of his impatience with Gareth, but none came. Turning back he saw Larec and Voyga locked in an intense exchange of words. A slight edge of concern started to overtake Gareth. He was about to dismount again when his two friends conversation ended in a whoop of laughter and a suffocating hug by Voyga.

Who in turn, waved for a final time to Gareth before turning and walking away.

Gareth watched Larec intently as the other mounted, then set off at a brisk pace. Gareth's steed quickly caught up.

"Is it your intention to remain quiet?" Gareth questioned.

"Of what would you like me to speak." Larec responded coolly.

"The conversation between you and Voyga of course."

"It was nothing but one friend expressing their concern for another's safety. And then he sternly addressed the consequences if I failed to ensure that safety."

"He had no right." Gareth spat, looking back over his shoulder. "He has no right to threaten you."

Sensing Gareth's growing anger at his friends actions, Larec quipped, "I thought it was actually kind of cute, his show of concern."

Gareth nearly fell from the saddle as he swung out at Larec, who spurred his horse to safety as they both laughed.

The glamour of riding a war-horse, hour upon hour and day after day quickly lost its appeal for Gareth.

Apart from the happened upon remains of other Märkén Thraüm towers, travel became a continuous, mind numbing droning of hoof-beat. On occasion the two men tried to outmatch one another's knowledge of the storied past of the towers and of the so-called wizards which occupied them. Only to realize that neither held much new insight to the ancient riddle.

Gareth had even become bored of the desultory pull of the darkness and the momentary glimpses of the pitch. It was almost frightening how easily one could become so complacent of an impending evil.

Their only respite from boredom came from a minor scuffle as the band tried to cross the border into the Kingdom of Alder.

A flaring of tempers, which quickly dissipated as soon as Gareth made his way to the front of the procession and proceeded to pull a scroll and quill from his pack.

Any thoughts of a violent encounter which would be chronicled by a Scribe, ceased. Neither party wanted history to see their actions as the catalyst to all out war.

This, at least, provided Larec with an additional two days worth of foolhardy ribbing.

The entire procession came to an abrupt halt. Gareth and Larec looked at each other with a mutual look that screamed, *what now*.

Before they could actually voice their question, a sweaty and panting page came running toward them from the front of the line.

"Your pre… presen… presence." He stuttered in between gasps of air. "Master Scribe, my apologies, your presence is demanded by the King. He request you join him with all due haste."

Finished, the young man quickly spun around and ran off again.

Larec looked gravely at Gareth. "And so it begins."

Gareth spurred his horse, guiding it quickly around all obstacles. As he reached the head of the column he spied a most humorous sight.

No less than five pages were attending to King Rhyce the IV, trying with severe difficulty getting him saddled upon a monstrous black stallion. And when they finally achieved their goal, the horse almost lost its footing trying to adjust to the heavy load.

Gareth waited until the beast regained its balance and several of the pages nodded to him. As he brought his own horse forward a dour and officious man appeared at his side and with a flurry of words, instructed Gareth as to Royal procedures.

"You will station yourself to the right and one half horses length to the rear of the King and will not speak or wave to any who acknowledge the King and or you through the King and you will not speak to the King even if he asks a question which will not imply that he expects an answer which he does not and you will proceed to follow the King until such a time that the King's Aide-de-camp feels that our sovereign has benefited from the pageantry of the occasion which is saluting the King's arrival home to his beloved kingdom and to the citizens that love him thusly. "

And just as quickly, he was gone.

A young boy, Gareth estimated to be under the age of ten, grabbed the underside of his horse's bit and gently led the animal to its proper position.

There was no acknowledgement from the King that he was even there, but the moment the little boy ducked away, there was a long blast of a battle horn. The King, after a moment of protest by the animal, moved forward and Gareth's horse obediently kept pace.

Gareth realized that they were about to cross the boundary into Rhyce's kingdom. And as the massive man led them across the border, a symphony of horns sounded. There were rows of peasants standing, cheering, and waving small banners. A proper tribute to their traveling King, now returned.

The sentiment felt forced to Gareth and with very little effort he could see palace soldiers dispersed throughout the crowd, prompting their revelry. He thought that he heard a slur cast at the King but by the time he could focus in the direction of the insult, all that stood in that place was a mass of soldiers.

The faux reception quickly dwindled after only a few hundred paces.

Just enough to soothe the giant ego, of a giant man.

The group of pages descended upon the King like a rabid pack of dogs. All of their might and choreography could not prevent a disastrous outcome to the King's dismounting.

The look of shock and anger distorted the King's face into a twisted glob of reddening flesh. At first Gareth struggled to contain his own laughter, but the realization that the King had landed on one of the pages sobered any thought of humor. Gareth watched in horror as the unconscious man was dragged away.

Gareth sat motionless in his saddle, not knowing how to react to such events. His thoughts were shattered, by the bellowing of King Rhyce, as he mounted the stairs to his personal coach.

"And that! Is not something that will ever see the likes of ink on scroll." His words and menacing glare burned their meaning into Gareth.

They reached the city and the Palace grounds the following morning. Gareth watched as parts of the procession broke off entering various secondary doorways and tunnels.

This time a suited, palace guard on horseback, approached. He nodded courteously to Gareth then brought his horse to stand directly in front of Larec.

"I commend your services, but beg you relinquish your charge. I, Captain V'ren of the Rhyce Guard relieve you of your duties."

He and his horse bowed to Larec.

"My lord I shall give you a moment to take leave of your aide." He said to Gareth and with that V'ren's horse slowly backed away.

Gareth gave Larec a bewildering glance.

"Occasionally, we are set upon by the true respect warranted to the Guild." Larec acknowledged. "Now do not waste time with colorful sentiments."

"I am grateful to have met you. It has been an honor to ride along side of you… even if you are just the lowly aide to a quill pusher." Gareth smiled.

Larec nodded in return and they reached out to clasp each other's forearm. Their eyes met and conveyed their true sentiment.

Nothing more was said, or needed. Gareth urged his horse towards the castle. Once even to the captain, V'ren's horse fell in stride.

Larec watched as Gareth and the other, disappeared through the massive archway of the castle.

Upon entering the castle, Gareth was led through a maze of corridors and rooms. At times he was quickly dragged and hurried, not allowed to even focus on where he was. At other times he was ceremoniously paraded through. A grand introduction was given to announce his presence and he was given a detailed explanation as to who, what and where they were.

He easily picked up the pattern: it was implied that he did not need to know who the servants were, although the younger ones, especially the girls, were very interested in who he was. They would move aside and bow as he and V'ren would pass. The older ones, who had spent most of their lives in servitude, could not care less who they had to wait on. They made their displeasure known by way of failing to move quite far enough to the side. On more than one occasion it took a piercing stare from the Captain to widen the way.

When being formally introduced to the various officials, dignitaries and guests... it was implied that Gareth, Master

Scribe of the Guild of L'uramentia was King Rhyce the IV's demanded choice, chief consult and personal friend.

It was told on more than one occasion, to anyone of any consequence that Gareth was the King's Scribe: that if it were warranted, their every action and word would be recorded for the King and all of history to learn.

Gareth noticed an immediate change in every one he was introduced to. A sense of awe followed him from that point on. And something else, a seething fear and distrust permeated from all of those around him. He was angered at how quickly he was being misjudged.

He also noticed that certain members of the court seemed to light up, their own desires beginning to take root in the opportunity to engage the King's Scribe. His anger turned quickly into discomfort and unease. It was as if he could read the minds of those he knew he should avoid and it made him feel slimy.

The show ended and without notice or word, V'ren departed, leaving Gareth in a back corridor briefly alone. A wretched looking old man grunted loudly, as he motioned Gareth to follow him. Several times on their journey to the upper floors, the old man paused, coughed and spat a disgusting wad of phlegm onto the ground.

Gareth began to be concerned that he was being led to another hidden nook and was completely surprised when the old wretch stopped and opened the door to a massive suite. He motioned Gareth into the room and as soon as Gareth had cleared the path of the door. It was slammed shut.

Gareth tried to find the appropriate word to describe the sight before him. Opulent, lavish, regal were a few that came to mind but ultimately would not succeed in doing it justice. He stood in a room, which was larger than the area of his entire house back home.

The ceilings were higher than most of the trees in any of the groves on the farms he worked as a child.

Paintings, taller than any window he had ever seen.

Windows larger than most buildings.

Colors from across the rainbow covered the walls. Every curve and edge was coated in gold leafed guilding, creating the illusion of a fiery sunset.

A massive bed filled the furthest wall. Long sheer strips of silk in the Scribe Guild's colors, spiraled from a center point in the ceiling and were intricately braided to the ornamental posts.

Off to the side an elaborately carved desk sat. Two beautifully hand blown oil lanterns stood on opposing ends of the leather, covered surface. Quills made from the rarest of feathers hung across the facing of one of the shelves, their gold and silver tips radiated the afternoon sun. While bottle after bottle of the deepest ink, seamed to swallow it.

Built into the wall itself, to either side of the desk, were scroll filled cabinets, tooled from the finest wood. In each cove were the most ornate scrolls he had ever seen. Made from the finest materials known. He wasn't sure if he would be able to make himself defile the purity of their surface with his hand.

He was overwhelmed...

Then startled, when he spun around and stared into the eyes of one of the most attractive woman he had ever seen. She stood at the entry to a bathing chamber and she quickly bowed as soon as Gareth had acknowledged her presence.

"I am Annalei. I will be your chambermaid and servant. Anything you wish or desire I will obtain for you, my Lord." And she bowed again.

The Master Wordsmith stumbled over his words again, eventually only managing a coherent, "Thank you." although it sounded more like a question.

Annalei began to unpack Gareth's bags, which he hadn't even noticed were sitting on the edge of the bed. She carefully hung his outfits in a cove that was hidden behind one of the draped curtains that adorned the corners to each side of the bed. She carefully laid out the few quills he had brought with and arranged his scrolls so that they were in the closest slots to the desk.

All this time Gareth stood in the center of the room, mindlessly watching her every move.

"Is everything to your satisfaction, my Lord?" Her eyes almost pleaded for a positive response.

"I… I couldn't have done it any better." He stammered. Which brought a huge smile to her face, which in turn brought one to his.

"The King has decreed that there will be a gala in your honor tonight. Though that will not be for some time. Would you like me to prepare some refreshments?"

Gareth hadn't even realized that the afternoon mealtime had come and gone while he was being displayed throughout the castle. His stomach rumbled at the mere mention of food.

"I will take that as a yes." Annalei smiled as she hurried from the room.

His eyes were locked to the spot in which she had previously stood. His thoughts lost in trying to comprehend the situation he found himself in.

How could such a fine lady be a servant? Why would anyone overlook that gentleness and sincerity, to forcibly rule over her?

The feelings that stirred inside him threatened to unhinge his mind, as if being in this place, at this time, in this capacity, hadn't already. Surely she was almost ten years his senior, but still…

He quickly shed any of those thoughts and tried to refocus on the true nature of his assignment. All else would have to wait.

Gareth was lying back on his massive bed impatiently waiting. The longer he lay there, though, his body melted into the comfort. He had never felt anything this soft. It was like being swallowed by a cloud and it was almost as large as one.

Annalei, despite his protests, had primped and primed him according to court protocol.

At first he was embarrassed to bathe, to let her see him in the buff. Then her amusement at his discomfort embarrassed him further. They finally settled on an agreement in which she would scrub the areas that he could not reach and he would take care of those parts that an unwed couple should not share.

All that was fine, until it came time to dry and dress. Gareth was prepared to be firm on his stance, this time around, until he saw Annalei's distressed reaction.

Looking into her eyes, he knew that he could not, would dare not, be the cause of any further anguish and he politely gave in.

He allowed her to clothe him in layers of garish colored garments. Though, when she stood back and declared him finished… He insisted that on top of it all, he would wear the vest he was given on his first day at the Scribe guild house.

As he smoothed out the garments underneath, he began to notice a comparison to something or someone else.

Both, his thoughts, and Annalei's admiring glance were rudely interrupted by a thunderous, banging on the door.

Gareth reached the door and began to pull it open just as another round of loud knocks had started. As he opened the door he heard an obnoxious voice deriding Annalei.

"Dreadful woman, would it be too much to ask that you have your charge ready for when the Ki…"

"Are all of the King's servants…" Gareth let the word sting for a moment. "As insulting and as impatient as you?"

Gareth recognized the man as the same page who "schooled" him on the proper riding order. Unlike then, though, the man stumbled and slurred his response.

"My, my apologies sir." Then his voice raised several octaves as he squeaked. "It's the King sir. Doesn't like waiting, sir. It makes it difficult to handle things in the proper, courtly fashion. There used to be protocol. Now there's only rush, rush, rush, rush."

The man began sweating profusely and for a moment, Gareth thought he might actually faint.

"We need never speak of it again, as long as it is understood that the Lady Annalei will never be spoken of like that again." Gareth said sternly.

There was a furious shaking of the head, which looked more like the page had gone into a seizure. It didn't stop as he began to side step down the corridor, waving for Gareth to follow.

Gareth reached back for the door handle only to see Annalei, teary eyed and smiling. He nodded to her and she curtsied. Closing the door, he turned to leave, sure that the broad smile on his face was lighting the entire passageway.

Although they traversed the same corridors, as before, this time there was the intent to make sure that there was time for all to behold, the Master Scribe. Guests and servants alike paused from their tasks to notice and acknowledge the presence of a member of the venerable guild.

Gareth was sure that he would sprain his neck from all of the bowing by the time he reached the Grand Hall. He was unaccustomed to this much attention. What made him most uncomfortable was that he could feel himself being pulled in by the false salutations. He knew how easily this intoxication could override common sense. He had already seen, on too many occasions, how quickly the admiration could change to deceit and distrust. As if there was always an underlying presence of the Darkness. He wondered if it was born from the Kingdom of Rhyce being almost completely surrounded by the lands occupied by the Mürken Rühle and their evil hoards…

Or if it was solely a projection of the vile tendencies of men.

The King's page suddenly came to a halt in front of the massive doors of the great room. Gareth in turn, almost walked directly into him, then noticed that several other of the guests, whom had taken up positions behind him, almost did the same.

The page stepped aside and motioned Gareth forward and then nodded to another regally dressed man standing behind a small podium. The man stared at Gareth, patiently waiting.

Gareth realized the implication of the man's action. He nervously brushed down the layers of clothing that had become misplaced in the long walk from his suite. Looking up, he smiled at the man, who in turn, gently nodded, then gracefully twisted.

The Herald picked up an ornamentally sculptured bronze sphere. He made a grand show of bringing it down to strike the metal surface of the podium. Gareth watched in awe as with each strike of the sphere, more and more of the huge crowd became silent and turned to face the doorway. By the time the third strike had echoed through the immense room, even King Rhyce the IV was standing quietly at attention.

"I have the honorable pleasure of introducing to my King, Rhyce the fourth, and to his many guests…" He swept his arm back slowly until it pointed directly at Gareth. "From the Guild House of El'Athandria, the Master Scribe, Gareth of L'uramentia!"

The entire room erupted in a thunderous applause. Gareth was almost concussed by the wave of clapping and cheers. He slowly began to walk forward, unsure of what to do, or where to go.

There was a surge of people in front of, and behind him, as everyone wanted to clasp his hand or feel the ruffle of his shirt. His movement was choked, as more and more well-wishers pressed to meet him.

Gareth felt suffocated by the onslaught. He was not prepared for this reception. He became paralyzed with fear and uncertainty. He wanted to scream out! Wanted them to leave him alone! Still they kept coming at him. He was ready to turn and bolt from the room. As he looked for the quickest path to try and achieve this, he noticed the crowd parting before him.

Captain V'ren, and several of his men had cleared a corridor through the masses. V'ren, looking resplendent in his dress uniform, led Gareth forward. All the while the cheers and applause continued.

As they approached the main table, King Rhyce, who also was clapping and cheering loudly, rushed to circle to the front of the table. His massive body dislodged several chairs and those in his path moved quickly out of his way, or were pushed by the bulk.

Gareth felt a brief moment of panic as the large man spread his arms to engulf him in a massive hug.

"My boy, my boy! Come and feast, for tonight we celebrate your arrival in our fabled land." He leaned close. "And it will be your words that make it so. Come! Eat! Drink! Until you feel as if you are about to burst. For this night belongs to you."

He began to lead Gareth around the raised table, again leaning in.

"And that is something you can write."

Gareth noticed a subtle change in the King's voice, and staring into his eyes caught the meaning. There were going to be things, that Gareth was expected to write, no matter what. And when he wrote those things, they must be glorifying the King.

Throughout the night, that was how conversations went. A funny joke: Write of that.

A veiled threat to another: no need to mention that.

A story of bravery and gallantry: write it.

A clumsy servant, a mess on the King's courtesan and the subsequent backhanded lashing: spare the servants shame from print that lasts a lifetime.

It was apparent that the celebration was going to last well into the night, but Gareth had had enough of the false friendship and phony show of civility. He was trying to figure out a way to excuse himself, as the King stood and bellowed to the crowd.

"It has been a most joyous of occasions, but our Wordsmith must take his leave of us to record our history. We have made him one of our own and expect great things… of ourselves and of him. Tomorrow will be an eventful day that through the grace of his quill, will speak holy of us for centuries to come."

A majority of the crowd applauded, but hours of food and drink had sedated a large portion of those attending. There was barely a notice as he walked through the large gathering and headed off in quest of the softness of his bed.

After what seemed to him, hours, Gareth finally found his room. He was actually proud of himself. He made only two false turns that he quickly recognized, before setting back along the proper course.

Several of the gas lanterns had been lit, but set low.

"Thank you lovely lady." He spoke under his breath, grateful that Annalei had left a few lights on so he would be able to find his way in this unfamiliar abode.

He paused briefly at the desk, contemplating if indeed he would write of this night. He was concerned though, that his doubts about the true nature of his assignment here, would bleed into those words. So he chose not to.

He reached up to extinguish the flame.

He couldn't figure out if it was the dozen or so tangled thoughts, or the copious amount of mead that was the cause of his dizziness. He mindlessly walked to the bathing chamber and splashed water upon his face. He held the cool liquid to his eyes, until the warmth of his skin removed the chill from the water.

He no longer wanted to think. He just wanted to succumb to the gentle fold of that cloud awaiting before him. But when he looked up. It wasn't a cloud that stood before him.

The light from the remaining lantern cast a soft glow on Annalei's sleeping gown. The plain cotton garment could not hide her beauty and Gareth thought she looked like one of the heavenly creatures of olde. He stood motionless admiring her. Not knowing what to do.

Annalei reached up to both of her shoulders and slowly pulled the ties that held her nightgown up. With no effort the garment slowly slid to the floor and she held out her hand to Gareth.

"Wait! No. What... I... What are you doing?" Gareth sputtered.

"I am yours, in all things." Annalei spoke softly and matter-of-factly.

"But you don't... I mean I never expected... You don't have to do that, this, you don't... I mean I would not expect that of you." Gareth's realization began to anger him and that anger seeped into his words. "Just because I am some King's play thing, doesn't give him the right to make you... anyone else's."

He turned away not wishing to cause her any discomfort and to allow her time to redress. He heard her faint sobs and spun to see her still standing there... beautiful.

Her shoulders rose and fell with each suppressed cry. Gareth could not stop himself from following a single teardrop as it glistened from the warm light. Its trail led down her cheek. He momentarily lost sight of it until it splashed upon the top of her breast and came to rest, above her nipple.

His only embarrassment came from causing her pain. He bent to pick up her garment and held it up to her.

"I am nobody. You do not need to bend to mine, or anybody else's wishes, if they are not your own." He said as he reached up to wipe away yet another tear. "You may sleep in your own room tonight. You are not beholden to me..."

But before he could finish, her sobs became a torrent.

"I have no room, but yours. And if not your bed... I have none." And her crying pulled at his heart.

He reached out and pulled her close, hugging her trembling form. The warmth of her body threatened to drive him mad, and yet he knew he must comfort her. The thin cloth of her garment did nothing to hide the sensation of her soft flesh against his.

"You will stay here." He whispered to her. "This room is yours, as well this bed. But not, in that fashion. Besides, there is a good chance that with the size of this bed… we may never even see each other." He smiled, which brought a much, needed laugh from her.

When Gareth awoke, the other side of the bed was empty. It was as if the events of the previous night were but a dream. Had he just imagine it? That in a drunken haze, had he brought forth an image that he wished for. If so, why didn't he take advantage of that desire?

Because. It was, real.

And it was not right.

After washing his face he proceeded to the desk. Sitting down he pulled a fresh scroll and was about to chronicle the evening's events, but his mind only returned to her.

Where had she gone? Would she ever return? Will he…

The smell of freshly cooked pork filled the room and mixed with the scent of several fresh fruits. Gareth turned to see Annalei carrying into the room, a large tray overflowing with food. She proceeded to fill a plate, then grabbed a mug off of the tray and brought both to Gareth.

"You are the most noble gentleman in this entire Court." She bent to kiss his cheek.

His eyes followed her, as she skipped away humming a lighthearted tune.

Gareth had to wonder how any scribe could succeed in their tasks, without an extensive military training. Forget the weaponry and swordplay, though knowledge of them could only enhance the narrative, but for the hours of field and horse training. Building physical stamina by subjecting your body to exhaustive motion, creating an instant muscle reflex to any given situation.

He silently thanked all who had made him train, hour after hour, in the saddle, so he could perform any task with either hand or if warranted, neither.

He had spent the better part of the day, accompanying Rhyce and his men during what was called a border check. He was again mounted on his steed, which he had now chosen to call Allegiant. His comfort with the animal, and its with him, allowed him to ride almost entirely hands free. Which made the task of recording the day's events, somewhat easier. He knew it would take time to perfect a steady hand whilst riding.

The one thing he was unprepared for though, was the constant pull of the Darkness. Having unknowingly succumbed to its presence before, it disturbed him that he now consciously felt that urge to meld with it. For all intent, there was nothing there. Just a lost history, buried under a blanket of evil.

No reason for any to want to understand it.

No bravery strong enough to want to recover it.

A sharp pain in his hand brought Gareth back from the edge. He stared down to define the cause, shocked to see that he had thrust the point of his quill through the scroll and into his palm underneath. A minor cut would barely be cause for concern, if he were training or helping his father in the forge, but he was not there.

The blood did not pool in the palm of his hand, but seemed to be drawn up through the tip of the quill to spread onto the surface of the scroll. He couldn't tell if it was the interaction with the ink on the quill's tip that caused it to turn a sickly shade of scarlet. It darkened as it spread across the page and for a moment it seemed as if it formed words, in a script that he had never seen. Only, as he tried to focus upon those words, they, and the blood, simply faded away.

7

He stared at the hole in the scroll for what seemed like hours. Only the faintest of traces were visible to where the blood had been. But no matter how much ink he used, not a single line would write in that spot.

He had wanted to write about the few conversations he was allowed to have with the local townspeople. He wanted to record their stories. Of how much life was worth, to endure the entirety of that life, living so close to the Darkness.

Of their encounters with the pitch.

About how, those creatures occasionally broke the border to steal away livestock, the elderly, or even on rare occasion, a child.

And even though the thought of such happenings twisted Gareth's stomach, threatening a violent release. He had to question the validity of the statements.

He knew only of the horror stories told to children by adults.

Describing, and defining, the most horrific scenes and actions, sometimes as a cautionary tale, but Gareth had also witnessed the use of those same tales as nothing more than cheap entertainment.

Still, his own experiences with the Lost Realms made him at once, a true believer of those tales and at the same time brought doubt to everything he had ever been told.

There was no denial that there were definite signs of an incursion into the Kingdom of Rhyce the IV. A choking black skin would spread like a disease across anything that had come in contact with... one of them.

Rhyce and his men, made a show of "peeling back the flesh of darkness to reclaim their home."

Gareth wondered to which side, that phrase was more symbolic.

The warmth from Annalei's hands on his shoulders stirred him from his impromptu slumber. Sometime during his musings of the townsfolk, his mind could no longer answer the troubling questions he asked and simply chose to shut down. There was something nagging at him about their careless attitude to the missing children that worried Gareth but…

Annalei's gentle prompting towards the bed, caused yet another thread of thought to unravel. Gareth decided to give in to his body's call for rest.

Once standing at the side of the bed, Gareth watched patiently as Annalei removed all of his dust-covered clothes. She had a bowl of warm water and a soft cloth at the ready and proceeded to wipe away a day's worth of riding through the outskirts of the kingdom. Each stroke of the damp cloth brought greater release from the tensions that clouded his mind. Instead of focusing on the problem though, his thoughts turned only to Annalei.

Watching the care she put into everything she did brought a smile to his face. And when she saw that smile, hers beamed even greater. But Gareth noticed something missing, something new.

Gone was the expectant desire, the longing for passion and compassion.

Present, was the deepening of feeling, of safety. Of comfort.

He realized, that even as they both shared the same bed, his gallantry through nights past, meant there would be no passion between them in the nights to come.

There would be no long ride on horseback.

No threat from the edge of the Darkness.

Today, the threat would come from boredom.

He sat, hour after hour listening to petty complaints, pleas for financial support, requests not to have taxes levied or enforced. The constant barrage of meaningless chatter was mind numbing enough, but what made the experience utterly excruciating were the blatant attempts to placate the King with boisterous ovations as to all of his greatness.

His mind quickly drifted and his eyes began the same journey. He marveled at how completely the vast hall had been transformed. There were no tables, no chairs, save for the ostentatiously large and obnoxiously ornamental throne of King Rhyce the IV.

Most of the room was shrouded in darkness, save for a corridor of light that was illuminated from above. Each new dignitary, guest, visitor, peasant or servant had to walk the entire length of the hall. Every footstep echoing back and forth creating a piercing sharp pitched drone and all the while Rhyce the IV glared at them, or worse, completely ignored their presence altogether.

Gareth's wandering mind snapped back, alerted by the loud protests of an elderly farmer. His pleas began to mix with the woeful cries of a woman who appeared to be in her late thirties. She was being dragged off under protest by two members of the Rhyce Guard. The old man swayed back and forth from the futile gesture of reaching out to pull his daughter to safety, back to the equally futile gesture of pleading for clemency from the king.

"There are laws in this land. And if, not upheld… tyranny and the Darkness shall take control." Rhyce's booming voice reached all corners of the large chamber.

And then, with a flick of the King's arm, the old man was roughly escorted out through the pillar of light while his daughter's cries faded into the stonewalls of the inner castle.

Rhyce turned towards Gareth and in a calming voice quite convincingly stated.

"I know it seems harsh, my lad, to extract such a heavy fee, for his unpaid taxes. But we have relieved him of the burden of another mouth to feed, body to clothe. She will be able to work off her father's debt, all the while being provided three healthy meals a day. And I dare say, looking at the skin and bones waif, she could use it."

Try as he might, Gareth could not think of a valid point to argue any different.

During the following weeks, there were more days spent chronicling the King's actions within the walls of the castle. Gareth attended every public session, political meeting and private meal. He wandered through every hallway and room with complete autonomy. He was invited to, or able to join at will any gathering.

He was privy to secret sessions between the King and the members of the Rhyce Guard. Any session, whether dealing with escorts for visiting dignitaries, or having to do with military matters and the minor border scuffles with the Kingdom of Alder. Once again Gareth found his training to be helpful.

At times he would spend the day walking the grounds with the King. Recording his musings, his joy, his laughter, his dreams and his fears. About his slightly off centered way of defining the existence of man, amongst the pressing weight of the Darkness and its menacing tool, the pitch.

He found that he began to at least understand the man, if not that, that he actually liked him.

All too soon though, that would change.

8

They were on horseback again. This time though, the escort was much larger. A whole company of heavily armed members of the Rhyce Guard rode in front of Gareth and the King.

The King, in turn, was on his own mammoth horse, which Gareth now learned was named "Boulder".

"It takes a rock to hold the likes of this monument of sovereign majesty!"

Rhyce's boastful statement was accompanied with a grand gesture of spreading his arms wide and then bringing them down hard to pound on his chest. The action caused every inch of the King's armor to vibrate, drawing attention to the fact that he too, was armed today.

All of these things only added to Gareth's puzzlement. He was told this would be nothing more than the simple matter of settling a minor land dispute.

Gareth saw wisps of smoke rising in the distance. Their spiraling trail mixed with the clouds that came down from the mountain slopes before them.

Instantly the demeanor of the entire troop changed. The reaction of all around him, including the King, told Gareth that they were approaching their destination.

As the silhouette of the tiny buildings came into view, several members of the Guard began to peel off, flanking the village to all sides.

Again, Gareth's training had taught him that this was not meant as a simple precaution, but as a preamble to action.

His senses became more alert, yet the confusion continued to increase as every sight that befell him showed no need for concern.

The remains of the company entered the dilapidated town and Gareth was appalled at the miserable living conditions that existed here.

Muck and Mud coated everything.

There was no growth...

No plants, no flowers, no grass. There wasn't even the faintest sign of food growing for harvest. Yet there were the remains of a carcass from some wild beast. Gareth could not decipher what animal it could be due to the heavy coating of flies that seemed to infest the entire place.

Again he wondered how these people could possibly be surviving, much less be the cause of unrest to the King's realm.

He tried to stare past that scene, only to notice the poor condition of each... He could not even bring himself to call them homes. The rotting timbers, which barely kept the hole filled, thatch roofs aloft were no abode fit for any living creature.

And by the looks of the few townsfolk that wandered aimlessly about, they had given up living some time ago. Occasionally one would cross their path and the vacant eyes that met theirs, showed no sign of acknowledgement to anything, lest the King's presence.

Gareth had trouble meeting their glances. Instead he turned towards the King, searching for any answer as to how anyone could be allowed to exist in conditions like this.

The King ignored it all. Instead he rode steadfast and calm. As he settled his horse in what would loosely be called the town square, he stiffened his posture even further.

The resolute sign of nobility.

Once there, he nodded to Captain V'ren.

The shrill blaring of battle horns shattered the morbid silence, throwing Gareth into a panic. All of his training had taught him to take arms, to expect danger and he cursed himself for the reflex action of reaching for a weapon that was not there.

He continued to anticipate the attack of an unseen foe…

But none would come from this putrid lot.

The women and children barely managed a whimper, as all of the wretched souls were extracted from their dismal shacks and placed before the King.

All were prompted, pushed or knocked down to their knees before him.

Even the younger men, whom Gareth would have expected to protest, barely managed to raise their heads to look at those that brutalized them.

Nothing at all happened.

Time seemed to stand still in relative silence. The only thing to draw Gareth's attention from his seething thoughts were the occasional sputtering coughs from one of the pox covered children or the snorting of one of the Rhyce Guard's horses as it hoofed another clump of mold-covered moss in apparent discontent at even having to be in this place.

He tried to push away the unwanted thoughts that kept creeping into his head.

Thoughts that, were as ugly as the environment in which they now stood.

Would it not be more humane to put these wretched souls out of their misery and to scorch this vile place from existence and cauterize the land in hopes that it may, one day, be saved by the future?

He absentmindedly began to jot down those horrible thoughts only to realize what he was doing, when the quill snagged on the parchment.

He looked down.

First with relief to see that not a single thought made it to the surface of parchment. But then confusion, realizing that the quill had dropped through the hole of that same, torn and stained scroll. And just like before, the sharp tip of his quill re-opened his previous wound, with the same puzzling effect.

Gone were both the blood and all of his words.

Almost with a sense of relief, Gareth's gaze was drawn to a distant commotion, as two members of the Rhyce Guard shattered a termite infested door from the inside of the building and began to drag its sole occupant toward the assemblage.

Unlike the other members of this undead society, this one was struggling.

As they came nearer, Gareth began to understand the extent of this man's struggles.

Were it not for the dried and caked clumps of mud and feces, his tattered clothes would barely have clung to his emaciated body. His long, ratty hair was also, discolored by the same, and here and there, scabbed patches remained where clumps had been forcibly removed.

What Gareth could see of the man's flaying arms, appeared to be covered with scratches and cuts. Some dried and healing, others freshly made and bleeding.

Loud shouts were followed by incoherent ramblings, cries, and bouts of maniacal laughter. A few momentary, calm sentences escaped the nan's dried, cracked lips, in a tongue that Gareth had never heard, nor could he understand.

This unsettling presence was forced down and held close to the ground before King Rhyce the IV in mock genuflection.

Gareth turned his gaze towards the King hoping to find strength in the larger man's indignant confidence, only to be disheveled by the sight of both man and beast struggling to maintain any composure in light of being brought face to face with this ominous soul.

The tattered man's ramblings became one low, raspy drone.

The King, who was still not entirely able to compose himself, managed a brief nod between a body-trembling shiver...

A shiver, which seemed to course its way from the man, through the great steed, Boulder.

A distance horn sounded, then, slowly throughout the mire and decay, others echoed the call. It was no battle cry, as such, but a definite call to action. As guard and horse began to pull down, then set ablaze each and every structure in the diseased town.

Gareth watched in horror and growing anger, as his thoughts became reality.

He screamed out! "I didn't mean it!"

"Mean what, son?" A puzzled Rhyce, asked.

Gareth just shook his head, trying to separate thought from reality. And the King took advantage of the pause to caution him.

"Take note, Master Scribe. For this, is what befalls those who deem to change the world with the written, Word. For those who do not come from the venerable Guilds, succumb to the deception of their own hand."

And Rhyce spat in the general direction of the miscreant, to signify the vileness of the act.

At the King's mention of the Scribe Guild, the self-tortured soul became increasingly agitated. He began rocking violently, causing the two guards to lose their grip on him.

Loud bursts of the strange language erupted as a chilling, violent glare, glazed over his eyes.

He did not see this world… this time… this place, but some other realm with horrors far greater than any seen here.

He abruptly became calm. Raising his head to the sky, he spoke two lines in that same, indecipherable language.

"Trét gäh MáCrèdüm: Mär Shi'ëlt ürmé rhüle ver Shàl."

He then screamed at the top of his lungs!

"Mürieté Scÿnth!" And then lunged at Gareth.

Allegiant, sensing the impending attack began to rear up in protection of his rider.

It was not necessary, though.

V'ren, who had taken up station behind the deranged man, drove his long blade down with both hands. The sharp-edged blade immediately severed the man's spinal column at the base of his neck. Freed from the support of his body, his head flopped forward. The finely honed metal continued its path as it shattered the sternum and exited the man's chest. Such was the force of the attack, the blade did not stop until it had buried its-self six inches deep into the hardened, clay-packed soil.

Gareth jumped from his mount and bolted across the short distance towards the vacant soul. He did not stop, though.

With all of his momentum, he slammed his shoulder into V'ren's chest.

The Captain, who seemed to be admiring his handi work, was caught off-guard.

Gareth, fueled by rage, was not content to stop. He pressed the flat of his boot across V'ren's throat. Not caring that the amount of force he was applying was not allowing V'ren to recover his breath.

"What the Rhule are you doing! He could have never reached me. Are you so filled with a lust to take away life, that you need to strike down such a helpless victim?"

A darkness, descended upon his own soul, as he increased the pressure on the injured Captain's throat.

V'ren began to struggle. Not only to breathe, but in an attempt to use injured limbs, which grasped in vain, at Gareth's boot.

Gareth was not sure, how far he would actually take this surge of hatred.

"If you want to experience death so greatly..."

The choice was taken from him. Not, by force, but by the pressure exerted on his shoulder by the oversized hand and bellowing laughter of the King.

"Now, now! Master Scribe." He sarcastically squeezed out between bouts of laughter. "I do believe you have more than made a proper impression upon my former Captain of the Guard. Mount up and return with me to the Keep, where we shall feast. There is no further need to subject ourselves to such indisputable defiance to the common code of engagement."

Rhyce directed Gareth back to his horse and prompted him to mount. He then began to straddle his own steed, but as he inserted the first foot into the stirrup, V'ren's coughing and labored breath caused him to pause. With one bestial gaze, he conveyed his true displeasure to his former Captain.

It wasn't until they had brought their horses to a brisk canter, that Gareth ventured a glance back towards the smoking remains of the fetid town.

He saw no buildings standing... just flaming piles of timber and ash.

He saw no townsfolk or the body of the troubled man… and he knew that, all, had joined together in that same pyre.

The only movement beyond the smoke and flame was a former Captain, struggling to stand on his own, trying to regain some semblance of self-respect.

The ride back to the castle was filled with wild replays of all of the day's events. Over and over, Gareth was tormented by the memory of each action… and reaction.

Through it all, one image kept invading his every attempt to make some rational sense to all that had occurred.

And then that image was lost.

Replaced by the strange speech that that impossibly deranged man screamed prior to being struck down.

What language was that… what meaning could there be to warrant the look in those crazed eyes?

He forced his thoughts back to the here and now. And was lost yet again in more unanswerable questions.

What did the King mean, former Captain of the Guard? Would he actually strip V'ren of his rank? Did it mean V'ren's actions were in conflict with the King's?

Wait!

His arms! The markings on his arms! Carved into the flesh as easily as script was written upon a scroll.

The script was familiar and yet, unknown.

A script he tried to duplicate to no avail.

A script that seemed to disappear, each time he had believed he had written it correctly.

And yet, both of the man's arms were covered from wrist to shoulder.

Why? Why was it there? Why did the marking stay on his arms, when it so easily disbursed every time I have drawn them out on the parchment?

What could it possibly mean?

They were questions that Gareth desperately wanted the answers to.

But these answers would ultimately shape and cloud the future of the Crescent Realms, the Darkness beyond and the role Gareth's own life would play in both of them.

9

There are times, when a ruler... a king, whether despicable or great... even the actual leader of men... must make the choice, for the betterment of the whole, which may seem, inhuman at best, from any viewpoint it is gazed... for which no decision, could be called just and good. A sweeping action, with broad implications for all that it enthralls... but an action, which may poison the very history it chooses to protect. When deciding that the continual bliss of ignorance of the majority of the masses, overwrites the pain, sacrifice, even the destruction of a secluded group of petrified souls.

These are the times when there is no right...

These are the times when doing a wrong takes a greatness of strength...

These are the times when true kings, become more than just a king...

When they set themselves amongst the...

"Ahh!" Gareth's scream echoed throughout the bedchamber. His flailing arms proceeded to sweep scrolls and quills off of the desk where they clattered loudly and spun on the stone floor. As he kicked back the chair, he grabbed the closest well of ink. At first, just slamming it repeatedly on the desktop was sufficient. But his anger continued to mount and he spun wildly, flinging the bottle with all of his force where it shattered and began to spread and flow down the wall like a darkening disease.

His ranting was incoherent even to himself. He was unable to put a voice to his frustrations.

Tears mixed with sweat. Which streaked through the day's dust and grime, burning his eyes. Ink soaked hands raked at the mess, adding to the haunted image he felt of his own soul.

Exhaustion finally collapsed his legs. Leaning against the foot of the bed, he drew his knees towards himself. His head bowed, in part from fatigue, in part from defeat.

The gentle warmth of her hands, cupped his and he slowly raised his head to stare at her glowing face.

She said nothing. No judgment of his insane actions. No rebuke for the destruction and mess.

She calmly waited, until that moment, when she knew that he was back.

Then with a soft squeeze, she let go of his hands, smiled, then raised herself to begin cleaning everything left from his destructive path.

Gareth watched her every move, losing himself in the gentle sway of her body as she walked across the floor. He caught himself trying to mimic the sweet tune she hummed as she knelt to sweep the shattered glass.

She was about to begin to wipe down the ink on the wall, when Gareth bolted upright…

"No wait!"

She stood there frozen, as Gareth walked up behind her and lightly rested his hands on her shoulders.

"That is the proof of what I have become…

… Or haven't become.

It proves what I have said all along, that I am not a Scribe. I cannot take the actions of a twisted man and write some superfluous soliloquy that justifies his deeds… even if, prior to them taking place, I, myself thought them to be the only actions warranted.

As I try to commit those actions to history…

… I choke on the very meaning of every word. I despise my own actions. Those I took, and all of those I should have taken.

Shouldn't my own complacency in these events be chronicled? Should there not be a scribe to archive the misdeeds of the Scribe?"

Annalei turned in his arms, which now became more of an embrace.

One. That neither of them chose to break.

"I do not profess to know or understand the ancient path and wisdom, or lack thereof, of the Guild. I do not know of your own role in and of that same sect. Is there a right inherent of you, to simply view the world from the outside? Or must you, immerse yourself in its actions, to be able to honestly tell of what you have seen and experienced? What point is there to history, if the past had not been lived in?"

Gareth choked through a wave of intense emotion.

"You see much more… than I could ever."

She reached up with both hands to cup his face.

"I only see that which is before me. Don't look for what you cannot see, what may not even exist, just because you feel that there should be some justification for what occurs around you. There are so many things in this world for which there can never be a logical explanation.

Goodness, evil.

Beauty and the Darkness.

Life and death.

I have seen an act of kindness destroy a person's desire to achieve for themselves, and the vileness of evil unite a community to unbelievable acts of heroism. I have seen the plague of beauty carve out the soul of a woman, and the Darkness alight, with the amber glow of a single Calla Lily. I have seen a man's life shatter as he watched both wife and child succumb to the birthing, and a family heel as the sickness that tore them apart finally takes the last breath of their anger.

I don't speak this because I feel that you can not see these things, but because you choose not to see that you recognize this, and so much more than I or anyone else will ever be capable of.

You only need to choose to acknowledge this in…"

He kissed her.

He kissed her with a ferocity that he was sure would harm her. It did not matter, though. Every emotion that had bottled up in him, released itself in the passion of the moment.

He traced the smoothness of her lips, with his.

He felt the moistness of her tongue, with his.

His hands molded to every curve of her dress. And when that sensation was not enough, he tore the fabric away and cupped the warmth of her flesh.

He raised her in his arms and carried her to the bed. Stripping off his own clothes, his mouth began the same path on her body that his hands had traversed just moments before.

Then, with a gentleness he did know he was capable of, he laid upon her.

He lost himself in the sensation, in the intensity of their coupling. And when he felt that he could last no longer…

She pushed him off and onto his back.

His brief confusion turned to anticipation as a wry smile arced its way across her face and she slowly mounted him. His thrust met her decent with a thunderous release.

Neither was satiated yet.

Slowly at first, but then with a growing intensity, the grinding of her hips brought them both to the point of collapse.

Gareth slowly continued to count, releasing a small bubble of his breath with every beat. Their ascent curled through the water, occasionally catching and nesting on his eyelashes. A quick blink released them to the water's surface. Only when he could force no others, did he give in.

He jerked his head out of the bathing tub and whipped his soaking head backwards. The cold trail of water bit into his warm flesh. Although the exhilarating sensation sparked his adrenalin, he measured his breath.

Steadied his heartbeat.

Control.

Then the memories of the night would flood back in and he laughed and smiled until his face hurt.

As he quietly walked back into the main chamber of his room, he gazed at her sleeping form. Her bare shoulder had worked its way from under the comforter and he gently covered her again.

He did not want to wake her. He was determined that today, he would be the one sneaking out early. That he would cater to her.

Not knowing the direct access that she and all of the other servants used, he decided to be practical, and quietly exit the room through the massive door.

The early morning light barely cast a glow onto the two massive members of the Rhyce Guard, who stood at the entrance to the room. Gareth screamed out, at the momentary shock, at almost having slammed into them.

His surprised curses woke Annalei in a start.

"What the rhüle are you doing?" Gareth growled out of the side of his mouth once he regained some semblance of composure.

"The King has declared that in light of your distressed state from yesterday's events… that you should remain in your chambers and rest until such a time that the King's Medician feels you have had ample time to recover."

Gareth began to raise himself to his full height, his hands clenched, as he fought to bring some control to his mounting anger. He was about to challenge the guard's authority…

"I demand you tell the Ki…"

Annalei's soft pull, guided him back into the room. She deftly closed the door with the bump of her hip as she opened the comforter and enveloped Gareth within the cloth and her body.

Neither saw, or cared about the exchanged smiles of the two guards as the door silently shut.

"You shouldn't have stopped me." Gareth stated, staring up at the canvas above the bed.

Annalei peeked her head around the corner as she laced up her bodice.

"I didn't have to try very hard." She smiled.

"Still…"

"You may lay there and ponder the afternoon away, if you so like. I, however, will excuse myself and get you some food."

And she disappeared, leaving Gareth with a sense of longing.

She peeked around the corner again. She smiled realizing that his gaze had not left this spot.

"And… maybe some answers."

This time, to his dismay… she really left.

He sat at the desk, tracing the few lines of ink stain that Annalei was unable to remove. Shaking off some distant thought, his hand moved to the quill. Yet he didn't pick it up. Instead both hands returned to the stain. Tracing the outline from both sides simultaneously.

The image reminded him of something.

Something unseen. Yet. Familiar.

Pulling himself away from the image, he reached down for a scroll. Out of the corner of his eye, he sensed a movement in the shadow off to his left.

Abruptly he pulled himself from the chair to stare down the intrusion in the corner of the room, to face the scars of last night's tirade.

He slowly walked directly to face the image of darkness. Sinking to his knees, he reached out towards the blackness, only to recoil in horror at the moist touch of…

Mürieté Scÿnth!

…He scurried back to the chair, grasping it as a feint form of protection.

He fought to control his panic, control his breath.

Still his heart, still his mind.

Whose voice?

Whose thought?

His hands shook uncontrollably as he tried to reach up and claw the vision from his eyes.

He forced himself to confront the image. Confront the Darkness.

All that met his gaze was the spot. Where ink fused with paint.

Yet. In the very corner where a shard of the broken well had embedded its talon.

A fresh flow of ebony coursed a sickening path, down the wall.

When Annalei returned. She found Gareth bent over the desk. His hand moving, at times, faster than the ink would flow from the quill. On that occurrence, his arm would quickly swing out and jab the quill in the general direction of one of the five bottles of ink that he had grouped off to his right.

She called to him repeatedly, but he ignored her.

She gently pushed several scrolls aside with her foot attempting to carve a pathway to the sideboard to set the tray of food she had retrieved from the palace stores. Once done, she made her way towards him again.

More scrolls.

She gently bent down, picking up one of the discarded scrolls. As she unraveled it, she was surprised. She had expected to see his artful hand, followed by what he would have perceived an error, then a dramatic flourish in disgust, then nothing.

But the scroll was complete.

Not a single error.

Not a single omission.

Each scroll was complete, without mistake. An unbelievable amount of work produced in such a short time.

Her second surprise was the content. Every word, every description was, as he claimed to be, a false interpretation of all of the kings actions and commands. A flowery, reenactment as to the cause and effect of what Gareth had previously described as one of the most horrific sights he had ever witnessed.

She dropped the scroll. Fear and concern cascaded across her body. Weak knees gave out and she dropped to the floor.

What could have caused this?

Had the rumors she heard from the other servants been true?

What could have made him change so quickly?

She slowly crawled closer towards him. Pausing briefly to swipe another scroll from her path.

As she reached out, her hand brushed yet another.

Fresher.

Wetter.

The ink, almost still running.

And she read.

Tears immediately welled in her eyes at the true, and honest account of the previous days actions. His thoughts. His admissions. His pain. And his fear. This was not the man she had thought she had grown to know. Seeing, through his words, his eyes, tore that perception apart. It reinforced everything that she knew to be true, but also showed her so much more.

It showed her, dare she admit it… that she loved him.

She stood, proud once again, but confused. She desired to understand what all of this meant. What had driven him to this path.

She gently placed a hand on his shoulder, but if he noticed it, it wasn't evident.

She was on the verge of panic. So she spoke the one word she had never uttered in all of their time together.

"Gareth."

He had never heard his name sound like that.

It was not just the melody of her voice, but the emotion attached to it. It became a destination.

A place of warmth and love.

A place, that he longed to be.

He hadn't realized, that once again, he had been pulled into the Darkness.

But that song called him back. Called him to the destination from which he was pulled. A destination he would always fight to return to.

He dropped the quill and reached up to cover her hand in his.

"I thought that I might be lost, again. That I might not be able to separate the word and the reality."

She bent down and kissed the top of his head.

"I'm not sure I understand what that means." She quietly stated.

He bowed his head.

"I'm not sure that I do, either."

"Many have left. They said it was like this the last time. Except how could any of them remember that long ago?"

His meal having been eaten and a selection of scrolls having been given to the Rhyce Guard outside his door, Gareth was now completely content to sit back and listen to anything that that beautiful voice uttered. So he nodded his answer, prompting her to continue.

Her narrative of the morning's events in the scullery continued.

"Even the King's personal servants seemed to be at ill-ease. Too many secrets. Too many hushed words and locked doors. Do you think any of this has to do with the events in Cellia?"

"What? Where?" Gareth mumbled.

"The name of the town you saw obliterated was Cellia. My Elders once called it home. Well before I or even my mother was born. But still, a memory from my family's past."

"I'm sorry. I didn't think to ask. I was so caught up in my own horror. I guess I chose to separate those events from anything… or anyone else, lest it make it even more unbearable."

"That's okay. You couldn't have kno…"

"What last time?" Gareth practically screamed out.

Annalei was caught off guard by Gareth's alarmed reaction. She slowly began, wary as to his state of mind.

"You have, no doubt heard and read about the last great battle that carved the Crescent Realms?"

"Many believe most, if not all of that history, to be fables. Tales to frighten ill-mannered children. Nothing more than a cautionary guise. Even my time at the Guild house has shown me nothing to disprove that." Gareth frowned, hoping that this will be something more than old wives tales.

"Believe what you may." Annalei stated harshly, a bit peeved at his dismissal.

"When one lives as close to the true Darkness, as to see it every day from her bedroom window… you don't believe in tales. You believe in the reality that confronts you. Always.

I have seen the effects it has on you. I have listened to your tales, so do give me the courtesy of a hearing, before you belittle my thoughts."

He reached out and took her hands in his for reassurance.

"I meant no disrespect of you. I simply meant to state, albeit poorly, that that history has been lost to us."

She smiled, then, continued.

"The Kingdom has had no less than a half dozen incursions from those that dwell in the Darkness. Not meaning, a single member of the pitch straying across the border and leaving their rot in their wake. That happens far too frequent for any to admit. What I mean is an actual raid by the Shàl Mïr Cri."

Gareth's eyes widen in disbelief. In no history, story or legend, had a name ever been given to the monstrous warrior race from the Darkness.

He struggled with the validity of this, but one look into her eyes convinced him not to challenge her words, only his inability to comprehend the truth.

"I know what you are thinking. That the end of the Last Great Battle… the end of the Lost Realms… the end of the Märkén Thraüm … meant the end of the Shàl Mïr Cri. Yes, their legions were decimated, their power to spread panic, greatly reduced. But they were by no means eliminated. Theirs was a force of numbers. Not skill or stealth. So they retreated beyond the Lost Realms back to the lands of the Mürken Rhüle, where they await their Master's call."

"And you believe that they are about to, or have already attacked again?" Gareth questioned. He now hungered for more information, more answers to newly forming questions.

"It is not I who believe this. Have you not been paying attention to what I am trying to tell you?" She snapped.

"I most certainly have. I just need to know." His eyes pleaded for answers.

"The elder members whom have spent their lives in servitude to this king and those before… claim that there were signs prior to the last occurrence. Towns lain waste to cover the intrusion. Troops sent off in the middle of the night. Meetings held in secret. Members of the staff, or guard who disappeared without a word. Even…" She looked up at him, with a heart breaking anguish.

"Even the death of the King's Scribe."

A faint, repetitive knocking on the door, pulled Gareth's attention from his attempts to comfort Annalei's concerns. He brushed a single tear from her cheek and then softly replaced it with a kiss.

She reluctantly allowed him to pull away.

He looked back to give a reassuring smile as he began to open the door.

Abruptly, the door swung back, catching his hand and twisting his wrist in a scream of pain.

A maniacal man, in miniature, pushed past him. Ignoring the injury he had caused. The little man spun around, his trailing bright green robe, pirouetted around his small frame. He frantically glanced around the room.

Once assured of his next actions, he reached out and grabbed a handful of Gareth's tunic. Dragging him across the room, he spun Gareth until the backs of his legs hit the edge of the chair by the desk. The force of the impact caused Gareth to collapse onto the chair.

Gareth began to stand and protest, but a quick smack to his forehead, put him back in his place.

Annalei, though as shocked as Gareth, could not help but giggle.

Both Gareth and the little intruder threw stern warnings at her with their eyes, causing her to have to fight to suppress another.

Reaching out with both of his short arms, the man grabbed and pulled down on both of Gareth's ears.

"Owww! Wha…"

Before Gareth could even begin to protest the man splashed a fowl liquid into his mouth, causing him to stick out his tongue in disgust. Which the curious creature then grasped tightly between his finger and thumb.

Ignoring Gareth's protests, he turned towards Annalei.

"How long has he had this strange aversion to taste?" He asked in a high-pitched quivering voice. Before she could answer through her tears of laughter, he continued.

"You do not have a bout of the…"

The implication and insult sobered her mood instantly.

"I most certainly do not!" She screamed.

Annalei's rebuke was quickly silenced with a dismissive wave as he turned his attention back to Gareth.

Still clutching Gareth's tongue, he began to rattle off a series of questions, never releasing the tongue and never expecting any answers.

Suddenly and just as abruptly as he had entered, he stated…

"Fine"

Then left in a flourish of robes.

As the door slammed, both Gareth and Annalei raced after. Reaching out, Gareth painfully flung open the door readying to spew forth a series of curses.

But as they looked, in either direction, the little man, and even the Rhyce Guard, were gone.

10

"My boy, it is so good to see you up and about, looking healthier than ever. You had us all worried there for a day or two." King Rhyce's enormous arm pressed down on Gareth's shoulder as they walked through the courtyard.

It was a bright but chilled day. Gareth couldn't help but squint through the sun's glare as he turned to judge the King's sincerity.

"But the Court's Medician has declared you fit and sound and that is all that matters." He let out with a thunderous laugh.

"And now we can get back to business… or should I say, the business … of recording history, of course."

And he laughed again.

But there was no comfort in it for Gareth, only more concern. A concern that grew with every shadow that lengthened to hide the truth.

With every sentence, that was twisted to mean two things or more.

With every subtle glance, thrown in a direction where no one should be.

He returned back to the room late in the evening, exhausted and ready for sleep, but determined to keep his plan alive.

He quietly set about creating a scroll with a version of the day's events, one that he knew Rhyce would want to see and believe.

He would then, as Annalei suggested, "Write the right" and create a scroll that hid no truth. Even if it painted his own actions or thoughts in a less than favorable light.

It would be time-consuming, but the proof of its effectiveness was already apparent by the lifting of his imprisonment, such as it was.

Though being confined to a room with...

Annalei wrapped her arms around him from behind. He leaned into her, drinking in her fragrance. Melting, with the warmth of her breath. He wanted to give in to the urge, and was about to, when she disengaged.

"I will leave you to your task, but be warned sir, your work is not done until you have satisfied all matters under the covers."

He leered after her, as she sashayed back to the bed.

With a renewed sense of urgency, he set to complete the first task as quickly as he could so that he could spend the remainder of the day on the second.

He was still getting dressed when Annalei burst from the servant's passage she used. His disappointment that she had no food, quickly passed as soon as he recognized her worried state.

"Something has happened. They wouldn't say what it was. But there were bodies. A lot of bodies. They brought them through the food stores. The women were screaming and… and…" She began to break down in tears.

Gareth rushed to grab her, to give her support and comfort. Her breath slowly calmed.

"Even some of the soldiers were crying."

He held up her face and peered into her eyes.

"You must stay here. I am going to go and see if I can find out what has happened, what is going on."

He tried to pull away from her.

"No! You mustn't. You don't know what he will do. What he has done."

"It's fine. They'll want to tell me so I can record the event. Don't worry, I'll be back as quickly as I can."

He let her go and hurried from the room.

When he reached the main floor he saw no evidence of any disturbance. Other than the hallways being unusually quiet, all seemed perfectly normal. A faint voice in the distance was the only clue that there was even another soul around.

Confused, Gareth went towards the servant's passages that he had originally been led through. Upon reaching the hallway his path was immediately blocked by the same two members of the Rhyce Guard that had been perched outside of his quarters for days.

"Let me through. Surely the King will want his Scribe to record the day's events." His voice failed his resolve and squeaked out as a pathetic plea.

"There are no events for you to record today, Scribe." They sang out in unison as they crossed their swords in front of Gareth.

He stared past them, hoping to gain any vantage, but all he saw was darkness. He began to lower his head in defeat and noticed a crimson pool directly behind the guard on the left.

"I'm sure the King will tell me in due time." Gareth stated matter-of-factly.

"In the meantime you might want to watch your step." He motioned with his head, then, began to turn and walk away.

"A pool of blood that large would be easy to slip and fall in."

He continued walking, ignoring the calls of the Guards and their threats to silence his lies.

Gareth wandered the main floor of the palace. Trying to conceive of some plan that would gain him access to the answers he so desperately craved.

His path, led him to stand directly at the entrance to the Grand Hall. The depth of the great expanse was shrouded in the shadows of disuse.

He was about to move on when he thought that he heard a feint sound emanating from the rear of the hall. He stared into the darkness, trying to perceive any movement. He hesitated to move, not wanting that action to create any sound that would drowned out the other.

Whether due to this added vigilance or because the sound was louder, he clearly made out the slight call of his name.

"Gareth!"

At first, he wanted to rush into the room, fearing for the safety of the only soul to use his name in this place. But the voice clearly wasn't Annalei's.

He slowly walked into the hall and cautiously headed towards the sound in the distance. Every footstep echoed, causing the misplaced perception of another unseen threat. His eyesight had become accustomed to the dark by the time he had reached the source of the calling. But it did not prepare him for what he saw.

King Rhyce the IV, sat slumped on the ground. His massive bulk leaned heavily upon the side of his throne and his sheer weight had caused it to become askew. He left arm was draped at the elbow on the cushion, trying in vain to support his effort to not sink completely to the ground. The once powerful and booming voice, let out a rasping breath, as the fallen man tried to speak.

"Whatever you think of me... do not judge me for these actions I take today. For even a king, such as myself, can show weakness against such a calling. Don't judge me until you read all of the..." The rest of his statement trailed incoherently into silence.

Gareth wanted to question him, probe for answers. But any attempts, were simply met with a slight nod of the King's head, signifying that there would be no more answers.

He was tempted to just leave the man there.

To continue on with his search...

But he quickly realized the foolishness of that action and how he would be able to use this better to his advantage.

Another thought he was not proud of. Those who would read this scroll would then have to judge him, for that.

It was a struggle that almost stole all of his strength, but he was able, with the weakened assistance of the King, to get the man seated atop his throne. He then pushed over a small block table to slide over and use, elevating the man's legs upon it.

He bent over to speak directly into the King's ear.

"Sire! Where is your Medician? I must get him to help you. Where is he?"

There was no response.

Gareth looked around, staring into the Darkness. Everywhere he thought he saw movement, but it was just a trick of light or shadow. His focus was drawn to one direct spot, only to feel his threshold of pain begin to elevate.

He shook it off and returned to the King.

Pushing, prodding, even lifting the man's inflated head did nothing to rouse him.

"Rhyce!" Gareth screamed. "I am trying to help you. But you must help me. Where is your Medician?"

The man's eyes flickered open, briefly. Gareth hoped that he had made enough of an impact on the King to elicit a response. The man's head lulled over as his eyes rolled to the left, before loosing consciousness again.

Gareth stared off in that direction. Suddenly, he remembered the doorway, positioned in the rear corner, and raced off in a hurry.

The scene, hidden here, was much different from the rest of the castle. Servants, aids and soldiers alike were stumbling about in a frenzied dance. Injured soldiers and townsfolk were laid out or propped up in any available space. The sound of the screaming victims, wailing relatives and those trying to help, cascaded off of the stone walls and concussed Gareth's ears.

He searched, frantically for the King's medician. His task made almost impossible by the shear number of people crammed into the narrow corridors. It had become increasingly difficult to discern the living from the dying. Most were covered with blood, some with their own, some with that of those whom they tried to help.

Gareth began to notice one major difference between the two. Of those that he knew were dead, or near death… any visible wounds oozed, with a blackness, along the edges. Their blood and its stains, darkened. A foul smell, stronger than the stench of death, emanated from their blood and seemed to intensify as it turned the color of pitch. He watched as the diseased droppings seemed to come alive in and of themselves. Curling to form symbols which quickly dissipated and faded to nothing.

Through the cacophony of voices, Gareth heard a high-pitched shrill, which he recognized as the King's Healer.

He struggled through the mass towards that voice, pushing servants and soldiers aside without care. Once or twice he slid in the pooling sickness that drained from the dead. He could spare no more time, and plowed straight to his target.

Gareth found the short man, whose once green robes, now were soaked down to a burnt umber. He was screaming out instructions in all directions.

The little man paused only briefly when he recognized Gareth.

"I have no time for interviews." He vapidly stated.

Gareth, in no mood to have any sort of confrontation or conversation, simply grabbed the man's tunic and lifted him in one swoop to his own eye level.

"The King is in need of your help and I mean to see that he gets it."

Gareth turned and began to drag the protesting and flailing little man through the hallways.

Gareth stood off to the side while the King was attended to. His abduction of the Medician had spurred a massive amount of activity. He cared not of the outcome as long as it had led them all to the King.

The entire hall had been illuminated again and no less than three-dozen guards and aids now attended the King, by means of the short mans orders.

A massive gurney was hefted by almost all of the available soldiers. And with a nod, they were off.

Stripped of his blood soaked robes. The squat little man seemed to disappear in the loose smock that he had left on. His stride, so small, it took several minutes for him to cross the floor from the dais to where Gareth stood.

"Though I highly disapprove of the timing and means of your intersession… Your concern was… justified."

He was about to leave and then turned back to Gareth.

"I am baffled though by your actions… I would not care to assume that you feel that his survival is in your best interest."

He shook his head, then, began to walk away, turning back to Gareth one last time.

"Or any one else's for that matter."

"What I saw, raised only more questions… And what I did, only makes me question myself, more."

Gareth continued to pace around the chamber. Occasionally he paused by the desk, as if he were about to stop and record the events of the past few hours. He knew though, that he did not comprehend the context in which those events had transpired and therefore was in no position to set them down to history. So the pacing continued.

Annalei had given up trying to calm him some time ago. So she sat, patiently on the edge of the bed.

Both were caught off guard by the door swinging wildly open and the unannounced entrance of the short-statured medic. His tightly woven gold overcoat caught the candlelight and cast an amber sheen all around him. He walked directly up to Gareth, but then talked as if he was not even there.

"I remembered… even amongst the turmoil, something I heard said." He stopped and turned back towards the door, then spun again on Gareth.

"Something you said… no read. No! Not something you read. Something you wrote. It was I who read it. Heard it read… Which doesn't matter."

Gareth and Annalei stared at each other in fear, confusion and even amusement at the actions of this little man.

"You see! It spoke to who you truly are. Not that trivial banal text you have force fed the King. And trust me, you needn't try that hard to hide the truth and to stroke his ego. He will gladly run with the smallest tickle."

"It was…" And it was his turn to start pacing the room frantically.

"The word. Words, plural. That you said, wrote, that the villager said. Wrote. Both. On his arms and on his tongue."

Annalei, not liking where this diatribe was heading, moved to head off the little man before he could focus directly upon Gareth.

They both seemed to anticipate the other's action but the frenetic pace of the medic brought him before Gareth first.

But before he could utter the words, Annalei grasped Gareth in her arms and whispered in his ears.

"I love you."   "Mürieté Scÿnth!"

Both phrases battled for Gareth's attention. He became oblivious to both of the speakers' presence. An internal struggle that threatened to loosen the very fabric of his soul.

He felt a darkness and fear… cold with despair. Pulling him to a place he did not want to go.

And a warmth and peace… a sense of where he knew he longed to be.

Mürieté Scÿnth!

It meant more than the Darkness.

But, what?

He longed for the answer, any answer. Yet, he wasn't sure he was prepared to go where that answer might take him.

Wasn't prepared to be drawn into that darkness.

And then, just as quickly… the Darkness didn't seem ready to accept him.

He heard shouting. A loud shrieking whine… and then Annalei's countering.

He focused his eyes on the ceiling drapery and quickly realized that he had been laid across the bed. His head began to pound with each burst in the argument. He wanted the shouting to stop, but did not feel as if he had the strength to rise and put an end to it.

"You had no right to barge in here and subject him to… that!" She screamed at the Medician.

"I have every right. It is you who has not even the slightest…"

"If you even think to complete that sentence, it will be you who needs the aid of the King's Medician." And the glare she shot across the bed at him stripped him of any semblance of authority that he may have felt that he had over her.

"Well then…" He squeaked out.

"I would greatly appreciate it if someone could please tell me what the Rhüle just happened." Gareth coughed.

Annalei jumped on the bed and smothered him with kisses.

"You had me…'

"Us" Shouted the little fellow.

"Us" Corrected Annalei with gritted teeth. "Worried"

Gareth read the concern in her eyes and glanced at the comical, head shaking of the intruder.

"You have been in some sort of self-induced state for several hours, my dear Scribe."

"What!"

Gareth bolted upright, instantly regretting his decision. Both the small man and Annalei rushed to steady him.

"We need to talk, my son." The man calmly stated.

Annalei shot him a steely-eyed glare.

"Hush woman! The man needs to know what he is up against."

"You know what is going on? What the symbols mean? What those words meant? Why the darkness speaks and pulls at my very existence?" Gareth's face pleaded for answers and he reached out to grab them.

"What! No! I have no idea what you are talking about."

"Then?"

"I meant that the King and the Rhyce Guard care not for your safety. Your acts of valor… mean nothing to him. It was just another extended right bestowed upon him by the makers. You just did what you were supposed to do. These walls do talk, but I know not of this darkness you speak of in here. There is, but one Darkness, and it has caused the misery you had witnessed earlier. But why it has chosen this time and this place is not a question any with color to their skin will ever know."

Gareth was about to question the man further, when a lone guard poked his head into the room.

"Antryg! We must go. Now!"

The little man stopped mid sentence and abruptly turned to leave.

"Take care, Master Scribe." And he paused and gazed at Annalei. "Make sure there is no path, that is hidden from him."

Annalei nodded in acknowledgement.

And the man disappeared.

11

He slammed his head into the overhang for the third time.

"Gah!"

He rubbed his forehead, checking for blood. Yet, again.

"Please! Stop!" Gareth pleaded to Annalei who moved through the narrow passageways and tunnels with ease.

"How do you do this? You actually carry trays of food and supplies through these… these things!" He screamed out the last words as he pounded the stone, wall.

She came up to him and kneeled at his feet.

"I know this is difficult. I know it is not the way of a noble member of the Guild. But if Antryg thinks that your safety may require this…"

"Antryg?" Gareth shook his head.

"Trust me, it makes my skin crawl to have to agree with that little weasel, but I will not take that chance. I am no longer willing to allow chance to keep you safe."

Gareth heard her voice trail off. He reached down to raise her head to face him.

She tried to brush away a tear without him noticing.

"That's my job." He stated as he rubbed the tear-streak from her cheek. He raised her to his height and gave her a gentle kiss.

"Lead the way, my lady."

There were only two points at which the labyrinth of tunnels crossed actual hallways. On each of those occasions Annalei went first and made sure no other servant or guard was within view.

Once in the main corridor, Gareth was amazed at how hidden or nondescript the entrance of those passages were. Whether covered by a loose tapestry or hidden in the shadows of a deep recess, any passer-by's vision would be drawn to the ornamental statues, paintings or enormous plants that graced the hallways before and after each opening.

He himself had walked past this very spot on several occasions without the slightest hesitation or attention to the secrets hidden within.

Annalei tugged at his sleeve to get him to refocus on the task at hand as she led him into the dark, yet again.

This series of tunnels, though taller, were narrower and seemed more ancient. Less used. At various times, the exact stone that Gareth reached out to grab to support his half-sighted journey, simply crumbled to dust in his grasp.

Another switchback, and their descent became much steeper. Annalei's caution to Gareth came almost too late, as his impatience caused him to nearly bump into her, sending them both off balanced, onto a cobwebbed covered, wooden platform.

They paused to catch their breath and Gareth thanked the fact that the wood, although old, was still in good shape and without rot.

He gazed over the railing into the shadows below.

"They must have built this platform to allow them to maneuver the bulkier supplies around this curve," he stated, trying to cover up the tension of his having almost sent them to their doom.

Annalei didn't seem to notice or care.

"The remaining way is all timber. We must be careful… but we are almost to the end," her soft voice reverberated off of the stone, walls and into the depth below.

Once at the bottom of the stairs, Gareth tried to look around and familiarize himself with the surroundings, but every direction he turned, his gaze faded in the never-ending gulf of blackness.

Even after Annalei had lit a few torches that were mounted to the walls, his vision failed past a few feet.

"What is down here? How far does the chamber go?" Gareth would have thrown out a hundreds questions of the like but Annalei cut the inquiry short.

"I do not know and you should not care. It is not what I brought you down here for. Come this way." She motioned him to follow her around a corner not more than ten feet from the edge of the stairs.

There was a feint glow coming from the outside wall. As the two got closer, Gareth recognized it as a vestige of remaining light from the setting sun as it wormed its way around the gnarled timber of the ill-set door.

Annalei did not hesitate. She grasped the iron ring hanging to the right and deftly twisted and pulled the old door open with an ear-piercing squeal, as un-oiled hinges protested their use.

Gareth's eyes struggled to adjust to the flood of natural light, limited as it was through a covering of bramble and overgrowth.

Again Annalei reached out and Gareth was surprised as she easily pushed away this obstacle. The obstruction being nothing more than a camouflage cover mounted on a wooden frame.

Garreth followed Annalei out of the castle, all concern of their being visible to any passers-by, quickly dissipated as he looked around at the trench like area they now walked in.

"If a time comes, that you need to get out in a hurry… If I or the other, tell you it is no longer safe… And if it is not possible for us to leave together…you… must head down and to the left. We will not go that far, for there are certainly others who will be at the side entrance of the gate.

Lose yourself amongst the crowd of servants and head into town. Straightaway from the gate, about four rows in, you will find a long narrow building. Go inside and tell them that I sent you. They will give you a room. Wait for me there while I arrange for a means to leave the kingdom."

Gareth was both amazed at the depth of her planning and baffled by the mere thought that it might be needed.

"This seems ridiculous." Gareth protested sheepishly. "I am supposed to be a Scribe. One who walks through battles… unscathed. The voice of the present, so it may echo throughout history… I wear the colors that say so thusly." And he yanked on the edges of his vest.

"I do not wish to argue the fact that protocol dictates your safe return to the guild-house in El'Anthandria. But there is something far greater than history's edict. Something more sinister than just the pitch in play here."

"How can you say that? How can you know that?" Gareth stubbornly asked.

Annalei's concern was quickly turning to irritation.

"Maybe you've hit your head a few too many times on the way down here. You seem to have forgotten everything that has happened to you since the time of your arrival. And if your own words are to be believed, the occurrences began even before setting foot in the Kingdom of Rhyce. So which is it?"

She stood there, hands on hips. Eyes demanding an answer and yet, Gareth had none to give.

Each moment asked another question of him, but nothing, or no one provided the answer.

Not a single word was spoken on their way back up to the room. Gareth's thoughts and mood kept darting back and forth from regret at having caused Annalei's anger, to his own anger at her not respecting his view.

The longer the trip took the more his anger turned to concern. Had he damaged the one thing, the one person, he held most dear.

This was a worry that intensified as they came to, and crossed the last hallway. Annalei did not even pause or check to see if the coast was clear. She just continued without hesitation, never looking back to see if he was even following.

Gareth was so concerned with her apparent apathy to the situation, that he himself did not bother checking the corridor before proceeding.

In his haste to catch up to Annalei, Gareth blindly pushed through the tapestry and walked directly into the path of the King's page.

"Ah, Master Scribe." The jittery man's eyes darted in every direction. The man's nervousness made it impossible for him to stand still for even a brief moment.

"Master Page." Gareth countered. Quickly realizing that the man hadn't noticed where Gareth had apparently come from.

"Hmm… What?" The man squeaked out, his thoughts torn from some deep introspection, to the now confrontation with the King's Scribe. He kept shuffling from side to side, peering around. Looking in every direction.

He didn't speak. Couldn't focus his attention on Gareth… and yet would not leave.

Gareth, slightly unnerved and anxious to be on his own way, slowly realized that now since the encounter had taken place, it was his responsibility to release the page to proceed with his duties. And yet knowing this made Gareth pause in doing so. He thought to take advantage of having this captive audience with one of the King's inner attendants.

"Might you be taxed with the King's bidding at the moment?" Gareth asked to begin, trying to determine if the man's uneasiness was due to the unobtainable demands of the King.

The man's demeanor changed instantly. Although the darting eyes and profuse sweating continued, the twitching and wringing of hands stopped.

He leaned in closer to Gareth and with a sideway glance, softly asked. "Would… may you… the King?"

Gareth stepped back. Wondering if the man had become unhinged.

Even more so than he already was.

The man pressed toward Gareth again.

"Wha, wher… might you have see… seen. The king? I mean… may, you, in your recent roaming, have come across and or know the whereabouts of… the King?" The man's voice trailed off into silence with the last words.

"The King is missing!" Gareth shouted.

With a ferociousness Gareth was stunned by, the measly page grabbed Gareth's tunic and swung him into the shadows of the alcove, which held the tunnel. The frantic man pressed his face impossibly close to Gareth's.

"Miss…missing? Nobody said anything about missing. Why? Why? Why would you even think, that. No need to even think, about… Why? What have you heard…know…have you seen?" The man's head shook from side to side with each incoherent babbling.

"I just thought since you…" Gareth tried to speak calmly, but was cut off again.

"It's his castle! I mean he could go wherever he wants. His kingdom, he could go…"

He let go of Gareth and began to slowly wander away.

Gareth took advantage of the man's distraction and faded into the tunnels, leaving the confused page with yet another mystery to ponder.

Gareth tried to quickly catch up to Annalei, but the Page's distraction had taken so long that Gareth knew that he would find her in their room.

If he was to find her at all.

He was suddenly struck with the panic of having lost her and he quickened his pace.

His thoughts kept wandering from the possibility of losing her and…

How could they lose the King?

He rushed past the last wall torch failing to remember the long stretch of darkened corridors he was about to enter.

There was a sharp pain in his head and he briefly thought. *But, I haven't hit anything…*

And the contact of his flesh and the mortar echoed almost as loudly as his curse.

Gareth felt and stumbled his way through the darkened maze. He thought that his eyes where becoming more adjusted to the darkness. He could make out the faintest of outlines, which helped him avoid smashing his head two more times.

As he peered into the distance the glow of another torch came into focus and he realized, he was at the back entrance to his room.

He heard shuffling from inside and froze in panic. He hadn't worked out what he would say. What could he possibly say to convey his guilt at causing her any distress, when all she cared about was *his*, safety.

Leaning against the wall, he looked around. He wanted to be anywhere but here, having to deal with his own failing. He turned and grabbed the torch preparing to bolt down the passageway.

This was not a torch to be held, but to be used as a guide and the heated metal stem quickly seared into his hand. He threw it down with a muted scream of anguish. The spilled oil flared across the floor alighting the grotesque shape of a figure pressed against the wall.

Before Gareth could comprehend and confront that form, the oil quickly burned itself out, plunging the corridor into the pitch of darkness again.

The burning of his hand and the sharpening pain in his head clouded his mind. He slowly slid to his haunches. Trying to sort out each thought, each emotion, every desire, every concern.

All moments of brightness quickly twisted into scenes of anger. Unbridled hatred that fueled unspeakable desires for swift and callous retribution.

It was not his anger and yet it veiled the truth. And even though he knew it, it was the force that drove him into his room and the waiting confrontation within.

12

"What the rhüle do you think you are doing?" Gareth screamed as he charged at the figure standing before his desk.

"Verit Glah!" Rhyce spat through gritted teeth as he turned towards Gareth, throwing several scrolls off to the side. "You really should rethink your choice of words Master Scribe."

Gareth, momentarily stunned, recovered his anger quickly.

"You have no right. Those scrolls are the property of the Guild. No man, woman, king or god… shall possess them until being presented them by a member of that guild."

"I possess all that is within my kingdom!" Rhyce bellowed. "At times I think you seem to forget that fact." And he turned back towards the desk, almost dismissing Gareth.

Gareth pressed forward not willing to be put off as something insignificant. He paused, noticing Rhyce shaking with laughter.

"I am amazed at how well you seem to grasp every nuance of guild protocol, when you haven't even been taught anything but to twist the perception of the happenings around you."

He flung another scroll across the room as he turned back towards Gareth.

"Are all of your brethren inbred with this air?"

Gareth realized that the King expected an answer and he allowed the venom in his soul, to do just that.

"It is as inbred as the arrogance of kings. A perpetual guise, worn by the weak…

To assert control and subservience over the masses…

A birthright, of sorts, contrived to allow an elite group momentary predomination of those whom would never allow themselves to take advantage of such a situation."

Instead of countering with anger, Rhyce seemed to alight with the challenge of debate.

"And yet! Does not the fiction you have written, either version." Rhyce swept his arm out pointing in the direction of the scrolls, strewn across the floor. "Of the happenings in Cellia, prove the words you render now, false?"

Without Rhyce's boastful pretext to fuel his anger, Gareth barely was capable of responding.

"What do you mean?"

"Whether one is to believe the call to duty of a venerable King, or the abstract horror of a people's decent into the ashes which claim them. You clearly profess, either respect for the King's courage to do what is needed done or your own self-loathing at having realized the only solution before a single action was even taken.

Either way. In action, or thought, you set yourself above those miscreants, in true noble fashion. So who is being a slave to their own arrogance?"

Gareth struggled to regain the momentum that his ire had supplied. It seemed for a moment that it had faded, but another sharp twinge at his temple refocused his indignation.

"One's thoughts do not need to become action. So to try a soul based on an intention that may never have manifested itsself, would be a callous form of justice. Just the same as your actions without thought have dire consequences. You misrepresent one in order to draw a parallel that couldn't exist until the thought, became action, in an attempt to appease your own self-doubt."

King Rhyce's own anger began to mount again.

"Have no doubt. Scribe. That there is never, any doubt, in any of my actions. Thoughts and truths are molded by my will at my behest. As are your words."

Gareth began to protest. "Never…"

"The mere existence of these scrolls, prove what I say. You believe to hold yourself on a higher moralistic plane than I. Yet you cave to scrawl a history that you think will appease me. Presenting a garish account of the day's happenings, in hopes of providing me an appetizing guise. You think so ill of me that I would not be able to handle, what you feel the truth to be set, would be. So you, the Master Scribe, distort history and shape it to my will. So in the end, all is as I say it is to be."

Gareth reeled from the truth. He was ashamed at how easily he had been manipulated. He struggled to form some rebuke.

"You are assuming that I will continue to do, just that. And you are assuming that I will not present to my Masters, the true accounts of history."

Rhyce approached Gareth, and chuckling loudly threw his large arm around Gareth's shoulder.

"My dear boy, you are as much a part of this kingdom, as those poor lost souls in Cellia. Mine to do with as I please."

"Gareth push himself away from Rhyce's grasp. "I am no one's…"

"Hush! I am growing tired of this reasoning. For a moment I thought that I had found in you a worthy opponent. But the moment you protest truth…"

"Truth!" Gareth shouted. "What truth could there be, when a King leaves his people and land to fester until the only solution given is to condemn them to the ashes?"

"The weak enslave themselves. To poverty. To subservience. To the Darkness. Their actions, or lack thereof, propel their future. It delivers them into the hands of the sovereignty.

They are given the means to exist, albeit in a limited capacity. And this existence need not degrade as long as they comply with the constraints that they, themselves have delivered their own souls in to."

Gareth pleaded the case of Cellia. "That is not what I witnessed the other day. What constraint did they fail to comply with that could have led to… that?"

"I thought that that point was made clearest of all." Rhyce let the statement hang in the air for a moment, then abruptly continued when it seemed that Gareth was about to respond. "History is not kind to those, who do not possess the appropriate means, that still try in vain to rewrite it. They only achieve placing themselves in the path of the unobtainable. Their attempt to reach beyond their station, fuels desires that need to be quelled. Swiftly and succinctly. At that point, there can be no hope left to be granted."

And the King began to head for the door.

In an attempt to find any sign of compassion in the man, Gareth again countered Rhyce's argument.

"Continuously demoralizing them, doesn't train them to be obedient. Pushing them as such, trains them to be animalistic. And sooner or later, they turn rabid. Then what do you do?"

His question hung in the air, momentarily.

Then as it seemed Rhyce would not even offer an answer, he turned back towards Gareth and coldly stated.
"Then we exterminate the vermin."

13

The intensity of their lovemaking threatened to drive Gareth mad. A desire on both of their parts reached out to consume them in a frenetic dance, each forcing their lead on the other. Only submitting when their energy waned, but then that submission lead to another wave of desire.

They found themselves begging for release and were lost in the other's screams when it finally overcame them.

Gareth shifted Annalei's body from the foot of the bed where their unbridled dance had threatened to eject them.

With each pant and exhale, he drank in her perfume.

She wrapped her arm and leg across his body and quietly moaned in contentment.

Gareth smiled at the absurdity of his concern. The wordsmith needed only two words to profess the honest sentiment and all was forgiven. "I'm sorry."

"When I returned to the room, I thought you wouldn't be here," Gareth whispered.

"I wasn't." Annalei responded with a giggle.

"I know, but Rhyce was."

Annalei abruptly pushed herself up, almost bruising Gareth's chest with the force.

"Why? What could he have…" And her thoughts and sight immediately went to the scrolls, strewn about the floor. "I thought that maybe you just… I'm sorry. I know you wouldn't. But that means."

Gareth finished her thoughts.

"He has seen all of the scrolls."

She bounced to the edge of the bed, searching frantically for her dressing gown.

"We must, you must… we have to do something." She rambled in a panic.

Gareth reached over and pulled her back to him.

"It's alright. For now, at least. We don't have to do a thing but lay here in each other's arms. And then maybe…"

"How do you know it's alright? What did he say?" She was pleading for any comfort that Gareth could give.

"There was a heated exchange. But…" He kissed the top of her head. "Things seemed to have been sorted out."

His calming manner had little effect. She sprang from the bed and quickly dressed. Finding his clothes in the semi-dark she tossed them at him, covering his face.

"You need to do it again. By yourself. In the dark. We need to know that you know… the way."

She frantically began picking up all of the scrolls and inserted them carefully into their appropriate slot.

Realizing that he had not yet moved, she turned to him and begged.

"Please!"

He was not about to deny her concerns again. He quickly dressed and with a parting kiss he made his way through the rear passage.

It hadn't taken as long this time. Even in the dark, with only the light from an occasional wall sconce, he made remarkable time. Fewer, were the collisions between his head and the stone archways.

After the first such occurrence, he realized that the nagging ping at his temple preceded each impact and so each following twinge caused an almost involuntary response.

In the light, it must have looked as if he was lunging sharply only to bolt upright and hop to regain his stride. A comical dance, that, was best hidden in the darkness.

Each time he exited the tunnels into a main hallway, he did so spinning around. Backing out, to appear as if all he was doing, was checking out the tapestry or had been admiring the adjoining painting. No one gave notice, though he was not sure if his ruse worked or if those he encountered actually cared what he was even doing.

He never slowed his pace the entire journey, until his feet hit the wooden planking on the final landing. He allowed himself a moment to catch his breath. Then slowly he grasped the railing and headed down to the cellar.

He stood at the base of the stairs motionless. No amount of time, or period of adjusting, would lend any sight in the utter blackness.

He forced himself to focus.

To remember the layout of the cellar.

But his thoughts were drawn to the vast cavern before him. He felt as if he could easily be pulled away from his intended task, but, as before, it was Annalei's warnings that pulled him back from that distant place, and a renewed focus of attention pushed him to the right and around the corner to the exit.

The faintest glow of moonlight illuminated the framework of the door. Gareth was about to pull on the metal ring when he heard a crash and the mumbled cursing of someone approaching from the outside.

His hand froze, grasping the cold steel ring. Paralyzed by disbelief, his mind struggled to comprehend the situation.

Nobody is ever supposed to use this path. How can anybody be using this path? Now! When I'm supposed to be the only one here.

It wasn't until Gareth felt the beginning pull from the other side, that his fear propelled him into a panicked reaction.

He stumbled, wildly, reaching for and stroking the cobbled wall as he spun his way back into the chamber. A growing sense of vertigo threatened to overtake him and the growing column of moonlight, as the door scrapped open wider, only intensified the effect.

He struggled to control his actions.

Struggled to remember the hidden layout of the vast chamber.

He knew that he must be beyond the point in which he would have turned to head back to the stairs. He remembered the rows of wooden stacks that in the dim candlelight, he thought, were wine racks. He slid to the ground and crawled, throwing his body against the slotted row.

The growing clambering, grunts and curses of the entering group, masked any noises Gareth made in his desperate attempt to find shelter.

His heart was beating so loud now he heard the thrumming of each beat echo in his ears. As he tried to control his breathing, the beating faded into a growing cicada call of ringing in his head.

His sense of worry escalated as the room started to glow as the intruders began lighting torch after torch. Although he was concerned that the growing illumination would reveal him to the group of men as they came closer, he could not control his need to see and understand what was happening and why.

He slowly spun trying to gauge if the answer was worth being seen. Would the importance of this moment be worth his exposure and the questions and consequences it would bring? Would it be worthy of his quill, to be recorded for all time? Should the true nature of his-own presence, in this location, at this time be included in that narrative?

He began to raise his head even as he continued the internal debate. Then his face became bathed in the torchlight through one of the many, long, dusty slots that made up the partition that he now hid behind and he also wondered, if discovered, would he ever again raise that quill.

He gazed, in surprise at a group of five members of the Rhyce Guard whom where struggling to move an immense shrouded object. Their muffled shouts and curses to each other seemed to fuel a sense of uneasiness that even Gareth felt. An unease that intensified with what sounded like a gravelly, hissing growl.

Gareth wondered if indeed the men were transporting some sort of animal. And yet…

The massive object was actually moving itself.

The guards, were struggling to keep whatever the covered thing was, from tripping, or stumbling blindly into a wall. The might of all five men was barely enough to correct its path when the mystery steered off course.

At one such point, a member of the Rhyce Guard placed himself between it and the wall. The resulting collision caused the young man to scream in pain, and through the growing chorus of hushes, the man cursed at their mountainous charge. He was about to kick out in frustration, but a massive hand struck out from under the cover and slammed him severely into the wall.

Gareth heard the shattering of the man's chest as the force of the attack drove his body into the stone, wall. A wave of nausea hit Gareth with the recognition of the moist thump of the soldier's head impacting, also.

A panicked cry rang out from the remaining members of the guard, which was quickly silenced by a ferocious roar that emanated from under the tarpaulin.

Gareth himself quickly turned and clutched his knees to his chest, trying to render himself invisible to the horror that now seemed present in the castle of King Rhyce the IV.

He lost all sense of time, locked in his cowering state, that when his mind regained focus… there was no sign remaining that any of the previous events had even happened.

The cavernous room was again lost in the blackest of pitch.

Unable to trust any movement at first, Gareth began at first, to slowly fumble at the pockets of his tunic.

Although he promised Annalei that he would do this venture in complete darkness, the remaining bit of soldier left in him was prepared, and he pulled out a small hand held lantern and flint strike.

The resulting covered flame barely illuminated the surrounding area. He struggled to discern between object and shadow. He reached out, preparing to steady him-self in an attempt to stand, when a deeper pain struck his temple.

At first he was concerned that his guiding ping had become a danger, but as he reached to rub the side of his head, his hand struck an object that was now sticking out from one of the unseen slots.

His hand grasped the roughly hewn finials and slowly began to slide the ancient scroll from its resting place. The dark wood was unlike any he had ever seen or felt. He had to reposition his body as the increasing weight and length of the mysterious object seemed to never end. Even with both arms supporting it, it almost slammed to the floor when it became free of its entombment.

Gareth ran his hand along the surface of an unknown type. Even before his time with the Guild, he had seen and was familiar with, what he thought he knew to be, every type of material used to create a scroll.

Wood pulp and hemp.

Lamb's wool or sheep's skin.

Even the elaborate process the Scribe Guild used, was known to him.

But this was, something else.

The darkly colored material though sinuous, had occasional rough fibrous patches on the underside. As he began to unroll the scroll, he could feel the light presence of oil. The surface, though mostly solid, had areas that were either torn or had holes that were created in its making.

His hand involuntarily stroked the text that was haphazardly scribbled on the material.

And then it froze and his mind screamed at the sudden realization of what it was that sat before him.

Line after line. In a script lost to memory and time. More elaborate than the carved tattoos of a deranged man…

Templ' Scri'!

The words pierced his soul.

He could have never conceived of its existence, or that any man or creature would ever create such a thing, but he knew this to be the true name.

Just as he knew his very own name to be…

Mürieté Scÿnth!

"Gareth! My name is Gareth!" He screamed out in to the darkness.

And though the answer was silent, it stated again.
Méü Mürieté Scÿnth, gà.

He screamed, "NO!"

And in his mind he threw the scroll aside and bolted for the stairs. Coming up short, in direction and strength, he collapsed against the wall. Only to find himself seated in a pool of congealing blood, as brain matter fell upon his shoulders.

This time the hoarse scream passed his lips and alerted his senses to the fact that he had never moved. Never let go of the twisted rune in front of him.

He did, however see a growing pool of blood, as the wound upon his hand was torn open again.

The blood, however, did not stay for long.

Gareth watched in amazement as it oozed from his palm and crawled across the surface of the dreaded writing. The scarlet liquid seemed to join with the ancient script. Slowly its tint faded to a sickly hue. And then each individual character seemed to morph before his eyes.

He could read the words before him.

Understood their meaning.

And he lost himself in their narrative.

"Gareth!"

Annalei called out as she descended the final stairs to the cellar. She paused a moment and raised the lantern above her head, casting the amber light across a greater area of the vast room.

Staring to her right she saw Gareth's body slumped against the wall. Fear caused her to move cautiously and yet she still began to slip as her foot stepped onto the edge of a large pool of scarlet.

She screamed and stumbled backward.

The glass on the lantern shattered as it hit the floor but it did not spill its liquid and the flame remained.

The commotion startled Gareth awake and he quickly stood in a panic. Scrambling away from the wall and the bloody patch on the floor, he frantically brushed at the chunks of flesh and muscle that clung to his tunic.

Annalei ran to him, and to steady him.

"Are… are you okay?" She pleaded through tear soaked eyes.

Gareth hesitated, lost in a memory that existed and one that did not.

"I… yeah, I'm okay. It's not my blood." He hesitated, "How did I get over here?"

"What do you mean? I sent you to come down here. What happened to you?"

Gareth ignored her questions.

"The last thing I remember…" He stared at the rows of wooden racks. "I was behind there. Hiding from the Rhyce Guard. And I found something. Something ancient. Something, that doesn't exit. Shouldn't exit."

"The Rhyce Guard!" Annalei looked around in a panic.

She grabbed a hold of Gareth's wet tunic and dragged him to the stairs. "We must return to your room. Before they come back."

She began to push him up the stairs.

"We have to hurry! They can't find you down here." Her impatience sparked an angered tone, which she regretted instantly, but knew was needed.

But before she took her first step upon the stairs, she stared back at the blood soaked stone and wondered, how much longer, either of them might have.

14

It was nearing morning.

Any and all who were ever in the service of the castle, had that internal sense branded into them. The hour of servitude approached.

Hers had never ended from the night before.

Annalei stood and paced around to the other side of the bed. Her back ached from sitting in that uncomfortable chair most of the night. The only time she had moved was to check her love's breath, during one of the few times that Gareth's intense dreams and fits had subsided and his stillness awoke a panicked fear.

She allowed herself a quick respite and turned from her vigil to enter the bathing chamber in an attempt to get a cool drink for her-self.

It was but a brief moment, but as she turned back, she let out with a faint scream at the sight of the now empty bed.

As she fought to control her panicked breath, she began to hear a feint tapping and then scraping sound off in the darkness of the room.

Slowly she approached.

He was crouched over the desk, enveloped in the shadows at this end of the room.

As her eyes adjusted to the darkness she caught the movement of his hand as it darted out to dip the tip of the quill into the inkwell. Three taps, then he proceeded to scratch the surface of a half unrolled scroll.

She was tempted to reach out, to coax him back to bed. She desperately wanted to quiet whatever demon had control of him now. She paused. Her hand hovering just above his shoulder…

And she nearly jumped out of her skin when he silently reached up and grabbed a gentle hold of her hand.

"I can't get it right. I write it… but it's not right. I know I didn't imagine it, or dream it or conjure it up during some concussive hallucination.

I sat there and watched my own blood flow across the scroll. Watched each letter, word… transform before me. I could read each. I understood it all. It was as clear as any scroll I had written, read…

And now it's gone. None of it remains. I cannot remember a single line, a single character of the text." Gareth dropped his head in anguish.

Annalei wrapped her arms around him from behind. She had no idea what he meant. She just knew how much it meant to him, and she felt how much its loss devastated him.

Annalei awakened from her exhaustive slumber, staring at the empty space next to her. She immediately knew that Gareth had not stayed in bed and she quickly glanced towards the desk as she sat upright.

Her chest began to pound as her breath and heartbeat quickened with each new dread thought at finding him not there. She pushed herself to and was about to swing her legs over the side of the bed, when she noticed the top of Gareth's head. She carefully moved over and slid from the bed to kneel before him.

He sat there, clutching and rubbing his, once injured hand.

Annalei took both of his in hers, as she gently searched for any sign of a deeper injury. Finding none, she woefully stared into his eyes.

Gone, was the torment and loss. Instead she saw his fierce determination and commitment.

"Please don't." She pleaded. "You need more rest."

"What I need are answers. Any answers. A single answer. I don't remember a thing that was on that scroll, but I remember there being a scroll. One that shouldn't exist. I know that when I held it in my hand… it was the single, most horrific thing, and the single most important thing, in all of the Crescent Realms…

…that, the message on it was paramount to the future of all living things, even those that avail themselves in the Darkness. That, that message was written in a language the existed before time its-self was recorded.

I need the answer to why I remember that…"

Annalei was tempted, in his brief pause, to convince him to alleviate her fears by staying with her. But as she prepared to coax him with a tempting stare…

His, convinced her that this was something she must let him do.

She squeezed his hands, a little tighter than necessary in order to make sure he listened to her words.

"Be careful. But above all else… be safe." And then she kissed him.

They used each other as support, rising from the side of the bed. There was the quickest of hugs and then Gareth headed to the door.

Pulling it open, he froze in place.

Annalei thought for the briefest of moments that he had decided to give up this dangerous quest for answers and return to her arms. That elation was very shortly lived.

Gareth's words were spat with more venom than she thought him capable of.

There was no time to question them though. As he furiously pulled the door closed and left.

Gareth struggled to keep his anger in check. He had to suppress an intense desire to strike out. He felt an unfamiliar fury in himself that increased, as the pain in his temples did also.

"So help me, if any of you tell me the King sent you for my own protection and that I am not well, I shall strike you all so ill, that the Medician won't even know how to begin to fix you."

Gareth's whole body shook in anticipation of an upcoming battle.

The lead member of the four Rhyce Guards, quickly and calmly responded.

"My Lord! Please forgive the intrusion, but it was not the King who has placed us in your charge."

Gareth could feel his face twist in confusion.

"Lord Antryg has placed us as such, to insure your safety. He is concerned that there are conspiracies afoot in the Castle Rhyce and wants to insure that you are safely able to record all for history."

"You will not bar me from seeking an audience with the King? Or to go to the cellars if I so choose?" He questioned with a cracking voice.

"We will remain in protection of your quarters, but our presence throughout the castle may warrant greater suspicion than you may want to court."

His anger deflated, Gareth threw back a parting retort as he cautiously headed down the hallway.

"Alright then… as you were."

Gareth nervously kept looking over his shoulder, never quite convinced that the Rhyce Guard were not there, to keep a constant vigil on him for more nefarious reasons. He felt that each step he took, led him further into the heart of the castle, further into the shadow of whatever darkness was now trying to take hold of these lands. His growing sense of paranoia seemed more justified with each hollow footfall, as every corridor he entered seemed abandoned.

He slowed his pace, trying to search out any sound that would indicate anyone's presence. But only silence answered back.

"How am I supposed to find answers when there is no one to ask my questions. No one to show me any solutions!"

His frustrated scream echoed down the vacant hall.

He continued forward, though for every few paces he advanced, his doubt would cause him to hesitate and wander back.

He tried to grab hold of the anger that had propelled him past the guard. He used what he could conjure to push past any hesitancy. As he rounded another corner he saw a quick flash of movement in the distance and as he trained his ear, he heard the faint sound of talking.

He hurried his pace. Each step increasing speed as the droning conversations grew in volume. His only hesitation came when he thought he heard the bleating of a lamb.

He entered the main cross-corridor of the castle, into a confusing scene of orchestrated chaos. It was as if every single citizen of the Kingdom of Rhyce was crammed into the passageways leading to the great hall.

Noblemen and their ladies, spectacularly draped with the finest garments and jewels, stood shoulder to shoulder with farmers and their livestock. Soldiers and servants, stood arrow straight with protocol, ignoring the taunts and tugs of scurrying children and small animals.

Gareth could think of no rational reason for them to be dispersed in such a procession. The only thing they all seemed to have in common was a great look of disdain towards him as he edged his way through the growing crowd.

He pushed his way forward, trying to ignore the occasional shove or poke to his side. He tried not to pay attention to the mumbled curses thrown in his direction.

He paused.

Taking a deep breath he tried to quell the growing anger that was threatening to escape in a scream of frustration. He choked backed the sour taste in his throat and as he was about to let his curses be heard, and then he saw the face of the King's Page, approach.

Unlike any of their previous meetings, gone was the frenetic movement, and the uncontrolled and squeaking voice.

"Ah! Master Scribe, it is so good to see that you have responded promptly to your summons to court."

Gareth was slightly taken aback at the calm demeanor of the page as he gently hooked his arm around Gareth's shoulder and began escorting him towards the Great Hall.

Gareth's own statement seemed to fall on deaf ears.

"I received no summons."

They continued through the crowd and into the Great Hall. Even more people were amassed inside than were even at the reception on his first day.

Gareth struggled to keep pace as he continuously looked around, searching for any clues as to the reason for such a massive gathering.

As he was finally led to the dais at the back of the hall, Gareth noticed one major absence. There was no indication whether it be, throne or guard, staff or banner that the king was to attend.

All that met Gareth was a large table filled with quill and inkwell. Bundle after bundle of scrolls laid to either side of the chair that he was prompted to sit at. Off to the side several servants stood holding trays of beverages and food.

"I thought you said I was needed at court?" Gareth was the one to now squeak out.

Standing resolutely, the page answered sharply.

"I said, you, would be holding court." And he turned towards the mumbling crowd and spoke with a booming voice that Gareth would not have thought possible.

"The Master Scribe, Gareth of L'uramentia will ask of all, whatever he so wishes, and as the King commands, you will answer with as free a tongue as you so desire. You shall not waiver or be dismissed until such a time as the Master Scribe shall deem."

He turned back towards Gareth and leaned in so that only he could hear. He spoke with a venom that Gareth felt came directly from the King himself.

"Ask whatever you so wish…" He paused and when he spoke again, he left no doubt to the meaning of his words. "But… and be very careful of this. Record their responses, thusly."

15

Gareth sat frozen for a moment as the Page's words echoed in his ears and the sheer enormity of the task set before him settled in.

He watched as the crowd began to panic as members of the Rhyce Guard started forcing their way through the horde.

How was he supposed to find a single truth from the unwilling masses? And if found, and written, would those words appease Rhyce, himself? Or did Gareth have something further to fear?

The guards abruptly and unceremoniously pulled out, and pushed the first of the citizens forward towards Gareth.

The young woman struggled in a vain attempt to cover her now exposed breast as the once suckling newborn was dislodged by the harsh prompts of the guard. She staggered forward as two more, dirt, covered little ones clutched at the hem of her tattered dress. They in turn, began to wrap themselves around each of her legs, putting an end to her struggle to move closer to the dais.

Giving up on any further attempt to cover the exposed flesh, the tired mother no longer showed any signs of vanity.

Only fear.

The much older man, to her left, paid no mind to his young wife's struggles.

After realizing that there would be no attempt by either, to cover the woman's body, Gareth tried to divert his eyes.

Taking a deep breath, he closed his eyes to allow himself to focus.

Then nervously, he began.

"How are you?"

It was the most innocuous question he could have ever thought to ask, but the response, or lack there-of, was deafening.

The woman nervously stared at her husband, who in turn, glared back. Then, as if on cue, both stared at the two members of the Rhyce Guard begging for guidance.

The wife started to speak, but a quick, backhanded slap from her husband, flared the flesh of the naked breast and her response painfully became a stifled yelp.

"We are fine, Sir Scribe." The husband sharply stated, as he failed to make any sort of eye contact with Gareth.

There was still some fire in this man's soul.

But, not much.

Gareth's thoughts immediately were brought back to those fearful moments before the fall of Cellia.

"What trade do you keep, sir?" Gareth questioned, trying to instill as much respect in those words as he could direct towards the man.

"I am but a smithy." Came the hollow response.

"I thought as much." Gareth stated.

Which brought a sharp gaze from the man.

"And a very noble trade at that. I have spent many the hour by my father's side, stoking the forge. I have to say I myself have more than a few burns upon my arms from the spitting oil of a wayward quenching or two."

The man slowly ran his hands up the landscape of his scarred arms and stood ever so taller.

"Take your fine family home and enjoy a well deserved meal." Gareth said with a nod.

Both husband and wife quickly bowed and thanked the Master Scribe.

Gareth noticed, with a smile, that as they turned to leave, the husband gently helped cover his wife. And the entire family proudly left the Great Hall.

The rest of the day primarily went exactly the same way. Each citizen brought before him fell in to one of two categories. Most were too frightened to speak, unless heavily prompted. At times all it took was his excessive pandering to what he perceived would pull them from their frightened shell. On occasion, when even that failed, the sharpness of a Rhyce Guard's stare or the threat of the sharpness of their spear, brought out a desired response. Gareth's anger would flare knowing that those responses held no truths in their stammered syllables.

The others. Mostly those of some stature in the kingdom, allowed their tongues to spill words freely, yet they said little of any consequence. Again Gareth's anger would flare as he found himself the recipient of the pandered flattery.

The never-ending theme throughout the entire day by all of those present was, one of joyful existence in the Kingdom of Rhyce.

Gareth was sickened by the choreographed fantasy.

His patience and anger were pushed to the limit as he watched a frail hag of a woman try to spout revelries of the magnificent King Rhyce the Fourth, as several of her teeth fell from her malnourished, crooked smile.

He began to quickly dismiss the peasants and hardened his approach to any whom would lay claim to any nobility.

And yet, through it all, not one strayed from the carefully orchestrated script.

Gareth didn't need to look at the sky to know that as he dispatched the last remaining nobleman, that it was closer to the next morning than the evening passed.

He rubbed his burning and tired eyes, noticing the increasing pain in each of his hands as he did so. The cramping in his right hand drew his attention to the haphazard piles of scrolls. Shaking his head at the recognition of the enormity of the task, now completed, he was somewhat startled to see both female attendants, still standing nearby. The trays they held aloft contained the remains of half eaten meals and flask drained dry.

"Please!" Gareth pleaded. "You may leave. You have done more than I or any king, could, or should have ever asked of you."

The two young ladies, in concert, looked to the remaining member of the Rhyce Guard, who nodded his assent. Their stature quickly deflated as they clumsily stepped down from the raised platform and staggered off to the rear corridor of the hall.

The guard was about to dismiss himself when Gareth called a halt to his departure.

"I have not had the pleasure of questioning you." Gareth sarcastically called out. "Though I'm afraid there won't be any available blades to prompt your responses, if needs be."

The guard snarled and hesitated, but seemed on the verge of continuing his exit.

"Did not the King's Page say I could ask any question of any and all whom were present?"

Reluctantly, the guard turned and stood before the scribe. "Ask what you will."

Gareth made a show of reaching for a fresh scroll. He also took his time in uncorking a new bottle of ink. Then he slowly stroked the crimson feather of his quill. First with his hand, then across his cheek as he made a show of pondering his first question.

He had to give the guard credit. None of his little theatrics seemed to phase, the man.

So Gareth took a different approach.

"What are you afraid of?" Gareth slowly asked.

"I am a member of the Rhyce Guard! We fear nothing." And the man stood straighter than Gareth thought possible.

"My father said that he was always afraid before a battle. He said that any man who wasn't, would quickly suffer a fool's fate." Gareth calmly stated staring the guard down.

"Then your father was a coward. And most certainly not one for the ranks of King Rhyce the Fourth."

Unfazed, Gareth continued.

"I don't ever remember hearing that phrase being applied to the name of Timeon, Captain to the armies of L'uramentia.

The man who held the entire forces of Predur at bay, and saved the sovereign land.

The man whom single handedly turned backed a mercenary hoard and their brethren of pitch, putting the Darkness at bay." He paused. "But… you may be right."

Gareth snidely made the last statement as he continued to scribble across the scroll before him.

"I meant no disrespect, Master Scribe." The guard sheepishly murmured through a newly formed sense of respect and awe.

Gareth looked up at the young man again.

"May we start again?"

"Most certainly." Was the guard pleasant response.

Gareth's body protested the long walk back to his room. He found himself quickly searching out the first opportunity to rest along the quiet and darkened route.

He rested his haunches on the base of an ancient statue, tucked into a niche carved into the stonework of the castle.

His exhausted mind tried to pull some semblance of relevant information from the day's long proceedings. His final discussion with the guard brought about no new insights. The answers to every question were the same. No matter how Gareth tried to rephrase or twist a question to trick the guard into revealing some form of unrehearsed truth, the answers remained unaltered.

Though, Gareth noticed a major difference.

Unlike the majority of the kingdoms citizens, who's answers were clearly scripted and forced upon them…

The young man wearing the resplendent uniform of a Rhyce Guard, believed every word he spoke to be the truth.

At the same time though, one discussion kept forcing its way through. One soul. Spoke of something other than the elation of living under the sovereign hand of King Rhyce the Fourth.

He closed his eyes, concentrating on the exact words.

"You must be resolute that you are at peace with the Darkness." The frail old man continued. "You must be at peace with the Darkness and what it holds… and the darkness, it will show you that which you hold within yourself. Or… you will not, can not, go on."

Gareth remembered staring into the man's eyes. Eyes as clear as his thoughts. Yet the man seemed to fade into the darkness, just as his words almost did.

Upon opening his own eyes, Gareth realized that he was leaning next to the entrance of the hidden passageway.

For a moment, the haunting meaning of the old soul's words moved Gareth to push the tapestry aside and head down into the darkness of the cellar. But the nagging pain that had now become a constant companion to any reference of the Darkness caused him to pause.

And knowing that the other direction led him to the comfort of his bed, and to Annalei… He began to head to the other side of the corridor.

He hesitated as a fresh wave of pain hit him. Shaking it off, he reached out to push back the tapestry, only to freeze at the sound of echoing laughter, as King Rhyce thundered down the hall.

The booming baritone of the King's laughter reverberated off of the stone, walls. Its concussive effect slammed into Gareth's head, assaulting his mind as it twisted and battled the ever-present pang.

Gareth reached up and pinched the bridge of his nose, trying to force his mind to expel both.

"It would seem that maybe the weight of the entire kingdom may have been too much for our young Scribe's shoulders to bear." Rhyce joyfully chided Gareth.

"If this was your not so subtle way of proving how the narrative can affect the outcome…" Gareth still failed to match the King's gaze. "I concede."

The King was about to let loose with another bout of laughter, when Gareth quickly continued.

"I concede the fact that fear and ignorance can be used as a tool to manipulate the weak minded. But no matter how many fools you get to call day, night… their eyes will still burn if they gaze into the heavens."

The King, visibly shaken and angered, struggled to maintain any semblance of control. His words brought a lathering of fresh blood from the corner of his mouth as he spoke through gnawing teeth.

"If I tell them to call day, night. If I tell them to stare at the heavens until their eyes burn. They will comply, for that is my will. And when their eyes burn and all sight fades from them… the reality of day becoming night will then be the truth it was first said to be."

Rhyce raised himself menacingly above Gareth.

"And that is how a King shapes reality."

His shoulder nearly slammed Gareth through the wall as he turned to stomp off in a rage.

For the first time in his young life, Gareth had thought that he might die. He struggled to control his breath and nerves. His heart was pounding so fast and loud, he barely heard the King's fading comments.

"No quill shall rewrite the events that we have set forth."

16

Gareth struggled to complete his narrative of the day's events to Annalei. Each time his retelling approached the disastrous encounter with the King, his emotions and fear welled up, strangling his voice. He couldn't speak of his self-perceived cowardice and on the attempt that he was able to push past his self-loathing, the raging pain in his head resurfaced.

Yet there was something more, nagging in the background. He tried to concentrate to the point beyond the pain.

And as he did.

He felt it give way.

Slowly. It seemed to part, to allow his ideations, clarity.

If they began to stray from the vital path…

It would intensify again and wrap itself around his thoughts and guide them back… to refocus, his recollection to the most meaningful part of the exchange with the King.

To his parting statement, and the implications of that chilling phrase…

Pain!
His encounter in the cellar…
Pain!
His body quaked with recognition.
The scroll. The Black Scroll!

Annalei had found herself becoming more distressed with each recounting of the day's events. She knew though, she could not let her unease add to Gareth's torment. She patiently, knelt behind him on the bed, occasionally stroking his head, or squeezing his shoulders.

Anything, to try and draw attention away from his growing concerns.

It had seemed that his retelling had ended.

His shoulders dropped as the rigid, paralysis seemed to leave his body.

Annalei took his relaxed posture as a sign, to continue with the growing passion she applied with her caress.

She undid the ties of her nightgown and let the soft garment slide from her shoulders. Her nipples flared, erect as they stroked the bare skin of his back. She leaned up to kiss the nape of his neck allowing her tongue to form warm wet circles from side to side.

She felt his body tremble.

As she slowly slid her arms around him searching for the binding of his trousers, she felt the quickening of his breath.

The pounding of her own heart, echoed in her ears, distorting the soft words that escaped his lips.

His body convulsed and his head shot straight, almost smashing into the bridge of Annalei's nose.

She recoiled in shock!

His body convulsed again.

Tears began to well in her eyes and she let out a harsh shreik as he bolted upright screaming…

"Et,il sï ï vérgrinäht si,tu glï Mür,ïlt Scynü'ilt!"

Slowly, the sound of Annalei's crying, penetrated Gareth's fugue state.

He painfully twisted towards her cries. Every stiffened muscle ached in protest, but her discomfort demanded the effort. Crawling across the bed to her tightly coiled body, he gently touched her bare shoulders.

At first her body tensed and her sobbing increased. His persistent coaxing and soft words began to ease her fears. Each apology, then kiss, then apology again, slowed the tears to an occasional hiccough of breath.

"I know not where you go… and I fear that I will not be able to bring you back." She stammered.

He wrapped his arms tightly around her shivering body.

"No matter where ever I go, I will always find my way back to you… as long as you will have me." He said choking back tears of his own.

She turned her head and their lips met, melting into each other and their bodies soon followed.

They had spent the majority of the following day and evening in bed. Only a brief respite to refresh or relieve themselves interrupted their bond. Hunger was an afterthought and quickly satiated with a small bite of cheese or fruit.

The interim of lovemaking was filled with talk of each other's past and their joined hope of the future.

But with those plans came the brief singe of pain, trying to steer Gareth's path in another direction.

He was determined not to let it envelope him again. Though try as he might, he could not disguise the growing discomfort from his lover's eyes.

"Tell me!" She sternly stated. "Tell me what you are feeling. What is it telling you? Where does it want you to go?"

"The problem is I don't know what it is trying to tell me. It feels at times that there is no common thread to draw upon and that is when the pain increases. I cannot always focus, but when I can… it seems to want to guide me to… glï Mürén."

"That! What is that? That sound. Are they words? Each time you come back you seem to scream those sounds or something like it. What is it? What does it mean?"

Gareth looked into her panicked eyes.

"What noise? What words!"

Together they tried to fight off the growing sense of dread.

Gareth's face twisted in agony as a new wave sliced into his head.

"A language. The language I heard… I saw, saw written, written somewhere dark, some where, alive, dieing…"

He vehemently shook his head trying to rid himself of the thoughts.

Of the pain!

"I remember. The pain, their pain, his pain… but I don't remember the words, do remember, should remember… but no one is supposed to remember, supposed to know. So. Very old. He, she are so old… am I, will I be so old?"

Annalei reached up, grasping his head, drawing it to her.

"Look at me." She whispered. "Listen to me, my voice. Always follow my voice."

She could feel his struggle. Felt him trying to come back to her and she knew immediately, when he did.

She began to smile as she felt him slowly nod his head.

17

He spent the better part of the evening pacing franticly around the large room. Occasionally, he sat at the desk. Sometimes picking up a quill, other times he cradled a fresh scroll. Hoping it would coax some kind of reaction or prompt a new clue, or even give up his much needed answers.

Even if they could, he wouldn't have stayed still long enough to listen.

Annalei, having given up on trying to calm him, finally put aside her concern and told him what he most needed to hear.

"Go. You'll never rest until you find some sort of answer, so… go."

Seeing the immediate change, the growing sense of purpose, and above all else, the return of his smile… Was worth whatever elevated trepidation she could ever have. She began to laugh as he almost stumbled over himself, racing for the door.

"Gareth!"

He skidded to a halt and turned back towards her.

The confused look mixed with his overanxious grin, brought out another laugh. Momentarily she couldn't speak, but managed a deft nod towards the back of the suite and to the hidden passage.

He repeatedly nodded as he reversed course and headed to the covered exit.

As his arm brushed back the furled tapestry, he hesitated, and without turning back softly declared.

"I love you."

He didn't wait for a response and pushed ahead into the darkness.

A single tear streaked down Annalei's cheek as her muffled voice called after him.

"Please come back… to me."

He moved swiftly through the passageways, allowing the twinges to guide him. As long as he trusted in the pain, it steered him true.

Racing towards the final corridor on the main floor a massive wave of gut wrenching agony slammed him to the ground. He wanted to pound his head into the stone floor, anything to give himself relief.

His hand clenched the thick cloth before him. As he tried to pull himself to a standing position, he reeled again as a fresh wave of pain gripped him. He felt a flood of tears roll down his face. The sensation did not seem to stop as it continued down his body.

A brief moment of clarity brought the realization that the sensation was the flow of blood stemming from the shattered skin of both knees.

Yet, he tried to press on.

Torment!

He struggled to force himself to breathe, and with that focus he was able to push back the fabric wall that was beginning to tear from his convulsive grasp.

Another assault shot through his head, collapsing his weakened legs. The throbbing pain of his battered knees echoed through his body.

As he tried to raise himself again he caught the movement of a shadow to his left.

He struggled to wipe the tear soaked blur from his eyes in time to see the large silhouette of the King cross into darkness. And then, just as it was in the cellar, four members of the Rhyce Guard struggled to guide the massive, cloaked figure into that same shadow.

"Where did you come from?" Antryg squeaked down at Gareth.

Gareth had failed to notice that he had landed just behind the left shoulder of the King's bizarre medician.

Struggling to stand, Gareth had no breath or voice to answer.

Boney fingers bit into Gareth's arm, as the elaborately garbed man made a half-ditched effort to help him stand.

Antryg gave Gareth's tattered body a quick glance and continued without showing much concern for his injuries.

"You are in no position. Shall I say shape, to be caught spying on, or interfering in, the King's secret dealings." He shook his head while a sharp tsk tsk sound, escaped his lips.

A booming voice exploded from the darkness ahead.

"Medician! Now!"

Antryg nervously turned to Gareth to plead with him to leave...

But the Scribe was already gone.

There was no pain in his head to help guide him down the ancient wooden stairs.

Not that his battered legs would allow a hasty descent. He struggled to navigate each step. Repeatedly sitting to catch his breath or to stem the recurring tide of blood from his injuries.

As rough as the weathered wood of the railings were, his now, scarlet covered hands slid whenever he put too much weight on the support. Again, he almost fell as he shifted his body to turn towards the last run of steps.

Reaching the bottom, he was awestruck and at the same time, dumbfounded.

Almost the entire, cavernous room was alight with the flickering amber of torchlight. Row upon row of support columns held twin metal sconces. The spiraling smoke of each rose and twisted on the high ceiling.

Where darkness had shrouded the room in mystery, the light of flame, bathed it with wonder.

Gareth quickly realized that its shear size went beyond the borders of the castle walls themselves. And he stood paralyzed with amazement.

Slowly that marvel, turned into a growing despair.

He had no reference to go by to figure out where he had seen the scroll that shouldn't exist. He paused, wondering if he should actually begin to search for something that may have just been a distorted memory.

He began to walk the rows of darkened wood racks. An assortment of wines and preserved foods filled many of the slots. Here and there, a bolt of fabric, disguised itself as a mottled scroll.

And on occasion, a tattered roll of parchment existed.

After several failed to be the blackened scroll he sought, he slammed the most recent one down onto the earthen packed floor. The brittle scroll shattered into a cloud of dust.

Through his curses, Gareth heard the cracking and shifting of some unseen object on the edge of sight.

Slowly he headed in the direction of that noise, only to stumble and fall again. He slammed his clenched fist into the earth and bowed his head, trying to gain control over his mounting anger and self-doubt. He struggled to find any reason to continue this fruitless search.

Not one of any worth presented itself to him, to give him a reason to remain. Though one kept pulling at his heart to admit defeat and return to Annalei.

A new determination told him to seek out the answers through, and with, the sensibility of his love.

As he reached up for support to stand and begin his quest upward, his hand grasped the over-sized finial.

It seemed strange to Gareth that the light did nothing to change the appearance of the ancient scroll. If anything, the wood, though it seemed older than he remembered, was even darker than the blackest pitch, the parchment a darker tone. The ink, a shade of burnt umber, had a scarlet hue when viewed from different angles.

What he had originally taken to be oil used in the making of the writing surface had congealed in the rough grooved areas caused by the combing of what Gareth was now sure to be some sort of leather.

It wasn't from any creature that he could plainly identify. He wondered at the possibility of it being from some creature only known to the Darkness.

A shocking thought had him bolting backwards as he thrust the scroll to the ground.

It had no skin!

When he saw it move, its body seemed to ooze that same gelatinous substance. Only then... it was the blackness that seemed to create the very essence, which the mortal realm called the Darkness.

Could this surface before him be the excised skin of those horrific, creatures? Was their only means to create such a scroll, self- flaying, then tanning their own skin?

How could any creature survive such a process?

Gareth cautiously approached the over-sized scroll again. As repulsed as he was to its creation... he was also drawn to its content.

Several feet of the aged scroll had unrolled when he threw it away in disgust. He now bent over it to try and read the text without actually coming in contact with it.

Nothing.

Though the words *Templ' Scri'*, rang through his head, what was comprehensible before, did not appear to be anything but displaced scratches and pools of ink.

Gareth stared off into the distance, blind to any movement. His vision turned inward, searching for any answers that might unlock the confusion and stem the growing tide of anger.

He did not see the stack of dusty wicker baskets rock and fall, and was only made aware as their decent dislodged several empty casks causing them to also plummet and shatter.

His head snapped painfully around towards the disturbance, but it was the intensifying drumming in his head that demanded his attention. The harder he stared into the darkness beyond the wreckage, his level of discomfort increased ten-fold.

Again the progression of pain to nausea to vertigo, made his legs threaten to give way. He chose though, to give in and spun, landing on his hindquarters. He collapsed backward against the roll of wooden stands, exhausted and out of breath.

The quiet was again disturbed by the clanking of various jars and bottles, as they rocked in their long forgotten tomb.

His head slumped forward just in time to see the last of the dried blood flake from his hand, that now rested on the edge of the black scroll.

At first the flecks of red dust spun in a cloud, stirred by some unseeable storm. Then, like a storm, liquid droplets fell to the surface and a ripple eddied across the entire leather parchment.

Gareth quickly grabbed the edges and pulled the tome as close as possible.

He knew that the chance of him retaining any real portion of the text was slim, so he concentrated on reading one sentence.

One sentence, word for word.

Over and over.

Trying desperately to burn the image of those words into his memory.

Every stroke.

Every serif.

The marriage of each letter to the other.

He began to comprehend that he was not reading a transfigured version of an ancient language, but that his mind had opened and was reading the actual script itself.

He read it again, and again.

Burning!

His hands, his knees and his head all alighted to the sensation, as every nerve was reawakened to the torment that this night had thrust upon his body.

There was another stirring in the distance, and though there was no sound, the effects were immediate.

His sight blurred and the words faded. All recollection lost as he slid into an unconscious state.

18

She awoke knowing that it was still the middle of the night. Knowing that her love had not returned. A cool wisp of air blew down her back through the void where Gareth's body should have been.

She rolled over and let her fingers slide to the spot where his softly rising chest had been but a few hours earlier. Then her fingers went to where his head had lain and she pretended to stroke his furrowed brow.

Finally, she reached with both arms and grasped his pillow. Closing her eyes, she hugged it tightly, and deeply inhaled his scent.

A new wave of concern swarmed through her, and even though she promised not to follow, not to interfere, she bolted upright and prepared to search for him.

Circling the bed, she noticed the feint flicker of light coming from the bathing chamber. Even from a distance she knew that the candle in that room was almost extinguished.

She hesitated, wondering…

Had he even left? Could he have gone and returned so long ago that the candle had burned so low?

She quietly walked to his side of the bed and carefully lit the lamp on the table. She raised it high, casting more light, and deeper shadows, throughout the room as she continued forward.

As she entered the smaller room, a broad smile arced across her face upon recognizing the back of Gareth's head peaking over the edge of the basin.

Setting the lamp next to the fading candle, she gently called his name.

"Gareth."

Slowly she began to slip out of her nightgown, intending to slide into the tub with him. Not sure if he had heard her the first time, she called out to him again.

"Gareth!"

He did not respond.

A growing concern, created hesitation and she reached again for the lantern. She walked to the side of the tub and holding the lantern aloft, she gazed down at her love…

And nearly fainted at the sight of Gareth, lying in a pool, of scarlet water.

A high-pitched squelch awakened Gareth in a start. His battered and tired legs failed to support him and he quickly reached for the side of the tub for support.

"Whu…?" Gareth's confused mind failed to complete even the simplest of inquiries.

Relieved that he appeared to be okay, Annalei dropped the lantern into the water and in the dim light, threw her arms around Gareth's neck. As she pulled him towards her, intending to lavish him with kisses… his uneven weight, threw both of them off balanced and they ended up in a pile of moist flesh, upon the polished, stone floor.

They both made a show of concern, checking to see if each was indeed, okay.

Then that concern turned to laughter.

Then laughter, to passion.

Gareth and Annalei woke to the increasing sound of clambering coming from the hallway outside of their room. Raised voices elevated to brief shouts and then the distinct sound of metal clashing with metal echoed through the stone, walls.

At first, Gareth had intended to rush to the door, but with the briefest of Annalei's prompting, he held back and remained seated in the bed next to his love.

Still concerned, he settled for listening intently to the ongoing skirmish, envisioning each thrust and parry, based on the distinct sound that each blade made. Every pause… then scuffle… then clash, played out in his head as he reconstructed the standard military tactic that each combatant must be using. He also knew by the sound of each gasp or yelp of pain, when a response was too slow or unanticipated.

Then! Almost as quickly as it had begun.

Silence.

The commotion was over.

Nothing held him back now and Gareth raced to the door. Throwing it back, Gareth almost stepped right into the chest of a member of the Rhyce Guard.

After a brief, startled pause, Gareth stared off to the side, and noticed the unconscious bodies of the previous guards being dragged away. A growing line of blood, trailed after.

"The King wants you to know that there have been traitorous thoughts abound and we have taken precautions to insure your safety. The unauthorized sentries' removal will ensure the health and safety of the King's Scribe."

And without waiting for any response from Gareth, the soldier spun on his heels and followed the other members of the Guard.

Gareth stood stunned. Wondering what this turn of events truly meant.

Could there have been a real threat to his well-being from a source other than the King? Or the Darkness, which constantly seemed to invade him?

The warmth of Annalei's hand sliding around to his chest, quickly pushed those worries aside.

As she slowly pulled him back to bed, he softly pushed the door close.

They weren't prisoners in their own room, but every time Gareth went to leave through the door, a massive member of the now, renamed Rhyce Elite barred his way. Informing him that, "maybe now wasn't such a safe time for him to be wondering about the castle." Or they flatly stated, "The King is too concerned for your safety in these troubling times."

Gareth would have pushed the issue, if it weren't for the fact that these members of the Elite were some of the largest men he had ever seen.

But through it all, he could not stop worrying about what was actually happening, what his eyes were not seeing, what his quill was not recording.

As he walked back to his desk after the latest of these encounters, he saw Annalei step from behind the drapes carrying a tray of fruit and cheeses.

It dawned on him, that it had been three days since the disturbance and removal of Antryg's sentries.

How did the guards think he was getting any food? Did they even care? Was it their plan all along to starve him to death, or more importantly... did they know about the hidden passage?

Gareth set on Annalei more harshly than he intended.

"You said none but a few servants knew of the passages. Is that true? Or could the Elite have learned about them from one of the other girls?

Or Antryg?

They dispatched his guards. What if the have gotten to him? Could he have told them about it?" With each question, his voiced rose in pitch and volume.

Annalei chuckled.

"You silly man. If they knew about the passage, why wouldn't there be a guard stationed there, stopping me? Though..." And now it was her turn to begin the wild speculations.

"Maybe they are waiting to catch you in them, so they can claim that you are part of this conspiracy."

Neither of them liked the sound of that. So they decided that both should remain in the room, for now.

Hours had passed and having run out of comforting or frivolous things to say to put each other's mind at ease, Gareth alighted on a new logic.

"What was the mood of the other servants?"

"The servants?" Annalei questioned, but quickly comprehended his reasoning, even as Gareth started to nod his head. "They... were acting... normal. Well! As normal as one could, being a slave in a castle ruled by a mad man, sitting on the edge of not only the Darkness, but also bordering the ancient realm in which all evil has ever been bred."

Gareth laughed.

"Well I'm glad you caught my subtle meaning there."

She wanted to slap him, but seeing him smile was intoxicating. She allowed herself to drift, momentarily, back to the time she had few concern but to make him happy. A slight frown crept across her face as she felt that feeling slip away, to be replaced with concern for their future.

Gareth, misinterpreting her changing mood, feared he may, have pushed her a little too far. He quickly embraced her and kissed the nape of her neck.

She warmed to the touch of his lips then realized what her answer would mean to him. He would leave the room via the hidden corridors at his earliest opportunity.

She grabbed his head and guided his lips, past hers, past the cleft of her throat. She didn't allow them to stop until they came to rest upon the hardening flesh, of her nipple.

She hated that she was trying to manipulate him, though at the same time she was pleased with the knowledge that he would not be entering *that* passage any time soon.

He waited until he felt the slow and steady rise of her chest brushing against his side, to slowly slip from under the covers.

Grabbing his clothes, he entered the passageway before he even began to put them on. There was a slight stumble or two as he tried to stick his leg into his trousers as he was walking. As he made his way through the darkened hallway, he ducked at the appropriate places while he slid on his shirt. And he made good time through several levels of the castle.

It wasn't until the point in which he crossed that final corridor that he realized no pain had accompanied him throughout this journey. Even as he was about to push back the heavy garment, he felt no twinge, no knifing through his sensibility.

That in itself was something he should have worried about. Instead, it gave rise to the debate of whether or not he should continue to the cellars and the Black Scroll, or should he search out the King's Medician, and seek out the answer to the identity of the mysterious figure that had now crossed his path twice.

Would the strange man have any insight for him? Anything that would actually, be helpful? Or would it be a case where-in Antryg would be in need of *his*, help?

A sharp ping, pressed into his temple, leaving Gareth to ponder its meaning.

The answer came quickly, in the form of a loud crash.

Gareth felt the rush of air and the movement of the tapestry, as shards of one of the statues smashed onto the floor.

He froze in fear, ready to race back to his suite, but the feint, garbled plea for help decided which direction he would go.

It would be a decision that would change everything.

19

Gareth peeled back the heavy cloth and stepped onto a field of shattered marble and stone. The shear weight of the large bust cracked, and tore chunks of the flooring away as it obliterated on impact.

Throughout the debris, a flushing liquid trailed after a fallen body draped in gold.

Gareth faltered in his decision to rush and aid the fallen Medician.

A growing sense of fear, threatened Gareth's ability to think clearly, to act rationally. He staggered, then took a step towards Antryg.

Stopping abruptly, he turned and stumbled in the direction the Medician had come from, and the shadows that cloaked it.

A growing pall seemed to block any avenue in which he moved, save the path back to Antryg's prone body. Any attempt to breach that barrier was met with a sharp attack. Not to his mind or sensibility, but to his physical body. As if he was being beaten by an unseen foe.

His growing anger at the invisible barrage cleared his thoughts. Though as the assault ebbed, his anger shifted to his own confusion and cowardice.

He could find no part of his own being that would walk away from a fallen friend. Turning with determination, he pushed past any force that kept him from doing so.

Although fading, Gareth still felt an energy trying to push him away as he knelt next to the frail man.

Antryg was trying desperately to push himself over and in doing so, his hand slipped in the growing pool of his own blood. A small brass disc attached to a chain, fell from his hand as it scraped the stone flooring.

A growing sense of revulsion emanated from the disc and Gareth rushed to push it aside. He stared in its direction, trying to comprehend its power. Once again his thoughts and actions were pulled from his intended task.

A blood soaked cough from Antryg, refocused Gareth. He grabbed the injured man's garments and gently pulled him over on to his back. Gareth slid his arm under the man, trying to elevate his torso to give him some relief from the liquids building in his throat. And as he did so, he shuddered at the sight of the Medician's injuries.

Closing his eyes tightly, he took a deep breath, clearing his mind of any invasive thoughts. He needed his wits about him if he was to have any chance of saving the King's healer.

Gareth opened his eyes, focusing at first, on the man… the friend he needed to help, not the chewed up flesh that hung from several gashes that had torn open brow, cheek and throat. The large claw marks oozed a grayish, mucus which bubbled as it mixed with the elder man's blood, releasing a noxious stench.

Gareth's eyes began to water from the fumes. He continuously had to rub them with the back of his free hand to keep his vision from blurring. And in doing so, smeared Antryg's blood across his face, creating a scarlet mask.

The failing man's eyes snapped painfully open and the accompanying convulsion, threatened to propel him from Gareth's grasp.

Adjusting his hold, Gareth's hand found the ragged edge of several more incisions in the old man's side. As his hand unknowingly pressed into the lowest area of shredded flesh, a stream of garbled bubbles hissed from Antryg's mouth.

Gareth pressed his brow to the man's forehead, willing strength into him. And failing, that… his apologies.

"I am sorry! So. So, sorry, Antryg. I should have come sooner. So, so sorry." Each word fell to mix with his tears.

"You must leave." A crackled voice whispered. "Your time here is at an end. But do not follow my path." Antryg coughed another flood of darkening phlegm.

"I need to find you help." Gareth pleaded. "Please, tell me… who heals the healer? I must get you help."

"Choose to leave, or the choice will be taken from you."

Gareth could feel the fading man's hands fumbling about, as if trying to gain a greater grasp on an object that was not there.

Putting his bloodied hand in Gareth's, he spoke once again.

"Take this… wear it… it may provide you with some semblance of…" And his voice trailed off.

Gareth checked the rise and fall of Antryg's chest, and although erratic, the medician was still breathing. He slowly laid the man onto the ground.

He paused, sitting back on his haunches, trying to decipher Antryg's requests. He repeated the man's last words and as he did, his hands fumbled about just as Antryg's had done.

The repeated motion of grasping air.

Grasping a medallion.

A chain.

In which to wear that medallion.

To offer protection?

Gareth's gaze bolted to the brass disc laying several feet away. He hesitated even approaching the object, fearing the effects of before.

But a clearer voice escaped the medician's lips.

"Take it and go…now!"

Gareth rushed and scooped up the pendant and without hesitation pulled the chain over his head. He felt… nothing.

A thousand questions swarmed in his head. He headed back towards Antryg in hopes of retrieving any answers, but the booming voice of King Rhyce the IV, sent him scurrying to the protection of the tapestry's hidden retreat.

"Antryg! Antryg my old friend, where have you gone?" Rhyce's voice echoed off of the walls as he rounded the corner and approached the fallen medician.

"Our guest was just starting to like you… and then you go and run off like that. Not very, sporting of you." The King's voice slipped into its harsher tone. Rhyce paused to look at the debris from the fallen statue, shaking his head. He then stood over the injured man. Posing, as the statue had once, with both hands clenched and seated on his hips.

A soft whisper of a reply escaped Antryg's blood stained lips.

"It is not sport to hunt a prey that does not know it is the hunted. And I will not be that game for you or any."

"My dear Antryg…" Rhyce calmly stated as he began to lower himself to one knee. "We are all the prey of someone or some thing. Whether you know this to be true or choose to ignore the fact… we all succumb to the cold embrace."

"But what of the coldness in your heart? To what wound is that owed?" The old man hissed between labored breaths.

Rhyce slid his bulky arm under Antryg and raised him to a seated position.

"There are some wounds, even you my old friend cannot heal." He paused, almost reconsidering. "And there are some wounds that you should never try."

The movement was subtle, but the result was devastating. Rhyce drove the entire length of his short sword under the old man's ribcage and into his chest.

The Medician's eyes flared in shock for an all, too fleeting moment, as the life quickly drained from them.

A steady flow of bloody froth seeped from the corner of the dead healer's mouth. With a brief show of affection, Rhyce pulled an embroidered cloth from his pocket and slowly wiped away the mess as he gently laid Antryg's head on the ground.

Any possibility of a moment of respect or regret abruptly ended with a muffled gasp and shuffled retreat of an unexpected witness.

Gareth cursed himself for allowing his shock to become audible. Closing his eyes and clenching his teeth, he repeatedly banged his head on the wall of his hiding place. Yet he knew that that action was not the cause of the increasing pain that rang throughout his being.

Gareth sank back further into the tunnel as he heard the enraged King searching out the source of the noise. Without thinking, Gareth reached out and cradled the brass pendant hanging below his throat.

Rhyce's massive hand grabbed the edge of the tapestry and pulled back the linen, exposing Gareth's shadowy presence… and yet, the King acted as if the frightened Scribe was not there.

Gareth could see the King struggle to fight off the ill effects of some unseen force. He quietly reached up with his other hand, and it too, grasped the pendant.

Rhyce seemed to notice the slight movement but like before he could not react…

A booming voice echoed throughout the hallway.

It was a cross between an injured animal's torment and the concussive bass of thunder. Raspy, but precise in the definition of each syllable it spoke. The nagging ache in Gareth's head became the screaming pain of a dagger, entering his mind with each of those syllables.

"C,mïr'sä Rhüle! Müg,é t'seo sëg mao'nähd gäh ve'glëth ï üré véid'h!"

Whatever was said and whomever said it was a mystery to Gareth.

But the effect it had on Rhyce, was immediate.

Even in the dim light of the tunnel, Gareth watched as the color quickly drained from the mountainous man's face.

Rhyce's shoulders slumped, as the once alert warrior, cringed and turned sheepishly towards the echoing voice.

Gareth swore that he even heard the slightest of whimpers escaping the King's lips, as Rhyce began to hesitantly shuffle towards the calling.

20

Disbelief, confusion, anger, fear, all these emotions and more accompanied Gareth as he stumbled back to his room through the ancient tunnels. He paid no heed to the guiding pangs or the sharp sensations as flesh, met stone. The emptiness, consumed him, clouded his judgement, and masked the urgency of the situation.

He had known death before.

Met it with the passing of an ill family member and the tragic accident of a fallen friend.

So why should this man's passing be any different? He was barely a friend. A bizarre stranger, who on occasion spewed insane comments and random thoughts his way.

Gareth fondled the brass pendant as his mind struggled to form parallels to another face, another time. And failing that, he searched for some meaning to what his own life had become these past seven months.

Time slipping.

He reached the second crossing and paused, not out of caution, but from a growing sense of detachment. The more he focused upon the events of the past few days, the more they began to fragment his mental hold on reality. Falling back against the wall, he broke out into a brief bout of laughter at the complete absurdity that his life had become.

He heard the echoing cadence of footfall from an approaching Detail of the Rhyce Elite. Their frantic pace and shouts of alarm, shattered Gareth's complacent apathy to the situation at hand.

An overwhelming sense of dread mixed with his growing, inner pain of alarm. All of the implications of the day's events, flooded into his head at once. He didn't need to sort through them, individually, because the resolution of each led to one place.

He pushed passed the fabric cloak and bolted through the other side, sprinting as fast as he could in hopes of reaching his room, reaching Annalei, before the Elite did.

He pulled up short of entering his room.

The shouts and screams of the Rhyce Elite were only drowned out by the destruction apparently being done to the room's furnishings.

As he reached out to push the cover aside, in attempt to steal a glance of what was going on, the sharp edge of a blade sliced through the cloth and nearly severed his fingers.

Gareth struggled to put his anger in check…

To not race into the room to stop the destruction…

And to rescue his lady.

As difficult as it was, he knew he needed to exercise extreme caution and to assess the situation fully, in order to form the best plan to save both of them.

He didn't even know if Annalei was even in the room. Rushing in would only thrust both of them into the growing threat.

Taking a deep breath, he tried to silence the pounding of his heart so he could hear clearly, all that was transpiring in the room.

Relief and trepidation raced through him as he heard the exchange between the Captain of the Elite and Annalei.

Annalei stood in the center of what was once Gareth's suite. The entire room was a scene of devastating carnage as several members of the Rhyce Elite tore through and smashed all they encountered.

The once, luxurious bed had been shredded. Each comforter and sheet was torn and left strewn about the cleaved remains of the wooden frame.

Every piece of artwork had been slashed and torn off of the walls.

The same went for the tapestries. Even the one hiding the secret passageway had suffered damage, though no guard bothered to check beyond it in their haste to cause mayhem.

Every piece of furniture had been destroyed.

The barbarians seemed to take extra pleasure in reducing Gareth's desk to a pile of splintered lumber. Every quill was snapped, the bottles of ink, thrown to shatter against the wall. Even the hand-blown lanterns were reduced to shards, the oil once inside, was splattered all over the ground.

The only thing untouched…

Were the scrolls!

Whether by command or some last vestige of reverence to the Guild, their history was left intact.

Six more members of the Rhyce Elite entered the room. The Captain of the Guard, bowed to his superior, who took a quick glance around at the destruction, then at Annalei.

"Get on with it." He spat.

The Captain, in turn, menacingly approached Annalei and without hesitation screamed out his interrogation.

"Where is he! Where is the King's Scribe!" The massive man shouted down at Annalei.

If his intent was to unsettle or frighten the chambermaid into submission, it failed.

"You tell me." She sharply snapped back.

His momentary look of confusion, allowed her to press her advantage.

"Have you, yourself, not stood guard outside of this chamber for nearly a week? If the King's Scribe is not to be found within these walls, it would seem that *you*, should be the one answering that question. Or do you not wish the General to know which side you truly stand in this matter?" She threw a momentary glance in the direction of the General.

The Captain raised his anger driven hand, ready to strike down Annalei.

"Why you…"

"Streygah! The General shouted. "A word!" He continued through gritted teeth as he started to exit the room.

"The rest of you… to your posts, Now!"

Annalei was amazed at the speed in which the entire Detachment vacated the room. Slowly she approached the door and peered down the corridor. There was no sign of any Page, Guard or Captain.

Leaning back into the room she gently closed the door. Dazed, she mechanically returned to the spot where she was almost stuck down. And that is when the emotions of the event, floored her.

Sinking to her knees, she buried her face in the palms of her hand, trying to stem the oncoming flood of tears.

Gareth cautiously entered the room. Once past the tapestry, he paused and turned to look at the damage done to it by the guard's sword. He was still amazed that he was not seen as he jumped out of the way of the blade as it slashed through the cloth.

The realization of coming that close to being caught hastened his desire to get Annalei and leave.

But when he turned his attention back towards the main room and saw Annalei's sobbing form in the middle of the chaos, nothing else mattered and he rushed to her aid.

Raising her in his arms, Gareth enveloped her entire body with his. Kissing the top of her head repeatedly, he assured her that everything was going to be all right.

All of their actions seemed to be moving in slow motion. Gareth rationalized the sensation as the desire that he did not want all that they had had together, to end. But, each time he stared past her face, he noticed another piece of their world that had already been destroyed.

Holding her tighter, he softly apologized in her ear.

Annalei's response stunned Gareth, as she quickly pushed back from him.

"Do not … do not say you are sorry for something that you had no hand in doing. That is not your fault. Never apologize to me for something you could never have stopped. I will not have you weaken yourself, in my eyes or any other's.

You cannot rob me of your strength. Not when I need it, when we need it, the most."

Without waiting for a response, she gathered that strength and meticulously began sorting through the remnants of the suite, collecting and packing those things that Gareth would need.

At first Gareth stood idly by, watching the whirlwind. He then noticed that Annalei had failed to pick up this item, or that, and he struggled to dive into the fray without getting run over.

All too quickly, the task was done.

Gareth turned to head towards the secret tunnels, but paused noticing that Annalei was not following.

"What are you doing? We must get going."

Gareth choked on the recognition of what her eyes began to tell him.

"No… no, no, no."

"I will follow shortly, I promise. But I cannot leave with you through the tunnels." Her voice broke several times.

"We must leave together. We must leave now!" Gareth demanded.

Annalei simply shook her head.

"We promised each other, that if this time came… we would go together. We would go home together." Gareth pleaded.

"I know, my love. And we will. It will be safer for you if we do not try to leave the castle together."

"How will it be safer for you? The guards have already threatened…"

"The guards are through with me. And even if they weren't, all attention paid to me will just guarantee your safe retreat."

Gareth struggled to find fault with her argument.

"Now go! Time is running out. Meet me at the building I showed you on the map. I will be there as soon as I can be sure that no one has found your trail."

Her anger elevated for each second he stood there, motionless. She was about to scold him again when his lips covered hers.

She allowed herself to melt into him as their tongues conveyed the message each needed the other to know.

And then he was off.

Gareth trusted that each sensation of pain was the guiding force for his quick exit. No sensation, no sound, no movement, met him at the first crossing and he raced forward.

He approached the last with trepidation. Would the fallen body of his friend, yes his friend, still be there. Unceremoniously displayed for any passer by?

Gareth hesitated parting the heavy curtain but there was no accompanied elevation to his discomfort, no sensation directing his actions. So he proceeded.

At once he was thankful, but also dismayed that the corridor was entirely empty. No sign of Antryg's body, or the aftermath of his death, remained. Not even the slightest speck of dust from the shattered statue, lay upon the floor. In fact, Gareth noticed that even that, had been replaced.

A slight twinge in his temple brought him back to task and he raced forward and down the final flight of stairs.

Upon reaching the cellar, he moved quickly, searching out the side door. As he turned the corner, his whole body was slammed to the floor with a forceful presence that went beyond any of the pain he had previously experienced.

He struggled to move forward, pushing against this unseen torture. Even the slightest progress was swiftly met with an overpowering urge to retreat back into the darkness.

Again and again!

Over and over, until Gareth found himself within the role of racks, that housed the Black Scroll!

All pain and sensation of discomfort flowed from his body. The sudden sense of relief threatened to paralyze him more completely than the pain.

A rapid procession of sharp twinges refocused his mind, as he comprehended, their meaning.

He could not leave without the Scroll.

Gareth began frantically searching around. He knew he would not be able to carry the Black Scroll, so he searched for anything that might help in that task.

Pushing over stacks of baskets and crates, he scurried through all the debris searching for just one thing.

He knew there must be one here. He had seen several of the kitchen staff using them. Then finally, next to a pile of large, broken, wine carafes, he saw them.

There was no time to estimate size or weight. So he pulled what seemed like the newest, and largest, from the stack. Gareth tested the fit and feel of the burlap sling as he rushed back to the ancient scroll.

The awkward size made it difficult to maneuver into the harness, but Gareth succeeded without too much effort. The harder task was lifting it high enough to slip his arms into the sling.

Once standing, Gareth had to shift the weight, in order to maintain his balance when he walked. He tested it several times and when he felt that he had gained control, he set out once again for the side exit.

Every action was a labor with the added weight on his shoulders and back. But, slowly, the task seemed to get easier and he pushed through the camouflaged thicket that hid the entrance to the outside world.

21

The bite of the early morning air, burned Gareth's lungs and made his eyes water. Even with Autumn's early chill, he felt the clamminess of his body's sweat, soak through the layers of his clothes.

He took advantage of the time of day, moving quickly through the semi-deserted and fog shrouded streets. On only one occasion did a single soul even acknowledge his presence, and that derelict was too overcome with ale to form any form of communication.

Barely a light was visible, until he weaved further away from the castle. Here, either the peasant's day started early or they had failed to yet end.

There was a larger gap between buildings here and Gareth hesitated. His destination lie on the other side of what he deduced was the main market road, leading through town.

Many farmers and tradesmen were shuffling their carts and animals, frequently crossing his path. Each time he was prepared to make his final dash, the hoof-beat of an approaching Sentry's horse, made him scurry back to the shadows.

The sun continued to rise and with it, more souls began to occupy the road.

Gareth knew he could wait no longer. His felt his only hope was to blend in with the growing crowd as he forced his way to the building beyond.

Although he tried to act casually and blend in, his growing anxiety forced him to make a mad dash for the front door of his destination. An action that he hoped did not draw the attention of yet another, approaching soldier.

Once inside, he slammed the door closed and fell back against it. He held his eyes closed and his head aloft, trying to catch his breath.

Suddenly he had the feeling that he was being watched. And as he lowered his gaze, he saw that his every action was indeed, being scrutinized by no less than a dozen, half dressed ladies, of the working class.

Gareth was tempted to turn and run back out into the road, into the waiting arms of the Rhyce Guard.

Shocked, was too tame of an expression to describe what he felt. There was no frame of reference for him to call on to know how to handle this situation, to handle the wall of jiggling flesh as it pressed in on him.

The only thing that was moving faster than the bevy of swaying breast was, the banter that each tossed out upon their approach.

"Ooooh, aint he a purty one."

"He's one of them Scribes or what-nots…"

"It's been a long one, simce we had one of them types, huh?"

"I remembers the last one, she was a feisty one. You sure as, had yur hands full with that un."

"She had her hands more full of me."

All the ladies broke out into a raucous laughter.

Gareth was finding it harder to breath, harder to tell which breast was talking and which was being pressed into his face.

Several more skin bare women approached, shouting to be overheard by the rest.

"Hey word man, why don't ya writes me the Queen of the castle. I'll show that fat-assed bastard how to mount a head."

"You's always did like 'em big."

"Theys just lay there. If they can get it up, you get on, they get off, you get off. No sweat."

"I tell ya what, girls. This pretty boy's got lots of energy. You should feel how he be squirming around already."

"I tell you, if his quills big enough, we'll be making some histrees to write about."

Gareth couldn't take any more of this... nonsense!

Though all he could squeak out was, "Annalei sent me."

"What?" Came a snide remark. "That bitch aint shared no one, with no one."

The boom of laughter erupted again, but was quickly silenced by a soft voice that Gareth only thought he imagined hearing.

All heads turned as a slim, dark haired, long legged, fully clothed beauty walked slowly through the parting wall of flesh. She seemed entirely out of place here. And the clarity of her voice accented that fact even greater.

"Weasa, you know I do not appreciate those kind of words being thrown at my sister."

A short, overly voluptuous blond, bowed apologetically.

"I'm sorry Mistress. I really didn't mean no..."

"Enough! If all of you have none to call on, there are plenty of dirty sheets to launder." She planted her booted foot and firmly placed her clenched hands on her hips. "So which is it?"

All of the, woman, began to scurry, shouting out as they went on their way.

"Whorin' or washin', washin' or whorin'" And their chant began to flow into melody.

22

Without a single word, merely a slight flick of her finger, Mereliéth lead Gareth down a dimly lit hall. Every few steps, a doorway opened to each side of the hall, revealing a small cramp chamber. In each of the rooms, one of the ladies of the flesh was either, stripping linens and scrubbing surfaces, or she was attending to someone else's flesh.

"Washin' and whorin'."

They reached the end of the hallway and Mereliéth made a big show of twisting the ornate knob, then pushing open the door with her booted foot. Standing in the doorway, she motioned Gareth into the room with a nod of her head.

Gareth had to turn sideways to squeeze past.

He felt her hip brush into him as she slowly slid sideways when he tried to pass. And as he did, she nonchalantly raked her perfectly manicured nails across his chest.

The momentary relief he felt from being freed from the mass of female flesh returned and he had to question his own decision to enter her room.

Unlike the rest of the building, the furnishings, or even the women… this room was meticulously clean. A delicate, shear elegance that would never, lower itself to the outside world. And the lady who, carefully took off, folded and draped her lace shawl at the foot of the bed, carried herself even higher.

"You'll have to forgive the girls. They are unaccustomed to having anything resembling true nobility, here."

She walked over to Gareth and stared into his eyes. Gareth in turn, tried to find any resemblance to the woman he left behind, the woman he loved.

Mereliéth reached up and stroked his cheek with the back of her hand, slightly raking it with those same polished nails.

"They are right about a few things, though." She smiled.

And that's when Gareth saw it.

The word, "What?" stumbled, out of his mouth!

"You are, quite pretty. And…" She let the word float in the air, like her hand against his face. "Annalei, has never shared anything, with any… one."

She made a slight biting motion towards him and Gareth jumped.

She turned away, laughing.

"Do not worry Master Scribe. I do not lie upon my Sister's bed. Though…" She sat on the edge of her bed and gently patted the spot next to her. "It might be nice to have hers lay on me."

Gareth was again, completely out of his element. Struggling for any means to steer this conversation into a safer one, he blurted out.

"One of the brea, um ladies, said that there have been other Scribes here? I mean in this establishment?"

"You don't need to say it like that."

"What do you mean? Like what?"

"With contempt! Like it pains you to even reference it. I hope your abilities with the quill are more deft than your tongue."

Again! Gareth was nonplussed.

"I truly meant no disrespect. To you... The ladies or your..."

"I'll finish the sentence for you. Whorehouse! That way you don't have to soil yourself. And yes we have had many over the years. There is no vow of chastity on entering the Guild. As well you know and have tasted."

Gareth's confused look prompted Mereliéth into continuing.

"It is in your eyes. In, my sister's, eyes. Every mention either of you hear of the other... it is in your eyes." Then she silently laughed and added., "I wonder if it is your hips."

She turned from him and busied herself organizing trinkets that were covering the top of a dresser.

"One of these Scribes was a woman?" Gareth pressed on.

"For such an esteemed member of the venerable Guild, you seem to have no grasp of it at all." She said, turning back towards him and shaking her head.

"Since the day I had entered that building I have been asking questions... only to this day. Not one has been answered." And it was Gareth's turn, to turn and walk away.

Even though, there, really wasn't anywhere to go.

Gareth shuffled around, staring at anything in order to continue his guise of self-deprication.

Mereliéth, on the other hand, enjoyed watching Gareth squirm. And in between bouts of quiet laughter, she mused.

"I am starting to see why my chaste little sister, is so enthralled with you."

She moved as close as one could without committing an act that would cost her customers a months worth of wages.

Gareth felt the warmth of her breath across his lips, the scent of her skin, with the rising heat of her body. He wasn't entirely sure what his reaction would be if she pressed in, to close the minuscule gap left between them.

Sweat from his brow, rolled down his nose and dropped, getting captured in the funnel of their lips.

Gareth felt the tip of Mereliéth's tongue brush his upper lip, as she pulled that drop in to her mouth. Then he felt the vibration, as she let out a little purr.

If there was ever going to be a time to stop this, he had to act…

"Mereliéth!"

Annalei's voice shattered the sexual tension, as Mereliéth turned nonchalantly, shrugging off the intrusion.

Gareth, meanwhile, nearly passed out from relief.

"You needn't worry, little bird, I wasn't going to eat him. Maybe just nibble here and there." Mereliéth said snidely as she walked past her sister. Looking over her shoulder, she continued. "Besides, the fun was in the testing. To see how far he would let me take it."

"Still, you should never have…"

"He wouldn't have betrayed you. If you doubt those words, check his pants."

"Must you be so crass?"

"I am merely pointing out that despite my best effort, even his independent parts, didn't forsake your love. That should make you happy, shouldn't it? You now have what you've always wanted. Unrequited love. The one thing each of us has sought since the day we ran from that putrefying hole. You found it, in your selfless servitude, and I push it vehemently away with each spent, pile of flesh."

Annalei, shaken by her sister's brief, but raw statement, slowly moved towards Gareth. She couldn't hide her disappointment in her sister's words.

"Why do you look at me like that? I know what I am, what I do. And just because I will not throw up a veil to hide the truth to those around me, it doesn't place me at a level that you or any one else can look down upon me." She turned away. "Save your pity for that fool you left behind in that castle."

Gareth could no longer hold his tongue.

"What do you mean? What do you know? What is going on in that castle?"

Mereliéth lips curled in a vicious laugh.

"Once again, the man with all of the words... who sat next to that bastard's side... who, as such a keen observer of events... Seems to have missed the biggest one ever."

Annalei quickly and firmly grabbed Gareth's shoulders as he tensed to pounce at Mereliéth.

"I have no patience left to play games with you woman!" Gareth's anger boiled over. "Tell me now what is..."

"Or what!" She shouted, and she was the one to close the gap between them.

"Mereliéth, no!"

"No? Your little quill pusher finally finds his words, finally finds the lost manhood in his pants, and you expect *me* to back down?"

Annalei pushed herself in between the two, facing Gareth. She reached up with both hands to cradle his face and to stare into his eyes. Softly she whispered her plea. One word.

"Please."

Gareth blew out a heated breath and sharply turned from them both, walking, again to the far corner of the room.

Annalei spun on her sister, the tone of her voice demanding a straightforward answer.

"Tell me, now!"

Annalei sat next to her sister on the foot of the bed. Gareth had pulled over the small stool that had been seated in front of the small changing table.

The tension and anger had been replaced with anxiety and impatience.

"As *you* know," Mereliéth held Annalei's hand as she spoke. "We receive *all* kinds of callers."

Gareth was almost annoyed at the tones she used while speaking. To him it was as if she was trying to imply his inability to comprehend her meaning.

"Yes. We know." Annalei softly stated as she threw a quick glance at Gareth that begged him, not to press.

"The Nobles, marry the finest women this Kingdom has to offer. Only, the finest, don't like to do the dirty things that the Nobles like best. So occasionally they come here... to cum, here." She smiled at her own joke.

"This is getting us no where!" Gareth started heading for the door. "We need to go back to the castle and find ou..."

"No!"

Gareth was stunned at the harshness of Annalei's response.

Without even acknowledging Gareth's shock, Annalei turned back towards her sister.

"Please, there is no time to play games. Please tell us, tell Gareth, what you heard."

"I'll admit, that not one of my girls would ever be mistaken for being a world class conversationalist, but plenty of the men, just want to talk. They tell us things they would never think of speaking to their colleagues, their friends, and especially their wives.

They will confess their greatest secrets, their greatest fears. Simply because they think so lowly of us, that we would never be able to comprehend what they say enough, to bother repeating it.

Some of these girls know what is going to happen even before the King does." And she turned to look at Gareth. "In a way, they shaped the courses of history like the Scribe, but by sexually manipulating the key players and their opinions.

And, as much as I love every last one of them… You do not want these women to be the narrator of public policy."

Gareth struggled to call up every last bit of his patience.

This time, even Mereliéth knew she could no longer stretch out her narrative.

"One such noble, and I use the term lightly, is one of Rhyce's war consuls. The King, even though he enjoys ruling with an iron fist, does not trust those fists enough to allow them to create strategy, less it be used against him.

He was here, the night everyone got word of what had happened to Celia. Some of the girls were screeching like an injure owl. Had to practically whip then into silence and he's, 'Oh that was nothing more than laying down a welcome mat. Clearing unwanted eyes, so that which doesn't want to be seen, could move freely'."

Gareth's eyes locked onto Annalei's. With a silent glance, they screamed. *See, I told you!*

"He kept talking about how the King's new allies would raise El' A Mür to new heights."

"El' A Mür?" Gareth questioned.

This time there was no sarcastic preamble.

"It is the ancient name of these lands. The elemental light, before the Darkness. Before the Family Rhyce. So… she asked, 'what could Celia's ashes welcome?' He said, 'the King of all of Mürén'. So she asked, 'if not Celia, what would be the path?' He said, 'El' A Mür would be raised when the Mürken devoured the Island of Souls'."

"Delgar!" Gareth shouted. "The Mürken Rhüle plan on invading Delgar."

He bolted from the stool and reached for Annalei's hand.

"We have to leave now. We have to tell the Guild…"

"No!" Annalei screamed leaving Gareth in stunned silence.

"What did you mean when you said that I should, save my pity for that fool you left behind in that castle?" She growled at her sister.

"One would call him a fool, others a page, I myself, call him nothing. But you, little bird may still refer to him, as father."

"Wait!"

"I have to go. You, yourself saw what he was willing to do to those around him." Though she tried to remain strong and adamant, Annalei's body began to betray the bravado. Tears began to stream down her face as she stared into Gareth's eyes.

"I know. What I meant was, wait for me."

"But Delgar?"

He stood there shaking his head.

"It will have to wait." He tried to sound convincing, but fooled no one.

"Regardless of lineage, might I suggest, one man's life may not be a fair trade for the souls of an entire kingdom."

Mereliéth's words, harshly cut to the truth and caused them all to pause.

"I will have Weasa take you back to find, and stow away our somewhat, supposed father." She plainly stated to Annalei. "And I will steer your Scribe to fetch a ride and be on his way. When you return, I will make arrangements for you to join him."

Without waiting for their response, she left the room, bellowing out…

"Weasa!"

"I should go with you." Gareth mumbled, trying to convince himself that he actually meant it, while knowing full well, he should not.

"And I want nothing more than to go with you, but just as we had no say in our meeting… we both know, we have no say in why we part."

As Gareth pulled her close, she bowed her head, knowing that if she looked into his eyes or locked her lips upon his… He would never let her go.

23

Gareth was amazed how quickly Mereliéth moved through the narrow passages and alleyways that wove their way in the shadows. They kept low and quiet, never uttering a word.

Every time they paused, Gareth chanced a look back, hoping to see Annalei, and when he didn't, he wondered if he should race after her.

A sharp tug, on his hair, spun his head around in anger.

Only the face that stared back at him was even more irate than his.

Mereliéth's lips mouthed the word *move*, as she in turn bolted across the road and into the slightly opened stable door.

Gareth hesitated, to make doubly sure no one was within eyesight. Then he too, ran into the barn.

Once inside, he slowed, allowing his eyes to adjust to the diminished light. The stable was much larger than it had seemed from the outside. There were two corridors that split to either side, with smaller pens on the outside walls. Down the center, accessible from both sides, were a series of enclosed stalls. Presumably for the higher paying clients.

To the right of the entrance, a raised recessed area formed the hayloft.

Gareth looked up to see the silhouetted form of Mereliéth standing on the edge of the rise.

"Fancy a roll in the hay Wordsmith? It may be your last chance for a while."

"I think I can wait until such a time as your sister and I are together again."

"There you go again with that better than thou attitude." Her voice took on its sharp tone again.

"What is it with you? Is it because I simply won't play your game? That every time you throw out a sexual innuendo I'm supposed to get all heated up like some jackrabbit? That just because some beautiful woman has made a pass at me I'm supposed to fall all over myself trying to crawl into your bed? Or is it because I know exactly who you are? What you are?"

"You don't know anything about me!" She screamed, losing control for the first time. "And the fact that you think you do, just proves my point."

She tried to push the veneer back in place.

To quickly wipe, the one stray tear away.

Gareth saw it though, it was exactly as it was in Annalei's eyes, and he immediately regretted his words.

"You're right!" He conceded. "The words that come from my mouth seldom hold the same meaning as they do from my quill. I'm sorry. I …"

"You're a man. I know." And the façade was back in place. "Now get up here! You can hide behind the bales while I make sure there is a suitable horse for you."

Gareth was amazed at how quickly she could turn the switch on her emotions. He did not want to trigger yet another one, so he began climbing the ladder.

"Not to sound disrespectful, but I do know a thing or two about horses, you know."

"And do you also know the owner of this stable may take less offense to a beautiful young lady handling his steeds, more so than a wanted criminal?"

"You may be right." Gareth said, as he reached the top and stood before her.

Mereliéth shoved him backwards and he fell into a makeshift bedding of hay. Before he could even shout his protest, Mereliéth had thrown herself on top of him.

Even with his own admissions, this was too much for him to bear.

But again, as he was about to speak his growing outrage, her mouth covered his.

He would have thought, that if her intention were truly to seduce him, and have her way with him. That she would be putting in more effort to make it pleasurable.

He looked up at her and her eyes seemed to be screaming at him.

A loud crash from below, finally brought his understanding to her actions, and he nodded. She withdrew her lips but did not move off of him and they waited in silence, pressed together, feeling the nervous beat of each other's heart.

The commotion down on the main floor lasted several minutes, then a guttural curse, followed its orator out of the stable.

"Stay here." Mereliéth firmly whispered. "Wait for me to call and tell you the way is clear. Then maybe…"

She dipped down and this time gave him a meaningful kiss. And as she pulled away she let her tongue linger on the edge of his lip.

He heard a slight hum escape hers.

Then she was gone.

Gareth quickly decided that he was finished with waiting.

Waiting to be found.

Waiting for someone else to save him.

He began searching out an appropriate saddle and bridle. A task, that took him close to the front door.

He heard Mereliéth's voice and he could tell that she was trying to use her professional charm, to dissuade someone from continuing their search. The exchange began to become heated as both parties' voices became elevated.

Gareth pulled back, wondering if he should intervene, or should he rush to mount up and exit through the other end of the barn.

The sharp crack of fist to flesh turned his gaze back towards the door, just in time to see Mereliéth's, unconscious, body fall to the ground.

Gareth pushed through the door and ran to Mereliéth's silent form. He dropped to his knees and reached out to see if she was still alive. Completely forgetting, that in doing so, he was exposing himself to the same danger.

A loud, slow clapping echoed through his head.

"All it ever seems to take, to get you to rush forward, is to strike down the less fortunate."

Gareth bowed his head upon recognition of the voice.

"Do at least, give me the honor of seeing your face, Master Scribe. I want to look into your soul as my sword bleeds it out of you."

Gareth hesitated, struggling between living up to the honored code of the Guild, or living.

Finding no means of defense within his reach, he slowly stood and turned to face, the once, Captain of the Rhyce Guard.

"V'ren."

"I notice you do not use my former title."

"Why should I?"

"Fair enough. But therein lies the problem in which we are both now faced. I truly do not hold any ill will against you for your actions in Celia. I know it is hard to believe whilst staring down the length of my sword, but I am sincere in that notion. My unceremonious demotion left me to ponder on a great many things. But unfortunately for you, I could not find one reason to continue, unless it was to the ends of getting my old commission back. And again, nothing against you, but at this moment, my returning with your corpse, is the only way that that has been presented to me."

"Then show that you still stand as an honorable guard. Honor the code and return me to the King, unharmed, as is mandated... I would not attempt any escape. That would serve you better, would it not?" Gareth hoped his argument was sincere enough to at least cause V'ren a moment of contemplation, so he could try to figure some way of escaping his blade.

And should V'ren decide to take him to the castle, he might still be able to talk, or write the means to his, or more importantly, Annalei's safety.

"It is a sweet notion. For you, at least. But you forget... you have already shown me that beneath that guise of ink and quill, lays one very adept with the engagements of combat and I would care to wager, you wield a blade more deftly, than that quill. So, I believe we have both placed ourselves beyond the edict of the code."

His arm began to tense and Gareth noticed the slight adjustment V'ren made, shifting the weight in his palm. Preparing to strike.

"So you understand, it would be foolhardy for me to underestimate you a second time. And even thrice, to ignore the fact, that you have a way of twisting thoughts and actions with words. I regret, for your sake, that your lifeless form will not provide as many complications."

Too many thoughts entered Gareth's mind at once.

Of strategies… to defend, to deflect, and advance.

Actions, that should be, should have been, or should never had been taken.

Words… spoken, and left unsaid.

Questions, never asked. Answers, never learned.

He found himself wishing for the sharpness of pain entering his head to quiet the thoughts and direct his way.

But it did not.

He barely caught the dip in V'ren's shoulder as the blade was thrust forward.

Against his own intentions, he flinched and closed his eyes, expecting to feel the biting pain as V'ren's blade entered his chest.

But it did not.

24

Gareth wondered if death could overtake him so quickly that his mind did not have the time to register the pain.

Fool!

He opened his eyes and stared down at the point of the blade. It had stopped just as it began to pierce his outermost tunic.

Something wasn't right.

The length of the blade was covered in scarlet, and the flow from the bloodline began to drip onto the ground.

Gareth looked up into the confused eyes of the former Captain. His own, mirroring that face.

The blade quickly withdrew.

Gareth watched as V'ren's eyes curled back to their whites, and his lifeless body crumpled to the ground.

"I said, never take up arms. I didn't say, never defend yourself."

Standing there, with his blade splayed out to the side, Larec allowed a smile to beam across his face.

By the time Gareth's mind fully comprehended what had just occurred, Larec had stowed V'ren's corpse in the barn, Mereliéth had been attended to and was, in turn, even mopping Gareth's dazed brow with a cold rag.

Larec had moved on to readying their mounts. He cinched the last saddlebag to the side of his ride, then, moved on to Gareth's horse.

It was Allegiant's whinnying and hoof clomping that broke Gareth's stunned lethargy.

"How in the Rhüle did you get here?" He stated as he bolted to nuzzle the horse's face with his.

"I see your time living in the civility of the Court, has done nothing to temper your need to spout obscenities." Larec teased. "Your lady, leaves nothing to chance."

Confused, Gareth looked back at Mereliéth.

"Do not look at me with those puppy eyes. I had nothing to do with it. The only person I know with caring forethought is…"

"Annalei!"

"Do not look around for shadows that are not there." Mereliéth chided. "She has not yet returned. And by the time she does… you cannot be here."

"She is right! We must leave now. Every moment we linger threatens your safety."

"My safety means nothing!" Gareth shouted.

"Clearly! As you have just stood, unyielding, in the path of a blade. But what would that have accomplished?" Larec asked.

Merelíéth quickly added. "Was your concern for the Isle of Souls merely a false pretense so you could separate yourself from…"

"I advise you to not complete that statement." Gareth's anger flared as he moved towards Merelíéth.

Larec hooked his arm around Gareth's chest to hold him back and steer he back towards the horses.

"I do not question your feelings. But… my friend. There is much more at stake and you, yourself realized it is greater than us all. Otherwise you wouldn't be in this place, at this time."

They both nodded.

Gareth quickly mounted Allegiant without another word.

Larec held and kissed the top of Merelíéth exended hand.

"Thank you for your service and care of my charge. I pray you safe days ahead." And he bowed before Merelíéth.

Merelíéth smiled and quipped.

"The sad part was, he never let me service him."

They both could still hear her laughter as they exited the far end of the stable and coaxed their horses into a full gallop.

25

They never slowed their pace.

They couldn't afford to.

Surprisingly, the Rhyce Guard at the border was not present. Gareth had wondered aloud that maybe all efforts were needed closer to the castle. Still it was a strange tactical disadvantage, unless...

Something darker was watching the border.

They met no resistance from the guard on the Alder side. They were only, too happy to allow someone apparently up to no good in the Kingdom of Rhyce, to pass.

As much as Gareth wanted to question them as to the disappearance of the Rhyce Guard, he knew they had no time. Could risk no chance of being detained and further delayed.

So!

They road on.

The days were long and hard.

The meals… sparse, and harder.

They slept in the saddle, one at a time, strapped in so they would not fall off, and guided by the other.

Their only respite was to relieve themselves or to give their exhausted horses a chance to drink and eat.

Conversation between the two was almost nonexistent, as they saved every bit of their energy. No words were needed. They both knew the importance of their journey and what could possibly lie ahead.

Again, they met no challenge at the border between Alder and Predür. But upon gaining access to the main highway, it was quickly decided that they should exit the busy crossway and use a less crowded route to the Capital.

Their horses did not protest, but at times needed extra prompting to pass on the occasional thicket of burrberries and the abundant patches of sugarstalk.

Gareth and Larec also appreciated the long stretches of shade provided by the canopy of the immense, ancient forests. They relished the cool air and admired the extensive color and variety, of each tree that rose above them.

Their journey, though rough, had been quick and uneventful.

Until, the rains of autumn crashed down upon them.

The wet leaves and rotting vegetation made the footing for the mounted horses, unsteady. The two riders were forced to spend most of their days on foot, and leading their mounts.

Each drop of rain bit into their flesh with an icy chill. The layers of clothing that had once provided comfort, and protection, had now become drenched, and cumbersome. The dampness smothered the two travelers in an irritating skin that pulled the remaining heat from their bodies.

Each step became a laboured motion that frequently amounted to nothing more than, a stumbled attempt to remain upright.

The rain's intensity increased and the ground beneath their feet churned into a mass of sucking mud and moss.

At times it was up to the horses to take the lead and pull their Masters, forward.

Owner and steed neared exhaustion and both Gareth and Larec knew they must find shelter from the never-ending downpour. They led their animals back toward the main road, hoping that they were near enough to anything that resembled a town or inn.

Every rut and low-lying area of the highway, although covered with stone and gravel, had been filled by several days worth of nonstop rain. The only benefit of having to wade through several inches of water, was, that Larec was able to figure out where they were and knew they were very near an outpost. Though reaching it before dark was out of the question.

No living creature moved, nor made a sound. The darkness of night and the intensifying storm, made sure of that.

Gareth struggled to focus his rain, blurred eyes to take in the features of the multi-storied building. Very few flickers of light emanated from any window. His only real chance, was when the occasional flash of lightning, illuminated the entire structure, revealing four floors, and corner bastion towers that stretched higher into the night sky.

Impressive as it was, they cared for only one thing.

Larec took the reigns of both horses and led them around the side of the main building, to what Gareth presumed was the stable or barn. He quickly returned and they both walked to the large oaken door and pounded upon it in unison.

The response was not immediate, and when it came, it was in the form of mumbled obscenities. The gruff language continued even after its orator looked upon their faces.

"As if ye can't already tell, we are closed. And with a seasons worth of weather in 3 days, we are full of our share of wayward travelers. So even if I had half a mind to care for your well-bein', I don't. So…"

The ill-mannered stick of a man began, to push the door closed on them.

Larec slammed his foot into the door.

The abrupt halt, caused the innkeeper to lose his grip. Sliding forward with his momentum, the slight man cracked his face into the back of the door. He let out a high-pitched yelp and his eyes glared at Larec.

"You mistake us as some common folk that you can impose your own twisted will on." Larec continued as he pushed his way past the innkeeper. "You evidently failed to recognize the coat of arms that is emblazoned on my chest. For if your sleep addled mind had, you would have chosen your words and courtesies, more carefully."

Gareth felt his friend's display was a bit over the top, but it seemed to have worked. The disheveled man, begrudgingly, mumbled his apologies, mostly towards Gareth, as he began to fumble around, lighting lanterns and readying drinks.

"I weren't lying about there bein' no rooms. The bests I can do, is give you some linens and a blanket to use down here in the alehouse. Maybe a bench or a table…"

"The linens will do just fine." Gareth announced, drawing a somewhat relived reaction from the owner.

"Would'ja be needin' any meats, or…"

"The drinks and sleep are all we require." Larec added.

The wispy little man hurried out of the room.

"Had I not witnessed the atrocious behavior towards the Guild in El'A Mür, I would have struck this man down for his impertinence. But times seem to be troubled and I am not sure what to make of any of it."

"Is that what my impending execution was? A slight against the coat of arms, emblazoned upon your chest?" Gareth quipped, half teasing, half serious.

"I would think that I would not have to define the meaning of these words to anyone. Even you."

Their tired laughter faded as the innkeeper returned and handed over the rough linens and blankets. He nodded and quickly retreated, leaving Gareth and Larec to set up their makeshift beds.

"We are but a half days ride to the crossroad that leads to the Capital and the Master of the Guild. Were we heading back to L'uramentia, it would be another days ride, beyond that, to reach the border."

"I understand the reasoning for going to Ba'sal, but I would feel more comfortable delivering this message to Lord Hadrion."

"Events have taken us beyond that comfort." Larec stated as he began to strip layer after layer of rain soaked clothing, and hung each by the small fireplace along the outside wall of the hall.

He grabbed one of the blankets and wrapped himself in it as he propped himself against the wall on one of the benches next to the table he had set his sword upon.

Gareth spent a few more minutes of contemplation, before he followed suit.

Leaning against a wall wouldn't do it for him though. He slid into the largest booth and stretched his entire length across the wooden plank. Balling up the linen, he shoved it under his head and wonder how he had gotten so far from the fluff filled comfort of the bed he had shared with Annalei. Those thoughts, though not comforting, allowed him to drift into a restless slumber.

26

In his dream-state, he recognized no images or shapes or colors. Just a disconcerting vagueness that accompanies the slight shift between shades of black.

He felt that he was being torn apart, and with that feeling, the growing pangs started to elevate in his head.

It was as if he was being pulled from one realm to another and a sense of weightlessness over came him with a final cracking pain to the back of his head.

Gareth tried to shake his head clear as he was manhandled forcibly to stand. He felt the cold, wet grip of his attackers hands as they increased the tightness of their grip. Then a stinging smack across his face drew his focus forward.

"I know this face. And it is not one of the Guild!" The rain soaked man screamed back over his shoulder to yet another. "Bring me that miscreant inns-keeper, so he can try to speak his lies to my face."

The fourth man of this band of brigands quickly, shuffled off.

Turning back towards Gareth, the man reached up and squeezed Gareth's face so tightly, that the inside of his mouth was split open against his teeth. The man edged forward and brought his face so uncomfortably close that each drop of rain that fell from his matted hair, splashed into Gareth's eyes.

The older man violently pushed back on Gareth's face as he began to spit out his displeasure.

"So! The son of Timeon fancies himself such a fine warrior that he mercenaried himself out to the Guild. Pretending to be the protector of a word worm. But look around you…" The man made a sweeping gesture. "You have fallen asleep during your watch. Your charge is gone. And there is nary a weapon in sight."

It was only now, that Gareth realized that Larec was nowhere to be seen. Had he snuck out before the intrusion? Or had this group already dispatched of his friend and, more importantly, protector?

It had taken his sleep addled, and battered mind, a moment to recognize the leader of this group. But once he did, he tried to use that knowledge to his advantage.

"General Kanther, my old teacher in the not-so-adept art of battle."

Gareth knew the blow was coming but was unable to avoid its impact while being restrained as he was.

"If only you were as quick with your sword, as you always seem to be with your imbecile words."

The General turned away and agitatedly paced to the other side of the room.

Gareth spit a mouthful of blood in his direction.

"If only you knew the benefits of those words and that of the mind that thought of them… then you may have begun to understand, and would have had the tools to defeat your opponents. But as my father always said after he saw me flailing like a wounded goose, following one of your, lessons… if you do not bother to know what is in the thoughts of your opponent, you are blindfolding yourself in battle."

And he spat out another glob of congealing blood.

The elder warrior closed on him so quickly, that Gareth did not have time to prepare himself for the succession of blows to his face and ribs.

His captors struggled against his weight as his legs gave out on him.

"That stupid gimp! He knew nothing about defeating an enemy!" The words spewed from his mouth as a fanatical cry. He reached down and yanked Gareth's head back by the hair.

"Tell me then, what does a beating such as this tell you?"

"You mean, besides the fact that you can not even defeat an unarmed man without the aid of three mindless thugs?" Gareth laughed, forcing more blood to trickle down his chin. His human restraints, yanked back on his arms in response to his insult.

"My one armed father could even beat you with one arm tied behind his back."

Gareth's jest drew an unexpected laugh from each of his captors, and in response to that… an immediate, and severe response from Kanther, in the form of a hard kick to the groin.

This time, they let him fall to the ground as each repeated cough and gasp for air sent a mist of scarlet across the wood planks.

Gareth barely heard the following exchange as he struggled to recover from the brutal assault.

"Father!" The shout echoed throughout the alehouse.

Kanther spun towards the back of the room and hesitated as he stared at Larec's silhouetted form standing in the doorframe, sword drawn.

The elder general finally broke the gaze of his son and looked back at Gareth's crumpled form. He flipped his view, back and forth several times, until the realization hit, and he broke into a raucous laughter.

"If you stand there…" He spat in Larec's direction, "then that means…" And he turned again towards Gareth, "that that fool is the one we came for all along."

Choking back yet another laugh he began to move in Gareth's direction again, slowly sliding his sword from its sheath.

"Don't!" Larec's voice boomed.

"Or what!" The General screamed as he reversed his direction and headed directly at his son. "Will you cry and blindly strike out as you did when I struck down that disrespectful bitch that spewed you out into this world?"

Larec's blood began to boil.

"You fail to remember that that was the day that I…"

"What! Beat me? Ha!... You did not, that day, or any day that followed. I laid before you to show you that by embracing your anger you could harness its power to defeat a stronger foe. Call it an encouragement, or courtesy of battle. But it was never my… defeat."

Stunned, Larec, barely managed to raise his sword in time to deflect the first arcing attack from his father's blade.

The two men that had restrained Gareth began to draw their knives and swords, preparing to accompany the general in battle.

Gareth used that distraction to make his move.

He bolted from his crouched position, driving his shoulder into one of the men's hip, sending him sprawling into the edge of the table. The man doubled over as it dug into his stomach forcing the air from his lungs.

Any noise he made was drowned out by the continuous clang of steel upon steel.

The other man, now alerted to Gareth's attack, grabbed Gareth in a crushing bear hug.

An audible crack sounded out causing Gareth to scream as the pain from his broken rib hit.

Though in spite of that pain, he had to act.

Gareth slammed his head backward, shattering the man's nose in an explosion of blood. He pushed with all of his remaining strength, ramming the larger man into a wooden pillar.

Instantly the man's grasp faltered and Gareth was able to break free. Stepping slightly forward, he pivoted and drove all of the force he could through a spinning kick, into the man's chest.

There was no counterattack from his combatant. Only the feint hiss of escaping air, that came with the sound of his shattering chest.

Gareth struggled to stand upright. Every breath caused his broken rib to pierce his lung with a debilitating agony. He felt himself slipping into an unconscious state and forced himself to focus on the battle at hand. He clung to any thought that allowed him to remain upright and continue.

The distant sound of a free blade hitting the ground echoed in his ears and he snapped his head up to see his friend and protector, stumble against the onslaught of the General's fury.

Gareth barely caught the movement from the corner of his eye, as the first of his assailants had recovered and was rushing at him.

Stepping back, Gareth grabbed the man's tunic and used the man's momentum to spin him around and back towards the table again.

This time though, the man's stumbling body hit at an extreme angle and there was a sickening snap, as his head bent, and distorted into an impossible form.

Gareth's own movements brought him to rest right next to the dead man.

Again, Gareth's attention was drawn to the other side of the room as General Kanther screamed, as he prepared to thrust his sword into his son's chest.

Without thought, Gareth picked up the dagger that his attacker had dropped. He hurled it towards his old teacher in hope of preventing his friend's demise.

The blade struck Kanther with deadly accuracy, penetrating the back of his neck and instantly severing the old Soldier's spinal column.

As immediate as the death was, it wasn't quick enough to prevent Kanther's blade from slicing into Larec's side and the young man sank to the ground in a growing pool of his own blood.

27

Gareth couldn't assess the damage in the dim light and through the blood soaked cloth. He turned and grabbed the dagger from Kanther's neck and quickly cut away Larec's tunic.

Although he had never seen, let alone dressed any battle injury, Gareth knew this one to be severe. His friend would not survive unless Gareth acted quickly.

Recounting the story of his father's injury, Gareth ran across the room, sword in hand, and buried the long blade into the heart of the fire. He anxiously waited until the blade glowed red and smoke began to rise from the leather wrapped handle.

Ignoring any pain from the intense heat, he grabbed the blade and returned to Larec. Without hesitation, he pressed the flat edge of the sword against the gapping wound in Larec's side.

Larec's eyes alighted as he screamed out in pain.

Smoke began to rise from the burning flesh and blood, carrying with it a sickly stench that threatened to overcome Gareth.

He dropped the sword and spun away just as his stomach released its contents. Each wretch mixed with the stabbing pain in his side, amplifying his discomfort.

Gradually both subsided and he was able to once again attend to his friend.

Whether from pain, or lack of blood, Larec was unconscious again. Gareth took this opportunity to move his friend and began to wrap his wound.

As he struggled to complete this task, his mind struggled with the implications of the night's events.

Why, in this place, would somebody be hunting for him? How could word or warrant have beaten them to this point in their journey? And if he was, indeed, a Scribe, why were so many willing to go against the code and strike him down?

The one thing that he was sure of though, was, they could not remain here.

Knowing full well that he would not be able to carry his friend far: he bolted for the stable. He had no sooner stepped through the doorway, when, he tripped over the prone body of the fourth member of Kanter's gang.

Gareth let out with a small laugh as he pressed on towards the stable.

"Larec was doing his job all along."

Larec's horse protested at first as Gareth tried to lead it into the alehouse, but when it caught Larec's scent it quickly moved towards his fallen master. From that point on, it remained perfectly still as Gareth struggled to mount and secure his friend to the saddle.

Packing every piece of linen and blanket available around Larec, Gareth tried to pad and make the journey ahead as comfortable and less jarring as possible.

Gareth knew that speed would be Larec's only chance. The horse whinnied and blew out a heated breath through it's nostrils, acknowledging this fact also, prompting Gareth to lead it outside where he mounted Allegiant and they sped off into the pale light of the rising sun.

He ignored the crossroads and stayed the course for El'Athandria, the Guild House and their possible salvation.

Adrenaline kept him going.

The enveloping pain in his head, guided him.

The only time they stopped was when Larec screamed out in pain or the horses protested at taking another step.

On those occasions, he checked and changed the dressings on Larec's wounds, gave him water to drink and even forced a bite or two of food into him. And at the same time, he ignored his own discomfort or need for rest, or food, or drink.

Although Gareth knew he was asking too much from them all, he didn't hesitate to do so. Upon checking Larec on the most recent stop, he found a growing stain through the dressing. The melted flesh was giving way.

Blood and life, was again draining from his friend.

He spurred the horses faster.

They approached the border between Predür and L'uramentia at a full gallop. Gareth struggled to rein the horses to a stop.

Standing before them, across the main highway, three abreast, was an entire company of Predür's army.

And standing alone in front of all of them, stood Gareth's old friend.

Voyga D'ianto.

"Stand down Gareth." The Master Sergeant commanded.

"I cannot do as you ask, Voyga. I beg you to step aside and let us pass."

"Now it is I, who must decline. There is a Royal Decree for your arrest. So again I ask you to… peacefully, stand down."

Gareth's anger pressed to the forefront.

"There can be no decree for an arrest based on recent actions, unless those who signed that decree had also put in to motion those events which caused my actions to be taken."

"I told you to take care… That there was an ugliness, clinging, to the underside of all things in this world. Now stand down!"

"Is this where you reaffirm your warning not to trust anyone, only to then turn on me yourself?"

"I would never do that. You are my friend. But I am a Sergeant of the Royal Army of Predür, and I must follow my orders. I promise you, that if you stand down, I will get the best care for your companion and that no further threat or harm will befall either of you."

Gareth let out with a cynical laugh.

"It is almost a pity that you will not betray me, Voyga… because that means, I must betray you. Now command your troops to stand aside and let us through or draw your swords and we will see whose justice prevails."

Gareth's hand slid to the hilt of Larec's sword, which he now had next to him.

Voyga searched for any sensibility in his friends gaze, but only found the stubborn determination he had so often failed to be able to combat any time their opinions had been at odds.

Shaking his head sadly, Voyga stepped to the side and commanded the guard to do the same.

"We did not see each other on this day. And by letting you pass, we most likely, never will again."

The meaning of his friend's words, struck Gareth hard. And even though that meaning broke his heart…he did not have the luxury of time to even respond. He spurred Allegiant and both of the horses raced forward.

28

He woke in a very large bed. It wasn't as soft as a cloud, and as his arm shot out sideways…

It didn't have Annalei in it.

He closed his eyes again, trying to wish everything back to a time when she was beside him.

Those thoughts and images quickly eluded him, abruptly being replaced by the events of the previous night's arrival.

Portions of those moments were hauntingly clear, as others eluded his desperate reach.

By the time they had reached the cobbled streets of El'Athandria, both man and beast were near collapsing from exhaustion. Blurred eyesight caused misguided routes through the Capital, both through the seedier side and its shadowy dealings, and through palatial estates, where unannounced guest were less welcomed.

Harsh responses sprang forth from both. And whether or not, that was the sole reason for the growing number of pursuing hoof beats and shouts, Gareth could not tell.

Though it had seemed, no attacking presence was present, until Allegiant had raced past the Governor's estate.

Gareth could not take the chance, that their pursuit was a case of mistaken identity. In every instant since they fled the alehouse, Gareth made note to fly the colors of the Guild.

Voyga's claims, and the reaction of all of those that they had encountered, since, cast serious doubts on Gareth's part, that the Banner of the Scribes, was truly as powerful, as it was said to be.

With a growing horde of both mounted soldiers and criminals on their heels, Gareth steered both horses to the main, front entrance to the guild house.

His booming voice screamed his intentions, and begged for the gates to be opened.

It was that same little boy, he had first encountered, that pushed opened the metal gates just in time, as Gareth, had no intention of slowing the horses. And once through, he did not look back to see if the gates were closed behind him, instead he galloped his steed straight into the massive hall.

The polished floors made reigning shoed horses to a halt, a difficult task. But a growing number of aids and Scribes alike, created a human stopgap.

It was at that time, in which his, and Larec's limp forms were being eased from their mounts, that he managed to pull the harness off of his back and he shakily held out to Lord Hadrion…

The Black Scroll.

Even though his consciousness was fading, his mind was forever imprinted with the sight of Lord Hadrion's face, as the staunch demeanor was overcome with horrific recognition.

And throughout his recollection, he had heard no noise.

No indication that anyone had entered the bedchamber.

But the slightest inhalation brought to the senses, the heavily over-spiced scent, of Guild House cuisine.

Without hesitation or care for the protesting aches, from all of his sustained injuries, Gareth bolted to the small table and greedily ate everything that had been laid out.

He was so consumed by satiating his hunger that he failed to notice the young lady standing by the door, smiling contently. And then, as she had almost every day of his previous residency, she quietly slipped away… unnoticed.

It had taken Gareth a few false tries, to navigate from the section of the residency in which he had slept, in which he had never been in, to the infirmary where his friend was being attended.

Several, older female aids were still dressing the freshly cleaned and sewn wound.

Though none verbally protested his presence there, several scoffed as they made their way brusquely past him. The remaining nursemaid smiled at him, and gently spoke.

"He really should rest. He's lost a lot of blood and will be very weak for quite some time." She moved aside to let Gareth closer. "He wakes… briefly, but those moments quickly pass."

Gareth sat next to his friend, struggling to hold in the raw emotions that the sight of Larec's pale face stirred within himself. Sadness gave way to concern, which was quickly overpowered by anger.

Anger at all that had transpired.

The more he tried to comprehend, the less anything made sense. He needed answers. And at this time and in this place, only one person might be able to provide them.

He pushed the chair away from the side of the bed and stood. Turning, he started to walk towards the door, when a raspy voice, pulled him, back.

"As I felt my father's blade bite into my side..." Larec struggled through parched lips to continue. "I thought I saw, out of the corner of my eye... a Scribe... take arms and strike, from across the room."

Gareth gently raised his friend's head and guided a mug of water to Larec's lips.

"It must have been the delirium of blood loss." Gareth flatly lied. "No Scribe has taken arms."

Though he felt a twinge of guilt, at having to lie to his friend; his anger mounted again.

He wanted an explanation as to why he had to do so.

And he wanted it now!

It was easier for him to double back and go up through corridors he was familiar with. And in doing so, he found himself, once again, standing on the balcony overlooking a large gathering of Scribes, taking sides in an ongoing verbal argument between Lord Hadrion, and...

The peculiar little man, draped in oddly colored clothes and layers of charms and necklaces.

Gareth's hands unconsciously went to the charm that hung from his own neck. He had to steady him self as the parallel between two lives, seemed to pull him forward, and almost over the railings edge.

He kneeled and leaned his head over, straining to hear all of the ensuing discussion.

"We are Scribes! We are not afforded the luxury of believing in fables and half-truths. The implications of what you suggest…" Hadrion's voice trailed off as he shook his head.

"You have seen with your own eyes, Elistir…" The squat man continued. "Power crazed warlords, bent on the annihilation of an entire peoples, suddenly break down and weep uncontrollably for hours, when faced with the written account of their deeds. You have witnessed whole governments crumble when faced with the accounting of their fabricated falsehoods used against its own people for nothing more than monetary gains.

The words that had sparked those actions have been written in your own hand. And yet you still will not believe their power. You preach these properties to every such apprentice, but choose not to believe what is in front of your very own eyes."

"It is not that I choose disbelief. It is because I must convince myself that I truly understand all that this means and the consequences that that belief brings with it."

Without waiting for any further response, Lord Hadrion turned with the intension of exiting the great hall.

"But what of the proof that sits before you? Will you not at least…"

Lord Hadrion turned with a fire that shocked every soul in the room… save, one.

"Would you have me say it, Mikal Syla! Do I need to admit to you, to everyone present… that what stands before us, is but a myth, born again? That imprinted upon its skin, lies the oldest, and darkest, most powerful script of all. The absolute.

Templ' Scri.

That very few even, have heard the rumor of its existence…

That, even less know of its true nature…

And not one living soul knows its meaning!

I am sure that if you would venture to any marketplace and offer a thousand drams for its translation… you would marvel at how many would know the words."

Hadrion was left shacking, on the verge of tears, before he finished.

"Is that what you want of me?"

"It is not a matter of want…" Mikal Syla flatly stated. "It is a matter of need. I, like you my old friend, do not want to hear any words spoken in that tongue. But I fear that all history begs that we do hear those words spoken."

"Roü sï té ë'tháin! Sëg vérhäin mügén gläh Mürén, Atrüs véid'h arüin sëg ver ëliét änfái c,rïnth!"

Gareth's scream echoed across the hall. Then he continued.

"For it has arrived! And when comes this Darkness, Evil will follow and all light shall perish."

29

The Great Hall was eerily silent, save for the low hum of scattered pockets of Scribes as they separated and cowarded into the dark recesses of the massive room, to express and share their own fears and opinions.

Only three bodies remained in the center of the hall, illuminated by the unseen light.

Lord Hadrion, Mikal Syla and Gareth.

"Why did you make those forsaken sounds and scream those ungodly words?"

"I spoke the words written on the Black Scroll, and for the uninformed, I spoke their true meaning." Gareth said defiantly.

"Didn't I tell you he was going to be a good one?" Mikal Syla giddily announced.

"Quiet!" Hadrion barked. "Your opinions have always been biased in that matter."

He then turned back again on Gareth to continue his condemnation.

"How is it that you read, what to ordinary men, and scholars, and Scribes alike, see, only as scratches and misshapen symbols?"

Gareth began to answer. To tell the story how the words, born of blood, morphed into a readable script.

But, Hadrion was not interested in stories.

Was not yet finished, with his own, diatribe.

"Black Scrolls!" He threw his arms in the air in an elaborate, mock, gesture. "What did you bring into my house?"

Gareth quickly replied.

"You know what I brought, for I handed it directly to you."

"Handed to me!" Hadrion's cynical laugh chilled Gareth to the core. "Even in your damaged state, you thrust out in one arm, something that took six grown men to move. You held with your pristine hand, that which scarred the flesh of all others whom touched that tainted skin."

Lord Hadrion leaned in closely to Gareth so that even Mikal Syla would not hear his next question.

"What might… *you*… be, that would allow… *this*?"

His breath and voice failed him as his retreating step, threatened to betray him.

Although he was not meant to have heard the question… it was Mikal Syla who provided the answer.

"There is but only one soul, who may do as you suggest, Elistir." Syla offered.

The elder man's pale skin flared red.

"I forbid you to speak those words, in, *my*, house!"

Gareth and Mikal's shocked gazed, never strayed from the now vacated spot. But Lord Hadrion was no longer there.

"What word?" Gareth mumbled quietly as he and Mikal Syla slowly wandered the halls of the Guild House.

"All, walls, have eyes and ears. And… with due respect to our honorable Lord, I will not go against his wishes and utter them here."

Mikal suddenly stopped, and turning towards Gareth, he reached up and grabbed both of the young scribe's shoulders. He locked gazes with Gareth and slowly continued.

"But take me to the Roasted Hog… and if you are buying, say… thrice! I may… let that, and more, slip."

His eyebrows shot up in a comical dance that Gareth remembered.

Gareth, in turn, struggled to stifle his laughter as he asked his next question.

"Why did you not tell me you were a Scribe?"

"I did not know it was my duty to do so." Came the curt reply.

"And will you tell me now, where it is that we are going? Or, is that also, not your duty as well?" Gareth jibed.

"Oh! Of that, I will, tell. And I won't be surprised if it does not send you screaming and running for the comfort and safety of your bed."

"I hardly think, that anything held within these walls can compare to what I have already experienced in my journeys so far."

"Ah! A seasoned veteran of the darkest campaigns, huh?" He mocked Gareth. "Though I do not wish to dispel your beliefs, or belittle your experiences… these walls contain all of history.

The good and the horrific.

They contain you. And by that extension, all that you have experienced, now resides here, as well."

Gareth could not let another opportunity for answers escape him, so he pressed on questioning Mikal Syla.

"But what of histories that have never made it to these walls? Deeds, so unspeakable… unwritable, that no quill has set them to scroll."

Mikal Syla abruptly halted, and seemingly reached out to grab a hold of Gareth's arm for stability, visibly shaken by this frightening thought.

"Could this be?" He wondered aloud.

A slight smile spread across Gareth's face, as he allowed himself a moment of self-satisfaction, for having presenting such a new, and bewildering hypothesis to the learned, Scribe.

His hubris was quickly shattered with the utterance of a simple word.

"Nah!"

A Mikal Syla walked away laughing uncontrollably.

The rest of the day was spent, almost entirely in the same fashion.

Countless, steps taken.

Hundreds of questions asked.

Very few answered.

Occasionally a tattered scroll was let loose from an ancient stack, its content mumbled, then tossed aside.

Over and over, the process repeated.

Gareth's feet and jaws were beginning to ache from a day long, marathon. He was about to announce his inability to continue. That he, unlike, the seemingly tireless, little man, had to take his rest.

As he was about to speak, Mikal Syla came to an abrupt halt.

"There are many things, we must do in the 'morrow, many thoughts to explore, words to write and even more to read. That is, if we are to find the answers."

Gareth finally noticed, that they had come to a stand still in front of the room, he, had awoken in.

He turned back to ask Mikal one last question, but the little man, was gone.

Shaking his head, with a broad smile on his face, Gareth entered the room.

Nothing, though, seemed right.

Even though it was not as gaudily adorned as his suite in the Castle Rhyce, it was equally as large.

No artwork or tapestries hung on the walls. No over-sized windows, with sills guilded in gold.

Instead, polished wood, gleamed, by candlelight.

Several, desks, were covered with scrolls and quills.

Every available surface was filled with the accoutrements of the Guild.

It was everything a Scribe could wish for, and yet…

It was missing the one thing he needed most, right now.

And failing that…

It was not for him.

As tired as he was, he had no trouble mounting the stairs, and traversing the dust covered corridor.

And when he reached his destination, he was somewhat surprised…

That, his little cubby, was lit and ready for him.

The bed was freshly made.

His clothes, neatly hung.

And a plate of steaming food, rested on the small end table.

He glanced down the dimly lit halls, not really expecting to see anyone. Though he still called out to the darkness.

"Thank you!"

They spent the following three days, holed up in one room after another.

Reading, and re-reading, scroll, after scroll.

Gareth had thought on his first term at the Guild House, that he had read and copied more history than could be read in a lifetime, and yet, here he was, going beyond even that.

With each scroll, they peeled back another layer of the history of the Crescent Realms.

The thousand-year, lineage of the Kingdom of Alder and its continuous battle for existence, against, an even older line of the House of Rhyce.

He read of the rise and fall of a hundred or more Governors of L'uramentia and the constant political war that was fought against the might of "the Prime", Predür.

He read the depressing accounts of the continuing struggles of Sonësia and Mariv', constantly battling the elements of their landscapes, in hopes of merely existing.

But the one thing he never read, throughout these long days, was any reference to the Darkness, the battle between it and the Märkén Thraüm, or the Black Scroll.

He smashed the palms of his hands into his eye sockets. Threatening to push them through the back of his head. Anything to end the painful, burning and watering caused by endless hours of scouring through centuries of dust and grime.

His patience was quickly dissolving.

At no time over the course of these last few days, had anyone acknowledge the Black Scroll or his ability to read and speak a mythological language. Not a soul seemed to care, or want to hear his account of how that transpired.

The events in the Kingdom of Rhyce, didn't seem to be of concern, nor were the threats that were implied.

He felt he could no longer sit idly by, loosing himself in the past, when so much of the future seemed in peril.

Gareth reached for the door handle and was about to exit the room… exit the Guild House itself.

Then Mikal Syla's laughing voice, sang out.

"Ah ha! I knew it was here. I told you, I told you, I told you." He clapped his pudgy little hands as he spun around, charms and layers swirling like the veils of an exotic dancer.

"I told you it was just a matter of time… and history. I mean what is history? Just time. And just like time, history repeats."

Gareth was beginning to get dizzy.

Dizzy from trying to follow all of the twirling…

And dizzy from trying to follow the twisting logic.

"Please, try and stand still and try to tell me what in the Rhüle you are talking about." Gareth had to rub, his already aching eyes.

"The reason why Delgar is so important to the Darkness. The reason why, as much effort was spent trying to overthrow the Island of Souls, as was spent trying to defeat the combined might of all of the Crescent Realms."

Gareth's heart jumped! Could these countless hours of drudgery have actually paid off?

"What does it say? Does it mention how the Märkén Thraüm defeated the Shàl Mïr Cri?"

"The who did what to whom?" Mikal seemed confused.

Gareth's anger threatened to scream out again.

"You said you found…"

"Yes! I found it. It says right here. Right here before us." And each time he repeated himself, he slapped his hand onto the ancient scroll. And with each slap, dust and particles of the frail manuscript puffed into the air.

"It says it right here. It says the secrets to that mystery, may be found in the words of the Eighth Denial. The Eighth Denial clearly states…"

"Wait! Wait, wait, wait, wait!"

"What!"

"There you go again. Speaking in riddles of cryptic things, that no one else seems to have ever heard of. As if it was taught to every child from the day they opened their eyes."

"What do you mean?" Mikal Syla clearly seemed confused. "You question me as if you know nothing of the Eighth Denial."

His eyes danced around, searching for confirmation.

"That is exactly what I am saying! No one… knows anything, about the Eighth Denial."

"Oh! Well then…" Mikal began to mope around the room, dragging his booted toe through the layers of dust, deposited upon the floor.

"What do the first seven say?" Gareth tried to bring Mikal's interest back into the conversation.

"What seven?" The older man grumbled.

"What do the first seven Denials say?"

"What! The first… Who cares! That's not important. Never has been. It's what the Eighth Denial states that you should be concerned with."

"So teach me." Gareth challenged.

"Teach you what?"

"The Eighth Denial."

"Am I now to become your nursemaid, who teaches the newborn babe through rhyme and limerick. There, once was an eighth denial, he shouted and cursed through a smile…"

"You don't know it…do you?" Gareth began to laugh hysterically. And after he found the confirmation of his question in Mikal Syla's down-turned gaze, he left the room.

Leaving the morose little man, to ponder the meaning of the ancient scroll, alone.

30

It wasn't that the bed was too small or too hard. That the blanket too short… or the number of the bed's occupants, also short.

None of those things contributed to his lack of sleep.

Even though he could see nothing in the near pitch black, Gareth's eyes were wide open, searching.

Only the faintest sliver of light illuminated the border of the small window next to his bed. The same crack that allowed the thread of light, also allowed the night's chill to creep in.

Too many thoughts, too many questions raced through his mind. So many so that he could not even focus on a single one. Each thought bled into the next. Every time he thought that he had the meaning of, or answer to one question, the next invaded the thought process and shattered the brief moment of clarity.

The Kingdom of Rhyce: why was he the one sent to the land surrounded by the Darkness? Was the task deemed so inconsequential that a mere apprentice would suffice?

The pull of the Darkness and the challenge of the pitch: was he being drawn into some dangerous game?

The attack on Celia: what could, the senseless destruction of its people achieve? Could his thoughts and writings have had anything to do with the King's final decision?

The crazed, tattooed man: and the writings on his body.

The Castle Rhyce: and the mysteries it held and the threats the King and his mysterious guest, presented.

The Black Scroll: and the mysteries of its writings, and the effect that it had on him.

Annalei: and the mysteries of how his feelings for her, had been the one thing to save him from those effects...

The Attacks against him: and by extension, the Guild itself.

So, many things, clouding, twisting, and shaping his thoughts and actions.

So, many things leading him to…

"Why Delgar?" Gareth screamed as he bolted through the door to Mikal Syla's room. "You started to allude to it before, but…"

He suddenly realized the inappropriateness of his action. He hadn't knocked, or waited to be invited in. He hadn't even considered that the elder man might be sound asleep.

He definitely hadn't expected to rouse a trio of completely naked young chambermaids from the Master Scribe's bed. Two of which, let out with high-pitched screams as they retreated to the hidden darkness of the bathing chamber. The third simply dove under the covers. Leaving Gareth to stare at the sheepish grin on Mikal Sylas' face.

"Go ahead, judge me for the puellaphilist that I am. Though I think you should not, knowing full well that you, like myself, enjoy the company of beauty."

It took several moments for Gareth to collect his thoughts and the reason for his intrusion. Every time he was about to continue with his inquiry, there was a brief stirring under the covers and Mikal would either jump and giggle, or close his eyes and release a slight moan.

"Clearly this is not the appropriate time." Gareth quickly stated as he turned to leave.

"Ah, Delgar… yes!' He heard Mikal scream and he turned in time to see the portly man scurry from under the covers and crawl to the edge of the large bed.

His bare feet made a slapping noise on the cool stone floor as he plodded across the room to his immense desk.

"It has something to do with the stone." He pronounced as he started shuffling through the pile of opened scrolls, haphazardly tossing any unwanted one aside. "Ah! Here it is. Come look!" He called over his shoulder to Gareth.

Who did not, move.

"What are you waiting for? Come and see…" He hesitated at seeing Gareth's nod.

"You, may, want your robe." Gareth hinted to the naked Scribe.

"Suit yourself. Mai'ella, my robe please!" The older scribe shouted to the darkness of the bathing chamber.

Without hesitation, one of the two retreating, young women emerged with Mikal's robe. And even though she was still undressed, she took the time to help him properly put it on and tied it for him.

He thanked her and kissed her cheek, giving her a light slap on the rump as she again headed for the shadows.

"Now! Where were we?" The elder scribe questioned as Gareth approached the desk.

What little sleep Gareth found, came and passed all too quickly. He haphazardly dressed and ate his spicy breakfast at the same time, anxious to resume his study of the information Mikal Syla had found in an ancient scroll.

He did not profess to fully understand the complexities of what they read, but it was his intention to not end this day until he did.

He raced to Mikal's room again, and barely remembered to press a light knock on the surface of the door before he pushed it open.

Though his intrusion went unnoticed.

There was no one there.

Gareth searched the room in the dim light calling out for Mikal.

Getting no response, he gathered the last scroll they had been reading in the middle of the night and went in search of the squat, little Scribe.

The halls and common rooms of the Guild House seemed uncommonly vacant today. It was more like his first day, not like the buzzing hornet's nest of activity, since his return.

But just like that first day, he ended up in the same place.

Mikal Syla and Lord Hadrion were locked in a heated debate, at the far end of the room. An, anger emanated from each. It seethed from their words and gestures. It grew in the aggressiveness they hurled towards each other.

Gareth began to cross the room intent on interceding in what ever discussion it was that could have caused such a disagreement.

As he neared the end of the table, his focus was pulled from the arguing Scribes, to the object of their ire.

Laid out before them, bowing the width of the table with the weight of its ancient, dark text.

Was the Black Scroll.

Gareth felt an immediate, nauseating pain strike his temple. He grabbed for his head as well as his stomach, as he began to double over in agony.

He wanted to run.

To set as much distance between himself and that accursed text.

But… instead, he found himself struggling to get closer to the object. He was lost in a growing fog, and the call of the Black Scroll screamed a false salvation.

He flung himself across the table in an attempt to displace the scroll. Hoping to push all of the pain and suffering, all of the anger and ill will away.

As his fingertips reached the edge of the darkened surface his momentum was halted by the staying hand of Mikal Syla.

He heard their discussion as his thoughts began to clear. They were no longer screams of anger, but whispers of concern.

He was seated in the far corner of the room, and as soon as the elder scribes realized he was conscious again, they hastened to his side.

"My boy, what do you think you were doing?"

Gareth only answered question with question.

"Why were the two of you arguing so?"

The two master scribes looked at each other in confusion.

"What are you talking about?" Mikal asked. "We were merely discussing how best to decipher a language, that was no longer a language. A language not spoken… or heard, for a millennia… or, longer. A script so foreign to the eyes, that the mind cannot distinguish its text, from that of the scriblings of a scatter brained infant. There was no, argument."

"There is a way!" Gareth whispered as he pushed away from the chair a marched towards the table.

The older men were too slow to restrain him and were forced to watch as Gareth grabbed the nearest quill and using its tip, sliced the palm of his hand.

Reaching it out, he offered it to the Scroll with no effect. Although several drops of blood had now fallen on the ancient surface, nothing happened.

He began to pull his arm back, but a sharp twinge of pain in his temple stop him. Closing his eyes, he tried to concentrate, to not give in to the pain. But the pull was too strong.

His arm dropped again and this time, the blood seemed to be pulled from his palm to flow across the scroll.

In Gareth's mind, each letter and symbol morphed to the legible and he began to read aloud, words not spoken for thousands of years.

Mikal Syla and Lord Hadrion stared in horror as the blood continued to flow from their young apprentice.

Mikal was the first to react.

But he did not run to the aid of Gareth. Instead he grabbed a fresh scroll and quill and began to frantically transcribe every word that Gareth uttered.

The words kept coming.

As the stream of blood, did not cease.

Hadrion moved to Gareth's side, supporting him as the young man began to wobble.

And still the words and scarlet leapt from his body.

"Mikal!"

Syla looked up from his task, to see Lord Hadrion struggling to maintain his grasp on the unconscious, and pale form of Gareth.

They gently laid Gareth on the floor.

Hadrion rushed from the room, screaming for the aid of the Guild's Medician.

Mikal Syla angrily cursed his weakened strength as he tried to tear the edge of his tunic in order to fashion a makeshift bandage.

Once done, he reached out for Gareth's injured hand, only to find a feint vestige of red liquid as it retreated into the already healing slices.

Concern turned to confusion.

Realization, to horror.

Mikal Syla sprang to the table, scrambling past the Dark Scroll and hurriedly, unfurled his transcribed text.

"NO!"

He let out with a hollow scream.

Each character, every symbol…

Was as it appeared upon the ancient scroll.

31

He couldn't understand what all the fuss was about.

He was fine.
He felt fine, looked fine.
His hand was healed, as he knew… hoped, it would be.
All he wanted was a little rest.
Away from the pawing Medician, and the fawning chambermaids. Away from the dour gaze of Lord Hadrion, and the sometimes, elated, sometimes morose ramblings of Mikal Syla. It seemed to take hours to convey that message to everybody.
He was fine.
And finally on his own, heading to his cubby, searching for the solace it held.
He knew that everything would be, as it should, light, bed… food.
And it was.
But there was something more.

Propped upon the pillow, stood the most ornate, narrow scroll that Gareth had ever seen. Its finials were solid white stone, inlaid with gold and set gems. Both of which cast the amber glow of the lantern and intensified, and spiraled its light throughout the stone niche. The writing surface was as smooth as silk. A brilliant beige that almost appeared to be wet from the gloss coating that seemed to protect the script that appeared on its surface.

The most elaborate form of Ornamental type swept across the surface.

Gareth was almost too mesmerized by its brilliance to read it. But the heading caught his attention, and he involuntarily pulled back.

The Eighth Denial.

He gently set the scroll down and took a deep breath. Rising, he walked to the edge of the nook and peered down the corridor in both directions. Partially to search out whom it may have been who left the mysterious scroll… and partially to make sure he was alone and secure.

Confident that there would be no disturbance, he began to read.

***There is no magic in this world, nor has there ever been.**

***The Märkén Thraüm suppressed the entirety of the Darkness by wielding staff and sword, and superior intellect, not magic. The belief that magic has ever existed is false.**

***Claims of the existence of the Towers of Thraüm, which supposedly contained this magic, which the Märkén Thraüm supposedly chose to connect in one final act of extreme desperation, which then supposedly expelled all of the forces contained there-in those massive stone monoliths, creating a final surge, which then held at bay, the advances of the Darkness, and which supposedly to this day, continue**

to deliver upon that promise of protection and sacrifice, which then were destroyed, utterly, within that final act of desperation. Simply do not, and have never existed. Any remains therein are simply misinterpretations of natural occurrences.

*The Märkén Thraüm, having seen the entirety of their potential's reach, did not reach out with that potential across the remaining realms.

*All of the rulers, in all of the lands, did not shudder at the potential of that reach, and did not choose to act accordingly.

*The additional known falsehood, that magic is shared through bloodline, rendering an almost immortal status to the Märkén Thraüm and their descendants, did not precipitate the action of severing said bloodlines by means of hunting down and dispatching all known members of the Märkén Thraüm.

*It is known that a falsehood prevails that some members of the hunted, may have used unwarranted means to hide their lineage, to escape a rumored justice.

*A falsehood may be known to except the fact that a mixture of lineages may retain aspects of Thraüm legacy. An even greater falsehood retains that those mixed lineages may have contained aspects of the Darkness its-self.

*The falsehood that the retelling of these events through the words written by the newly formed Guilde of Scribes, would preserve the history, avail all accounts to the past, and even shape the future by revealing their truths within.

Gareth hesitated before he began to reread the denial again. As his eyes followed his fingers edging across the ornate border of the scroll he noticed additional text contained within.

***and... having found the means, to alter that existence, they chose to hide that means in the words of others, and it shall pass that even those words shall be hidden in a thinly veiled skin of truth, and that truth shall reside in the soul of the one true Mürieté Scynth.**

Gareth read it, and reread it. He tried to gleem some semblance of understanding. Some way, in which it applied to the current circumstances. And when he thought that he had achieved that understanding... he reread it again, and was no longer sure.

Over and over, the cycle repeated, until exhaustion claimed him once again.

The dawn of a new day brought with it an overbearing sense of unease.

A confusion, as to whom, he should trust.

Until the moment that he had returned to his alcove and found the Eighth Denial waiting for him, he had felt that the Guild house was the safest place in the world. The place he felt most sure that all who surrounded him, had his best interest at heart. He had no reason to question anything different.

But knowing that someone thought that it was he, who should know and have the Eighth Denial, and not one of the esteemed members of the Guild, like Hadrion or Mikal Syla, caused him to reel at the possibility that that may not be the case.

Unless...

It was one of them who had placed the scroll on his bed.

Even so, that would mean, that they did not trust someone else with the knowledge of the existence of the denial, and therefore, Gareth's own distrust grew even further.

But where to place it.

He tucked the small scroll into the waistband of his trousers and covered the protruding end with several layers of his tunic and vest.

Each step he took in the direction of the staircase caused another moment of hesitation.

Another moment of doubt.

Gareth felt as if he was being watched, being judged, and he found himself, wishing for that sharp ping to ring inside his head to either warn him, or guide him.

But none came.

He tapped on his temple with the tip of his finger, hoping to stimulate himself into reaching the proper conclusion.

All that that achieved was to blur his vision and numb his finger.

Slowly he made his way to the copy room where the Black Scroll, laid.

He was immediately grateful that the room was empty and quiet. He was unsure that he would be able to hold a conversation with Syl, Hadrion, or anyone else, without acting like a lying lunatic.

Gareth crossed the room and approached the Black Scroll cautiously. There was no longer a fear of the object, just an uncertainty as to when or if, it would strike out to meld with him.

Control him.

Show him.

Nothing happened.

He instinctively gazed down to the palm of his hand.

No blood was present, or seeping out of reopened wounds.

Pulling his arm back, his hand bumped into the end of the small scroll tucked into his pants. Pulling back the layers of clothing, a charged thought crossed his mind.

Light and Dark.

Quickly he laid the small form of the Eighth Denial upon the surface of the Black Scroll, and jumped backwards, preparing to take cover from some impending reaction.

None came.

Other than the extreme contrast of the two surfaces… light becoming brighter because of the darkness, dark becoming complete pitch because of the shear brilliance…

Nothing happened.

Were there any other member of the Guild present, they would have surely seen Gareth's immense disappointment at the lack of any calamitous happening.

Gareth was so displeased, he angrily grabbed the Denial and stormed off to exit the room, completely failing to notice that where the Eighth Denial had sat upon the Black Scroll, the surface seemed bleached.

But the implication of what it revealed would have been too much to comprehend.

Gareth was nearly at the doorway, when he happened to see, draped across the back of a chair, the leather harness he had worn to carry the Black Scroll from the Castle Rhyce.

Without thinking, or reason, he snatched it up and returned to the scroll. As before, there was only a brief moment in which the weight of the scroll seemed too much for him to bear, but that quickly dissipated and again… he was off.

Gareth was unsure as to where he was headed. He just knew that he needed to find some place, any place, where he could feel safe. Where he could try to piece to together the few answers that he had and try to weave them into all of the other questions that were unanswered.

As he passed the landing to the balcony of the Great Hall, his attention was diverted by the raging voice of Lord Hadrion.

Gareth rushed to the edge of the balcony. The scene below, in the Great Hall, shocked and angered him.

A large contingent of the Guild's personal guards and some Scribes, themselves, had barred the advance of a mixed company of soldiers from both L'uramentia and Predür. Small scuffles began to break out, as the intruders pressed forward, trying to gain access to the inner passages of the Guild House.

And in the center of it all, raged Hadrion's taut figure.

"No army may enter these halls unless invited by this Guild. To do so would be a declaration of war against the full might of all of the houses. The laws of every kingdom, proclaim this." His voice echoed throughout the hall.

"The laws do not protect one, such as this." The General of L'uramentia's Army bellowed back. "Besides, he is but an apprentice."

"An apprentice would not have been tasked with such an important posting as dealing with the likes of Rhyce."

"A member of the Guild would not have fled that post, under the veil of darkness. Retreating from the deeds of murder and theft."

A wave of nausea struck Gareth at the realization that he was being accused of murder.

Whose murder?

V'ren's? Surely the revealing that the Scribe's protector was merely fulfilling his duties would quell that accusation.

But what of General Kanther? Had somebody seen him throw the blade that brought down his old teacher?

The answer to his questions came as soon he stopped thinking and began listening, again.

"King Rhyce the Fourth's emotional state has been rocked by the murder of his personal Medician and close friend."

Gareth was about to scream his denial to the claim.

To scream out the identity of the true murderer.

But as he reared up, a sharp pain gripped his knee as the flat of a foot collapsed it from behind, dropping him instantly. And before he could react or even scream out in pain, a clammy hand forcefully clamped over his mouth.

32

Gareth struggles to break free were halted as a heated breath began to whisper in his ear.

"Now is not the time to become an orator. We must retreat and vacate these premises post-haste." Mikal Syla's voice demanded immediate compliance.

Gareth quietly nodded as Mikal withdrew his hand. Slowly they began to back into the stairwell, and Mikal Syla spoke a single word.

"Up!"

Gareth lead the way, but was unsure of where they were heading. He spun to question Mikal, but was met by those darting eyes and comical brows.

"Ah good." Mikal stated, "You brought the scroll. Good! Glad to see you were thinking ahead. That means we don't have to risk going back for it now. Follow me." He giddily stated as he turned and headed back down the stairway.

Gareth was about to protest heading back into the path of the pressing armies, but was stunned silent as he watched Mikal Syla apparently disappear from right in front of his eyes.

Stumbling forward in shock, Gareth let out with a slight yelp as Mikal's hand reached out and grabbed him.

Gareth was amazed at the sight of the portly little scribe smiling up at him from a recessed pathway. Searching for the answer, Gareth noticed how the edge of the wall was offset and the brickwork was colored differently to disguise and distract the eyes from the passageway.

Content with the how, Gareth readily followed his mentor's lead, down the narrow path.

Gareth was amazed at the speed in which Mikal Syla moved. The squat little man deftly navigated narrow tunnels and darkened hallways. He led Gareth through sections of the Guild House that seemed impossible to traverse. Areas, that Gareth had never seen. Through hatches and doors, crawl spaces and grand galleries. Rooms that seemed to double back on themselves and stairways that went neither up nor down.

On more than one occasion, Gareth had taken his eyes off of the elder scribe, only to lose sight of him again.

He quickly angered himself for his lack of concentration and could only imagine the growing rage Mikal must be feeling at having to constantly backtrack and tug Gareth in the right direction.

But each time, Gareth was met with that jovial smile.

The pattern did not change even when the two scribes had made their way from Guild House to city-street.

From Reekstown, to countryside.

Again Gareth was stunned as they covered vast areas of his homeland through pathways he had never traversed.

There was a beauty and sense of wonderment that each new landscape brought.

But, also something else.

Something, bordering on a sense of, darkness.

A feeling, as if he had never really known, who he was or where he had come from.

He felt a stranger in his childhood home. So much so, that he barely recognized the fact that they had just exited a thicket of burrberry bushes next to his father's forge.

Mikal Syla did not bother to wait for Gareth's shock to wear off, before entering the shop.

Gareth's mumbling question was quickly cut off by the other conversation already taking place.

"It is good to see you again, olde man!" Timeon's greeting boomed as he released Mikal from a near torturous hug.

"I trust all things have been made ready?' The little man said sternly.

"As if I could ever disappoint…"

"Hello!" Gareth shouted. "What the Rhüle is going on?"

Both Timeon and Mikal Syla turned their gaze on Gareth and then laughed heartily.

"My, you have grown. Not my little boy any longer, eh?"

Timeon closed the gap to his son swiftly and scooped him up with his one good arm.

Although embarrassed, Gareth also felt a wave of emotion overwhelm him. And he found himself wishing that his father would never release his embrace.

All too quickly though…

"Your provisions and horses, as well as escorts, are beyond the east field. I wish there could be more. That I could be going with you."

"You have done more than any could ask of you already." Mikal sounded off. "This next battle is the provenance of the Guild."

"The Guild fights NO battle!" Gareth found himself echoing his father's voice.

Triggering a raucous laugh from Mikal.

Gareth and his father joined in, and the jovial exchange seemed as if it would not end.

Except it did… abruptly.

"What the Rhüle is that man doing on our property?"

"Mother!" Gareth alighted, as he reached out to her.

Only to be met by the flat of her hand and a sideways glance.

"Child." She coldly greeted him, as she stomped towards the other two men.

"My Bäe'ilia!" Mikal Syla said cheerfully, holding out his arms.

Which she vehemently slapped aside.

"I am nobody's…"

"Bäe?" Timeon stated firmly.

"Of course, of course. I am yours husband. Just as you are mine. But this… this, so called man… regardless of what my mother has said…" She spat through gritted teeth. "Is nothing, and no one, to me and mine."

Gareth noticed the down-turned gaze and wave of melancholy that washed over Mikal Syla. As if he was just told that the love of his life was no longer…

"Wait!" Gareth shouted. "How do you know? Are you related?"

All three adults seemed to ignore his outburst of questions. And his mother once again pressed forward with her anger. Except this time it was focused on Timeon.

"I told you never again. Not here. Never!" And she turned to storm off. Only stopping when Timeon yelled after her.

"Bae'il! I know you did not only come out here to insult our guest, ignore our child, and to drive a wedge between us."

Gareth's mother's demeanor warmed. Ever so slightly, as she turned to speak to her husband.

"It would never be my intention to anger you, my love." She sheepishly stared at the ground. "Word has greeted their arrival, that a company of Predür marches this way at first light. I thought that you should know this." She curtsied to her husband, then, turned towards Gareth. "Come here my child."

Gareth slowly approached and as he neared, she reached out to tug at both of the lapels on his tunic. As he continued to lower his head down towards her, she slid a chain around his head.

"For protection… and remembrance."

Gently she kissed his forehead, then, pressed hers to his.

"You are always in my heart. Be safe wherever you go."

Then all too quickly, for Gareth's liking, his mother pulled away, and left.

He stared after her for a brief moment, then turned back towards his father and Mikal… only Mikal Syla was no longer there.

"You may want to hurry." His father stated with smiling eyes.

"But?" Gareth struggled again with the words.

"There will, be a time." His father smiled. "Now go."

33

"Are you my Grandfather?" Gareth called to Mikal Syla as he caught up to the plodding scribe.

"Well there has always been room for debate and doubt there." The old man said, not breaking stride.

"So you are saying my Mother was lying? And, by extension, that my Grandmother lied to her?"

"No! No, no, no, no! I would never say that. That woman was beyond reproach. I loved her dearly."

Gareth waited, for the statement to be finished, but nothing followed.

"But?" He nearly shouted.

"But! I am a Scribe. I live in history, to record, history. I cannot have one of my own. I had to travel, constantly… leave at a moments notice. I could not give her what she wanted. What she needed!" Then he whispered. "What she deserved."

"So you *are*, my Grandfather!"

"No!"

"But you just said that she never lied."

"Yes."

"So, yes?"

"Yes."

"Should I call you Grandfather?"

"No."

Gareth gazed at the rotund little man's face, trying to find any trace of the truth.

"You have no clue as to what we have been talking about. Do you?"

"No…pa." Syla made a popping noise as he stretched the word into multiple syllables.

"Is every conversation we have, going to be like this?"

"More or less." Mikal plainly stated as he kept sauntering on.

Gareth was pleased to be seated on Allegiant's back once again. Though, at the same time, he had to question the why and how, that he now found himself on his trusty steed, and why, he and Mikal Syla, were accompanied by four members of the Guild's sentries.

Everything that he had ever been told about the Guild of Scribes… Everything Lord Hadrion and Larec had told him about the Guild of Scribes: said that they were to be revered and treated with the utmost respect.

That they would be given shelter when needing refuge, even if that meant the owner had no room.

That they be given food when hungry, even if it was the last piece of cheese.

They could walk through a battle, but never be part of the conflict…

The last part, especially was what caused Gareth the most trouble in comprehending, the most concern in its apparent inaccuracy.

Over the past few months, even though he was deemed a full Scribe, no longer an apprentice, there were too many incidents that would seem to disavow those tenants. On each of those occasions, Gareth had to suppress his anger at the lack of protocol, as his life was put in danger repeatedly.

And although, everything he read, every word that was preached to him, said this should not be the case…

He had been pursued like some common criminal.

But the most surprising aspect of each of those situations was, someone was always ready for that betrayal of the code.

Gareth wanted answers.

"Grandfather."

"Who? My name is Mikal Syla. But you may call me Sil, if you wish. And please, dispense with that archaic familial title. But, if titles are what you crave… you may address me as Lord Sylabis."

Gareth had to stifle a laugh.

"You do know what a Syl…"

"Yes, yes yes! I know exactly what it is… and that is why I have chosen to use it as my moniker." Syla sharply stated.

"But, why?" Gareth puffed out with another laugh.

"Ha, ha, ha. Because that is the name I have chosen. It is the name my mother had always called me. Because she said I always had my nose in a scroll, always reading… studying. So if you feel that you must mock my choice… at least consider the reasoning first. Then by all means… laugh away."

Gareth lowered his head, too embarrassed to even try to apologize, and therefore never saw the sly little smile, creep across the older Scribes face.

34

Allegiant was the only horse that seemed undisturbed as they crested the hilltop before the remains of the Märkén Thraüm tower. Gareth reined him to a soft halt as he studied the landscape before them and the Darkness in the near distance.

There was no great wave of pain, or nausea. No pull or calling to cloud his thoughts or vision. Just a sensation that he felt through his bones… something caught between elation and an aching in his soul.

One of the sentry's horses bolted throwing him from the saddle and sending the remaining horses, save Allegiant, into a panic.

Gareth was surprised at how adept Sylabis was, at handling his unsteady horse. He was about to commend the elder Scribe as such, when another rider was thrown from the saddle, beside him.

The sentry's heel became entangled in the stirrup and the uneven pull on the saddle, panicked the horse even more, causing it to race frantically down the hillside dragging the man helplessly behind.

Gareth spurred Allegiant forward and the massive steed shot down the hill in pursuit.

Even at a distance, Gareth could tell that the sentry was unconscious, by the way his body dangled and flopped about, offering no resistance or vain attempts to free himself.

Whatever damage had been done to the young man at present was nothing compared to what would happen if Gareth could not catch the stray horse before it reached the scattering of stone remains.

Baring down low in the saddle, Gareth steered Allegiant on a steep intercept. The incline so sharp, it threatened to topple both rider and horse. Allegiant's footing seemed to waver, and Gareth struggled to remain atop him.

Though a struggle, Gareth let loose of the reigns and placed his arms around his steeds neck. Leaning forward, he whispered a simple encouragement to the animal, which seemed to steady the horse's stride.

The risk paid off.

Without a single effort from Gareth, himself, Allegiant pulled abreast of the other horse and pushed the smaller animal into a curving arc away from the rocky debris.

After several attempts, Gareth was able to reach out and grab the wayward horse's reigns. Pulling tightly, and with the added assistance of Allegiant's strength, Gareth brought the animal to a halt.

Bolting from his mount, Gareth rushed to tend to the fallen sentry. First, freeing his now mangled leg from the tangled leather.

Taking stock of possible injuries, Gareth noticed that the young man's right wrist was also, severely broken. And although unconscious, and covered with a multitude of scratches and cuts, his breathing seemed regular enough for the trauma just endured.

The three other sentries, as well as Mikal Syla arrived, and all quickly got to work attending to their fallen comrade's injuries.

It was immediately decided that they should camp amongst the mammoth stones. But, the discussion on how to proceed, or even if they should, became heated on all accounts.

"It doesn't matter if I am arrested, if there is even a chance we can get him the help he needs. If my mother was correct, and a whole company is in pursuit… they will surely have a medician of their own. Something, I will point out… we… do… not!"

"Saving this man's life will mean not a thing… if we fail in the duty we have been tasked with!" Mikal Syla's voice raised in an anger Gareth had never heard.

And yet, instead of emphasizing the elder Scribe's point, it only fueled Gareth's own, growing anger.

"What is the point of our… *duty*… if we allow even one soul to perish, that we could have otherwise saved?"

"That point should be the clearest of all!" Mikal screamed out, before turning and stomping off.

Instead of pursuing the Scribe, pursuing the argument… Gareth turned to the three soldiers of the Guild.

"At first light, secure him as comfortably as possible and I will ride back to meet the men of Predür. You will all, safeguard Master Syla's journey to Delgär."

Gareth's order, were interrupted by the slow, cacophonous echo, of Mikal Syla's clapping.

"So the selfless hero I met long ago, re-emerges. Willing to give up the quest for the sake of one who pledged their own life, to the completion, of, that, quest." Mikal Syla stared intently at Gareth's shocked face. "How proud must Timeon be, of the little soldier he has made… I think, not."

It was Gareth's turn to storm off in a rage, but unlike Mikal Syla, he had no intention of returning to the argument any time soon.

He ignored the dinner call, not trusting himself, or his anger to be near Mikal Syla, or anyone else for that matter. Instead he kept wandering the massive stone remains of the ruined Thraüm tower.

He ran his hand over the surface of every slab, marveling at the precise, cut-lines. The detailed grooves were so exact, he could easily piece together how several of the stones would have been paired and stacked.

The only instances where he was unable to do so, were when he came upon a section that had been chard or obliterated from the tremendous force of the explosion that had ended the reign of the Märkén Thraüm, and halted the advance of the Darkness and all of its evils contained within.

Once again he found himself near that Darkness, but unlike the last time… he felt no pull. No pain.

No faceless challenge, greeted him.

There were, in fact, two sensations. Though neither came from within.

Around him, on three sides, there was a sense of guarded elation. A joyful relief of being in a place, that should be most welcoming.

And yet, from the darkness ahead… there was an underlying sense of fear and loathing.

Gareth thought that he heard a feint cry as he approached the edge of the gelatinous, darkened ground.

As he stepped forward, he watched in amazement as a small portion of that ebony… retreated, several inches.

Gareth found that if he made small strides and then waited… the Darkness tried desperately to scurry away.

Though if he moved too quickly, or if the Darkness was too intertwined within the thicket or tangled around the root from an ancient tree… his foot was met with an almost violent hissing.

That action was met with the return of the numbing pain. But instead of conveying anger or fear, Gareth felt awash with a somber fate. A sensation that began to filter into his own feelings, bringing to light, but also distorting, the sense of separation he was beginning to feel.

From home, and family…

From the comfort of love, and Annalei…

Even from the guild, and now Mykal Syla.

Shaking his head, he turned from the Darkness and sought the refuge of one of the monoliths.

He crouched low, seeking shelter from the oncoming nightfall's, chilling wind. Burying his face in his hand, he struggled to push away the negative thoughts, which dragged him into a fitful sleep.

A harsh scream, dragged Gareth from his ragged slumber.

A quick survey in the direction of the foggy dawn, showed the labored attempt of the Guild Guard, trying to mount their injured companion with some sort of comfort, for the ride ahead.

Gareth closed his eyes again, no longer fearing an imminent danger, or attack.

Though he wasn't allowed the luxury of drifting off, again.

The horns blazed from the crest of the hill, and down throughout the valley. The sound echoed off of the large stones, and resonated into the Darkness, its-self.

Gareth struggled to focus his sight to the hazy distance where an entire company of Predür's Elite, began their descent. The war, hardened steeds, showed no sign of unease, as they filed down the hillside in an even canter.

He struggled to stand, but a searing pain filled his mind, pushing him down. Digging his heels into the dirt, he tried to find some form of purchase, to force his way up, through the agony. But now an immense weight tugged him back down. The straps of the harness tore into his shoulder blades, making it impossible for him to move.

Gareth screamed out for Mikal Syla, for any help… but his voice was drowned out by the droning footfall of a hundred horses.

His view of Sylabis, and the others was obstructed by the massive rock, but he caught a glimpse of a lone rider, trying to lead their fallen comrade toward the approaching army.

Not one rider seemed intent on slowing their pace, threatening to crush the pair of Guildsman.

Gareth went to scream his protest and warning but was unable to inhale sufficient air in to his lungs to do so.

A silent inrush drew it all towards the waiting Darkness. Every blackened bush and tree wavered in its path as the life of the land seemed to bleed from the light, to the dark.

The charging forces broke ranks, as riders and their mounts struggled for breath.

And then, just as quickly as the vacuum had formed… a concussive wave erupted from the Darkness and rapidly ripped through the hillside.

Several riders were thrown from the backs of their horses, just as those same animals and several wagons were flipped to the ground.

An uneasy calm, replaced the commotion.

Gareth returned to his struggle, to free himself from the unseen force pinning him to the monolith. As he felt that he was beginning to make progress, that same unseen force, directed him to look towards the growing shadow... towards the Darkness.

35

The sound started as a feint hum and grew to a piercing scream just as four creatures sliced their way from the tendrils of the black mass.

The pain inside Gareth's head turned to a thought… and then a scream, as it found the means to use Gareth's voice.

"Behold the Shàl Mïr Cri!"

They stood a head taller than the tallest man Gareth had ever met. Their massively muscular frame was covered with reddish-brown skin that was dry and creased like old, tanned leather.

Each warrior's naked body was covered from head to toe, with what appeared at first to be scarlet paint or tattoos. The patterns unique to the warrior they adorned.

But on closer inspection, Gareth realized that they were the results of a form of ornamental cicatrisation. A self-mutilation in which the skin was cut away or pulled back, allowing the wound to heal, while exposing the muscle beneath.

A ritual that did not spare their genitalia from the same fate.

Their heads were covered with a long, black, flowing mane which seemed to move of its own accord, lending to the effect that the creature was moving, even when standing still.

Gareth started to become ill, trying to filter out the movement and realized the tactical advantage this must give the massive warriors.

The only thing they wore, save for the harness and sheaths for their weapons, were, leather straps fitted around each bicep, from which hung the braided hair of their fallen enemies. Each clump was twisted and knotted, with the rotting remains of torn flesh still attached.

The men of Predür struggled to control their mounts, as they tried to reform their ranks against this new threat.

And just as it seemed that they had, and prepared to advance, one hundred strong, towards the motionless four...

The sound of cracking timber, and torn earth, disrupted the landscape, as blackened trees, brush and boulders were flung through the air.

Gareth watched in horror as a massive beast tore its way out of the Darkness.

His mind struggled with an explanation for the sight before him.

It was the perverse marriage of two forms that, should never be. And yet the dripping, oozing blackness, which slid from its body, suggested that that evil, made anything possible.

The body of the creature resembled a massive plow-horse, easily three times the size of Allegiant. But where one head should be, two massive, curved heads twisted and smashed into each other. The blackened skin, rubbed raw from the constant collision. Their elongated jaws were filled with gnarled, razor-like fangs that carved, and shredded the flesh that tried to contain them.

As disturbing as that sight was, Gareth was shocked by the protruding sets of extra…legs?

Easily as thick as a tree, the front pair of multi-jointed spider-like legs, ripped through the flesh of the creature, above the front shoulders. The heavily, plated appendages reached several body lengths in front of the monster and were covered with thorn-like hairs, capable of piercing most armor.

The shorter, but bulkier hind legs, ripped through the flesh in front of the hindquarters and were able to lift the enormous beast and propel it forward at an alarming rate.

Gareth watched in amazement as one of the front limbs reached up and curled around the waist of its rider and gently, lifted and set it in front of the Shàl Mïr Cri.

Unlike the other soldiers, which now dropped to one knee and bowed… the leader of this band, was a woman!

Gareth couldn't help but marvel at the stunning presence before him.

Equally as tall and muscular as the others, but that was where the similarities ended. The smooth perfection of her reddish brown skin glistened with oil. Her large, exposed breast gleamed like polished metal. Her head was covered with the same mane of black hair, but was highlighted with streaks of flaming reds and oranges.

There was no mutilation of this skin, only the highlighting, white streaks of war paint, accentuating every curve.

And just like her male counterparts, she wore the trophies of conquest. But for her, they hung from a belt, cinched around her waist. The multitude of colors, blended with the amber patch of pelvic hair that tapered down the inside of each of her legs.

A distant cry, from the fleeing guildsman, seemed to break the trance of the moment and then the leader of the Shàl Mïr Cri let out with her own.

If the future ever held a moment in which Gareth could spend the time to chronicle the events that followed, the word *battle* would never grace the surface of a scroll.

The blades of the Shàl Mïr Cri never ceased their carnage.

No number of Predür's Elite would slow their advance. The frail form of man and beast, offered no resistance to the evil now unleashed.

Gareth felt the weight lift from his shoulders. Thinking he had somehow freed himself of the Black Scrolls harness, he bolted upright and quickly stumbled as the weight shifted again, on his back. As he regained his balance, he slowly, slid around to the backside of the mammoth stone.

Once under sufficient cover, he surveyed the slaughter before him, trying to devise any scenario in which he and his friends might avoid a horrific death.

A large, black streak passed his field of view. His eyes and mind, struggled to follow the creature. He watched in amazement as the massive jointed legs propelled it across the plateau. The beast quickly caught up to the fleeing Guildsmen.

It slammed down its barbed appendages, crushing both men and their horses to the ground. Those same limbs then scooped up the shattered bodies and guided them to the awaiting, gnarling rows of jagged teeth.

Gareth heard the final screams of his men, even above the din of battle.

He fought back his anger and fear, vowing that no more of his party would parish on this day.

He searched out the others and their horses, only to be dismayed at the sight of Allegiant and the other three mounts, bolting in the opposite direction of the creature.

With that means of escape, now lost… Gareth knew he needed to rally his companions and make a dash for the only place that they may be able to seek cover.

The Darkness, itself.

A small ping of protest entered his head and Gareth hesitated to try and comprehend its meaning, but Mikal Syla's raised voice, spewing forth obscenities that Gareth had rarely ever heard, shifted his attention.

Gareth stared in horror as he watched the portly scribe curse, and holler as he made an elaborate show of tearing through every pack, pouch, and bedroll.

Gareth turned again towards the massacre, desperately hoping that the elder man's outbreak hadn't caught the attention of the warring Cri.

He caught sight of a group of the Elite, eight strong and still mounted… They had encircled a lone warrior of the Shàl Mïr Cri, and began closing in tighter, with swords and pikes pressing in on their opponent.

Gareth had hoped that this might be the turning point of the battle. He watched as several of the steel blades began to pierce the sides, and shoulder of the Cri. He was startled that it gave cry, no indication as to being injured.

Then a flurry of motion raised a mist of scarlet.

The creature spun its body, and blades, separating the inner legs of the Elite's mounts from their torso. And as the tortured animals' weight caused them to cave in towards the Cri… it meticulously separated each member of the Elite's, head from their perspective bodies.

Gareth turned away as the creature, now bathed in blood, set about retrieving his trophies.

His urge to flee, was almost sickening. He bent over and took several deep breaths before he bolted from the cover of the stone in the direction of Mikal Syla.

The elder scribe's tirade had now moved on to the various layers of his own clothing. Pockets were torn open and the contents within, were meticulously searched then, discarded with another bout of obscenities. When every pocket laid bare… overcoats and vests were peeled away.

Gareth tried to grab at and shake some sense into the old man, but each attempt was deftly shrugged off. He hesitated to raise his voice, in fear of drawing attention to their exposed location, but each attempt to do so only brought a louder response from Syla.

His final scream of warning reverberated, across a now eerily silent battlefield.

Gareth looked back, over his shoulder as the blood soaked warriors of the Shàl Mïr Cri, having finished off the last of the Elite, converged and slowly headed in his direction.

His legs threatened to buckle under him, as a panic he didn't know was possible, overwhelmed him.

Turning towards the elder scribe, his voice broke, as he pleaded with Mikal Syla to run.

"A-ha!" Sylabis screamed as he had ripped one of his sleeves completely off and began spinning around as he twisted his own arm in an attempt to read the strange symbols and script tattooed below his elbow. He then looked at Gareth with his face alighted with a massive grin. "I knew it was here, some where."

Gareth ventured a gaze in the direction of the Cri, surprised that the hoard had not overcome them already.

They seemed to be frozen in confusion. Searching for something they knew was there, but could not find.

Gareth felt a tug on his vest and turned to stare at that comical gaze.

"You might want to follow me." The rotund man said as he bent and scooped up the layers of his discarded clothing.

Gareth hesitated following, as Mikal plainly walked across the field and circled around another large stone as he passed. When he, himself also left, what should have been, the direct sight of the Shàl Mïr Cri… he heard their leader's scream of discontent and the frantic movement of her steed as it rapidly approached from the distant hill.

It… was not confused or distracted.

With a dual bellowing scream, it locked on to their scent and charged headlong for them.

Rounding to the backside of the stone, Gareth was shocked, but relieved to see the two remaining guides, whom instantly, put themselves between the two Scribes and the approaching danger.

Gareth turned back, and stood behind Mikal Syla, who had suddenly stopped.

The older man seemed to stagger backward and trip, off-balanced against the stone… Gareth reached out in a vain attempt to catch Mikal, but to his amazement, the old scribe… disappeared.

Gareth stared at the stone, perplexed, seeing nothing but faint cut marks, weathered smooth. Shaking his head, he ran his hand along the surface, but as he did, he felt, and began to see elaborate symbols and script, finely chiseled into the stone.

He let out with a soft yelp as a hand reached out and tugged him inside a narrow gap. He could barely see Mikal

Syla's profile as they both stood side-ways in the narrow passage.

"B-but how?" Gareth stammered.

"It is all a matter of perspective or should I say perception?. Now you may want to grab the others before they become yet another meal for that horrendous beast. I fear the field, doesn't work on such a creature."

Gareth lost sight of the little man as he began to shuffle further into the passage.

Poking his head out of the seam in the rock, Gareth called to the other two of his party just as the monster's front legs crashed down upon the field beyond them.

Gareth stepped from the passage completely to allow the other two, entrance. And in doing so, exposed himself to the swiping leg of the beast as the rest of its body cornered the massive stone.

36

Diving for the safety of the passageway, Gareth felt one of the barbs pierce his leg. Instinctively, he kicked out with the other, using it as leverage to tear his injured limb from the blackened spike.

Struggling to stand, he moved deeper into the stone, ignoring any pain or the damp feeling of the flowing blood as it soaked through the leg of his trousers.

The bulk of the two heads struggling to grasp their prey, blocked any vestige of light from the narrow tunnel.

Gareth tripped, and began to fall down a curving staircase. His only saving grace was that the gap was too tight for his body to twist, therefore, other than a few more scrapes, Gareth never fell to the ground.

He heard a distant voice call up to him.

"Sorry! I guess I should have warned you about the stairs. Never mind, you'll get down… one way or another."

Gareth let out with his own string of obscenities as he heard the distant echo of Mikal Syla's laughter.

By the time Gareth had reached the bottom of the narrow, winding staircase, the two Guildsman had already lit several torches, and Gareth marveled at what they revealed.

The immense, cavernous tunnel stretched beyond the light in both directions. The smooth polished surface seemed to absorb the torchlight and radiated it further into the fading dark.

Gareth noticed that Mikal Syla was already some distance away, and he ran to catch up to the old Scribe.

Reaching the center of the chamber, Gareth tripped and fell over a row of timbers laid the length of the tunnel.

His exasperated breath raised a cloud of fine dust as he slowly began to raise himself onto his injured leg. Instead he twisted and sat down again, reaching for the once soggy pant leg. He was confused by the sight of the red streak, that instead of flowing down from his injury, seemed to rise and twist to his back. He was about to reach for the Black Scroll when the two Guildsmen reached him and began to help him up.

Shaking off the growing mystery, Gareth moved, hesitantly with the others, along the track.

Two lines of massive timbers were laid to each side of a row of carved, stone wheels. Their surface was covered with some form of blackened, grease that still allowed the wheels to spin freely.

All three men were offering their guess as to the purpose of the tracks, when it dawned on Gareth… this must have been how they moved the massive stones for the towers. Another clue to dispel the Denials.

Either Mikal had tired, or he decided to wait for his traveling companions, as quite quickly, Gareth and the others were walking abreast of the old Scribe.

"How did you know about a secret passage, held inside the stone of a tower that was never to have existed?" Gareth did not hold back any of the anger or fear that the last two days had grown. "We could have camped down here last night and we would not have lost any of our men."

"The how… I read it somewhere." And Syla let out with an amused giggle as he twisted his arm, exposing the tattooed script. "The why… I did not think it was something we needed. Plus how would we be sure that those creatures were not down here waiting for us? What ever they were."

"The Shàl Mïr Cri." Gareth flatly stated as he continued walking.

"The what!" Mikal Syla cried as he raced after Gareth. "How do you know of such things?"

"I read it somewhere." Gareth coldly replied.

The small party continued to walk in silence. Only the muffled echo of footfall on the polished stone, broke the silence.

They decided to camp for the night, though down in this cavern, there was no telling what time of day it was.

Although he was amazed at the shear number of supplies the two Guildsman were able to salvage, Gareth knew, that if they didn't find a means of exiting this tunnel, those supplies would not last them till the end of their journey.

"Do you know of any other means in which we can exit this passage?" Gareth asked. And he recognized the contempt in his voice. Feeling ashamed, he tried to apologize. "I'm sorry for how that must have sounded. I should be grateful that you were able to save us, and provide us with shelter from our enemies and the elements."

"There is nothing to apologize for, my dear boy. We are men of thought. Sometimes those thoughts oppose each other, nothing more. There can only be a problem if we completely fail to listen to the others thoughts… or viewpoints… or errors."

Gareth laughed as Mikal's eyebrows shot up in a comical salute.

"At the risk of creating another impasse…" Gareth hesitated. "How is it, that we appear to be inside the tunnels that the Märkén Thraüm used to move the stones for their towers? Towers I might add, that aren't supposed to have existed."

"Why would you think that? A long time ago, Delgar supplied the finest quarried stone to all of the Crescent Realms. This is must merely be a means by which they moved that product." Mikal dismissively stated.

Gareth pushed past an instant of doubt, and pressed on for more truth. He reached inside the harness and produced the ivory colored scroll. He held it out towards the older man.

"This may have planted the seeds to those thoughts." Gareth stated.

Mikal Syla barely glanced at the scroll in Gareth's outstretched hand.

"Hmmph." He mumbled. "I take it, you deny the denial."

"The denial is but a thinly veiled wording of the history that, had actually occurred." Gareth pleaded.

"Interesting, that you would take it to mean the exact opposite of the words which grace its surface."

"How do you know what exact words…"

"I know of, have read, or have written, every scroll that has ever graced those hallowed halls in El'Athandria." Then the old man turned his shoulder away. "Let us speak no more of this tonight. There is plenty of our journey left for us, to do so."

They pushed on their way, rarely stopping to rest, and eating less than the time they stopped.

There was a sudden change to the surface of the walls. The bright colored, polished stone shifted to a rougher hewned form of bedrock. Several shades of blues and purples, streaked their way throughout the stone.

And with that change, came elaborate carvings and script. The Crest of L'uramentia, complete with colored tiles and gilding, was emblazoned on both sides of the massive chamber. Then delicately carved timbers ringed the entire shaft. Immediately thereafter, the crest of Marìv' appeared, signifying that they had crossed the border into another realm.

Several other apparent changes signified that they were now passing under the "Kingdom of a thousand marshes", as Marìv' was commonly called outside of its own borders. Moss and other forms of lichen grew on the surface of the walls and through small seams in the stone. Many cracks, wept a constant flow of water, which swirled and created its own drain, never flooding the tunnel.

The water at times, tasted a little salty, but on the whole, was pure enough to drink. Each man made sure to fill his belly to help stave off the rumble of hunger.

Again, there was no telling the passage of time, but each man was exhausted, and without a single word, it was agreed on to stop for the night.

They had stopped where a larger section of the wall had crumbled in on itself. The entire surface was covered in a dark, slimy moss that gave off a slight sweet fragrance. They all joked about the scent helping cover the rising stench of the unwashed travelers.

Although, there had been no apparent pursuit, each time they chose to stop, the two Guildsmen took turns guarding the group from a slight distance away.

In the open air, it was a sound, tactical practice.

But in the shadows, underground…
It would prove to be deadly.

37

Gareth and the others were awoken by the piercing scream. Dazed, they stumbled to grab the torches and raced towards the sound, which had now become a gurgling whimper.

They froze in shock at the devastating sight before them.

What remained of their companion was covered in miniature versions of the creature Gareth had seen on his first trip to the Darkness.

No less than a dozen, infant pitch were gnawing and tearing the remnants of the man's body apart.

The group watched the sickening scene as one creature grabbed a section of intestines and ran to the black moss, dragging the entrails behind it.

Gareth had seen enough. He raced after it swinging the torch violently, unsure if the flame had hit it, or not.

The small pitch seemed to boil into a gelatinous form, and seeped into the moss. Gareth wondered if he had actually killed the creature and had caused the effect or if…

Syl and the other Guildsman were also striking out at the tiny pitch.

Gareth watched in amazement and horror as each body of blackness dissolved into the cracks in the ground. Several ran up the side of the walls only to melt into the crevices at the edge of the light.

They needed no further prompting.

Quickly they grabbed their remaining provisions and ran as fast as their tired bodies allowed. Hoping that in the distance, safety would avail itself.

What they found instead, was the complete collapse of the ceiling of the tunnel. Rock, brush and water alike, spilled down from the surface along with the blinding, blaze of sunlight.

They did not hesitate.

Each man scrambled as swiftly as they could away from the shadows and the evil that the darkness held.

Once at the top, they paused a moment to soak in the warmth of the sun. Gareth couldn't help but smile and let out with a mild yell of excitement.

Mikal Syla, though smiling also, admonished Gareth with a sideways… "tsk, tsk." Then quietly turned, and began their journey, anew.

They ate berries and fruit from an abandoned orchard along the way, but all too quickly the bright green fields and pastures of yellow flowers faded to the churned, grey mud that symbolized a growing metropolis.

Only there was not a single soul to be seen.

They pressed on past a dank, smelly swampland, across a now, marled, timber planked bridge. The palling silence began to get unnerving as they entered the outskirts of a sizeable town. Not one voice, or dog's bark met their approach. Even the occasional gust of wind produced no whistle or howl.

Every building and surface had the appearance of being scorched and covered in ash, but there was no sign as to the cause of either. Dry grass and hay bales sat, untouched, proving no flame, but the same grey covered all.

Gareth hadn't realized at first, the close proximity of the border to the Darkness. As they continued to travel to the far end of the hollow city, the ghosts of Cellia screamed out to him.

And as he was about to voice the similarities and the story of that fateful day…

A raspy baritone shattered the silence.

"They've been through here, twice now. Searchin'…"

Gareth and Mikal almost screamed out in unison.

"Who!"

"Hurt some people. Didn't kill not a soul… but hurt some people. Which… all in all, is somewhat surprizin'."

Again, both Scribes questioned.

"Who?"

The mud covered man seemed to ignore their question. Instead he pushed past the trio and went about his own task of collecting small stones and twigs.

He seemed perfectly normal to Gareth, other than his appearance. He wasn't sickly, or malnourished. There were no outward signs of injury.

Just a cloak of apathy.

"Who has been searching? What have they been searching for?" Gareth asked again as he stepped in front of, and handed a rock to the man.

"The Cri. Came riding in on her Mïténà äin'öch. That's what you call those things… right?" He paused, expecting an answer from Gareth.

"Yeah! Right." Gareth agreed, shaking his head as he turned to Mikal for confirmation.

"You're the one whose… read about them, somewhere." Syla chided as he shrugged his shoulders.

"She said, they said… had those monstrous drones following on foot. But of course, can't understand a word of what they were sayin'. So! Who knows what the Rhüle they were searchin' for."

"How long ago?" Gareth asked, twisting to search the horizon, and every avenue for a possible approach.

"First time was about three days ago. Most people left after that. Some though started building a wall…" And he pointed back in the direction that the small party had been heading. "But, they came back a day and a half later, circlin' around or somethin'. Wall didn't stop that beast. Crushed half of it with its weight. But still, didn't kill none. Hurt more that time… but didn't kill em'. That's when the rest left. Figured they be back again until they found what they been lookin' for. Some kind of scinth. I think."

Gareth's pulse pounded and he had to suppress the panic. He turned to Mikal Syla and nearly screamed at the elder Scribe.

"We have to leave now!"

Sylabis didn't have to question. He read it in Gareth's eyes and shook his head as he turned to speak to the lost soul.

"From which direction did they last leave and what path did your people take to escape?"

"They left in the direction you came, surprised you didn't meet up with them. And as to where the town's folk went… as you can see by that rising dust… I think the Cri might be coming from there."

A panicked gaze to the distance, showed the looping segments of the Mïténà äin'öch's spider-like legs as they rose above the cloud of dust it stirred up.

The group turned, readying to race away.

"You won't be able to get over that gate in time… They built it too good… for men, at least. The only other choice would be the border itself."

They hesitantly began to move in the direction of the Darkness. The man followed close behind, giving a constant update on the Cri's progress. The group paused at the edge of the sea of black, and the lone resident, noticing their reluctance, spoke one last time.

"Imagine if you could, not the sound of crunching leaves and rotting timber... but a sickly hiss and painful cry as each step is sucked into a gelatinous, sinew that chokingly, curls around each footfall... and yet, it hastens its own retreat. Causing the ground to undulate and moan, creating a nauseating vertigo that threatens to upend any traveler."

They all turned to him with a pained and disgusted look.

"I have been in there before, you know." Syla snidely spat at the man. "Plenty of times." He tuned his gaze to his traveling companions, shaking his head. "And I've lived to tell the tales." His voice trailed off as he took the first step into the Black.

38

Gareth had long since pushed the dull throbbing in his head aside, forcing himself to ignore the sensation that every step that he took in the Darkness was wrong. He had also silenced the faint, high-pitched scream, the ground itself made, when it met each and every footfall.

The one thing he couldn't ignore was the growing pain in his leg from his previous injury.

His ability to heal each previous wound had seemed almost miraculous. That since he had first encountered the pull of the Darkness and the discovery of the Black Scroll, any letting of blood or bruise, quickly faded or was drawn away. He witnessed it time and again.

But the gash from the äin'öch's barb was different somehow.

Or was it the land on which they traveled?

Although the trio had hoped to keep from view of the pursuing Shàl Mïr Cri, it was their intention to skirt the edge of the Darkness, to keep the border in constant view.

To not lose sight of the light.

But as day became night in the Crescent Realm, the perpetual black of the Darkness, became absolute.

They lost any reference for telling how deep they had penetrated the evernight, but pushed tirelessly on.

Until Gareth could go no further…

His body succumbed to the energy draining pain. He pitched forward, hovering briefly at a weird angle, before his eyes rolled back and he lost consciousness.

There was a sharp, wet slapping sound as Gareth's body met, and began to mold into the viscous surface of the land.

Gareth awoke to a sickening mixture of smells that immediately made him regret his return to consciousness. His eyes began to water from the acrid aromas assaulting his senses. The mouth-watering scent of freshly cooked meat twisted into the putrid rot of diseased flesh. Decayed and stagnant vegetation fused with the sweet and spicy blend of a medicated salve.

Pushing himself up to a seated position Gareth looked around the makeshift campsite. He was somewhat surprised to see a burning fire, although, here in the Darkness, even that sight was twisted beyond the norm. A dark blue flame, with an undertone of blood, red scarlet seared the meat that hovered above it on a spit.

He reached his arms toward the flame, but felt no warmth. So how could it be cooking their meal?

Gareth turned to ask that same question, but saw no one to ask.

His growing sense of concern, was abated by the sight of Mikal Syla pushing through the thick, undergrowth.

"Ah! Splendid! Good to see you have chosen to return to us."

Gareth had to smile at the ever, present theatrics that Mikal Syla seemed to employ each time he made an entrance.

"You must be starving." The old man stated as he bent to pull a chunk of dripping meat from the flame. "You need to keep your strength up. Not sure what it is that ails your leg, but I imagine it must be the results of some sort of poisonous tincture or some such thing. Never you mind that this equates to the last of our provisions. Though I fear we may need to head back to the light in the morrow, to search out some fresh form of sustenance."

Gareth greedily ate the mass of stiffly spiced meat. Only pausing occasionally when Mikal's own sounds of gluttonous delight, rose in volume, above the tortured background noise of the Darkness.

Once finished with his meal, he laid back and stared at the starless canopy of the Dark. No light, faint or bright, penetrated the choking veil. Gareth found himself trying to comprehend how any life, be it plant or animal, could sustain itself amidst this aptly named, evernight.

The chattering form of the pitch, forced its way from his memory, but it gave no new insight.

Only more questions.

Gareth was about to ask Mikal what he knew of the landscape, when a brief, but haunting scream cut through the dark.

Jumping to attention, Gareth let out with his own scream of pain as his poison filled leg, almost gave out on him. He sucked in a lung full of night air and forced himself to slowly exhale, trying to control his body's intent to shut down again.

"Wh… Where is Evril?" The words barely pushed past his lips.

"He felt the need to scout ahead. To make sure, we… would be safe in stopping, at this location, to provide the time you needed to recover… by alas, I fear…" And the elder Scribe's voice faded.

"We need to find him. To help him!" Gareth shouted at Mikal.

"We must move… yes! But not to aid. But flee. If in fact, the sounds we heard were the last he has made in this lifetime… it was, to give warning, not to call for help. If he is fine, he will in turn catch up to us. But if not, let us not dishonor his service by rushing into the danger he has suffered to spare us from."

Mikal Syla closed the gap between them both quickly and hooked his arm around Gareth's waist.

"Let us move as quickly as a cripple and ancient sloth may." And he let out with a disarming chuckle that forced Gareth to join in.

"When darkness turns to shadow…" Mikal Syla pushed out the words through dried lips.

Gareth thought it was another one of Mikal's attempts to force his mind to think past the pain and exhaustion. A tactic, that had been needed several times throughout their escape from the unseen horrors, which pursued them. Gareth had been amazed at the elder Scribe's stamina and unrelenting determination to keep them moving forward, even when he, himself could find no strength left to carry on.

He turned to look at his friend, and quickly realized that that was not Mikal's intent this time at all.

"See!" Syla said, as he pointed to the defined outline of the treetops. "That's how you know when daylight breaks in the Darkness. The dawn of a new day, casts only shadows here. It is as bright as we will see all day."

Gareth smiled at his friend's self-satisfaction.

But, the feeling quickly faded as he now saw the toll that their trek had taken on Mikal Syla. The old man was panting. Every other breath let a slight wheeze escape through his parched throat. His stubby legs trembled and his large bulk wobbled, threatening to upend the old man.

"If you wouldn't mind. I think I need a bit of a rest." Gareth pleaded, hoping to hide that his thoughts were actually on Mikal's needs, instead of his own.

"Too right." Mikal's head bobbed as his body fell back against the blackened bulk of a tree trunk. "I hate to admit it, but I feel I may need one myself."

Though he tried, he could not force out the customary laugh that accompanied each of his quips.

The old man's eyes slid shut as his head bent to rest on the tree.

Gareth had to stifle a laugh when the deep guttural rumble of a snore, echoed throughout the small clearing they had stopped in.

Gareth hadn't realized that he had let himself drift off until he heard the startled gasp of Mikal Syla. Looking across to his friend, he saw the old man clambering to stand, angered that he had seemingly fallen whilst asleep.

But as the Scribe grabbed hold of the trunk again to gain a purchase to heft his large bulk, the trunk shifted, sending Mikal to the ground again.

Gareth slowed his approached towards Syla, looking upward as the blackened limb rose and flexed its multiple joints.

The Mïténà äin'öch spun lithely, extending its legs to their fullest height so that the hulking body could rise above the chaparral. Twin sets of raging eyes, blazed down at the wayward travelers. The duel, massive heads, smashed against each other as each gaping jaw snap at the other in a self-challenge as to which would lead the attack.

Then in concert, they both let out with a horrifying scream.

39

Gareth needed no prompt.

He raced to Mikal Syla and lifted the stunned man. He tugged so hard on the scribe's arm, the portly figure was propelled through the air, his feet barely touching the ground.

They could hear the clambering response to the äin'öch's call. As the Shàl Mïr Cri, converged on their location from multiple directions.

Gareth allowed himself, only the briefest of hesitations as he looked back to judge the pursuit of their enemy. Through the slight opening of the forest, he saw the leader of the Cri take a tremendous leap. She landed gracefully on the back of her beast and spurred it to attack. All the while shrieking a staccato, rhythm of commands, to her unseen, soldiers.

Gareth turned to see that Mikal Syla hadn't stopped running. And although fueled by adrenaline, it took the younger Scribe a few minutes to catch up to, then, slowly pass the elder man.

The sound of each frantic, step was drowned out by the groans of every painful, gasp of air.

Every gasp… was drowned out by the cries and hollers of the Shàl, as they steadily gained on the two Scribes.

Suddenly, Gareth slid as he tried to come to a sudden stop. At first the slimy vegetation gave way, but then his weight seemed to sink into the blacked ooze.

He took a deep breath, thankful that he hadn't rushed, headlong over the edge of the steep hill.

As Gareth turned to shout a warning to his approaching friend, Mikals Syla's bulk slammed into him and they both tumbled over the edge.

Their descent was a blur of flailing limbs and uncontrolled twirls. The few times the Scribes seemed to land on their feet, their momentum quickly sent them sprawling again.

The only benefit of this brutality was the speed in which they landed on the bottom.

There was a quick nod of ascension, after each took a brief assessment of their own, wellbeing. Then they turned and raced off.

The spider like legs of the Mïténà äin'öch lifted the creature deftly over the edge of the hilltop and unimpeded down its side.

The four pursuing Shàl Mïr Cri leapt furiously over the edge, landing more than half way down. Their massive bodies absorbed the impact and shifted the momentum into a smooth and rapid assault on the remaining distance.

Gareth and Mikal never slowed their pace, but it was painfully apparent that the Shàl Mïr Cri's hunt was drawing to an end.

Either fatigue, or miscalculation, found both of the Scribes running into the horseshoe shaped enclosure of roots of a massive tree. Turning to face their approaching demise, each pressed their backs into the malleable flesh of the tree, wishing that it would swallow and protect them from the approaching…

The Shàl Mïr Cri did not advance.

Gareth stared in disbelief. He could conceive of no reason why, he and Mikal Syla should still be alive. At first he wondered if their pursuers might not see them, as it appeared to have happened, at the Thraüm tower. But he quickly dismissed that theory knowing that even if the Cri could not see them, the äin'öch had no trouble. That was why his injured leg had hampered their escape.

Gareth's gaze was drawn to the jagged hook on the beast's articulated leg, amazed to find the limb severely injured. The spike that had pierced his leg, oozed a steaming flow of scarlet.

The animal, though mostly still, occasionally had to shift its weight to compensate for the injured limb.

The leader of the Shàl Mïr Cri made a small chirping noise, trying to steady the increasingly, uncomfortable animal.

In that moment, Gareth did not see a monster of the Darkness, but caught a glimpse of a caring being. He locked eyes on the female leader of the Cri and found himself being pulled in by the fierce beauty that lay under the sweat-streaked war paint.

She in turn, quizzically returned his gaze. Tilting her head as if she was trying to figure out her own confused thoughts.

A sly smile arced across her face.

Then she barked a high-pitched command, and one of the Shàl Mïr Cri advanced, drawing both of his swords.

The entire, surrounding area seemed to sway and begin to undulate.

Gareth believed that it was his mind, struggling to find a suitable way to compensate for the terror of their impending doom.

A low, synchronous, chattering raised in volume, as the forest seemed to come alive. Each tree and bush let out its own cry as they expelled a member of the pitch.

It was a painful display, as branch and leaf cracked and twisted… then bone and limb, cracked and twisted into the physical form Gareth had witness, before.

Dozens, if not hundreds of the living Darkness emerged.

Though more cautious, the Shàl Mïr Cri continued forward, echoing each call of the pitch, with his own.

Reaching striking distance, the warrior hesitated as the chattering of the pitch reached a thunderous level. It searched for any resistance, then, raised both arms to strike.

40

A massive, branch like appendage, swept out and crushed the Shàl Mïr Cri's body, sending it flying across the clearing. No sooner than it had landed, the body was set upon by a host of the pitch, which disassembled it with horrifying efficiency.

Gareth and Syl turned. Craning their necks, they gazed up at the female form of a massive pitch.

A thunderous bark and chatter rang out from its gaping maw, which sent the entire clan into a frenzied dance. Even the younglings that twisted and curled around her ribs and innards, took up the cadence.

Not to be outdone, the female leader of the Shàl Mïr Cri screamed out her own intent. And began to move forward on her beast.

Gareth was impressed by her determination against such incredible odds, but quickly realized what her success would mean.

He found himself, once again, shrinking back into the malleable flesh of *"Big Momma's"* thighs, as the matriarch of the pitch, slowly and carefully wrapped her massive legs around the Scribes in protection.

Although, his vision was impaired by the mammoth limbs… Gareth was still able to see, that the entire clan of pitch had taken up position, creating a wall, three deep in front of their Mother.

Another chorus of protest rose from the Cri, but was silenced by one, final deafening roar.

The unnerving silence was peeled apart as the mother of the pitch spread her legs to reveal a Shàl Mïr Cri free forest, prompting a giddy, uncontrolled bout of laughter from Mikal Syla.

An uneasy smiling broke across Gareth's face in response, though he was still hesitant to move.

Syl had no qualms, as he proceeded to spin about, repeatedly stopping to bow in acknowledgement of their savior.

Gareth was about to join the joyous Scribe, when the loud snorts and sniffing of the clan Mother, caused him to pause. He looked up at her face, which began to contort in apparent disgust.

Her long arm reached out and poked at Mikal as she took another long sniff. Quickly dismissing him as the source of her discomfort, she gently patted him on the head. Sending the portly man, spinning and jangling again.

Suddenly, she reached down and grabbed Gareth by his injured leg, spinning him upside down. Ignoring his protests, she drew the wounded leg closer to her face, and repeatedly sniffed.

She let out a pained scream as she flung Gareth to the ground, some distance away.

The semi-softness of the Darkness' coating was no comfort as Gareth landed brutally on its surface. Immediately a much smaller female raced from the cover of the woods and latched onto his leg. It frantically tore at the cloth of his trousers, shredding it away.

Gareth tried to kick away in protest, but even this smaller pitch was too strong to escape from.

It raised his leg to its face and clamped its gaping maw onto the injured section of Gareth's leg.

Gareth screamed out in pain as the jaws of the pitch increased its pressure and an intense suction felt like it was ripping the flesh from his body.

Then just as abruptly… the smaller female let go.

He felt an instant relief and he sat up, grabbing for a wound that was no longer there.

Gareth turned to the pitch to say thank you, only to see the contorting and distressed face shudder. The entire head, then body, began to convulse violently as a frothing scarlet stream spewed from the creatures mouth and eye sockets. Falling to the ground, the tremors increase in their ferocity.

Then with a last quiet shriek, the pitch died.

There was no moment of grief, no chance to express sorrow.

Just as quickly as before… a group of pitch, descended on the lifeless body and reduced it to fragments, which then were quickly disbursed.

Gareth felt a twinge of anger at the terrible mistreatment of the being that seemed to have given its life to heal his. He turned his tear, blurred gaze to the Mother of the pitch, intending to demand an explanation, only to witness Mikal Syla and the massive female engaged in a dance of chattering and head bobs.

Stunned into silence, Gareth stood transfixed by the exchange.

Mikal Syla turned and walked up to his friend and placed both of his pudgy hands on Gareth's shoulders.

"I told her how saddened we are for her loss. But! How grateful we are for her daughter's sacrifice." He bowed his head in sorrow.

"Ha…how did you… do you? How do you know how to speak to the pitch?" Gareth struggled to speak.

"I do believe that I may have told you. I have been in the Darkness several time before and, I must ad, have lived to write the tale." He then laughed a joyful laugh, and turned to walk away.

Gareth awoke, not only nestled in the protection of the Clan Mother's thighs, but also surrounded by several of the smaller females. He pushed passed the initial revulsion of having been encased in the slimy, black flesh… to the sense of comfort and warmth that those same bodies had provided.

He tried to slip from their embrace quietly, so as not to wake anyone else. But his movement did not go unnoticed.

Mother's deep voice gently echoed through the entire clearing, which set off an immediate whirlwind of activity.

Without hesitation, his female sleeping companions, seamlessly joined in as the clearing was transformed into a ceremonial banquet arena.

Row after row of small, tray-like platforms were laid out in an increasing arc, circling the Mother of the pitch. On each platform, was then set, a platter of glistening, dark, raw meat.

In the center of this array, stood two larger settings. Fashioned to resemble, human chairs and tables.

Gareth smiled as Mikal Syla approached the center of the ring, through the growing throng of pitch that had begun to take up station behind the smaller trays.

His smile quickly faded though, as he saw that the same viscous looking meal appeared on the two Scribes plates.

Mikal Syla made a show of bowing and bobbing his head towards the Clan Mother.

A move, Gareth tried to emulate.

The clearing rumbled with Mother's laughter, at Gareth's pained attempt.

An infectious, chorus that spread throughout the clan, and even to his friend.

Gareth checked his anger and tried to find the comedy in the situation in which he and his traveling companion had now found them-selves, in.

But the more he thought, the more other pressing questions invaded. So much so that Gareth had failed to realized that every other soul in the clearing had now taken a seat and had begun to eat.

"What is wrong?" Mikal Syla's voice intruded on Gareth's introspection.

"What? Oh! Nothing… I guess." Gareth mumbled his reply.

"Exactly. You are doing nothing, cept' standing there with your mouth agape, sifting the air for every dot-fly floating upon the forest breeze. You are not conversing, and more importantly… you are not eating."

"Not hungry, I guess. All of this being chased with an imminent threat of death and dismemberment, and being tossed around like a…"

"There are certain protocols…" Mikal interrupted. "That a man, a Scribe, even a civilization must follow to maintain what little semblance there is to order. And when the world, on those rare occasions, does choose the right path… we must uphold our end of the balance.

We eat. What they eat, because they would give their final bite, so we could be sustained."

"So what is it that we are, eating?" Gareth grumbled as he prodded the fleshy meal.

"You are seated amongst a hundred pitch that until they presented themselves to us, you were unaware of their existence. Just because you fail to be aware of any other creature that could be consumed as a meal, does not mean one does not exist."

Gareth bowed to Syla's logic and began to gingerly peck at the cold, fleshy meat. He took small bites until he was sure, no imminent death was apparent. The flavor surprised him. Even though the meat had not been cooked, the pitch had taken care to subtly infuse, each separated portion with a variety of spices and herbs, familiar to him.

Gareth's hunger, then spurred a gluttonous intake, which included a second helping and even a portion of a third.

Feeling satiated, Gareth leaned back to stretch as Mikal expanded upon his previous comments.

"The pitch, as you have become aware, are a matriarchal society on the whole. Those clans that have not been tainted by the darker influences, that is.

In each clan, a Mother may have several, lesser, male counterparts. Which is not the envious position, it would seem. If the clan suffers… such is the fate of the highest male.

Defeat in battle. Means death.

Harm to the clan. Means an equal response to the one-father.

If the clan goes hungry, he becomes the means to which the clan is fed."

Gareth suddenly took note to what exactly Mikal had been saying.

"You mean we could have just eaten the father of every pitch we were sitting with?"

"I don't believe that that is how their species, furthers itself. But. Yes!" Mikal stated flatly. "There is, however unpleasant a thought it would be… that the meal may have been a recent, unfortunate traveler."

Gareth stumbled backwards. His stomach twisted with the possible implication.

Mikal Syla watched the color drain from Gareth's face. Recognizing his friends growing panic and discomfort, he quickly tried to diffuse the reaction his misspoken words had prompted.

"I didn't mean to imply…" He was unable to finish his explanation, before Gareth had bolted from the clearing, and had disappeared, into the blackened thicket.

41

Gareth ran as far as he could before he doubled over and the contents of his stomach were painfully voided. Even after the last remnants, had passed... his whole being, shuddered and heaved in a desperate attempt to repel every vestige of his so-called meal.

Left in the wake of the purging, was a body, sweat soaked and aching. Trembling hands, raked at tear blurred eyes. Smearing their salty contents with the acid soaked, spittle that dripped from his chin.

Movement on the ground below drew his attention, as he watched in disgust as the oily surface of the ground, undulated and wrapped itself around each pile of his expelled meal.

Gareth frantically scrambled backwards, in horror. Each clawing, handhold and desperate footfall, opened a scar upon the surface of the Darkness. Then, just as quickly... the hissing mass, covered each patch with a living scab.

It was some time before Gareth had gained controlled of his panicked, breath. Still unsure of the stability of his ability to walk, Gareth scuttled to a nearby stump and was shocked by the discomfort of the Black Scroll biting into his shoulder as he tried to lean back and rest.

His anger mounted at the inappropriate time that the otherwise invisible relic, seemed to pick to make its presence, known. Gareth ripped at the harness which held it to his back, in a hurried attempt to be rid of the discomfort.

For the first time since he had encountered the ancient scroll, the shear weight of it made it impossible for Gareth to do much more than drop it at his side.

A slight incline caused it to roll further still. Before it came to rest, the end of the skin caught on some darkened edge and it began to unroll slightly.

The entire area of ground seemed to rush towards and rise up in elation, to form a ridged, outline.

Gareth cautiously crawled towards the scroll, pushing the resistant ooze aside. Unfurling even more of the ancient text, he raised it closer to try and make out the symbols in this darkened landscape.

A part of him had hoped that the congealed surface of the Darkness would act upon the scroll, as his blood seemed to.

Not a single symbol morphed.

Dejected, Gareth sat back. Frustration and exhaustion fueled his desire to have answers. Now!

Reaching into his tunic, Gareth pulled the spare tip of a quill from a small, side pocket. He raised his hand above the surface of the Black Scroll and plunged the sharp tip into his palm.

He screamed out in pain!

Not from the injury. The tip never pierced his skin.

A presence he had not felt in a long time shattered every nerve of his body causing his arm to fall short of its goal. Every muscle burned with fire and he threw back his head in anguish as another bellowing cry ripped out of his throat.

The entire landscape rumbled as the ground took up the chorus of his pain. The entire essence of the Darkness recoiled.

The surface around Gareth and the scroll cleared, and land that had not seen even, diminished daylight in a thousand years, instantly grew green.

Patches of virgin soil appeared and disappeared, as the Darkness seemed to stagger about, confused as where it should retreat.

Fighting through his own pain, Gareth struggled to roll the Black Scroll as quickly as he could and harnessed it to his back once again.

He turned to head back to the clearing and to find Mikal Syla, but a wall of pitch stood in his path.

Each creature seemed to be fighting off their own discomfort, and agony. Their swaying bodies tensed, then withered. Only to reform again. The massive jaws chattered in anger and warning, increasing in tempo and pitch, until it became one unified wail.

The unseen presence seemed to use Gareth's tortured voice to match the howl of the pitch.

The ground rumbled, nearly upending Gareth.

He gazed up in fear as a cloud of debris rose behind the pitch. Splintered trees and bushes, blurred with shattered rocks and massive clumps of earth.

Any obstruction was smashed aside, including the pitch, as the Clan Mother stormed into view.

Her screams silenced all others.

Gareth fought back the start of an uncontrolled response. Instead, throwing himself on the ground. Prostrating before the Mother of the pitch, begging for forgiveness.

Another bellow raised his head.

"I don't know what I did! I didn't mean to…" Gareth threw his hands up, hoping his vulnerability would convey what his words could not.

Gareth's pounding heart counted out an interminable amount of time.

Each time he thought that the situation had calmed and that he might be safe, a bellow from one of the pitch would insight the Mother. On each of those occasions, she had reached out with her immense paw and swatted the offenders, into oblivion.

The dark forest stirred off to the side of the Clan Mother, as another group of pitch entered the patch, dragging the wildly protesting form of Mikal Syla. Carefully, they approached and deposited the elder Scribe in front of their leader.

Without hesitation, she flicked out her arm and sent the portly figure tumbling towards Gareth.

Gareth carefully helped his friend to his feet, as they both took stock of Mikal's well being.

"What is going on?" Gareth whispered to his fellow Scribe.

"Why are you asking me!" Mikal shouted. "I warned you about showing common courtesy."

"I don't believe this has to do with my eating etiquette." Gareth returned the harsh tone.

"Everything was fine. Even after you ran away. Nature calls. Happens to everyone. But when you started the wailing… mind you, I thought the Shàl Mïr what's-its had gotten a hold of you. Then everything went crazy. And Mother…"

As if on cue, she let out with another, trembling roar.

All of the pitch seemed to fade and pool into one mass. A part of, but also separate to, the land around them. The Mother of the pitch, reached up and grabbed both Scribes by their collars and deposited them on top of the mass of melted pitch.

She growled an ominous warning at the Scribes as she shook her head. Then with one final gesture and howl, she spun around and headed back to her clearing.

Gareth looked at Mikal and they both smiled, feeling a sense of relief. Then both were knocked to the ground as the mass of pitch they had been standing on, quickly propelled them through the ebon forest.

42

After days in the Darkness, the brilliance of the sun was blinding, but provided little warmth. The ice covered peaks on the not too distant horizon signified that the pitch had deposited the fellow Scribes somewhere within the borders of Sonësia.

"If I am correct, taking in the lay of the land… the capital city Urä-néyd lies not too distant to the north." Mikal pointed off to the left. "There is a Guild House where we could, re-provision and get further aids. Of course we would lose a day or two in our travels. But maybe we could gather horses also. Although I do so detest riding on those beasts. Maybe we would be able to make up our time, that way."

Getting no response from Gareth, Mikal turned to question his companion, only to see his distant figure, steadily walking towards their ultimate destination.

They were able to find sufficient fruits, nuts and berries along their journey to stave off starvation. Though that did little to revive any sense of enthusiasm, and they continued to wander along their way, in silence.

After several days of minimal food and even less sleep, it was becoming painfully aware, that they needed real sustenance and rest.

Wisps of distant smoke curled into the sky beyond the rise of a hill, lending the hope that refuge was near. But before the two travelers were able to reach the top, a stiff breeze brought the thickening black cloud to them. And with it, the acrid scent death.

Gareth and Mikal stood at the top of the hill staring in disbelief. The landscape before them was a mass of charred earth, destroyed buildings, and shattered bodies. The skies above twisted, as the remnants of torched timber danced with swarms of ravens and every other form of carrion scavengers.

Mikal Syla wiped away the blur of tears and was the first to step forward.

Gareth, struggling between anger and pity, filled the silence with every heated curse his memory could call forth, as he slowly descended the gentle slope.

As they entered the devastation, Gareth began to give voice to his questions and fears, but a gentle nod from Mikal told the young Scribe that it was not the time.

Instead, Mikal Syla began to rummage for, and examine any scrap of parchment, leather or uncharred flat surface. He pushed through half burning timbers to gain entrance to the few semi-erect buildings and sheds.

His intense search became a frenzied, destructive force in its own right, as his patient, focused investigation… became a frantic, rush to find his own answers.

Gareth struggled to keep pace with the elder Scribe, as the portly figure tore through what remained of a sizeable country town.

Mikal raced up to the smoking, but still standing remains of another cabin. Throwing his bulk, shoulder first into the soot covered timbers, he easily shattered the hinges and he and the door tumbled into the darkened hut.

Gareth raced to check on the safety of his friend only to find the half crazed Scribe pushing aside the deceased body of the building's soul occupant.

Gareth couldn't take any more of the madness and he screamed his protest as Mikal Syla greedily unfurled scroll after scroll, only to toss them aside quickly thereafter.

"What the Rhule are you doing! What madness have you succumbed to that you would so easily defile the fallen?" His questions started out as anger but instantly turned into a plea for civility.

Gareth's outburst seemed to snap Mikal Syla from his possessed investigation. It took the elder Scribe a moment to regain his own composure, and to come to terms with his actions. He began to form some explanation, but the words seemed hollow in the wake of his disrespect.

"I have… had to, find a reason. The scrolls. The scribe. I knew a town of this size would have their own scribe. That if I could find them… the scrolls… I, we… might be able to piece together what. Why?"

A wave seemed to wash over Mikal Syla, draining the last vestiges of his mental and physical strength. Slowly he slid to the floor, weeping. His balled fists, pounding his temples.

Gareth kneeled before Mikal.

Knowing that at this time, no words would suffice. He reached out and encased his friend with the strongest hug he could manage, rocking the elder man as the torrent of tears continued.

Gareth had managed to find enough, unburned grains, and prepared some of the freshly killed poultry, making their first real meal in over a week.

It was his intention to wake his sleeping companion when the food was done, but the scuffling in the dirt behind, told him that there was no need.

"I do say, something smells mighty fine out here."

Gareth tapped on the overturned log next to him. "Have a seat. It's almost ready. It seemed like an added insult to allow the birds to go to waste. Even amongst all of this carnage."

He pulled one of the seared carcasses off the spit and gingerly set in on a resting plate. After he spooned out an ample helping of élan rice, he handed the plate to his older companion. Then he set to filling his own.

"I have always loved the flavor of the élan." Mikal Syla spoke matter-of-factly. "It has a certain tang. Like those sea-side melons you can buy in the dock stalls in Bá Sal."

"As I have never been to the Port of Crowns, I'll have to take your word for it." Gareth countered in-between bites.

"The Master's Guild house is there. We use to make a pilgrimage there every other spring. The smell of the sea gave a tint of salt to every fragrance on the breeze. Surprisingly enough…" He looked at Gareth with that long unseen, comical gaze. "The fish tasted sweeter than the fruit. I do believe it was the women who caught all of the salt."

The last statement confused Gareth and as he was about to question his friend, the man added, within a bout of laughter.

"Cuz they are the spiciest of the breed, you will ever meet."

The laughter felt good.

It seemed to give the otherwise, lifeless town, a voice. For a moment, the hollow screams that clung to the whistling wind were replaced with the joy that had lived there for ages.

The sentiment was not lost on the two Scribes, and as their laughter subsided, the reality of their situation slowly weighed down upon them again.

"You should try to rest." Mikal's voice was now barely a whisper. "We should honor those whom have passed, properly… before the rapacious skies, rob them of any more of their souls."

Gareth quietly agreed, and began to shuffle towards the shelter of the former scribe.

"Aren't you coming?" Gareth asked over his shoulder.

"I believe my weeping shame has afforded me, my remaining lifetime of sleep."

Gareth was too exhausted to console his friend. Instead he allowed his own shame to accompany him to oblivion.

Their task began before sun-up, and lasted well into the darkened skies of night. Each, pushing aside hunger and fatigue, until they had fulfilled the unspoken vow of completing the mourning for each fallen townsfolk.

They only wavered momentarily, when it seemed that their task of finding fresh wood for each pyre was hindered by the lack of virgin lumber. As Mikal was about to start disassembling the Scribe's hut, Gareth arrived with the news of finding fresh stores of wood that had been laid to dry, beyond the borders of the town.

It was only now, after the last funeral was lit…

The final grieving, spoken…

That the two, tired souls, took care of themselves. The poultry was a little burnt, but neither cared. A large canter of mead would moisten each bite.

Whether the somberness of the day, or the loosening of the ale, the conversation slowly turned to the regrets of every yesterday, and the hopes for each tomorrow not yet promised.

"If I am to be honest…" Mikal Syla spoke, staring at the night's stars. "I simply wanted to live my life out in a caravan. Visiting far off lands. You know, there is said to be, vast empires on the other side of the Push. Many think the Crescent Realms are all that exist of humanity… by I believe the stories. At least I had always hoped."

"Have you not seen more of this world by being a Scribe?" Gareth countered.

"To do so, because of an obligation, or a requirement of one's vocation, pulls the sweetness from the fruit. If it were my volition… my…" His thoughts drifted.

"I had no choice. It was never granted to me. And yet, even after the tasks of this day, and all that has led to it… I find my self more indebted to my father for each experience I encounter." Gareth had to choked back his emotions.

"In all of the years of this life, the previous, and the next… it still pains me, that I did not forego my vows, and wield a sword to his aid."

"You wrote the account?" Gareth questioned, as he struggled with the turmoil of his wavering, feelings.

"I may have chronicled the actions of that day, but I have been told, that you, my young friend, transformed those mere words and created history."

"It was only my intention to pay proper tribute to such a noble warrior. To pay the respect, ever so slightly, that my father deserved." Gareth's voice abruptly ended as Syla quickly raised his hand to silence him.

Both Scribe's strained to hear the sound of a distant stirring, over the crackle of the waning fire. A growing fear replaced curiosity, as a familiar sound grew into a drumming cadence.

43

They bowed, as close as they dared, behind separate pyres, hoping that the waving flames would shadow any movement... that the burnt flesh would mask the scent of the living.

The distinct sound of hoof-beat approached. Gareth was surprised that his first thought was not of danger, but that the cadence of the clapping was wrong.

Rising from his hiding place, Gareth tilted his head, questioning what his ears were trying to tell him.

Mikal Syla gave up trying to wave Gareth back into hiding instead he bolted across the short distance that separated the two.

"What is the point of hiding if you are just going to jump out into the open as soon as the potential danger nears? Mykal was incredulous. Throwing his arms in the air in a grand show of dismay, the portly Scribe spun to storm off only to find himself face to face with the blood soaked face of a snorting stallion.

Gareth reached out to secure the reins of the animal but had trouble locating the leather straps in the dim light. He gently patted the animal's neck, encountering instead, the hardened surface of full battle armor. His hand brushed over the smooth surface, and continued probing for the leads but stopped short as it encountered, what would be the first of many damaged and missing sections of plating, and the gashes and cuts that laid beneath.

Although it seemed that the extensive armor it wore had spared the animal from certain death, it was apparent that it had not fared well in whatever battle it had encountered.

"Gareth! Quickly! This side." Mikal's voice wavered.

Circling to the other side, Gareth saw the shorter man struggling to brace the slouching body of a soldier. The figure had almost completely slid from its saddle. And in trying to help his friend free the unconscious figure, Gareth had to untie the rider's wrist, which was heavily bound to the pommel.

Once freed, the weight of the fallen soldier slammed both Scribes to the ground.

It was a struggle for the two grown men to free themselves from the increasing pressure.

"How could one, as slight as this… carry such weight?" Mikal struggled to question, as he forced one leg free and began to use the leverage of his own short stature to push himself free.

Gareth had momentarily given up trying to extricate himself from under the fallen warrior. Instead he marveled at the type of plating, the soldier's battle armor was made of. It did not feel like any form of mail or metal that he was familiar with. The size and texture, was wrong.

The sharp sting of Mikal Syla's slap to the side of his head, brought a renewed focus to Gareth. He took hold of his friend's outstretched hand, and with some difficulty, they were able to pull Gareth free.

"We must get him inside, to the cot. Into the light, if we are to have any chance of... saving him." Syla paused to wipe his blood soaked hand on his trouser leg.

Their task itself was difficult enough due to the fatigue of their day's work, but the constant flow of blood onto the smooth plating, made the task of holding and moving the stranger almost impossible. Gareth struggled to maintain a grasp of the injured warrior, but the promise of being able to save at least this one soul... fueled his efforts.

"Try to get that, that... whatever that plating is, off. Whilst I get some water and linens. Take it off. Take it all off so we can assess every injury. We must see them all."

Gareth hesitated. He struggled to find any way to break the encasement of the intricately woven... stonework. The protective overlay was made up of hundreds of meticulously, cut tiles. Their thickness varied in concert with the vital areas they covered.

Gareth searched out the source of one of the strongest flows of blood. He had to partially roll the warrior on its side to gain access.

But there it was.

A thrusting blade had shattered a grouping of the tiles. And Gareth could see the remaining shards protruding from the wound itself.

It also afforded Gareth a view of how the brigandine was laced together with a steel filament. And just like the beaded links of normal chain-mail, once broken, this section of the armor was easy to unweave. With a greater area of the undercoat exposed, Gareth thought he would be able to easily reach in and undo the clasps that secured the plating together. Whether by design or damage, the suit was bound so tight around the warrior's chest... Gareth struggled to push his hand inside.

Continuing his efforts, redirected the blood flow from an unseen injury. The scarlet covered his hand and began to drip down his arm to his elbow. The momentary slickness it produced, allowed him to complete his task and the remaining bulk of the stone armor crashed to the floor.

He took extra care around the surface of each apparent injury, making sure not to dislodge any of the impaling fragments. Then he set to removing the undergarment. Again the areas around each cut and puncture had adhered to the congealing mass of blood and flesh.

With each layer Gareth removed, a new flow of blood revealed yet another wound to tend. And he had to wonder how anyone, even with that extensive armor, could survive such a brutal assault.

When the task was finished, Gareth let out with an exhausted breath and sigh of relief.

Then he froze at the realization of what laid before him.

44

Mikal Syla struggled to control his breath as he pushed his bulk through the narrow door of the small abode. A task made more difficult with his arms full of the provisions he was able to collect throughout what remained of the town.

"I believe I was able to find sufficient dressings and medicinal…" Mikal paused at the lack of any reaction from Gareth. "Am I too late?" He questioned, almost dropping the supplies.

The only response Gareth managed was a slight shake of his head.

"Then by all means, boy, why haven't you completed the one simple task I asked of you. Don't tell me you've developed a shock to the sight of blood."

"It's a… He is a… I mean, he's not a he. It's a girl. The soldier is a girl. And I touched… I can't keep touching…"

"In another time and place, your chivalry and attempted chastity would be amusing. But now, it will be damned, if it is the cause of our failure to render the appropriate care this valiant rider needs."

Mikal's anger and abrupt actions refocused Gareth's attention. He grabbed the handful of rags from Mikal and after drenching them in the nearby washbowl, set about cleaning the young soldier's wounds.

Gareth was still somewhat taken aback, by all that the tight armor had hidden from sight. The body of the young woman laid before him, was as curvaceous and ample as Annalei. But that form also held the tautness of the underlying muscles born from years of training in the arts of battle. The overall effect, accented each one of those curves.

Gareth found his memory flashing back to the glistening form of the leader of the Shàl Mïr Cri.

He cursed under his breath as he shook both images from his mind and renewed his focus on saving the life before him.

It was some hours later, with the threat of a new day's sun rising, that Gareth and Mikal sat exhausted, next to the dying embers of their fire. Both were too tired to even lift, what remained of their mead.

"Do you think she'll make it?" Gareth pushed out the questioned through tired gasps of breath.

"I feel confident in saying that the combined might and supreme intellect of the Guild of Scribes, has vanquished the arrival of death this night." Mikal unconvincingly boasted.

Gareth forced a smile and hoped that his friend's fantasy would come to pass.

Gareth was awakened by a gentle pat from Mikal Syla. He tried to raise himself quickly to pretend that he hadn't really been asleep. That he had remained vigilant of his charge through the night. But, the abrupt movement wrenched sore muscles and caused tight tendons to pop.

"Ahh!" Gareth yelped.

The figure on the bed stirred slightly.

"Take a break, get some food. There is a fresh pot of mü'rï. Lay down and rest." Mikal made a shushing sound as his armed motioned to sweep Gareth outside.

Gareth was grateful for the break, and stumbled out of the small cabin. No sooner than he had passed the threshold of the doorway, Mikal Syla was on his heels.

"I'm not sure if you have taken notice of the horse?" Mikal questioned.

"Does it need looking after? I must admit, I have forgotten all about it. I've been preoccupied with… by… her." And Gareth tilted his head in the direction of the resting soldier.

"I'm sure you have." Mikal teased.

"Not like that! I leave those actions to you."

"As well you should." Mikal Syla flatly stated.

Gareth couldn't tell if the old Scribe was still ribbing him. Especially when Syla continued.

"I did not mean the state of the animal."

"Isn't that a little rude. I thought she was quite cute, once we scrubbed the blood and mud off of her."

And it was Gareth's turn to smile as he watched Mikal try to figure out whether Gareth was talking about the girl or the horse.

"The colors! The colors, boy! On the horse."

Again, Gareth was put at the disadvantage of not knowing what Mikal was talking about.

"The horse wears the colors of Delgar. The Island of Souls. The young lady… also is branded with the coat. She was, is, of the Elite."

Gareth looked back towards the hut.

Mikal continued, his voice rising in pitch and intensity as he went.

"That means that the battle has already begun! They haven't a Scribe that I am aware of… So how could they begin… the battle… how could they start the battle without our presence? It goes against everything that has ever been written, taught… the code. We must go! Now! I have to be there."

Gareth had never seen Mikal so distraught. He wanted to do whatever he could to put his friend at ease, but he immediately regretted the words that blurted out of his mouth.

"I'll stay. You go."

"What!."

"We can't leave her, not if we want her to live. And by the same token, we cannot take her with us."

Gareth watched Mikal's eyes dance around as the elder Scribe mentally ran through every possible scenario.

"It is done!"

Gareth was stunned as Mikal Syla spun on his heels and headed off in the direction of the tethered horse.

"Wait! What? I didn't mean… what if something goes wrong?" Gareth had to run in order to catch up to the portly man.

Mikal Syla adeptly mounted the horse without hesitation. As he settled into the saddle he looked down at his friend.

"No need to worry. I'll be fine. And as for you… her injuries are no more dire than Larec's were, and you managed to keep him alive in far worse conditions. You'll do fine. I'll be fine."

Gareth stood in stunned silence as Mikal spurred the animal into a full gallop.

Then he screamed over his shoulder…
"Meet me when you can."

45

There was no gentle pat this morning. It was the cold bite of the air that awakened Gareth that following day. He struggled to stretch his stiff body without screaming in pain. Spending each night asleep bent over the edge of the bed or leaning on the hard surface of the small desk was beginning to wreak havoc on his body.

The freshly fallen snow crunched under his footfall as Gareth stepped from the small building. It was his intention to light another fire outside, but the temperature and the drifts across the fire pit, changed his mind.

Instead, he quickly gathered as many of the smaller branches he could. Anything that would fit inside the small iron stove, that was tucked in the corner of the Scribe's hut.

Once he had stoked the fire to a self-sustaining burn, Gareth sat back in the sole chair and nibbled on a piece of dry bread that he and Mikal had found in one of the food stores.

His thoughts turned to concern over the well-being of his friend and of regret for not accompanying him to their destination. He was dismayed at not being able to write the account of the historic battle that was unfolding on the Isle of Souls. Of, not being there to help his mentor. Of, traveling all this way, suffering and surviving through all of these hardships… only to miss out on how those events would ultimately play out.

And yet a part of himself was grateful for not having to witness further death and destruction. He was unsure if he would be able to disassociate himself from the battle, and bodies… just to commit the acts to the surface of a scroll. To, reduce anyone's life, or the manner in which they may leave it, to mere symbols on the surface of a skin, simply because he carried a pen, and not a sword.

A small, throbbing pain tried to push the seething truth to the forefront of Gareth's thoughts, but the figure on the bed convulsed into a retching cough and pushed any further reflection, abruptly away.

Gareth held the young lady in a sitting position, leaning her to the side of the bed. Occasionally he lightly patted her back helping her body to bring up the congealed masses of blood that she must have inadvertently swallowed. At least, that is what he hoped was the cause. The alternative, meant, that he would be gathering wood for yet another pyre.

The coughing stopped and once her breathing returned to normal, Gareth carefully laid her back down, and covered her. He took care in gently wiping the blood from her face. Then with a clean cloth, he dripped small amounts of fresh water over her parched lips.

The sound of the wind whistling outside the hut gave Gareth the chills and prompted him to add a few more logs to the fire. He tried to occupy himself with tidying the small abode, anything to pass the time. But the dim light made it difficult, and the fact that there really wasn't much that needed to be done.

He did manage to find a few hand made scrolls and sat back in the chair to read whatever accounts, this small town Scribe had written. He began to pull open the first scroll only to take pause with the realization of an obvious lie. One that now hung over his own life.

Delgar has no scribe.

How could an entire country, be without a single member of the Guild?

Granted, the Kingdom of Rhyce had none. But that was more out of the arrogance of the King himself.

Delgar however, has always had an almost mythical reputation as the land that was able to stand, alone, against the Darkness. How could there be no one to chronicle such a history?

Of all of the questions that this thought seemed to raise, only one truly mattered… why would Mikal Syla lie?

The question nagged him throughout the entire day. Each time though, the comedic image of an arching brow on Mikal Syla's quizzical face, served as a reminder that there were plenty of things, he himself was not aware of.

Anytime that that thought seemed not enough to push away the doubts, his eyes would catch sight of the soul lying on the bed, clinging to life.

And that image renewed his resolve.

It was time to change the dressings and check whether or not Mikal's attempts at being a field medician were as effective as the older Scribe had boasted.

After heating some water and preparing fresh bandages, Gareth began removing the old ones. Most were blood stained, but dry, giving Gareth cause to be optimistic of the young warriors recovery.

He took the time to bathe each wound, carefully so as to not open any. In doing so, he had to reach over the young lady's body and raise the soft tissue of her breast to clean the most extensive of the wounds.

"Mmmmm, your hands are warm."

Gareth jumped back so swiftly he stumbled, off-balanced. Tripping over and then landing on, the now shattered remains of the chair.

A muffled laugh, mixed with bouts of coughing, drew his attention back towards the bed.

"Don't make me laugh. I don't think these broken ribs can take it. But… they could use those warm hands again."

Gareth was both embarrassed and angered at the forwardness of the young…lady. Without haste, he bounded across the room and quickly covered the smiling soldier.

"I guess that means no." And she stifled another laugh.

"Even if I was so inclined, I don't think you'd be up to the task." Gareth spat.

"I do likes me a challenge."

"Why do you talk like that? Like some common…"

"Soldier!"   "Whore?"

As Gareth said the word, he realized the answer to his question. She was just like ever other soldier he had met. Using humor to offset the fear and pain. It was her response that confused him now.

"Why would you think that I thought that of you?"

"I caught a hint of pious indignation. So I assumed that I must have stumbled into the care of some house of worship. Though I must say, there really isn't room for a pulpit in here."

Gareth looked around and smiled.

"This is no sacellum. It is not even a true guild house. It is merely the diminished quarters of Scribe, somewhere in the outskirts of Sonësia."

"Sonësia? That mürkened horse must have had its head bashed one too many times, to lead me all the way to Sonësia." Gareth was slightly puzzled by, but also intrigued with the young warrior's expressions. He was about to question her about it, when she beat him to it.

"You don't sound like anyone I have ever met from Sonësia. Where might you be from? No wait... don't tell me. I don't really care. Just tell me that you have some food somewhere in this guild-hut. It feels like I haven't eaten in days."

Gareth spun on his heals, searching. Throughout the day's musings, it had not even occurred to him to prepare a meal for himself.

"I can heat some broth. Yes! That would probably be best for you." And he set about his decided task.

By the time the simple meal was completed and he turned towards the bed... he heard the soft breathing, of the now sleeping, young lady.

46

Gareth paced back and forth, outside in the snow, flapping his arms for warmth. Although it was he that insisted on leaving the hut when Tyresa, as he now knew her name to be, needed to relieve herself. He wished that she would hurry up, before he froze to death.

A high-pitched whistle seemed to indicate the all clear.

Upon entering the cabin, Gareth was about to complain, but as before, she seemed to know his thoughts and beat him to it.

"I wasn't the girly one who thought it was necessary for you to go out in the frigid air. When you are surrounded by a hundred other men, and the urge hits… you go where you have to go." She stated flatly.

"It wouldn't be proper…" Gareth started, slightly embarrassed.

"At first I would have thought that maybe you don't like the company of women… but the care you take, the gentleness in which you touch my body… tells me otherwise. So?"

"I did not touch you like that!" Gareth flatly stated. "And don't assume that I did, simply because the situation afforded me the opportunity. I would not do that to any woman. And I would not dishonor Anna…" He turned away sharply and forced out a hollow laugh as he reigned in his anger. Trying to hide the pain he felt for not being with the one he did want to hold.

"Ahh! I see it clearly now. It is rare indeed to find someone as young as you who can be betrothed to but one woman."

"We are not be… are we?" Gareth slumped down to the floor to ponder his own question while a smile began to arc across his face.

"What are you doing here?" Tyresa asked, staring down at Gareth's hands as he finished securing a new dressing.

"I am trying to take care of you before you spout another lewd reference as to why I don't take care of the rest of your body. Or some such thing."

Gareth turned and tossed the dirty bandages into the stove.

"That's not what I meant. At least not entirely."

"We are heading to… were heading to… Delgar. In hopes of warning, preventing… an attack by the Darkness."

"Delgar is always under attack from the Darkness!"

Her vituperative response stung Gareth.

"Sometimes it may just be the annoyance of the slimy pitch. Other times there may be a whole company of the inferiors…"

"What do you mean?" Gareth interjected.

Tyresa shook her head, almost as if she did not want to recount the images, but she continued on with her narrative.

"The main warring party of the Rhüle, are the creatures that seemed to have been rejected by both the pitch and the Shàl. They are Cri, but in name only. They are smaller, deformed versions of the true, Shàl Mïr Cri. As if the process of their creation went wrong. They are mindless creatures that are simply weapons to be pointed at an enemy. Their sole purpose is to kill or be killed. If not an enemy… then each other."

Gareth tried to reconcile this new image against the one of that statuesque warrior.

"Tell me why you felt the need to cross the Darkness, and interject your superior knowledge into our constant fight." Tyresa demanded.

"Your battle is not with two Scribes, struggling to survive long enough to warn and aid an ally against the might of the Mürken Rhüle."

"I know nothing of Scribes… or these allies you speak of. Delgar has been a single island in a sea of darkness for over a thousand years. No one has come to our aid, nor have we needed it." She defiantly stated.

Gareth had to check, his growing anger, but he managed to growl out one last statement before he turned and walked out into the cold.

"Without this ally… you would be dead."

It was his intention to find another building or shack to spend at least, this night, in. But no semblance of a building stood, that would provide any comfort or protection from the weather.

By the time the heat of his anger had ceased to provide him with warmth, he had, however, traveled to the far end of the town.

Gareth stood, shivering, staring into the grey shrouded distance. There was sense that this place, this time, had been abandoned, even though he knew that that had not been the case.

It was as if memory itself was shifting, bringing forth, and distorted other images and thoughts from his head.

He felt that he had abandoned Mikal, only to have his memory remind himself that it was he, that had volunteered to stay behind so Mikal could complete their quest.

He felt that he had abandoned his father, only to remember that although he was reluctant at first, he was now actually following through on his father's greatest wish.

The one thing that Gareth assured himself he would never be able to reconcile though, was how he abandoned Annalei. Simply, in the name of providing aid, to the Isle of Souls.

Only, they cared not for the salvation of a lowly, apprentice Scribe.

A seething resentment grew and gave way to a desire to simply walk away. And Gareth began to take those first steps, only to be floored by the sharp pain that screamed out to him from the darkness.

He was convinced it was a voice speaking directly to him, but no words followed. The thought had been imprinted directly, and Gareth was overwhelmed by the message.

His arm reached instinctively over his shoulder for the large finial, hoping for, but knowing that it was not there. He had laid the Black Scroll in the corner of the Scribe's hut, while he had tended to Tyresa's injuries.

The sudden affirmation that the Scroll was not with him, bore with it the pang of alarm, and an increasing sense of dread.

Gareth began a frantic run, back to the hut.

47

Every step was mired in the slush and mud, threatening to upend him.

Gareth struggled against not only the elements, but, the panic… the pain… the warning.

Each step bringing him closer…

Each step intensifying every sensation.

Ignoring those warnings, Gareth lowered his head, and pushed forward. He raced around the corner and began down the last stretch of snow, covered street, towards the small hut.

The commotion in front of Gareth, drew his attention, but only served to propel him forward in a growing, fit of blind rage.

The female leader of the Shàl Mïr Cri cursed loudly as she struggled to control her mount. The Mïténà äin'öch bucked and pulled wildly against its reins. The only thing that prevented it from bolting, holding it in place, was the fact that its rider stood on one of its appendages, clambering for purchase, in order to mount the beast.

A task made more difficult from the effort of trying to raise the Black Scroll with her one, free, arm.

The creature screamed in horror and pain each time the ancient text even briefly touched its skin.

Though now there was another growing scream that drew her attention.

Gareth knew the voice that emerged from his throat was not only his own, but something that had become a disconnected part of himself.

The thunderous chorus was joined by the cry of alarm from the Leader of the Shàl Mïr Cri and the terror of her mount.

Gareth slammed his body into his enemy. The momentum, coupled with the weight of the Black Scroll, caused the two combatants to slam into and collapse the trunk-like appendage.

Several of the thorny barbs tore through, impaling the female Cri's side. Ignoring the pain, she continued to reach for and try to free her blades to counter Gareth's attack, but the combined weight of both Scroll and Scribe made the task nearly impossible.

Gareth used every bit of his strength to force the large scroll downward, in hopes of suffocating his… enemy.

The briefest of moments, seemed to last an eternity as their intense gazes met.

Understanding. Confusion.

Compassion. Hatred.

Revulsion. Lust

The moment shattered, as their two bodies, were jolted by the force in which the Mïténà äin'öch pulled against the shear weight, entrapping its leg. The limb snapped and tore as the creature screamed out its final attempt to free itself. A large section of its bloodied, hindquarter fell to stain the white snow as the creature, now free, raced away.

Taking advantage of the shifting weight, the Cri tore herself from the barbs and threw Gareth to the side. She raised herself and unsheathed her blades. Slowly, she turned back towards Gareth, raising her arms and voice in a final attack.

Gareth spun wildly, and in defense raised the Black Scroll.

The ebony, surface caught and shattered both blades as its path never faltered. It slammed into the Cri with such force, Gareth heard several bones break. The intensity of the blow sent the female warrior sailing into the side of the hut, her body landing in a crumpled, heap.

Exhaustion threatened to drop Gareth next to the unconscious form, when a stark realization gripped him with fear.

Gareth slowly entered the Scribe's shack, afraid to confront the image he knew would meet him. There could be no way a severely injured, unarmored, and unarmed soldier could protect itself against the onslaught of a leader of the Shàl Mïr Cri.

He stood in disbelief. A cold chill burned through his body.

The bed, the hut… was empty.

His relief was clouded with confusion.

The growing chill though, drew his attention and provided the answer his tired mind needed.

Dropping to the floor, Gareth gazed under the bed, and through a gaping hole in the side of the cabin. Several planks had been pried loose. Gareth noticed the stain of scarlet that coated the edge of the remaining boards.

He rushed to the outside of the building and began to follow the compacted trail Tyresa's body made in the snow as she dragged herself to safety.

Gareth was elated to know that she had escaped the fury of the Cri, but his joy turned to fear as the trail quickly became a rose colored trench.

He found her unconscious body tucked inside the crumpled remains of a small shed. He struggled to squeeze inside, hesitating to check her, fearing that she may not have survived the ordeal.

"Took you long enough."

Her voice startled Gareth and he slammed his head into the broken beams of the small structures, low roof.

"Gah! Why did you do that?" He screamed in pain.

"I thought I'd save you the trouble of having to probe my body again."

She was somewhat surprised that instead of an angry rebuff, he let out with round of laughter.

48

"Why'd you do it?"

"I don't know. It's just not in me, I guess." Gareth shook his head.

"I get it. From what you've told me of that code stuff. You're not supposed to, but… this is the Cri were talking about. She won't stop. She'll keep coming."

They both shifted their weight in unison, as Gareth adjusted his grip on her waist.

"Lean more in to me, not away. If you keep this up I'll have to just throw you over my shoulder."

"I think not." Tyresa snapped back. But she allowed herself to sink into the fold of his arm and let him bare the majority of her weight.

"I'm not even sure she'll survive. She was broken up pretty bad." Gareth mumbled as they continued to walk along.

"Still… you didn't need to stitch up her wounds and wrap her in a blanket. We could have used that out here."

"If you remember correctly, I restrained her with that blanket. Probably to the point that she won't be able to survive."

"No loss." She vehemently replied.

"By the time she regains consciousness, if ever… we will be far from that place."

Gareth expected another snide remark, but none came. The rest of the days travel, continued in silence.

The anger had passed, as so the first threats of winter. The warmth of the sun was welcomed like a lost friend, and its warmth did more than simply melt the snow. Although their conversations were of brighter things, they were still sparse. They agreed that it was best for their safety and the conservation of their remaining energy.

The sunlight also seemed to aid in Tyresa's healing, as she was able to spend more time, moving without the constant support of Gareth's shoulder.

It was not long though, before the mountains closed in and swallowed most of the days sunlight. Making their questing days shorter and shorter. Gareth knew that being this close to the Darkness, it would be all too easy to wander into the evernight, and it was not his intention to ever have to do so again.

They had barely begun their sixth day, when Gareth noticed the stones in the distance. Masked by the layers of mountains, which rose behind them, Gareth instantly recognized the smooth edges and gleaming surface.

Tyresa was not as convinced, but also confessed that the only tower she was aware of was nearly intact.

"You know of the Thraüm towers?" Gareth could barely contain his glee.

"I have grown up within a stones throw of the mightiest of all of the towers. As a child, we would steal away to the ramparts of the cities outer wall, and actually throw stones at it. Each one gaining a point if you threw it far enough and hit it." She laughed at the memory. "You would win the day's toss if you managed to get your stone within any of the massive windows."

"And what of the tunnels? Are they accessible, or have they caved in?"

"You mean the mines?"

Gareth was puzzled by the question and was unable to answer quick enough before Tyresa's next statement.

"The mines have always been, and are operational to this day."

"That is how we are going to do it."

"What are you talking about?" Tyresa's voice cracked with the beginning edge of anger.

"I had no desire to traverse the Darkness again. Not that it would allow it. But knowing that the tunnels… the mines, as you call them, are operational… we can simple gain access from here and travel safely underground." Gareth had to refrain from dancing around.

"You mean to say, you put us on this course, not even knowing if we would be able to find, let alone use these tunnels? What if it didn't work? What if it still does not work?"

"Doesn't matter… does, it?" Gareth screamed as he sprinted towards the massive stones.

As much as she wanted to be angry, Gareth's joy was infectious and she laughed the entire time it took to catch up to him.

Gareth's elation at having found a more complete tower base faded with the passing of each, unmarked, stone. The pristine surface was polished smooth and showed no signs of even a single blemish, let alone the intricate carving that signaled the hidden entrance.

A wave of melancholy pressed down on him and he allowed the emotional deluge to drag his body to the ground. It was as if the exertion of every step, every struggle… every lost friend… manifested itself at this moment, to take its toll on the apprentice Scribe.

Gareth shut his eyes, even as he raised his head towards the heavens. Hoping for any sign to dispel the sense of utter defeat.

But none came.

Instead he kept his eyes clenched to stem the welling, tears of anguish that now threatened to flow.

"So you found it then?" Tyresa's voice whispered through labored breaths.

Gareth's eyes snapped open to stare beyond the harsh, back-lighting of the sun, to just make out Tyresa's head nodding towards the section of the wall just above, and to the left of his own.

He wanted to bolt upright, to continue on their journey, but as he was about to move, Tyresa stumbled, and her body crashed into the wall and slowly slid to a halt next to him.

"Good idea you had…" She labored. "To rest, I mean."

Gareth watched as Tyresa's eyes rolled back and the young warriors unconscious form fell over into his lap.

49

The strain of their journey, and lack of rest had taken its toll on Tyresa and on Mikal's needlework. Several of the stitches had torn loose, and a fresh flow of blood soaked the entire side of her tunic.

Gareth struggled to settle his mind on a course of action, but knew that he had to stop the bleeding. As there was no fire or hot metal to use to seal the wound, it meant he would have to re-sew the wound if he was to have any hope of saving the young woman.

Thankful that he had grabbed every supply that he and Mikal had assembled, he set to work preparing the needle and thread.

Only when the time came to begin, the trembling in his hands brought about a panic of self-doubt.

Kneeling beside her unconscious form, Gareth held out his arms in front of himself and willed the shaking to end. Each time though, that the needle began to pierce the skin, they wavered.

Tyresa's raspy voice drew Gareth's attention away from his nerves and brought back the focus he needed.

"If you could make it look like a bird of prey... that would be cool." She choked out between coughs. "But if that scare ends up looking like a butterfly... you can start writing about your own demise."

She winced in pain as Gareth tightened the next stitch.

"Be careful for what you wish for." He quietly stated with the vain attempt of a comforting smile.

"Back home, they make a Charbury distillate that melts the pain out of any body. If you make it there... make sure to have a mug for me."

Gareth was about to admonish her for her negative thoughts, but his voice caught in his throat as he watched her eyes slowly close.

Tyresa's head lolled and the swell in her chest faded with her last, rattling, breath.

It was as if it took every sound from nature with it.

Even the sharp breeze that blew away the warmth of that breath, was but a whisper. Its cold bite stripped the hue from her already pale skin, fading it to the pallor of death.

"No!"

His scream echoed off of the ring of stone and raced into the mountains nearby.

"I refuse to give her to you!" Gareth screamed in the direction of the Darkness.

It was the blackness staring back at him, ignoring him... defying him. That gave him the idea.

Pulling the Black Scroll from its harness, Gareth laid it on the ground and unrolled almost the entire length of it. Carefully he stripped the remainder of Tyresa's tunic from her body. He then lifted her pale form and set it upon the surface of the scroll.

Nothing seemed to happen at first, and when it did, the movement was so subtle that Gareth merely thought it to be the blur of tired and distraught sight.

Wherever Tyresa's body touched the skin of the Scroll, the ancient symbols slowly flowed around her form. The pooling, blackened cruor, pulled the fresher scarlet from her wounds and the two swirled until they became one.

The congealing mass rose, and coated every wound and curve of the young woman's torso with a, viscous, ooze.

Gareth reached out to touch the dark slime but it retreated from his touch. Falling away from Tyresa's body, it retreated into the ancient text, once more.

The faint hiss was slowly drowned out by Tyresa's congested breathing.

Partially out of relief, partially out of necessity, Gareth pulled Tyresa into a seated position and wrapped his arms around her. He softly patted her back as the last remnants of blood soaked phlegm were expelled and her breath became clear and even.

50

Gareth finished wrapping every available garment they had brought, around the sleeping woman. Pushing the small satchel of their remaining supplies, he made sure everything was within her reach.

He stood and looked around the small alcove. Enough of the remaining daylight could still be seen through the narrow opening, so he was confident that if Tyresa needed to exit the ruins, she would easily be able to find the entrance.

He felt a twinge of guilt at the thought of leaving her here on her own, but a growing tenseness seemed to signify that he needed to be somewhere else…

"I'm usually the one tucking them in and sneaking out with the morning's light."

"Man or woman?" Gareth questioned with a grin as he turned back to kneel by Tyresa's side.

"Depends on how much I had to drink." She smiled through cracked lips. "The way I feel right now…"

Gareth dripped several drops of water from a damp rag, across those parched lips. After he finished lightly wiping her entire face, he bent over and kissed her forehead.

"It is way past morning." He smiled as he pulled away and turned to walk into the darkness of the Thraüm tower.

He felt it the moment that he stepped into the vast tunnel.

Something greater than a sensation…

And yet the closest he could come to describing it to himself was… life.

Whereas the tunnel they had entered in L'uramentia was covered in ancient dust and silence, save for the occasional drip of water echoing in its self-made pool… and just as the moss covered run through Mariv' stank of the decay of passing time…

A hum of life radiated through every vein of the rocks that now surrounded him.

An energy, pierced the air.

Whether it was a real effect or simply Gareth's own excitement to be moving forward again, it made each step seem lighter, faster.

He felt no need to rest.

No passage of time.

It was no shock then that he quickly, happened upon the border markings that divided Sonësia and Delgär and the Darkness that separated the two.

Though, unlike the simple and ornamental carvings and markings that signified the change of territory of sovereignship he had previously encountered… what greeted his sight, filled him with wonder, awe, and fear.

The tunnel seemed to end. Swallowed by an absolute, beyond Darkness itself.

The ground gave way to a cavernous expanse of an indeterminate depth, and the breadth of the gap was defined merely by a pinpoint of light almost lost in the distant.

Gareth stared in horror at the only means of crossing the chasm and turned away.

The wooden timbered tracks, encasing the grease covered wheels had seemed large when one was simply standing next to them… but with the reality of their width being the only means of crossing the immense blackness, they seemed to shrink before Gareth's eyes.

Several times Gareth began to straddle the track only to immediately loose his nerve and walk away.

Frustration at his inability to conquer his own fear quickly mounted, and triggered outburst, after outburst.

"It's not fair!"

His voice echoed into the blackness, but what returned was a distorted, and twisted bellow. Mocking his every attempt to summon the slightest semblance of courage.

Dropping to his knees, Gareth crawled to the edge of the abyss. No matter how long he stared, or tried to focus… not a single feature revealed its self.

The longer he tried to find anything familiar or calming… his body would tremble like an infant lost in the forest at night. Images and phantoms would rise up to claw at him… only to shift and fade away with the blink of a watery eye.

As much as Gareth hated the feeling of being toyed with, the childish response sparked his plan of action.

He made sure to grasp both sides of the timber so that his fingers would curl over the outside edges. Allowing him to maintain his course when all sight could possibly fail him. Drawing his knees in tighter, he would allow the greased surface of the stone wheels to smooth the friction between cloth and timber.

The only thing he was not sure of… was how he was going to shut down the growing panic in his brain.

He found himself longing for those warning pings to the temple, that had so often helped him navigate the tight tunnels and corridors of the Castle Rhyse.

And almost in response, a sharp tingling sensation ran up his spine.

The signal he needed to proceed.

Staring ahead, Gareth tried to focus his sight on that small pinprick of light. Only lowering his head to help alleviate the stiffness and sore muscles that built over the countless minutes of slow, travel.

He cared not how long this journey would take, as long as there were no incidents.

No slips.

No stumbles.

Gareth nearly jumped off the track, as he felt something lightly brush across the fingers of his left hand. Flinging himself back on his haunches, Gareth struggled to maintain his balance and to stifle the urge to scream.

Gareth brushed frantically at his hand making sure the unseen assailant was now gone, but what was a guiding sensation down his back, became a darting, flame, attempting to purge Gareth's entire body of this invisible aggressor.

There was the briefest movement, and the slightest sound coming from below. Shadows bent out of the Darkness, where even light could not exist.

He cared not whether it was real or imagined.

Gareth needed no further prompts to scurry forward at a pace that he would have thought impossible on hands and knees.

A distance that had seemed, unreachable, quickly grew into focus. Which drove Gareth only harder to push the limits of his body.

His heart pounded in his chest, and the frenetic rhythm concussed in his ears.

A growing scream pierced the droning thunder… though Gareth was certain that the voice was not his own.

Once he reached the glowing surface of stone that was adorned with the golden inlaid seal of Delgär, he scrambled to his feet and ran.

He ran until his body could push its self no longer.

He ran until he fell…

But not from fatigue, and not by choice.

51

The smooth surface of the mine-shaft sharply descended at an improbable angle. One, that, the weary traveler was unable to navigate.

Gareth's body rolled and slapped the hard surface as he struggled to gain control of the decent. Every time he was able to steady his body in a controlled slide, the sole of his boot would catch a seam in the stone, or the edge of the scroll would tangle with the ridged, gears of an elaborate pulley system, twisting his body, causing already pummeled limbs to collapse and fold under him, starting the process again.

Although the bottom of this impossibly long shaft curved in a smooth arc, the abrupt end to his fall caused Gareth's leg to twist at an unnatural angle. His scream of pain and string of curses echoed into the distance, beyond sight.

Whether brought on by extreme fatigue, or paralyzing pain... Gareth quietly embraced the darkness that swallowed him.

He knew not how long he had been unconscious, nor how long, since waking, that he had been wandering the mines of Delgär. The throbbing pain in his head helped to distract him from the burning agony coming from his ankle and knee.

The continual downward slope of the tunnel, though, only added more stress to his injuries.

Gareth knew that he should be focusing his attention on these new surroundings, but his mind was a jumble of twisted thoughts and sensations.

His eyes tried to comprehend the stark contrast of the rock face to either side of the shaft. Off to the left, the brilliance of the milky white stone, with its silver threads, radiated any available light… And on the right, the absolute of the black surface hid its every feature, and at once, swallowed that same light while diverting the gaze of any onlooker.

Gareth felt the pull of that darkness, feeling as if a part of himself was being drawn into that void, but at the same time a relief as the pain also, slowly left his body.

He reached out to touch the stone, to see if he could also merge with this Darkness, but a gentle music filled the tunnel and Gareth was overpowered by its call.

52

Following the melodic chime, Gareth slid along the edge of the tunnel. The smooth surface became rougher as the shaft began to widen.

Hesitating at the sight before him, Gareth cautiously entered the massive chamber. Here again, the floor of the shaft descended at a sharp angle, but unlike before he did not rush carelessly over the edge. In the dimming light, he marveled at the intricate pulley system that was attached to the center tracks. Long, grease covered chains were attached to large counterweights that hung above boreholes off to the sides of the main shaft.

Gareth was pleased to find a stairway carved in to the flooring, allowing him to begin a controlled descent. All the while his gaze shifted from the cathedral like ceiling that seemed to create its own version of the heavens, complete with minute specks of light.

Then a new chorus of chimes would draw his attention to the distant, dim figures moving about piles of rock chips and gravel.

And then again, a ping of caution forced his vision to the ever shifting, blackened figures that seemed to be forcing immense blocks of the ivory stone, down yet another shaft.

A sharper tone rang out, and Gareth focused upon the entrance to a darkened shaft, smaller in size than the ones he had traveled on his journeys, but still impressive in the precise way it was cut out of the main cavern.

A soft, lilting voice followed one of the melodious chimes and Gareth couldn't help but smile at the joy that simple sound brought.

A gentle rap on a metal chisel followed, and Gareth felt a small tremor in the ground.

Inching further in to the recess, Gareth saw the outline of the frail figure tilting its head slightly as it stroked the seam it had cut through the slab of rock.

"You don't have to try and hide. I heard you when you fell and hurt your leg." Although Gareth could not see the young girl's mouth, he felt the beaming smile that accompanied the cheerful voice.

"Your curses were…" And she struggled to contain a giggling fit. "Amusing to say the least."

"How could you, that was easily a day a go. You couldn't possibly have hear…" Gareth's voice trailed off, as the young lady turned and stared in his general direction.

The sight caught him off guard, and he rudely stood quietly as he gazed into the pale grey of her eyes. Their color or lack there of, seemed to draw out and reflect the surface of the stone that surrounded her, and at the same time, they bled the color from all that was around them.

Gareth continued watching her in silence, taking in her simple, faded, beauty. Watching in amazement as each tilt of her head seamed to gather answers to her unasked questions.

Then a slight giggle turned into a louder laugh.

"What's so funny?"

"I was remembering your curses. How you cursed." She pushed out between the harmony of her amusement. "It was like a small child who is just beginning to be able to speak. How they confuse the words that their tiny ears have heard for the first time. Not knowing how to properly form the statement."

"What's wrong with the way I curse?" Gareth snapped, before he could check his anger.

"Oh! You mean you do not know? I guess, I should have guessed. Your accent places you from somewhere beyond the borders of Delgär. Does your kind generally mean to call out the leader of the realm, risking his wrath, or are you cursing the existence of the Darkness in general?"

She continued to smile as Gareth fumbled for a reply.

"What are you talking about?"

"Your usage of Temple Speak, the language of the ancients. Most would curse the existence of the land of Mïr, or Mürken as named by the many whom have known it, for its ability to steal all light from the world and soul. But you..." And she could no longer contain her glee.

Her laughter was infectious and Gareth's anger melted away.

"I see what you mean. I will have to yield to you on this account." He smiled, though he doubted that the young woman could see it.

"What brings you to wander the underskin of Delgar?" She asked.

"I was about to ask you the same thing." He said with a chuckle.

Another round of melodic sounds escaped her gentle mouth.

"That's funny… I live, here… but, you don't" And she reached out and brushed her fingertips across Gareth's face.

Gareth leaned towards her and bowed his head to her embrace.

She traced every feature, the curve of his lips, and even tugged on the length of his now, raggy hair. Then when she had committed those features to memory, she slid her hands down his shoulders and across his chest. Stopping to trace the outline of the guild crest embossed upon his vest. Her fingers paused there for a brief moment, then both hands shot towards his throat.

As her fingers entangled the various charms and pendants that hung around Gareth's neck, she froze. Her head tilted and an almost pained expression flowed across her face.

"What's wrong? You don't have to stop. I wasn't offended by your touch." He prompted.

She spoke in a hushed tone.

"I have heard of your kind, but… I do not remember or know of any who have ever met you or yours."

"My kind?" Gareth questioned. "I am from L'uramentia. And you are correct. I know of none of my kin that has ever found themselves within the Isle of Souls."

"The alluring realm." She whispered so softly Gareth did not fully hear. "I am sorry for my misidentification. I thought, ever so briefly, until corrected, that you may, be, of the Thraüm."

53

"My name is Gareth, and…" He paused realizing that it was the first time he was about to admit. "And I am a Scribe."

She did not seem to recognize the title Gareth gave of himself, and continued on with her previous thought.

"It would have explained why one such as yourself would have traveled such a distance, intent on discovering the inner workings of the mines of Delgär. I was beginning to wonder if in fact you were sent directly to assess the quality of each cut."

Gareth had to restrain himself from spouting a continuous stream of questions at the young lady, but the first question returned to one of her earlier comments.

"What do you mean, you live here? You mean in the land of Delgär right?" Gareth checked his rudeness. "Forgive me. And… I must apologize again, for I haven't done you the courtesy of asking your name."

Her laugh did little to dispel the effect of her chilling response.

"I have no name. We are but the Resonant. Chosen because we are connected to, and are one, with, the vibration of all things contain within this world." Her lifeless eyes seemed to drift even further with every word she spoke. "From the earliest of ages, when it is known that one is in tune with the land, the stone, the water… we are brought to our calling and remain there, here, until our gifts no longer ring true."

She moved passed Gareth and picked up both her chisel and a bent rod that Gareth had never seen before. Leaning into the stone she gently tapped the edge of the rod on the surface of the stone.

The sweet chime rang out and Gareth watched as the young woman leaned into the rock face and began to trace one of the thin veins of silver. Stopping abruptly, she struck the exact spot with the sharp tool and following a slight tremor, a minute fissure spread the length from floor to ceiling.

"We, I, am tasked with pulling the perfect stone, so that the power of the Thraüm might resonate against the might of the Mür'Ri once again."

The frail creature seemed exhausted but Gareth could not lose this opportunity to gain any of the answers he so needed.

"Are they building the tower of the Märkén Thraüm here again in Delgär? Do these mines connect to the starirway that enters that tower?" He rattled off the questions without giving her an opportunity to even answer them.

Her laughter once again checked his impatience and he had to join in.

"The stones, once cut, are removed from the mines. But to where… I know not. The trail down, and through, will get you to the path you seek… but I have not seen…" And she made a show of furiously, blinking her veiled eyes. "Those passages since I was pulled from my mother's breast."

Gareth's thoughts and sight were pulled away from the young woman's face. His body swayed in the direction back towards the stairway that led to the bottom of the cave.

"You need not worry. No insult will be taken if you rush away. I simply thank you for the momentary distraction. They tend to help refocus one's purpose."

Gareth turned and began to step towards the large chamber. Then hesitated.

"I wish there was something I could do for you."

"What would that be, for I exist for but one reason." It wasn't a question, just a simple statement of fact. "Please do take care though… Scribe Gareth, there may be others whom will not be agreeable with your presence here."

This time, she turned, and went back to her task, humming in perfect tune to each chime struck on the stone.

54

Though eager to be on his way, Gareth heeded the Resonant's warning and slid as quietly through the shadows as the journey would allow. He paused at every opening and side chute, trying to determine if others were working, within.

Occasionally the melody would pause and Gareth's body would tense, preparing for an encounter that never came.

Gradually, his fear waned as he realized that if the Resonant intended to raise a warning to his presence, they most surely would have already. It would be almost certain that most, if not all, would have heard his encounter with the first young lady.

Reaching the cavern's floor, Gareth found it impossible to remain hidden if he was to reach the far end, and the continuation of the tunnel that would lead him to the tower of the Thraüm.

He darted from one pile of debris to the next. Pausing briefly to admire the intricate work that several younger Resonant were doing.

Here, girls of the age of ten seasons or younger, as far as Gareth could determine, were delicately chipping squares, scales of the white and silver rock. Smoothing and polishing each one's surface, over and over. Then they would raise the stone platelet, stroking the surface with a more delicate rod of metal. The process continued until both the stone and the humming of the child joined in perfect pitch.

Racing to yet another pile, Gareth found this group of slightly older girls, threading the polished plates into the gauntlets and breastplates that made up the armor for the Delgär Elite and their mounts.

Although impressed with the detailed work, Gareth felt a spark of anger at what surely amounted to a life of slavery. He turned his gaze, searching for a captor to vent his growing rage to, only to witness a scene that brought an overload of fear, anger, and confusion.

He made his way up to a small rise that threaded in and out of the stone facing, to gain a better view.

It took a moment for his eyes to adjust to the blinding sunlight that blazed through a massive opening in the side of the rock face. He could also hear, as well as smell, the nearby ocean as its waves crashed into the shore.

But it was the sight, now below him, that drew his interest and his ire.

Several of the mammoth blocks were situated upon the tracks of wheels and timber. Large chains were attached to each on both ends to guide and pull those same blocks. It was, however the means of locomotion that enraged Gareth.

Dozens of pitch, were shackled to each block.

Ten or twelve in front to pull.

Four in back, to push.

Gareth noticed that the shackles that bound them to the blocks, were made of the very same stone of which they now struggled to move.

For the first time, Gareth caught sight of several of Delgär's Elite armored soldiers as they whipped and then prodded the pitch with long pikes, tipped with sharpened wedges of the blackened version of the stone.

As much as Gareth wanted to interject in these horrific proceedings, he knew that he could not risk yet another delay to his quest.

Peering into the fissure along the outcropping that he now stood, he saw a glimmer of light.

Squeezing through the narrow opening he found himself in what was surely a man made passage hewn from a point where both the light and dark stone met, and intermingled. The flooring was polished smooth, but the vaulted ceiling arced roughly overhead, with what seemed to Gareth was going to be an elaborate carving, mimicking the canopy of the forest.

He moved towards the light, finding a series of three windows that opened out, revealing the view of an ocean cove and very busy port.

Four massive vessels sat anchored, bobbing with a steady rhythm in time with the lapping of the water upon the shore. Around each, the flurry of activity, drew Gareth's attention as even more pitch were guiding larger stones, onto the decks and into the cargo holds.

Gareth couldn't imagine how these ships could be constructed in order to be able to handle such weights. Or more importantly, where were the ships going.

It seemed strange to Gareth that the mines and ports would be operating as normal, ignoring the battle that would be raging above…

And as if to emphasize his thought, a faint scream rang out from the distance, and Gareth rushed into the fading light of the tunnel.

Another muffle cry began but quickly cut short.

With the way the sound echoed against the stone, it was impossible for Gareth to judge the distance to reach its source.

He slowed his pace then paused, as a throbbing began to pierce his temples.

It was the briefest of sensations, but the preceeding breath of air caused Gareth to flinch out of the way of the wildly, arcing blade.

The corridor flashed brilliantly as metal met stone and the wall erupted in a cascading shower of sparks.

In that instant, Gareth saw the crazed look of his attacker as she drew her arm back for another attack. She was almost an exact copy of Tyresa. Same build and height. Same hairstyle, and… same damaged body.

But those hollowed eyes, bore the weight of terrors seen, that this young warrior, unlike Gareth's companion, was not prepared to handle. Every semi-coherent phrase or thought that she spat between each exerted action, pushed her mind further from reality.

Her body faired no better. Large sections of her stone-plated armor had been hacked away, while other threads of platelets hung down to the ground. The bright polished surface was marred with blade chiseled crevices filled with dirt, flesh and blood.

Any semblance of a functioning member of the Delgär Elite was gone. All that remained was a feral, wounded animal.

Her scream threatened to shatter the stone itself as she intensified her attack on Gareth.

There was no grace, no attempt at following a proven method of engagement. Just a flurry of random hacks and parries.

Gareth used his attackers lack of discipline to his advantage. Managing to stay, slightly ahead of the crazed melee. Using the uneven balance of the soldier, to push aside any real threat.

One last thrust pierced the edge of Gareth vest, but allowed him to grab the soldier's sword arm as she stumbled past. Swinging her around, Gareth ended the encounter simply by letting her go. The exhausted form slammed into the wall with a dull thump and a trickling sound as broken shards of her armor fell to the ground around her.

He wished that he could care for her, heal her, but the mere fact that she was in the state that she was in, meant that the situation had progressed beyond battle.

His every action must now move him forward, in hopes of preventing further damage.

55

A narrowing archway signaled his arrival at the spiral staircase. He paused with a moment of self-doubt. Wondering how he, a lone apprentice Scribe, could or should, affect all that may be transpiring above. And at the same time, he knew he would not be able to merely join Mikal Syla to observe and record the events that could possibly lead to the annihilation of the Isle of Souls.

An echo of tormented screams, and angry shouts of pursuit, propelled him forward, signifying that he could no longer… go back.

With each step, those same sounds faded, only to be replaced by the growing din of the battle that seeped through the narrow passage, yet to come.

A thin vein of sunlight signaled that he had reached the entrance to the tower, but Gareth hesitated... for that same glimmer showed him that the staircase did not end there.

He stood there trying to resist the sudden pull towards the upper level of the tower... trying to resist the growing pang that called for answers.

He called upon the crescendo of metal on metal, scream over horrific scream, to silence that call. So that he may take his place on that grisly field... but...

A flood of distorted memories rained on him...

A sight seen, but from a different vantage.

The voice screaming out in the darkness was but a remnant of the cascading echo.

Fingertips brushing across weathered skin, tracing the veins of history...

The play of shadows, reaching out of the darkness to distort the vision and memories of all it encountered...

A different stone passage, in a land separated by Darkness.

By the time his focus returned to the present, he felt a cool wisp of stale air swirl around him, just as his foot failed to make contact with any surface at all.

The scream in his head came too late.

Off balanced, he twisted his body, trying to use the weight of the massive scroll on his back to check the momentum. Every muscle burned with the effort. He felt the cloth and flesh being scraped from his arms, as he began to fall into the abyss.

Then his fingers bit into the edge of the stone.

Frantically his legs kicked out, as the flailing limbs desperately tried to find some form of purchase, threatening to dislodge his feeble grasp on safety.

The repeated thrusts slowly allowed Gareth to raise himself, first onto torn elbows, then to drag knee, after knee, on to the flat surface of a landing.

It was some time before he would trust himself enough to navigate the darkened interior of the tower. Instead he drew himself inward, leaning back against the cold stone.

A familiar curse began to pass his lips.

"What the Rhu…" The words quickly changed to a raspy chuckle at the remembrance of the ghostly Resonant's lilting laugh and revelation.

Gareth's hand slid slowly outward, feeling for any other edge or danger. Leaning over he allowed his body's weight to propel the search quicker, only to jam his fingers into the rise of another section of stairs.

He began the new ascent on hands and knees, but slowly rose to his feet, as the hidden stairwell seemed to continue. Every few steps, Gareth reached out with his left hand to rake the outer wall with his fingertips, wanting to make sure not to stray towards another unseen hazard.

The monotonous echo of each footfall served as a constant reminder as to the vastness of the Thraüm tower. The growing pain and cramping in Gareth's calves began to cause frequent stumbles, threatening to launch him over the edge.

His pace slowed, and even though he should be perspiring from the exertion of the climb… a growing breeze of cool air flowed where rising heat should dwell.

Gareth raised his head to enjoy the freshened air and noticed that in the path above a glow of light appeared.

With every step forward, both light and air became stronger.

The arc of the curve became visible.

And Gareth marveled at the breadth of the massive tower.

A tremendous shockwave rumbled through every stone of the structure, threatening to push Gareth in to the abyss.

Staring upward, he saw the focal point of the light's source, and how it defined the ceiling that covered the entire spiral of stairs.

Racing forward, Gareth reached the upper level and was immediately blinded by the afternoon sun as it glared through a gaping hole where a large portion of the outer wall and roof, should have been.

56

The sounds of battle, though muffled, filtered into the tower as an ever-present summons to the carnage below.

Gareth cautiously neared the crumbling edge of stonework and ventured a momentary gaze at the happenings so very far below. A wave of nausea gripped his stomach, although no ping of imminent danger brought it about. A growing knowledge that he stood where only the birds should reign, twisted his senses and he turned away.

Another shockwave tore at the tower, and Gareth dropped to his knees to avoid being thrown out.

Slowly he rose, finally taking in the view of the remaining chamber.

Gareth stared across the width of a circular expanse that was easily the length of the great hall back in the Guild house. A long center aisle divided the room, separating row after row of concentric racks. Each rose higher than the previous, the nearest starting at merely waist height… but by the time they reached the outer walls, the darkened wood reached to the base of the domed ceiling. At one time they must have held thousands of scrolls, but now, all that remained was dust and fragments of decaying wood.

As Gareth reached the center point of the room he marveled at the intricate stone work that was imbedded into the flooring. Overlapping circles and lines, each of a different type of polished stone, drew out the patterns of the stars themselves. And, as if to accent that fact, pin point beams of light focused down from the rooftop.

Gareth passed his hand through one such point, feeling the warmth on the back of his hand. He raised his head to follow the focal point of that beam, to a small point off centered from the rest. In fact each bolt of light, emanated from completely separate areas of the dome...

Only to meet in the precise matching pattern as the stones below.

Gareth moved further towards the far end of the tower's room. Through the dimming light he could make out what seemed to be a large mantle, carved from the stone of the tower itself. The same twisted vein of light and dark stone, wove through the wall, as ran through the caverns below.

His thoughts were so fixated on those veins that he stubbed his foot and tripped, falling on to a bed of that same stone.

Though it wasn't a bed.

Too small to be a bed.

The smooth surface angled upward from its base, to the point at which it melded with the wall.

As Gareth followed that flow, he noticed a series of circular holes bored into the wall itself.

Four smaller circles haloed a much larger irregular hole, in both the light stone... and as Gareth allowed his sight to focus... the dark.

Almost without thought, Gareth loosed the eighth denial from the harness across his chest. Moving to the side to gain access, he reached out and slid the small scroll into the lowest of the slots.

It fit with such precision, that the minute veins on the finials lined up perfectly with those of the wall.

"The Eighth Denial, has a home."

Slowly his fingers ran over the edge of each of the other slots, pausing as his entire hand began to slide into the center hole.

"Could it be?" Gareth questioned aloud.

Reaching over his shoulder, he grabbed the larger scroll and brought it to bare before the center hole.

As he began pushing the blackened edge towards the opening in the white stone, the pains raced up each of his arms, focusing their warning towards his head…

… but a moment too late.

As black met white, light met darkness… a blast of energy arced across the scroll and sent Gareth spiraling backwards.

57

He landed with a painful thud.

"Stupid! Stupid! Stupid!"

He slowly pushed himself into a seated position, noticing the faint cloud of smoke as it rose to dance with the beams of light above.

Once again reaching the wall-piece, Gareth picked up the Black Scroll, which had fallen and cracked off a corner of the surface below.

He moved to the other side.

To the darkness.

And there, it seemed as if the scroll, melted into the stone itself.

Gareth stood waiting…

And nothing happened.

"So we know where they came from. Great!" The pitch, and volume of Gareth's voice increased with his mounting anger. He swung wildly at the air, catching instead, the end of one of the ancient racks.

There was no resistance as flesh met brittle wood…

No pain from mangled bones, just coughing from a raised cloud of dust.

Gareth dropped to the floor again, tracing his own patterns on the floor through the dust of centuries passed.

"Just one clue would have been nice." He whined.

He reached over to pick up the edging of stone that the Black Scroll had broken off. Twisting it over in his hand he noticed the smooth curve carved into its surface.

A shape that his hands had molded to before.

With a renewed sense of growing excitement, Gareth knelt and ran his hands across the smooth surface of the bed-like slab of stone.

There again, on a smaller scale, were the same style of notches, hollowed out of the stone.

He jumped to his feet and retrieved the Eighth Denial.

Carefully he placed it into the grooves and slid the bright surface of the scroll across the disparate shades of stone…

The massive tower rumbled as the entire domed ceiling began to rotate. The small beams of light disappeared. Then shifted positions. Only to rearrange in some other spot, creating a new constellation of light upon the floor.

The whole of the tower seemed to darken as the section of the wall that had been destroyed, reappeared.

A chorus of voices began to echo in the chamber and Gareth stared in disbelief as the ghostly image of a dozen or so men and women, appeared around him.

He stumbled backward, sinking low to lose himself amongst the taller racks, unsure of the reality of anything before him.

Each man, and woman wore long layered robes, covered in a multitude of those same constellations and glyphs that adorned the center of the floor. The material glowed as each caught the light from a solid beam falling from the ceiling above.

Gareth watched in amazement as a handless quill, recorded the every word spoken by the gathering of mages.

And even without seeing the words inscribed on the pristine scroll, he knew what he was hearing to be the absolute truths.

- **The world, as known, exists because of magic. All that it has ever been, or will become, is such, because it was crafted to be thusly.**

- **We, the Marken Thraüm, need never, the use of staff or sword to vanquish fear or foe. Knowledge has begotten the power that was then used to suppress the entirety of the Darkness.**

- **The energies of Light, resonate through the core of every Thraüm Tower. And as such, the vein of each stone has amplified and focused the magic within. The Towers combined, then linked to amplify and focused the forces used to halt, for all time, the approach of the Darkness.**

- **The surviving members of the Marken Thraüm, sought to spread that knowledge throughout the known light to guide all men away from the darkness that will eventually infest all.**

- **A generation of Kings, fearing for their trivial reign, chose to side with that infestation, and fought to cast out the Thraüm and all of their knowledge.**

- **Upon confirmation of the true nature of the Thraüm lineage, that same generation of Kings,**

> sought to severe all of the ties that bound the Marken Thraüm to the mortal realm.
>
> - Those of the hunted, chose various means to ensure the survival of the Thraüm lineage. Whether by choice to hide and cower, or to raise staff and sword. Some chose a marriage of both.
>
>   Some of the enemy of the Darkness, when endangered by the darkness of man, sought the protection of the Darkness. Even to the extent of embracing the Darkness and all that their seed would sow.
>
>   The Thraüm, fearing the loss of all light, have chosen to commit the sum of these acts to history in the words put forth by a Guilde of Scribes, in hopes that a true account of all deeds, shall preserve the past, guide the present, and shape the future.

Pleased with their actions, the group of shades slowly disappated, leaving a lone figure that Gareth hadn't noticed before.

A young boy, barely ten seasons old, stood staring at the newly written scroll. He shook his head and his chubby cheeks, rolled.

Gareth was struck by the similarity to the man he knew, but before he voiced his thoughts aloud, he watched as the youth climbed upon the surface of the slab and took quill in hand.

Slowly and deliberately, he scrawled the words within the border of the scroll, rotating his position as the words passed from one edge to another.

Then with a final swipe of his hands, and mumbling of words...

Gareth watched the entire surface of the scroll change, and the ghostly image of a very young Mikal Syla... fade away.

58

Gareth leaned over the tableau and placed both hands to the edge of the stone. He was amazed to find that the words had not changed back. That what he was reading, was the original intent of the denial. He was also amazed that it was his friend and mentor… that made those words become the denial itself.

He had wanted answers, but instead he was plagued with an even greater question.

But as he raised his head to contemplate the implications of that question, Gareth watched as the Black Scroll seemed to bleed from the hollows of the wall.

Quickly he grabbed the denial, failing to notice that as the scroll was removed from the surface of the slab, the words returned to the form he had first read.

Instead, he anxiously watched as the blackened skin took its place on the alter of words.

The domed ceiling did not rotate.

No shades of the Darkness appeared.

Though a single bolt of light did, illuminated the surface.

Although he was unsure as to what he thought would be revealed, Gareth fretted the fact that nothing was.

The Black Scroll remained, as it had always been… a mystery, wrapped within the serifs of a dead language.

He knew that he should be overcome with some form of regret, anger, or even a melancholy of sorts, but there was an overpowering sense of jubilation. It was as if every dark vein that ran through the bleached stone was rejoicing, and the large patches of pitch, black stone, echoed the sentiment.

His pains of warning seemed more confused, than alert. That growing inner voice did not know whether it should answer the call… or should it force Gareth to take flight.

He fought to push through every sensation that was not his own. Knowing his only task, now lay in deciphering enough of the ancient tome, to provide some form of aid to those sacrificing below.

Reaching into his pocket, Gareth pulled the tip of a quill free. His hand began to shake as he hesitated.

Unsure!

The last time he attempted this, he barely survived. If not for Lord Hadrion and Mikal Syla aiding him, the scroll surely would have drained every last drop of his life's blood.

Leaning over the blackened skin, Gareth held his breath as it may be his last. Then he prepared to plunge the sharp metal into his own flesh. A rotting shade of scarlet seemed to bleed from symbol to symbol in anticipation of a fresher course, but as Gareth lowered his hand towards the surface of the Black Scroll… its blood seemed to leap forth and flow upward towards Gareth.

First his hands, then the length of his arms, became covered in the diseased ink.

But more than single words appeared.

Whole passages emerged. And with them, came… memories.

It was as if he was hearing the final passages of the *Truths* again. This time though, history was being recorded from the vantage of the Darkness itself.

✘   *** The enemies of all that thrive in Mürén, when faced with their own destruction, brought on by the darkness of their own leaders, sought the protection of Mürén and its comfort.**

✘   *** Some even embraced the Darkness and chose to hide within the seeds they sowed. And within those unions, a darkness coursed through the Thraüm.**

✘   *** The Mürken Rhüle have sought out, and joined those lines, so that they may one day breathe life into the one, true, MürRi.**

✘   *** And it shall too, find the magic hidden in these words, stolen by the Thraüm, so that all of Mürén may rise to proclaim…**

✘   *** "For it has arrived! And when comes this Darkness, Evil will follow and all light shall perish."**

As if to accent that statement, the entire tower rocked with the force of a blast. Larger sections of the wall and ceiling crumbled, threatening Gareth's path to the stairway.

He quickly rolled the Black Scroll, harnessing it once again… and only as an afterthought… retrieved the Eighth Denial.

Each step that brought him closer to the edge of the shattered room, seamed to loosen another fragment of stone. He angled his approach to the stairway trying to stay as far away from the gaping hole, but the visceral roar from the army of the Darkness, pulled him to the edge.

A mass of Cri surrounded a central figure. One that even at this distance, Gareth could tell, rose in height, greater than all others.

He watched in awe and fear as a flash of blue energy emanated from that figure.

The shock-wave produced, spread forward, and slammed the outer walls of the main Delgär battlements, even before the sound of the blast reached Gareth's ears.

The walls held, but every soul that had stood upon the upper reaches, was sent flying. Many shattered as their lifeless bodies made contact with the surrounding stone. Others simply sailed to the streets below.

Gareth's thoughts… his fears, became vocal.

"The Mür'Ri!"

"He has the power of the Märkén Thraüm."

He knew that only that same power might have a chance to stop this Evil. Quickly he surveyed the line, praying to find the one, ancient soul, that may still retain that, secret.

59

Throughout all of the history told and written, battles trained for and practiced, even those scurmishs fought and the lives lost in front of his own eyes…

They did nothing to prepare Gareth for the trail he now weaved.

The pretense for any form of controlled engagement had long since faded, ground into the blood soaked earth. The once golden field of grain was a churned, sickly hue, of death.

Ashe and bone.

The remnants of both man and beast.

The land itself had been tortured, and trampled to death.

As quickly as one foe was felled, another rose up to take the charge.

The only thing more abundant than man or Cri, was their dead and the dying left in their wake.

Gareth was horrified by the animalistic foot soldiers of the Shàl Mïr Cri. Their hunger for death and slaughter did not prejudice itself to the flesh of man. On more than one occasion,

Gareth watched as one of the deranged beast turned on its own brethren and even the Shàl itself.

Whether it was that lack of discipline, the superior armor of the Elite, or simply the will to survive... from Gareth's standpoint, the soldiers of Delgär seemed to be winning the day.

Then suddenly the ground shook as another blast of energy sent its concussive wave towards the walls of the city.

Gareth had seen that Mikal Syla had been struggling to make his way across the immense battlefield towards the source of the destructive blasts. His only hope was that Mikal understood the implications of the source of that power.

A power, never seen in this realm.

A power, lost in the myth of an ancient scroll.

But hadn't the visions of the Denial shown Gareth that his mentor was equally as ancient? His blood, the source of that power?

The closer Gareth reached, his breathing and the panic that propelled it, quickened. And with every approaching step, the intensity of the pain elevated.

Gone was the twinge of warning.

This was the pure scream of horror.

Fighting through the nausea, Gareth pushed his way through the surrounding ring of Shàl Mïr Cri. He cared not whether it was his clothing, the code of the Guild, the magic of the Thraüm, or even an unseen fear of the Black Scroll that allow him to pass so easily. His only concern was to reach his friend to give the briefest of warnings, in hopes of saving some semblance of the reality he knew.

The weight of the Black Scroll began to crush him. A voice inside told him that if their combined fear would not stop Gareth... then, the reality of what they carried, would.

Gareth reached out, clinging to the nearest of the Shàl for support. Trying in vain to maintain the ability to continue forward.

But he, and everything around him, collapsed under the immense weight. Suffocated by the forces driving down upon them.

Gareth was left to watch the fate of the future play out before him. Unable to stand by the side of his Master, his mentor… his friend.

60

Gareth continued to struggle against the weight of the Scroll. Each time he tried to scream out a warning to Mikal Syla, the fear of the voice inside him, around him, choked those words into a whispered scream.

He watched as the silhouette of the portly Scribe was dwarfed by the rising bulk of the leader of the Mürken Rhüle.

The creature had all of the beauty of the leader of the Shàl Mïr Cri, while embracing the visceral traits of the pitch.

It raised its massive arms, mumbling softly, ancient words that grew in pitch until its voice roared like thunder.

Words!

Words that were foreign to even the pain inside Gareth's head.

Spiraling bolts of lightning slowly engulfed the creatures upper body: Its screams shredded the senses, and then with a concussive thunderclap…

Was gone.

The creature had doubled over, falling to one knee. Slowly it stood, trying to control its breath. With each passing moment, a sickening calm, and composure, came to rest before the Master Scribe.

Slowly at first, the creature forced out a deep, resounding voice.

Forcing out words that it had never spoken, in a language never learned. But with each sentence it uttered… it gained more and more control.

"You are of magic blood." The statement was no more a question, than it was an accusation.

"There is no such thing as Magic." Mikal screamed back. Trying as much to convince himself. "Only the wisdom that knowledge brings."

"Words!" Was the thunderous, response.

Gareth watched as his friend stumbled from the onslaught of the massive creatures voice.

"You are of magic blood. You wear the iron casts around your neck." And it gestured to the chains and charms that hung around Syla's neck. "You speak the vagueness of its misdirection. Conceal it in the words written in your ancient texts."

Gareth watched in horror as Mikal Syla stood and began to approach the hulking beast. His calls of warning and struggles to free himself, to help, were futile.

"And who do you profess to be, that speaks so freely of things, that if indeed they did exist, would bring about the fires of your own demise?"

A haunting laughter filled the battlefield.

So alarming, so engulfing, all of the combatants halted their aggression and drew their focus towards this major presence.

"I am your blood, redefined. The blood of a thousand Märkén Thraüm purified with the Darkness of Mürén itself. I am the ultimate extension of all Mürken Rhüle." He raised his arms in exhaltation, "I am A'trumir. I am of the legend! I am the one, true Mür'Ri REBORN!"

A million voices rose! It was as if all of the evil, from every point of existence, echoed the chorus of its rightful heir.

Gareth watched as a visibly shaken, Mikal Syla tried to counter A'trumir's voice.

"A myth! You are claiming to be but a myth. Born from the distorted legends of but another myth. Exhaulted by words. Words that have no meaning. Words that have been twisted… to simply create, a… myth." His last word trailed off. The effect of which, seemed to draw all of the breath, from those million voices, and an unnerving quiet settled over everything.

A'trumir started again. "You are of the magic. But it is not you that I seek!" His massive clawed hand swung out violently. First raking across Mikal's chest, slicing through layer upon layer of cloth.

Then tearing flesh from bone.

Before the force of the blow could move the Scribe's body, the creature's other hand impaled Mikal, and raised his failing body, so that the gasping Scribe could only stare into the eyes of the evil reborn.

"It is a pity that you have convinced yourself that there is no magic left in this world. For if you believed, you might have saved yourself and the one that you are hiding from my sight."

Mikal Syla smiled as a trail of blood escaped his cracked lips.

Then A'trumir, the one true Mür'Ri, cast him aside.

61

The flow of tears blurred Gareth's sight. His throat, raw from his screams of anguish, choked back any curse into a phlegm, soaked rattle. His legs ached from the exertion of trying to free himself… trying to save his friend.

And all that time, A'trumir searched.

His fury grew as each body, which was torn from sight, failed to reveal the presence of the one it sought.

Gareth!

For a moment Gareth thought that he had been found. The creature seemed to be staring directly at him, through him. It took several steps towards Gareth then hesitated, mumbling its confusion.

"Someone… something else. There is something else, beyond the blood of magic."

Gareth realized with relief, that even though A'trumir's gaze was locked on him… the creature could not actually see him. He gently reached up and grasped the charms spilling across his chest.

The creature suddenly turned and screamed a command into the throng of gathering Shàl Mïr Cri.

Another figure pushed its way into the opening.

What Gareth could only describe as a twisted, distorted version of Mikal Syla, stopped to take up station next to A'trumir.

Without looking in the new arrival's direction, A'trumir held out his arm in the direction of the new-comer. The creature in turn, pulled a massive black quill from the tattered sack that was strung around its neck.

Gareth was shocked. *Could these creatures actually have there own Scribes?*

But still, there was nothing to write on.

No well of ink to draw from.

As the scribe of the Darkness moved closer to A'trumir, Gareth saw the tip of the quill, flash in the midday sun. This was no tip for ink or parchment… it was but a refined blade.

And indeed, the twisted, little scribe began to carve upon the forearm of the Mür'Ri.

A massive wave of energy struck Gareth and he felt as if he was about to be torn apart… swept away.

Then as quickly as the sensation hit…

A crippling blast of pain ripped through his voice in a massive scream.

The Demon Scribe screeched out in terror as it was blasted backwards into the mass of the surrounding Cri.

Another, raspy scream raised in protest as Mikal Syla rushed forward, on trembling legs, swinging wildly away at A'trumir with some procured weapon.

The pitiful attempt did nothing but draw the Demon King's attention away from Gareth.

Which was its only intent.

A slight backhand sent the injured Scribe, spiraling again.

"No arms raised, no arms against." A'trumir's recitation of the Guild Code seemed to be the final insult as he turned once again towards Gareth.

Another wave emanated from Gareth's unseen other, contorting his body in agony… hurling itself into the Mür'Ri.

The creature stumbled in confusion.

Then screamed out… in pain!

Using the distraction and the last vestige of his strength, the prone Scribe jabbed the tip of his long-sword into the calf of the towering monster.

A'trumir spun and kicked away the blade.

Looking down at the battered Scribe, he raised his bloody leg, and drove it into the chest of the elder soul.

Slowly, the leader of the Mürken Rhüle drew its own blade. The razored edge was blackened from the layers of rotting blood that crusted its surface.

A'trumir placed the tip of the blade so close to Mikal's throat, that every labored breath made it pierce the skin, ever so deeper.

Again the Mür'Ri spoke words of enchantment and amber bolts of lightning raced down his arms and through the sword. Small tendrils of energy bit out at Syla's skin. The smell of burning flesh filled the air as each of the Scribe's wounds, seemed to boil and heal over.

A'trumir stared down the edge of his blade, and into Mikal Syla's glazed eyes.

"Your words are no longer needed Master Scribe. Man has no future. And what will remain, will be scattered, running blindly to hide like the vermin it is. They will have no need of the past. And their only thought of the future will be of the comfort of death. Who shall reign in their place… my brethren. And they will have no use for the words of a creature that no longer exists."

He began to raise his sword, preparing for the final death stroke.

62

Gareth could not let this happen!

Struggling to stand, he fought violently against the forces that struggled to contain him. Using the severe contortions brought by the increasing pain, Gareth twisted his body wildly. Freeing himself from the harness and the power of the Black Scroll.

It fell to the ground with the force of the tallest tree. Sending out a shockwave across the entire battlefield. Men and Shàl Mïr Cri, were knocked to the ground.

A'trumir, merely turned and smiled as the wave blew back the fine hairs that circled his face… as well as the veil that had hidden his quarry.

Even without the weight of the Black Scroll, Gareth struggled to move. Each step was unbalanced as a new force threatened to pull him down.

Realizing the source, Gareth clawed at the twisted mass of his own pendants. His fingers split open, and the mass of chains torn at his neck as he finally broke through their binding.

Dropping the bloodied pendants to the ground sent another, more violent force, ripping through the surrounding area.

The Shàl Mïr Cri raised their voice in chorus, screaming a battle rythym that stunned the remaining soldiers of Delgär. Throwing their swords aside, most turned and began to run for the supposed safety of the city walls.

A'trumir lowered his sword. His eyes focusing, as if he was seeing Gareth for the first time.

He spoke but a single word.

"Apprentice."

The Mür'Ri's mouth mimicked the clacking jaws and staccato beat of the pitch. The sound drew the attention and the unease of all of the Cri.

It also drew in, something else.

The darkness of the tree line seemed to writhe and melt. Slowly, flowing into the open field, it took shape again.

The shear number of pitch that advanced was too great to comprehend. The speed in which they began to move caused Gareth's vision to blur, and his head to swim with vertigo, as he tried to keep track of the advancing hoard.

Even the Shàl Mïr Cri cried out in fear as the mass of pure darkness closed in and began to devour anything that was in its path.

Man and beast shared the same fate.

As the flood of darkness momentarily solidified and quickly tore apart flesh and bone. Then absorbed all into their ebony mass.

The leader of the Mürken Rhüle continued his call.

Gareth chose this time to act. Grabbing the nearest weapon, he charged.

The distance was too great.

Before Gareth could even cover half of the ground, A'trumir turned his sword upon the young apprentice.

A massive bolt, leap out and leveled Gareth.

His gasping breath turned into a tortured scream as the metal of the sword began to burn and liquefy into the flesh of his hand.

A'trumir's chatter returned to the speech of man, and his message pounded away at Gareth's soul.

"Again, the Scribe has taken up arms."

Gareth tried to pull his burnt hand from the boiling pool of metal… tried to roll away.

A massive foot crushed down on his chest.

The Mür'Ri leaned over, searching for something in the torment in Gareth's pain.

"It seems that this apprentice has learned the wrong lesson from his Master. Yet I smell more than just his failure on you. In you."

Dropping to one knee, A'trumir reached out his massive hand and scooped the molten remains of the sword and Gareth's hand, along with a mass of dirt. The Mür'Ri continued to increase the pressure of his grip as he crushed the hardening metal into the molten remains of Gareth's hand.

Gareth's agonizing scream quickly turned to a mere whimper as the dirt and metal crumbled away, leaving just the bloody, destroyed, flesh.

Again A'trumir called out and his Demon Scribe scurried forth. Hesitantly, he once again pulled his quill. This time, however, he closed in on Gareth, as A'trumir turned to walk away.

Gareth was in shock and awe as the Dark Scribe dipped its quill into the bloody remains of Gareth's hand. It quickly scribbled a line of distorted text onto the torn pulp.

Almost instantly, the burnt flesh flaked and fell away.

The twisted bone, bent back into place.

Gareth was amazed!

Amazed by the healing.

Amazed at the self-satisfied grin the twisted scribe gave as he stood to shuffle away.

There was a crescendo of thunder as the Mürken Rhüle called out to his remaining troops.

Gareth once again used the distraction, not for an offensive move, but for one of stealth, as he deftly lifted the black quill from the retreating Scribe's pouch.

Struggling to his feet, Gareth called after A'trumir.

"Why do you walk away? Why won't you face me? This mere, apprentice. Why can't you wield your sword in a fair battle, instead of using parlor tricks?"

Gareth hoped that his rouse would buy him time to conceive of any plan to save his friend.

But the Mür'Ri wouldn't play along. He simply paused and looked at Gareth with pity. Then flatly stated as he began to walk away…

"Because, I don't have to."

Reaching down, A'trumir grabbed Mikal Syla's leg and slowly dragged the unconscious Scribe away.

Gareth had no time to protest, or to pursue.

The entire landscape swelled again and the mass of living evil, began to close in on him.

Spinning around, Gareth's searched for any retreat.

A thin line of clear earth stretched back to the spot in which he had dropped the Black Scroll and his charms.

He raced towards them both.

Scooping up the charms, he twisted the broken chains around his neck.

The hope of their protection, quickly faded as the Darkness closed in.

He struggled to get the harness of the Black Scroll on again, but unlike before, there was no relief from its extreme weight. No pings of warning, no protection, from the impending doom.

The oozing blackness slowly began to coat and crawl the length of his leg.

He heard the chattering chorus of a million pitch close in around him.

Raising his head, he closed his eyes.

He wanted to scream out his apologies to all of those whom he felt he had failed. He wanted scream out every regret… but he knew those words would go unheard.

He pushed himself free of the harness again. Struggling against the suction of the congealing evil, he pulled a section of the scroll free.

His body was almost completely covered now, making every movement nearly impossible.

He could no longer see the surface of the Black Scroll, but guessed where the edge might be.

And even though he had no ink… he drove the tip of the Demon Scribe's quill into the black oil.

Then he traced his words upon the roughly hewn, skin.

The final wave of Darkness covered him, choking the last breath from his lungs.

His final memory was of a thunderous scream of torment that rippled through the Isle of Souls.

63

It wasn't the first bump in the road, or even the second or third. His body knew the difference between every rut. It was that constant, incessant arguing that pulled him from the depths of his final sleep.

Two voices… long gone… never to have met, were prattling on like colic little babies.

"I don't care who you think you are. You will not bring those mange ridden animals one, step closer to this wagon."

"What you carry in that rickety, old wagon is mine to protect, above all else. And if you so chose to not stand down, I will…"

"What!" Tyresa screamed. "I owe my Master a life debt, and any who think they can threaten him will quickly be dispatch by my sword."

"The Guild has placed me in charge of my Master's well being… and life debt or not… you shall yield." Larec raised his voice.

Some time ago, Gareth had wondered if there could be anything worse than the silence of the pitch.

A thin smile cracked across his lips.

And the wagon rolled on.

www.ingramcontent.com/pod-product-compliance
Lightning Source LLC
Chambersburg PA
CBHW020641120726
47906CB00001B/72